Nobody leaves Q
and an authority problem are the only immigration requirements. Emigration is banned.

Ember spends her days cruising Queen's endless sand
dunes, hunting sand pirates and wallowing in memories of
her dead wife. After an ambush, Ember is dragged to the pirate camp and learns her wife's biggest secret—before her
death, she'd joined the pirates, built an illegal spaceship,
and plotted to leave the planet.

Ember's sister, Nadia, hatches a desperate rescue that leads
her to the very edge of the habitable zone. There, Nadia
stumbles across other secrets kept—a flourishing, impossible ecosystem and a New Earth mining installation. Queen's
hidden resource, highly sought after and limited, should
have made its inhabitants rich. Instead, Queen's scientists
live in decaying houses, battle the elements, and struggle to
eke out a living.

Ember, Nadia, and the sand pirates must take back the
planet and expose the corrupt New Earth mining. Taming
giant beetles, wrestling stinkhorn fungi, and enlisting
Queen's rabbit population in a high-stakes aerial battle are
just part of the hijinks that will determine Queen's fate as a
galactic player, as well as the futures of all its conscripted
inhabitants.

The newly minted outlaws must also grapple with Queen's
narrow concept of "womanhood" and where trans and intersex people belong in its future.

QUEEN

Hidden Earth, Book One

J.S. Fields

For Anna—

A NineStar Press Publication

www.ninestarpress.com

Queen

ISBN: 978-1-64890-492-9

First Edition, June, 2022

Also available in eBook, ISBN: 978-1-64890-491-2

CONTENT WARNING:

This book contains depictions of depression over the loss of a loved one/family member, discussion of a cancer death (past and off-page).

For my sister, who punches first and asks questions later

Chapter One

During May, the trees died. The shrubs withered. The grasses curled in on themselves. Humans could live without vegetation. Earth could not.

Ember

Mornings on Queen always looked like blood. Ember stood at the edge of the habitable zone of the tidally locked planetoid. She scanned the crimson and rust horizon all the way to the perpetual sunrise. Her wife's body was out here somewhere, buried in the coarse red sand. Desiccated, mummified, likely stripped naked by the roaming packs of sand pirates Ember was out here to track.

Well... Track. Kill. The line was blurry when it involved a spouse, and it wasn't like the presidium—the administrative body of Queen—really cared one way or the other. Ember had cared, once, but she was on day seventeen of perimeter duty, and her whole plan of dealing with Taraniel's death by shooting grave robbers was starting to look a little thin.

A rabbit shot across her field of vision, registering in a halo of blue inside the face shield of her envirosuit. TOPA—the suit's AI—scrolled data across the screen, but Ember ignored it. Without thinking, she yanked one of the wide, flat stones from her exterior right thigh pocket (they were supposed to keep her calm, according to Nadia) and threw it at the flash of white, fluffy tail with precision honed from years of dealing with Queen's nuisance rabbit population.

The rabbit's hind legs skittered out from beneath it as it slipped on the sand. Ember wrapped her fingers around another stone, preparing to hit the head this time, when the damn thing started digging with its front feet, sand funneling around it, so that Ember lost her clean shot.

She stepped forward, grinding her teeth with an adrenaline surge that would again see no release if the little shit got away. She wiped sand from her face shield with a gloved hand, smearing red across her vision.

The area where the rabbit had dug settled flat with a slight pock. Tiny fans on the outside of Ember's face shield blew the particulate from her vision.

The rabbit was gone and her stone along with it.

Ember cursed, the words bouncing around the inside of her rabbit-hide envirosuit, wasted on recycled air and a generic TOPA. Queen didn't have stones like that—perfect for skipping over lakes that didn't exist on the barren planetoid. Those she carried in her pocket were some of her last reminders of Earth. And the rabbit... Ember knelt at the soft indent in the sand. It'd descended into one of Queen's giant beetle galleries. Of course, it had.

TOPA pinged as she reached a gloved hand into the depression. Ember debated the possibility of Queen's native beetles—approximately the height of a small school bus and twice the length—grabbing her wrist and pulling her down in pulp-era sci-fi fashion. She dismissed the idea. If beetles hadn't accosted her yet at this site, it meant the gallery was abandoned and being used by the feral European domestic rabbit population. They'd been brought over as food stock on the colony ships. Some had escaped. Big surprise.

Please read your notes, scrolled across the interior of Ember's face shield, in lettering so large it blocked most of the landscape from view.

"The rabbit got away. I was stupid for throwing a rock that can't be replaced. I wasted oxygen on the exertion. That about cover it?"

TOPA didn't respond directly, but it did fire up a series of reports.

Landmass stability: within ten meters radius: moderate.

Sand for at least three meters below the surface with scattered hollow tunnels reinforced with clay

from the temperate zone. Sand transitioning to silt loam noted in geographic surveys, with increasing occurrence toward the colony dome.

Silica content of the air: unbreathable.

UV index: ten point five.

Ember snorted. That did explain the suit smell.

She balled her hands as tightly as she could in the double-layered leather of her gloves wishing, not for the first time that day, that Gore-Tex was still a thing. Leather didn't breathe, though both the buffer and the electrical linings of the suit were supposed to. *Nothing* from Earth breathed outside the habitable zone, and as much as the filters of her suit tried, they couldn't filter out the smell of human, slowly marinating in her own sweat.

Awaiting input. **Continue scan?**

"Yeah. Sure. Why not?"

Ember stood, swallowing the dry air the suit pushed at her. The AI had a newly installed personality patch, but Ember would need to get a lot more bored before she turned it on. Instead, she pivoted on her right foot, keeping level with as much of the horizon as she could see, and let the suit feed data into the AI. Dunes and small valleys surrounded her, and TOPA disassembled each for content.

Silica: 100%

Silica: 97%, Chitin: 3%

Silica: 78%, Cellulose: 10%, Lignin: 10%, Chitin: 2%

Suggest moving 1.7 chains northeast for better visibility.

"Picturesque view?" Ember asked TOPA. *Maybe a body?*

"Hey, Ember!"

The red dunes faded into a semitransparent image of her sister, Nadia, displayed on the interior of the face shield.

Ember clicked her right canines together to increase volume. The winds were too fierce outside the colony dome to hear much of anything without enhancement, even when the sound came from inside the suit. That wind was the same reason the damn rabbits tended to stay in the beetle galleries. Wind screwed with everything out here.

Nadia's transmission showed her just outside the dome, her image picked up by one of her suit's sleeve cameras. Sand licked her calves. Her goggles were up but her face shield down, and red soil caked her envirosuit. The only parts of her skin visible were her lips, chapped but grinning as she tapped the front of her shield and instructions scrolled across the inside of Ember's own face shield. At the bottom of the message was a clear add-on from Nadia.

Your sentry duties now extend to Outpost Eight. Leave immediately.

–Dr. Narkhirunkanok

Hope you enjoy the sand. I'll make you dune-nuts when you get home. Extra sprinkles. Served on a tablecloth of rabbit hide since you love the little shits so much.

Ember read the short message and scowled—a facial contortion Nadia would see in detail from the camera inside Ember's suit. Puns and throwaway comments about the excess rabbit population had no place on an official director request. If Nadia was willing to deface government messages, it meant she was worried. But she wouldn't *say* she was worried because, historically, the sisters' ability to communicate was right around "bug and speeding windshield."

"Leave for Outpost Eight? I'm supposed to be here for another three days." Ember cinched her mouth into a caricature of a frown. "TOPA will be heartbroken. It hasn't cataloged every dune within a one hundred-chain radius."

"There's been a change. Director Narkhirunkanok thinks the mella pirates are going to hit one of our storage units, the one where we keep sticking all the glassware we probably don't need but can't get rid of. We need a sentry. You're the closest." The wind whipped her words away, but the auditory sensors on Nadia's suit caught them anyway.

This time, Ember did frown. It was one thing to *watch* for the mella and daydream about shooting one so you could avenge your wife, who didn't actually need avenging because she'd been about to die from cancer and had chosen to walk into a sand dune. *Chasing* the mella to one of their targets, even if only to spy on them, so they could shoot *you*, was something entirely different. She didn't have a death wish, just a need to see her wife's body and maybe punch some-one.

The solitude came as a bonus though. You didn't get a lot of it living in a pimple of a dome on an all-woman planet, especially if your wife had recently died. At the very least, out here, Ember didn't have to unwind spools of hair from the shower drain and had half a moment to remember her wife the way she wanted to, not the way everyone else de-manded.

"It's a two-day ride and a four-day walk," Ember said. "They'll get there before I do. They have beetles. I don't even have a flyer. The director turned down my requisition re-quest."

"That's because, first, it's the presidium that approves those, not the director, and second, you suck at flying. You are *terrified* of flying. You're terrified of ships, even those that don't leave the atmosphere. Which, I get; yours almost didn't make it to Queen, but still. This is a big group of mella. They're not moving fast, and they're still at Outpost Two. You'll make it. Move like a beetle. You kind of look like one in that suit when you have the antennae out."

Nadia leaned into her video feed until her eyes consumed the whole screen. Ember could see through her goggles, to the rich brown laughing eyes behind them. Nadia always had a smile, even when Ember thought the dunes might as well sweep her to the cold side of the planet, where her bones would crack and her marrow freeze, or to the hot side, where her skin would turn to leather in a day without the envirosuit, two days with it. Her sister smiled because she didn't remember Earth, not in color anyway. Not in sound, or smell, the way spring daisies gave way to buttercups in fields wafting a perfume of silage. Nadia had never seen redwoods touch clouds, had never slipped on moss-covered stones in streams alive with nutria and frogs and ducks and migrating geese.

Nadia had been ten years Ember's junior at the Collapse, but they'd been put on different ships. She'd been too young to go into stasis, at eighteen, but she'd made it here, eventually. They'd been in transit nineteen years, Earth time. Their time here on Queen, only five years, felt like an eternity.

Now Nadia was older than Ember. Older visibly, in the silver of her hair and crinkles around her eyes, and in the way she kept rotating her wrist to ease some unspoken pressure. They had the same skin though, a pale tan that flushed too easily. Nadia still smiled and joked as if Queen wasn't a desolate, isolated colony planet. As if Earth's memory didn't oppress them, hundreds of light-years away. She joked because she didn't want to leave. Queen was her home, even if they had no family here and precious few friends.

For Ember, it was a way station. A bad aftertaste. A future gone horribly wrong. "Botanists are not good with sand."

"Well, you know what they say about sand, sis." Nadia smirked. "*Dune't* forget your—"

Ember shook her head but couldn't help smiling. "You've used up all the world's puns. Please don't invent more."

Nadia's eyes relaxed. The crinkles smoothed. A somberness took over, and it looked wholly alien on this sister she'd never seen grow up. "We're just trying to give you what you want."

"If I wanted to look for Taraniel, I wouldn't have waited two months to do so."

The name burned Ember's mouth, and she sucked in her lips as an explosion of pain shattered her insides. Only sisters could make you hurt like this. Only sisters could dig up your most painful memories and talk about them as you would the weather at Sunday brunch.

"Doesn't matter. You have to go." Nadia's voice held no laughter now; no light shone in her eyes. "Maybe after, you'll finally want to come home. You're no good to yourself like this. You're a *botanist*. Finish your task so you can get back here and into the lab where you belong. Enough with your funk. The mella are done. There are two troupes left, and then it's just the outliers in their outpost, wherever that is. We've got a satellite reading that looks promising. We think it's the same group that raided the hospital last month. Find this group and send the coordinates to Dr. Narkhirunkanok. She'll send them to the presidium, and they will send out the flyers. One of these times, one of the mella will have a GPS on them, and our satellites will function correctly, and we'll finally track them back to their main base."

"The plan sounds about as well cooked as most of the presidium's brains."

"Oh, for fuck sake's, Ember. Just take the job. We'll get the coordinates to their home; the presidium will take it out."

Ember kicked the side of a dune, then squatted and crossed her arms. She kept talking, because poking the presidium would only get one of her minor research grants revoked, but poking Nadia got her much-needed human interaction. "Yes, but then *I'd* be out of a job."

"*Lab*." Nadia pointed back toward the dome. "Baby

trees and whatever else you have growing in your greenhouse that won't survive two days once you plant it outside the dome. Science pays way better than this, and you've got tenure coming in, what, a year? Get a raise. You need a hell of a lot more money than you've got if you want to leave Queen. Leave us. I know what you and Taraniel talked about at night. Your voices carried through the walls."

Nadia's voice turned sour. "Aside from that, think about your future, Ember. Not this shit. Come *home*. Taraniel may be gone, but visit your bestie Dr. Sinha, at least. Call Taraniel's mother on Europa. Talk to her about her daughter."

"Stop talking about her, Nadia. Please."

"Why? Someone has to."

Ember wouldn't let the tears fall. She'd never be able to wipe them away. Instead, she slapped the dried red blood of the barren planet and watched the sand spray into oblivion.

"I'm going to record that as your verbal consent." Nadia sounded smug. "You leave immediately. Should just be you and the grit the whole way. Enjoy."

Nadia's image clicked off. Ember's viewscreen reverted to the red landscape, where a wall of sand rose with the wind. The world turned russet for several moments, and Ember's respirator whirred into high gear, filtering the air it brought in. It smelled of crisp nothing. It smelled of heat. It smelled of loss.

Ember stood at the base of the dune and waited for the small storm to subside. Nadia's words stripped her mind of every other thought, and she gasped mouthfuls of hot, processed air.

Taraniel. It had been two months now, give or take a few days, and Ember still expected to see her around every dune. Hoped for a mistake. Hoped the doctors had been wrong.

Cancer.

Earth's legacy, the one enduring gift that had come with

the immigrants that nothing could kill. Taraniel had preferred to meet death on her own terms. She'd taken no respirator, only clothes and things that entwined with her memories, and left Ember with no body. No closure. No peace.

The wind died to a low rush. Ember turned and started the slow, plodding walk back to Outpost Seven, where she could recharge her envirosuit before going out again. Sand slicked under her feet. TOPA told her that giant beetles scuttled along the parallel dunes, just out of sight, knowing better than to attack while she still moved. A sand funnel swirled. Her face shield registered the distance in the logging unit of chains, but the landscape remained fundamentally unchanged aside from the occasional dotting of twisted trees—Ember's work as part of the terraforming project. These trees were the farthest ones out from the dome. After here, nothing grew in the sand, not even small plants, no matter how many genes Ember edited and how much irrigation Nadia installed. They were two scientists with futile science, although their PhDs had gotten them quick acceptance onto Earth's newest outpost. Well, PhDs had helped, and their anatomy had sealed the deal. Vulvas got you onto Queen. Nothing could get you off. A pun worthy of Nadia.

Ember looked out at the patchwork desert forest she'd grown from Petri plates. The trees were maples mostly, reds and silvers, but a few white aspens took the genetic modifications well too. They couldn't grow upright with the winds, so they branched more like bushes, staying low to the ground and fanning out their crowns to make the best of the perpetual morning. They caught sand and died when their leaves became too covered for photosynthesis. But, well, that was job security if nothing else.

TOPA chirped. Another tooth click brought up a readout.

Wind dropped to 14 knots.

Funnel increasing in diameter by 0.35 meters

per 5 seconds. Shape unstable and likely due to animal interaction.

Probability of human origin: 95%

"Well, yes, noting the data, that would be the obvious conclusion, wouldn't it?" Ember muttered to herself. The adrenaline hit like a punch anyway, snapping her body to attention. She stopped walking and watched the funnel continue to bloat across the horizon like a wave on a long-dead ocean. The wind wasn't strong enough to kick up that much sand, but giant beetles definitely were.

"TOPA, can you get a heat signature?"

The face shield blanked momentarily before a heat diagram splayed across it. Human signatures weren't discernable from the sand, but the five-legged beetles native to Queen ran colder than their surroundings due to a quirk of planetary genetics Ember didn't understand, likely because she'd managed to completely avoid entomology in her undergrad.

Beetles: two.

Her face shield blinked the words, and Ember pivoted. The beetles swarmed, were seldom solitary or in pairs in the wild. Her suit's artificial intelligence quickly confirmed her suspicion.

No ID sent. Not of the colony. Strong possibility of mella attack. Retreat or find cover.

Two riders on beetleback exploded from the sand.

Shit.

Ember ran.

Her face shield blasted packets of data at her as she did so. The beetles had shells of Earth-dirt red-and-brown on the sun side of the planetoid, and palest ivory on the cold side. The colonists had never bothered to do much with the damn things since they couldn't live in the temperate zone and had a huge appetite for plastic, which was the only material, outside of rabbit leather, that lasted longer than two seconds in the winds. The beetles could move faster than any of the colony's mechanical sand flyers. Watching the scrolling feed out of her left eye as she ran into the wind and around a short, sloped dune, Ember recalled their resemblance to Earth click beetles with their rectangular bodies, squarish heads, and funny antennae. Click beetles, however, were never ridden by pirates.

Two beetles three chains away.

Ember cursed again, crested a small dune, and slid behind it, panting in the dry air. She drew an avalanche mortar from the thick hide pocket on her right hip and tapped the tube to make sure it was clear. She had twenty seconds, maybe, before the beetles reached her, and she'd no desire to see their mandibles up close. Still, avalanche mortars didn't have great range. At the very least they'd have to get close enough for her to hear their clicks. That meant close enough for the pirates' weapons' range and maybe being blasted into sand herself.

Ember crouched into the dune and waited, peering around so her suit could get readings. The surface of her face shield clogged with grit, cleared itself, then clogged again. Five seconds passed before her interior shield again read **Riders: 2**, and another five seconds before they were close enough to make out distinct features.

The beetles and their riders swelled out of a mahogany sand funnel. The riders wore wraps upon wraps of canvas, cotton, and nylon—all scraps from supply ships since Queen didn't produce any plant or animal capable of generating textiles (the imported angora rabbits had all died of heatstroke) or have the mechanisms for synthetics. They'd have weapons though; that was a given. The riders' arms and hands were bare for some asinine reason, which meant not only sunburn but sand and windburn, too, if they weren't careful. Their beetles toddled more than scuttled toward her, drunk on never-ending sunlight.

Drunk was a condition Ember would have preferred.

The riders pulled up on the leather reins as they approached, slowing the beetles to an awkward sidestep. One of them waved in an almost friendly way. So, they clearly knew where she was, and she'd likely get robbed before she got killed. Lovely.

Ember stood and ran up the dune to face her attackers. "You're trespassing," she yelled, amplifying the sound through her suit's speaker. She loaded the projectile into the tube and tried to steady her breathing. "You have to show official colony badges to move past an outpost. What the hell are you doing out here?"

The riders didn't stop, but she really hadn't expected them to. Why should they? The presidium wanted the tech that allowed the pirates to survive outside the colony, but it was two against one, and Ember didn't have a beetle. She was a sentry, not a flyer. She was supposed to watch and report, not get close enough for an altercation no matter how much she might have wanted a little action. Extenuating circumstances aside, she was still expected to follow the rules.

The beetle clicks finally registered on her face shield, though Ember couldn't hear them. *Screw the presidium. Altercation it is, then.* She pointed the tube, waited for her face shield to confirm angle, and let the projectile fly.

A *BOOM* echoed and smothered the soft *clickclickclick* of the beetles, and the dune the riders were cresting yawned with sinkholes as the explosion collapsed the beetle galleries underneath. The riders shrieked. The beetles screamed. Ember's suit trilled happy notes of success and *Nice work!* scrolled across the face shield as the dune sucked the beetles and riders down. Ember briefly reconsidered activating TOPA's personality protocol just so she'd have someone to feel smug with.

Instead, she watched the struggle, the beetles with their legs and little sharp toes, the riders with useless hooks and ungloved hands. The wind began its warning keen, which meant the sand would soon be flying too fast to see, and Ember stayed rooted to her dune. She probably should have felt bad about it all; on Earth, you didn't kill people for sneaking up on you in a desert. But Queen had taken Taraniel. Queen's complete lack of resources had taken Taraniel, and the mella pirates stole what few resources the colony did manage to store. If the mella wanted to stalk sentries in the sand and live by their own code, well, they could die by it too.

Death, however, was apparently not on the schedule for the day. The beetles climbed from the sinkholes, perfectly adapted for their environment, and half trampled a rider in the process. That particular swathed head sank below the surface, and Ember remembered she'd need to ping Nadia to dig up the potential GPSs later. The second mella had a grip on one of the low, wind-bent maples that strangled the sand out here, but the sinkholes were still growing, and the small amount of stable ground she'd found would give in another minute. Still, the mella grabbed at the tree, trying to pull herself into its branches. Her head turned to Ember, eyes wild. Ember shivered in the heat.

Recovery? the suit asked.

"No," Ember said. "These aren't the ones I'm supposed to find, and there's no backup for days. Let her die. The colony can send a flyer later. Send the visual data to Dr. Nadia Anne-The-Frying-Pan O'Grady."

TOPA's screen blinked twice as it sifted through the database of seven hundred scientists, trying to decode a childhood nickname. Earth was a wasteland, Ember mused, and computers still couldn't do sarcasm or rhyming.

Confirmed. Data sent.

Ember resumed walking, giving the sinkholes a wide berth.

"Dr. Schmitt!"

The name caught in the suit's auditory sensors, and TOPA piped it both to Ember's ears and scrolled the text across the screen. Ember pivoted, scanning both her face shield and the horizon for the caller.

"Dr. Schmitt!"

"TOPA, where is the audio feed coming from?"

TOPA's response came instantaneously. **Audio external to suit. 72 degrees west. Follow arrows.**

Arrows, blinking and marginally patronizing, flashed on her face shield, pointing west and...down. Ember turned her head until the shield lit up bright green, to the mella centered in her vision, clinging desperately to one of Ember's gnarled silver maples.

"Dr. Schmitt, we came for you!"

"Errr," Ember managed, forgetting to tell TOPA to turn off the speaker. The mella shouldn't have known her name. Sure, there were only a few thousand humans on-planet at any given time. But Ember certainly couldn't name any mella, though half had their faces plastered all over the rec spaces with WANTED under their chins and, occasionally, bad mustaches drawn on in marker.

Ember hadn't drawn a good handlebar mustache since Taraniel's march into the dunes. Bottom line, there was no way this mella knew who she was unless Taraniel had told them about her. But that was ridiculous. It'd been two months. Taraniel had been less than a day from multiple organ failure. She was *dead*.

"Just die already!" Ember yelled into the wind.

"Wait!" the mella shouted back. "*Look.*"

As Ember watched, the mella surrendered precious security on the branch to reach one hand into a shallow pocket. She pulled out a piece of hide dyed deep blue, ocean blue, *Earth* blue, and looped it around the thick branch, giving herself a better handhold.

Shit. Again.

Ember had no breath. The sand swirled red around her,

and the sky was the same hot, unending fire, but all she could see was the blue leather—a headband she'd given Taraniel for their fifth wedding anniversary. Ember had drawn the dye from a shawl she'd brought from Earth. The color had come from a rare fungus Queen would never know. Taraniel had lived on the Pacific shore before the Collapse. The ocean filled her dreams and her paintings; the ocean was her heart. Though Ember had also grown up near the waves, they'd never captivated her the same way. On Queen, she couldn't give Taraniel the ocean, but she could give her blue.

Taraniel had worn the headband the day she walked from the habitable zone, taking an unrecoverable part of Ember with her. They'd dreamed of leaving Queen *together*, both of them breathing and alive. Now, here Taraniel stood—if only in spirit, if only in some grave-robbing pirate's scavenged clothing—about to die again.

Well, screw that. This time, Ember wouldn't let her.

Chapter Two

June brought hurricanes, tornados, floods, and tsu-namis. The glaciers finished melting, and seawater turned brackish. The oceans died.

Ember

Operation not recommended.

Ember ignored the TOPA. "Hold on!" Her words sounded tinny, suddenly, through her suit, but that was irrelevant. Ember ran toward the woman, toward the tree, down the dune, into the sand funnel and death. "If you let go, I will kill you."

She'd started higher than the mella, but her boots slipped, skidded, and she rolled down the dune side, too fast to have any control. The opening of the hole she'd created drew closer, swallowing the world. Her suit and left leg registered chitinous impact, and an unidentified root grabbed at her elbow, but she couldn't see anything except red sand.

ABORT ABORT ABORT

TOPA flashed the word over and over across her face shield. A hideous klaxon, one part fire engine and three parts angry two-year-old, blared in Ember's ears. TOPA had never made that sound before, and if she survived this fall, Ember swore she'd pay the upgrade fee to make sure it never did it again.

She kept slipping, past the opening, sand pulling her legs down. Tiny little air jets whirred into action. Ember's shield cleared, then darkened again with sand. The air intake valves clogged. Red flashed across her face shield. The interior of the suit turned damp with her breath, and she had to take deeper and deeper breaths to get enough oxygen. The sand under her gloved hands went soft, giving her the disturbing thought that she was about to be sucked down a giant funnel.

Ember kicked like she was clawing her way up from a dive off a diving board, an Earth activity she'd been passably good at until pools were banned due to water rationing. One of the intakes cleared, and fresh air blasted through the suit. The mella's ungloved hand grabbed her, bringing the bent tree into focus as the suit's air jets finally caught up. Ember's vision cleared.

Bless maple trees and their stubborn desire to grow anywhere. Ember swam up the side of the funnel and flailed for a branch, the mella's pants, anything that might hold her in place. Trust looked really different when you didn't want to turn into beetle fodder. Ember's fingertips brushed something firm and slipped off, just to have the mella grab her wrist, yank hard enough that Ember was certain something popped, drag her up the side of the funnel, and wrap Ember's fingers around smooth, sand-worn bark.

"Taraniel," Ember demanded as she tried to pull her knees up. The sand sucked at her legs, and the blue leather punched her heart, and the only thing that mattered in this godforsaken moment was her wife's memory.

"Later. Wrap!"

The mella pointed at Ember's leg, but Ember shook her head. There was barely enough soil to shore up her knees. Sand had wormed its way past a popped seam at her elbow, and bits of spiked, red granules static-clung to the inside of her face shield.

"Where did you get it?" Ember yelled back, trying to be heard over the growing wind. "Is she alive?"

The mella growled and grabbed Ember's thigh, fingernails pressing into the leather of her suit. The face shield scrolled warnings about pressure and other seams. It was conscious work to not let go of the tree and slap the mella's hand away. "*Wrap*," the mella said again and pushed Ember's leg up until her heel hit the trunk. The mella's own leg came up next, and she wrapped it around the tree, twisting her leg between branches.

"Oh." Realization smacked as fast as the sand, and Ember did the same. The silver maples had impossibly long taproots, anchored to a lower base layer, and wouldn't be going anywhere. The sinkholes were already slowing filling in. If they held on for another few minutes, the ground would be stable, and they could walk away. They could walk to Ember's wife, or her body, or whatever remained of her out in the dunes.

Four minutes to ground stability.

That was a long time to spoon a woman she didn't know, especially on the edge of a sand funnel. The mella apparently agreed and released as soon as the ground stopped sinking, and the sand in the wind settled to only slightly shitty visibility. That meant the sun was that much brighter, the temperature back to brick pizza oven levels. God, Ember missed pizza.

The mella tested the sand, straightened, and walked far enough from the edge that 1) Ember couldn't readily kick her, and 2) she wasn't likely to fall back in if she stepped wrong. She brushed sand from her mismatched clothing tatters, rewrapped the layers of leather and cotton around her feet and ankles, unwrapped the headband from the tree, and shoved it into her pocket. She oozed defiance in a way that caught Ember's attention and would have held it if they weren't in danger of actually baking to death.

Ember scowled, though there was no way the mella could tell through the reflective sapphire-reinforced glass of the face shield.

Send report to Dr. Nadia Anne-The-Frying-Pan O'Grady?

"No," Ember said, making sure to click off the speaker this time so she couldn't be heard outside the suit. "Just record. We'll wait until we have more data."

Confirmed.

Ember clicked the speaker back on. The ground no longer swirled like a budget funnel cake, so she dismounted the tree and stood, prodding sand with her thickly booted toe every few pivots, keeping her face toward the mella.

The woman still didn't say anything.

Ember kicked a plume of sand at her midsection.

"Give me the headband," Ember demanded. "And then I promise not to kill you, and I'll take you back to the outpost." She blew upward, trying to clear more clinging sand on the inside of her face shield. "It's nicer there, anyway, than a dune."

"Taraniel wasn't so demanding. Have you always been an asshole?"

Taraniel's name did not belong in the mella's mouth. Her name didn't belong in the scalding wind of the desert, and her headband sure as hell didn't belong in a tattered pocket that probably smelled like crotch.

Ember punched her. Thumb out, because scientists weren't complete idiots, and connected with the top of a shoulder as the mella twisted and sprang back up a few paces to the left. Ember made a grab for the peak of blue she saw among the wrapped tatters, and the mella grabbed her arm, pulling her forward and off balance.

Ember landed, face shield down, in deceptively firm sand. She rolled onto her back, and in doing so, a few of the sand particulates from inside her suit fell into her eyes. Ember swatted ineffectually at her shield and blinked furiously, eyes streaming saltwater with no way to wipe it away.

The mella held Ember's shins while she thrashed, not striking until Ember landed a blow to the woman's belly. Then she did punch, the first hits coming from her feet. When the strips of cloth she used for shoes started unraveling, the mella dropped to her knees—right on Ember's midsection.

Ember, vision still blurry, groaned, then sucked in as much breath as she could and tried to roll her hips over. Her suit was bulky white leather, and the mella's shitty clothing, coated in sand, proved too slippery to dislodge. So, Ember batted at the woman staring down at her—with punches, with knees, with curses—until warning lights blinked onto her face shield about excessive oxygen use.

"We came here to find you, not to die," the mella said as Ember resigned herself to being slowly sucked into a dune. "But after all that, you can go right to hell."

"This *is* hell. Where did you get the headband?"

If they'd been indoors, the mella probably would have spat on her. Here, though, the wind was too strong and the sand too thick. Instead, she reached into another pocket and pulled out a piece of petrified wood. At one time it had been a spoon. Taraniel had carved the handle herself. Every morning, she'd eaten Galactic Standard Oatmeal, another Earth legacy they could never escape, with that spoon.

Now, its bowl had been cut off and the end sharpened to a point. It didn't matter that the mella might be able to pierce Ember's suit leather with the thing. The outposts and the colonists didn't matter. If Taraniel wanted her treasured possessions buried with her, that was fine, but they didn't belong to *this* woman.

Ember screamed, "Damn you! Where is her body?"

"She was alive when we found her." She said the words, snarled, brandished her stolen spoon-knife. "Now back off and *listen*."

Ember stopped thrashing and lay under the red sky, stunned.

The mella got up.

Ember edged first to her elbows, then her knees, then her feet. She stepped back, not looking behind her, not reading her face shield. There was *no way* Taraniel was alive because if she were alive, she'd have come back to the settlement to find Ember and they would be *together*. Ember wouldn't be playing whack-a-mella on the uninhabitable sun side of a planet that was so red it looked like it was perpetually on its period.

"You're lying," she whispered, hoping the mella could hear the words through the suit. "She can't be alive. Are you saying she is alive?"

The woman shook her head. "No. But she left a message for you. It would have been nice if she'd mentioned what a complete sandhead you were in the process."

Ember blinked. "But—"

The mella took out a tranquilizer gun, and shot her.

Chapter Three

In July, we lost the squirrels, the voles, the chipmunks. The rats. For a moment, the number of predators swelled, and then in August, they fainted in the scarred forests, among cellulose skeletons. Humans harvested what they could. The rest rotted.

Nadia

"What do you mean the pipe broke? Humanity can colonize the Milky Way, but we can't keep pipes from freezing? Go out and fix the damn thing!"

Nadia's lab assistant, a short woman with sharp blue eyes, coal-black hair half shaved on one side, and pale, freckled skin coughed, then ran from Nadia's lab, her eyes on the floor the whole way. Nadia doubted Olive was more than nineteen. Her walk was too crisp and her fingers too jittery. She'd been working under Nadia barely three months—a recent immigrant from a planet that had a minimum birth rate law. Queen had to keep its population low due to limited resources, so it was a good refuge if babies weren't your thing. Nadia had been in Queen's pregnancy lottery for seven years before finally giving up. Apparently, babies weren't her thing either. She wasn't bitter about it; she certainly understood the rationale behind the birth restrictions, but that didn't make her heart hurt any less when she spotted a young girl occasionally among the crowds of women.

A high-pitched crash sounded from down the hall. Olive had likely taken the left turn too fast and run into the centrifuge Nadia had decided to decommission. Someone's absentminded graduate student had balanced a box of broken lab glassware on top of the centrifuge. While it had been taped shut, that wouldn't stop the glass from breaking further.

Nadia rolled her eyes, slumped onto a round stool, and flipped open her lab notebook. She flicked through the plastic pages and briefly mulled how likely the director would be to greenlight new piping before slamming the book closed.

She shouldn't be so angry with her assistant. It wasn't her fault, of course, that New Earth hadn't bothered to develop tech suitable for Queen's extreme climate, and that half the decent stuff they *did* develop had to be shipped to New Earth for testing before it could be legally implemented. The orders came from the presidium, who worked directly under New Earth governance. It would be Nadia's fault, though, if the biyearly report she owed the science director, which the director would then send to the presidium, came late. It'd be especially problematic if it was late because she couldn't finish gathering the data on their new irrigation project. *Her* report got combined with half a dozen others from around the colony and then sent on to New Earth, where yet another council would look at it and decide how much aid Queen would get over the next six months. If Nadia fucked up the data or the analysis, then she fucked the colonists, too, and she fucked her damn sister, whom she'd come to this ass-backward planet to be with, even if she was a giant sand maggot. The last message she'd sent Ember had been a real zinger though. Two could play stupid nickname rhyming games.

"Dr. O'Grady?"

Nadia perked up and turned toward Dr. Varun Sinha who stood in the doorway, fanning several sheets of plastic paper her way. A tall, willowy man, he had wavy black hair, sepia-brown skin, and a graying mustache that he gelled into handlebars. He'd been an architect back on Earth and had helped design most of the housing on Queen. The settlement hadn't been meant to expand however. The habitable zone was too narrow. So, he'd managed a remote PhD in… Nadia didn't remember what field, but it had something to do with beetles and how they used butt-lights to communicate. Now, he hung around the science complex pinning things to boxes of mothballs.

"What is it?" Nadia asked, more irritably than she intended. Dr. Sinha had just as many reports to file as she did. Wandering the halls chitchatting was academic time suck number one, and today, Nadia just didn't have the patience for it, even for her sister's drinking buddy.

Dr. Sinha smoothed one of the perpetual lateral wrinkles on his collared shirt, and Nadia took a deep breath in empathy. Being a man on Queen had to be a special kind of hell, especially since the surgeries he might have wanted would get him punted from the planet. At some point, the presidium would have to review their concepts of what made someone a "woman." That was way above Nadia's pay grade, however.

"One of the sentries called in," Dr. Sinha said. When Nadia's eyebrows rose, he added hastily, "Not your sibling. I've not heard from her since this morning when she sent me a 'selfie' of her…" Dr. Sinha mouthed half a word, swallowed it, then tried again. "A photo of the back of her envirosuit with an endearing caption. But the sentry I'm talking about, Thikhamphorn—"

"You know she goes by Apple," Nadia cut in. "She's told you that, like, fifteen times."

Dr. Sinha waved at Nadia irritably, and she tried not to laugh. He was a lot more animated when flustered, and he was often flustered when drunk, which was half the fun of drinking with him. "Her envirosuit is more formal, and so am I. Thikhamphorn was assigned sentry duties on the cold side last week. She sent images of the damaged pipes, and I confirmed markings consistent with beetle predation." He paused, thoughtful. "I haven't heard from her in two days. I wonder what else she has found?"

Nadia let her head roll back and stared at the painted yellow ceiling, random dreams of getting Ember and Dr. Sinha smashed at the same time and making them ride a beetle while wearing pirate eye patches slipping from her mind. "Mella."

"Yes."

Of course it was the mella. It was *always* the mella. Every broken pipe, every stolen piece of glassware, every resource New Earth had stopped sending because it wasn't worth the risk of piracy. Queen could have, *should have*, been a paradise, but it wasn't, because *mella*.

Nadia jumped up from her chair, rolled her notebook, and slipped it into the elongated pocket on her blue lab coat. "Fucking fuckers," she muttered as she elbowed Dr. Sinha out of the way and stalked down the hall, weaving around her assistant, who was sweeping spilled glass into a dustpan.

Broken glass, another import that couldn't be replaced until the next supply ship arrived and only *if* the ship had any on it to begin with. The colonists still lived in the same military-style barrack rooms the original settlers had brought over twenty-two years ago. They still didn't have a proper community library or anything set up for active recreation. A hard-packed sand track was available for a run around the dome perimeter. Anyone wanting to play soccer was screwed. They had barracks, a science building, a community mess hall, a medical center that had once been a lorry, a *tiny* school, and a ship landing pad the size of a pancake. The buildings were packed so tightly together they might as well have been humping one another. They also had an *entire planetoid* they could colonize and terraform if New Earth would give them half a chance. Part of Queen was obviously way too cold, part was hot enough for second-degree burns after a hot second (hah!) outside a ship, and the temperate zone was the width of her index finger. But they'd put a dome up once; surely, they could do it again.

Nadia stormed into the building's main office. The room was roughly the size of her lab, but instead of benches and glassware, it had imported wooden bookshelves, end tables, and, on the west wall, a dilapidated antique loveseat upholstered in avocado-green floral print. Nadia smelled forget-me-nots, which she'd thought had died with Earth. They had a synthetic equivalent used in perfumes, but she could definitely smell the difference. The bookshelves mostly held lab reports, not books, but with the constant messaging about limited space, limited resources, limited *everything*, every square meter rankled.

Nadia kicked the leg of an old wooden chair just to watch the thing wobble. The lab director, a middle-aged woman with sharp eyes and an even sharper chin, motioned for Nadia to close the door. She then pointed to one of the chairs that sat in front of three wooden secretary desks, placed side to side. Each tiny drawer of the desks overflowed with a mixture of plastic notes, pen refill cartridges, and pieces of electronics. Dr. Sureeporn Narkhirunkanok— nickname "Maew," but Nadia would never call her that—had been the science director of Queen since the first day of colonization, and Nadia was certain the woman would mummify in her office before retiring. They'd met once outside of work at one of Ember's "Variance is *Fucking* Awesome" club meeting thingies that Nadia tried really hard to be supportive of, though a part of her still wanted to flat-out ask who had come with factory-installed labia and who hadn't. As far as Nadia knew, Ember was the only intersex woman on the planet. But there were plenty of trans men— pre-surgery (if they wanted it), of course—because of Queen's stupid residency requirement. No trans women because the people that had platted the planet were bigoted as hell. At their two-minute meeting, Dr. Narkhirunkanok had been marginally less irritating, speaking about her pet rabbit, Sir Hops-A-Lot, and the diet of button mushrooms she'd adapted him to since they couldn't get hay imported anymore. That wasn't enough to make up for the head-in-ass way she ran the science center.

"The presidium already authorized flyers. But you know the mella are likely long gone," Dr. Narkhirunkanok said in a carefully controlled monotone. "There're better ways to spend your anger than yelling."

Nadia was in *exactly* the right place to spend her anger. Residency on Queen came with life tenure. They could fire her, but it wasn't as if they would kick her off-world, and there wasn't a line of hydrologists itching to move in either.

"What about the mellas my sister is tracking?" Nadia demanded. "Can we at least shoot *them*? I mean, Jesus

Christ. We've been hunting the mella since the colony started, I thought. How are they so robust? They're like Queen's version of the bubonic plague. They can't possibly be surviving just on stolen colony scraps anymore. *We* barely survive on the scraps New Earth sends."

Dr. Narkhirunkanok tucked a strand of rich black hair behind her ear and produced a look that was something between "I'm sorry I kicked your puppy" and "I really wish you would leave my office." Nadia recognized it immediately, and a weight dropped in her stomach. That look had driven Ember into the sand wastelands, and here, now, in the director's office, it stripped all of Nadia's anger and reduced it to panic over Ember.

How did one ask if their sister was beetle fodder? Dr. Narkhirunkanok had plenty of experience in theory, dealing with these types of conversations, and yet, they both sat there, staring at each other. Nadia gripped the edges of the chair. The sides were splintery from too many colonists having too many conversations like the one that was about to come. Nadia didn't have time for it, just like she didn't have time for the conscripted (stolen, if you asked her) experiments, poor management of resources, and the bad decision some nitwit had made about where to send her grieving sister. Even if that nitwit was her.

"I came here about the busted, beetle-gnawed pipes. Don't you dare tell me my sister has been injured. I talked to her three hours ago. She's *fine.*"

Dr. Narkhirunkanok couldn't meet Nadia's eyes. In the silence, a chill settled in. The momentary fear swirled back to anger. Ember was fine because Ember was always fine, Nadia rationalized. She'd made it to Queen on a ship that had practically limped through space, where 99 percent of the stasis modules had failed. She'd been out in the sand for weeks with nothing but TOPA for company, and there hadn't been even a blip of mella activity. One lone woman, especially without a flyer, wasn't worth anyone's attention, even pirates.

"We don't have a full picture," Dr. Narkhirunkanok said, drawing out the words as her eyes finally flicked up to meet Nadia's. "One data point is never significant."

"Tell me what you have."

It was a command, and Nadia didn't care if Dr. Cat (she'd never get over that Maew meant "cat" in Thai) docked her pay for academic subordination. Nadia hadn't left a husband, her parents, and hope of sex with a penis ever again, for giggles. Earth's failure had broken up billions of families as new planets were found and colonization rules made. Queen was the only planet that would take Ember. The *only damn one*. Nadia hadn't thought twice about her decision. She'd been eighteen and newly married, as were lots of people during Earth's decline. Something about the apocalypse made social milestones much more urgent. She'd left Sean O'Grady six months after their marriage and five months after Ember's colony ship left for Queen. Sisters stuck together.

"We know her TOPA is damaged. It keeps signaling us for pickup. The face shield was cracked, and TOPA reports numerous openings in the leather. The GPS in the suit tracks her to over thirty thousand chains past the habitable zone, cold side. She's almost near the equator. If she's out that far, in a broken suit, then she's dead. Now, or within the hour."

Nadia shot up from her chair and slammed her hands onto the desk. "Then send a flyer! Go get her! She's the only botanist you've got left. Surely that merits the fuel."

"We can't, Dr. O'Grady. You know that." The sticky finality to Dr. Narkhirunkanok voice spiked Nadia's anger to unhealthy levels. "Flyers can't take the extreme temperatures that close to the equator. It's a no-fly zone for a reason. Our satellites don't send data from those regions either. There's nothing to see, and I don't have codes for reprogramming even if I wanted to. How she even got out there is a scientific wonder."

"She probably got dragged by a feral beetle that took flight! If it is the mella, you can just blast them. That's literally all the flyers do, anyway!" Nadia pointed out the round window that took up half the south wall. "That's my *sister* out there. She already lost her wife because New Earth wouldn't hear her medical asylum case because of the computer chip shortage. Don't you *dare* let her die too."

"I send a flyer and the pilot dies, Dr. O'Grady, well before they would likely even reach Dr. Schmitt. Then what? I send another flyer for someone else's sister and *another* pilot dies? When does it end? Dr. Schmitt knew the risks of her job. You convinced her to take this last one. The presidium is clear about travel restrictions, and Dr. Schmitt signed the waivers for being a sentry. She can go places in service of the presidium. You can't. We can't. You have to let it go."

After a momentary pause, Narkhirunkanok added, "I can authorize new piping for your project, if you'd like."

Nadia clamped down on a hurricane of emotions and stood. She'd yelled at the director enough times to know when she'd already made up her mind. Hell, Nadia had barely gotten a blip of emotion off the woman when "someone" had carved a urinating penguin into the front of her lab door. The director had kept her maddening deadpan as she'd interviewed everyone in the building about it.

Ember had made it near the equator, which meant the envirosuit had been fine for a little while. She'd managed to send a distress call. She wasn't on the actual equator, and a thousand kilometers or so from the colony was marginally habitable. Right? They didn't need satellites for a rescue mission.

Also, generally, what the hell? Forget that Ember was the only family Nadia had since their parents had pulled winning lottery numbers for a retirement resort planet...*an entire planet* of old people playing rummy and having wild bunny sex, with a few younger employees to keep things running. Queen had started with five botanists, but three had successfully transferred to other worlds, and the fourth had died of exposure on the cold side when her envirosuit malfunctioned during a planting. Ember was their only hope of keeping vegetation on the planet, so that should have warranted at least *some* kind of emotional response. Panic, at the least, since botanists didn't grow on trees.

Nadia couldn't even laugh at her own pun. Dr. Narkhirunkanok just kept staring, and Nadia's insides kept churning until a tiny voice in her head suggested that she could stew anywhere. Somewhere with fragile glassware would be more cathartic. If everyone could waste resources, then she could too. She made a rude gesture—covertly, because raises were due to be reported any day now—and walked out of the office when every cell in her body screamed to run. Ember was depressed, sure, but she wasn't suicidal. If a few stray mella had found her and killed her, well, Nadia owed her sister a proper burial, if nothing else.

The trouble was, she didn't have many options. Nadia had spent a lot more time "awake" than Ember during transport to Queen, much of it in the stunted laboratories of her transport ship. Nadia could design a culvert for sand or snow, she could computer-model what Queen would look like if the snow side all melted, and she could build a passable water filter out of basic household components. But that was where her skill ended. She didn't have any medical training, couldn't operate a flyer, and didn't have security clearance to order underlings to help her.

That was why, several minutes later, she slammed open the door to Dr. Varun Sinha's lab. Nadia normally avoided the place like the plague since the chemical smell of whatever he used to preserve insect parts always smelled like cheap vodka. The lab made her feel claustrophobic and reminded her of what she could be downgraded to if she didn't get the irrigation system working reliably.

Dr. Sinha's lab was maybe a quarter the size of Nadia's, with two rectangular benches, six stools, and a broken laminar flow hood that they couldn't fix until new filters came in on a supply ship. He had a full set of fleakers displayed on one of his benches, which Nadia deeply coveted and had definitely mentioned wanting to borrow at least half a dozen times.

Outside of those, however, the lab had very little. The bare, white-painted walls were made of cinderblock—a material Queen could actually produce enough of to export. Concrete quality sand had become a surprisingly limited resource on Earth. Queen was full of the stuff, which *maybe* explained why the Earth leaders had thought it warranted colonization. The lime had to be imported, which was ridiculous. Three interstellar transports arrived per day just to haul cinderblock and raw sand. In return, New Earth sent a weekly supply ship with shitty dry goods. The value difference was statistically significant, and it sucked.

The room stank, as it always did, of viscera and ethanol. As the door banged against the jamb, Dr. Sinha looked up, startled, and dropped his scalpel into the cavity of the beetle spread out across the left bench. The beetle's two left legs twitched, and one of the antennae curled in on itself. Nadia took a reflexive step back.

The ass part of the beetle—abdomen maybe—had turned blue. Nadia had no idea what that meant and didn't care. Not her PhD thesis, not her line of research, not her problem.

"Dr. O'Grady? I didn't realize you were interested in the signaling patterns and colors of Queen's beetles."

Nadia swallowed the preservative-laden air and grabbed the frame for support. Behind Varun, rows and rows of reddish, penis-shaped forms sat on a low shelf, floating in what Nadia hoped was ethanol. Probably fungi. God, she hoped they were fungi.

"I'm not. I need a flyer."

Dr. Sinha sat back on his stool and crossed his arms, oblivious to the purple beetle innards that smeared across his lab coat as he did so. "Did you ask the director?"

Nadia made it a point to never ask Dr. Narkhirunkanok for anything before she was about to do something incredibly stupid. Dr. Narkhirunkanok reported directly to the presidium, and the presidium were the "peer review" for all Queen-specific grant funding. Nadia didn't need that attention. They already watched everyone's research output like turkey vultures. Nadia wanted them well away from sister-rescue operations.

"Can't. I need a flyer *now*." She took a deep breath. "It's Ember."

"I see." He stood and walked around the bench to the emergency eyewash station, which he activated and proceeded to rinse his hands in. Nadia could have pretended to be grossed out, but she'd definitely done the same a time or two, and right now, nothing mattered as much as getting to Ember.

"Are you going to fly it?" Sinha dried his hands on his pants and shed his lab coat onto a pile of similarly purple-gooed coats in the far corner of the lab.

"Not if you come with me. You still have the small one, right? That they gave you for carcass recovery? It has all the same tolerances as a normal flyer, right?"

"Yes, it does, yes, I do, and it's cleared for ground transport. We'll have to bring back biomatter that I can file. The presidium will check. Let's go."

He could have asked why they were going out. He could have asked where. He didn't, which was why Nadia had chosen this stinking lab over all the other potential chloroform and formaldehyde–perfumed labs on her floor—though she doubted many other scientists had their own personal flyers. Dr. Sinha and Ember's friendship had bloomed mostly out of necessity, but that didn't make it any less meaningful. The little support group used to get together once a month at Ember's dorm—single occupancy since Taraniel's death—for beer and bullshit and probably a lot of ranting. Before her death, Taraniel had come over to Nadia's place a few of those nights, and they'd binge-watched old Earth serials and talked shit about the stolen science on Queen. Taraniel had always been welcomed to stay for the meetings, but Nadia understood why she didn't want to. Those meetings had been a place of refuge Taraniel didn't want to intrude on. That fundamental understanding had been a core element in Ember and Taraniel's marriage working to begin with. They'd always allowed each other their own space, their own time. They allowed some secrets. It'd been the key reason Nadia had liked the woman right from the start and why Ember and Nadia's parents applied, year after year, for a travel visa to visit.

Besides, body semantics were weird to talk about when you had only a secondhand frame of reference. But Dr. Sinha's and Ember's unspoken alliance gave Nadia enough street cred to demand favors, even without mentioning Ember's name. Also, Nadia had walked Dr. Sinha around the dome for an entire night once while he vomited his homemade vodka, and really, if you weren't friends after that, you were never going to be.

Nadia spun around and all but launched herself down the hall toward the flyer bay, Dr. Sinha walking silently behind her. They passed several colleagues: Dr. Craig who did potato research, and Dr. Riggio who did something or other with microbes. Neither of them more than nodded to Nadia or Dr. Sinha because walking with purpose warded off questions. And because Sinha still reeked of mothballs.

When they reached the bay, he thumbprinted the controls. A plastic door rolled up and they walked in. Lights flickered on above them. A triangular, wedge-shaped flyer sat on blocks just past the entry. Smaller than the more cone-shaped standard flyers the sentries used, it shone a bright turquoise instead of the flat gray of the other ships. Yellow racing stripes blared down either side in lines that were clearly hand-painted and really delightful considering Sinha's personality, and gender, and his middle finger to the lab director's dictate about paint waste.

With a *click*, the top hatch of the flyer opened, revealing two seats and a wide, rectangular flat space behind, streaked with beetle blood. Nadia didn't care. She pushed herself onto the wing, then jumped into the back seat and clicked all the appropriate buckles.

"Envirosuits," Sinha said, pointing to a rack several meters away. He already had his on and was getting ready to snap the helmet in place.

Nadia looked down at her formfitted, fireproof-blue lab coat with black cuffed sleeves. It would take time they didn't have for her to get out of that, and her closed-toed shoes and blue jeans, into a suit. Sinha's looser clothes had come off much more rapidly. Instead, Nadia slid down the side of the ship, grabbed a helmet and a pair of gloves, and returned to her seat. "Let's go."

Sinha sealed the last section of his suit, grabbed a spare from the rack, and tossed it at Nadia. He then hopped into the pilot's seat, leaving his face shield up to be heard.

"Where are we going?" The question sounded tinny through her helmet, which bobbed awkwardly on her head without a suit to attach it to.

Nadia huffed at her recklessness. She'd forgotten to get exact coordinates, and marching back to Dr. Narkhirunkanok and demanding them would be beyond suspicious. "Can you receive distress beacons on this thing?"

"Of course." He tapped a series of commands onto the touch screen and, after a moment of fizzling static, a marginally British-accented voice sounded throughout the hangar.

GB-877 – Ember Schmitt. Mayday Mayday. See attached coordinates. Twenty-seven minutes of power left, and I'm several meters under a snow drift. Please send aid.

Sinha tapped the audio off, brought up the GPS coordinates, and fed them into the ship's navigation. He popped his helmet back so it rested on his back and shoulders, still partially attached. "It's sending on a loop and looks like we can't receive due to damage. This what we want?"

"Can you get us there?"

Sinha spoke into his right shoulder. "Location?"

A set of very long coordinates displayed on the flyer's screen. Nadia puzzled briefly over Sinha speaking to his shoulder and not to the inside of his helmet, where TOPAs usually resided, then shrugged.

"That far out?" Sinha pointed to the coordinates. "Not without freezing the computer."

"Would you be willing to try?" Begging was always an option, though not preferable. "We could turn around the moment the computer says we've exceeded whatever tolerances it has. I can't not try. You understand? She's probably dead, but what if she isn't? What if that same beetle dragged her back a bit?"

Sinha's brow furrowed. "Even with that, you won't be able to get out of the flyer without a full envirosuit for more than a few minutes."

Nadia waved the comment away. "If we wait any longer, if she *is* alive, there won't be a reason to go out. I realize I am being irrational. I realize science is rational. Still. *Please.*"

"I won't go any farther than is safe, and I will not be party to you dying of frostbite, but yes." Sinha nodded at her, and mercifully, his face didn't contort into a pity mask as he put his helmet back on and latched his face shield into place. The hatch closed, and the flyer whirred to life in a sputter of electric battery power (with a backup fuel tank because practicality). It lifted off its blocks, and Nadia sank into her leather seat as the TOPA in her helmet clicked on automatically with the ship's computer sync and pinged her for a user code.

"Turn off," she whispered into the face shield. The interior illumination of the helmet dutifully dimmed until Nadia only saw the inside of the flyer, tinted faintly yellow from the UV coating on the face shield. She probably should have told Sinha to do the same, just in case he decided to say Ember's name out loud, and his TOPA thought it was worth reporting. Too late now. Her TOPA wouldn't let her send an audio file without logging in, and there was too much noise inside the flyer to shout and be heard through two helmets.

Nadia kept silent, beyond thankful Sinha did as well, and tried to keep her imagination from spinning wildly out of control. Trying was better than sitting and wondering, and Nadia had never been good at sitting still. If they could get even a few kilometers within Ember, maybe they, or rather, Sinha, could walk out and drag her back. If the mella showed up, maybe Nadia could shoot a few in the process. After they defrosted Ember or whatever medical stuff she required, she and Nadia could give Dr. Narkhirunkanok hell, and maybe, just maybe, the whole experience would be enough to shake off the Taraniel funk that consumed Ember.

And if Nadia ended up dying on the snow side, well, at least she'd be able to torment Ember with puns for the rest of eternity.

Chapter Four

In August, the humans started dying. Not the rich ones. Not yet. The poor died, and the rich built rocket ships and looked for a future in their telescopes.

Ember

Stun guns did amazing things to the mind, Ember mused as she blinked in and out of consciousness. Half of her felt Queen's sun, with the other half convinced she was once again seventeen and sliding into a creek filled with tiny leeches, which would attach to every millimeter of exposed flesh. Earth had been overrun with leeches before the Collapse. Then fungi went wild, and all the trees rotted, while standing. Rabbits had dispersed them, right? Wasn't that what the news feeds had said? Rabbits were scavengers (surprise!) and fungi were scavengers (duh!) and the two had made an unholy alliance for the apocalypse. Not cockroaches. One of her postdoc friends had been really mad about that.

What else? Ember's mind spun. Earth had produced microprocessors and various other types of computer chips for a while, too, when pure silicon dioxide deposits had been found under a few formerly well-colonized cities. Then, everything kind of exploded.

Ember shuddered. None of these were good memories. Besides, she hated leeches and she *really* hated fungi.

The water, though, that felt...too real. Ember wrenched her eyes open, happy to leave behind the leech-infested memory, and saw...a lake. An orangish-blue lake with a tan sand bar that stretched meters past the water's edge. Above her beat Queen's blood-orange daytime sun. A densely-packed maple plantation edged the north side of the lake, except these maples grew straight, like on Earth, with red leaves the size of her palm instead of twice the size of her face, like in the dome.

They were not her maple trees, and there was no way this was her planet. Her planet didn't have fine sand and pale green grass—grass! And god, were those *daisies* ribboned through that endless expanse of green?

She was either dead, or the mella had a secret interplanetary transport service with zero resources and low-level technology. Ember took a moment to process both options. Either worked. One (being dead) got her to Taraniel; the other (being alive but off-world) got her away from her sticky memories. Both would piss Nadia off.

Four split seams greater than two millimeters and two broad tears over five centimeters. Suit compromised. Do not leave habitable zone until repaired. You are an idiot.

"Did your personality function trigger?" Ember hissed into her suit.

It got turned on. At least one of us has to function.

Ember groaned. If TOPA was still around, in whatever mode, then she was alive. It wasn't blasting readouts at her, either, so she was probably not on a luscious tropical paradise planet.

Ember clicked her molars in the pattern that would restart the suit's computer and waited the forty seconds while the previously clear face shield snowed with gray. A chime sounded, and the gray cleared, leaving the screen once again transparent. New data scrolled across the interior, but just then, a boat, an *actual wooden boat* with a little white sail, glided across the lake. A woman in tattered jeans and no shirt leaned casually against the mast.

The boat is made of teak wood which, just so you know, does not grow on this planet and is not a reported crop on any colonized world. Also, restarting won't shut me off. The mella downloaded and removed the personality-free version. I'm the backup.

Ember sat up, far too fast after lying under a hot sun without water. What the mella had or had not done to her suit was irrelevant. This ecosystem simply could not exist on Queen. They could have bioengineered it, maybe, in the habitable zone if New Earth had had resources to spare, which it did not. But here on the sun side, everything was far too hot. Queen orbited in the goldilocks zone of the red sun, but tidal locking meant you were fucked on 90 percent of the planet. None of this was possible.

"Good afternoon. You're heavier than you look, and my beetle doesn't appreciate how you smell. We had to rig up a sleigh to bring you in. My friend survived, by the way. If you'd been anyone else, we'd have just killed you."

Ember recognized the voice of the mella who had both saved her and shot her, though technically, she had shot the woman first. Ember turned, her head complaining the whole way. "Where in hell am I?"

Queen, TOPA provided, its voice reset to factory basic: Midwest US Earth male. Ember hated that voice. It was the only thing she'd ever programmed on her TOPA. She mashed her back right molars together, turning off the suit's audio.

To turn TOPA off, you must manually override safety protocols, said TOPA, switching itself back on. **Either this is your first time using your envirosuit TOPA or the use logs have been wiped for a new user. Would you like a five-minute tutorial?**

"The equator," the mella answered with a half-smile. "Welcome, Dr. Schmitt."

Ember ignored TOPA. "The *what*?"

The mella smirked.

Goddamn it, she wasn't joking. The mella woman loomed over Ember, arms crossed and her cool, khaki-brown skin patchworked with her own shadow. She had black hair, close-cropped with the hint of curls around the lobes of her ears. She'd changed out of the shredded clothes used for protection in the dunes and now wore battered Old Earth biking shorts and a T-shirt that read "The Upper Peninsula. A Special Place."

"This is not Queen," Ember asserted. "No way."

Remote satellite data stored in the envirosuit indicate your current location to be Queen.

"Stop it," Ember breathed. "Go to sleep."

TOPA didn't shut off, but neither did it respond, which was just fine.

The mella crouched and canted her head. She was so close Ember could see the frayed hems of the shorts, the start of a hole on an inner thigh, the torn collar.

"You steal from our recycling pile?" Ember wrinkled her nose and eyed the pit stains. "You know you could just meet the supply ship with the rest of us and requisition clothes, right? You know we would just *give you stuff*, if you asked. That's how Queen works."

"I thought you said this wasn't Queen?"

Three more women came up next to them. None had suits, and all of them wore the same hodgepodge of Old Earth castoffs. Jean shorts with tattered hems. Moisture-wicking runners' shirts that had clearly lost their antimicrobial coating. A neon-pink silk skirt with fading gold embroidery at the hem and knees, and *that* embroidery edged in tiger-lily orange.

The mella formed a loose circle around Ember. Ember kept her butt in the impossible grass. She was going to drown in all this color. Her eyes would explode. It was like having an LED light shined directly in her eyes while she stumbled around a dark bathroom. How in the hell did people live like this? How had she ever lived like this?

Ember mashed her right molars again, and TOPA clicked to attention, cutting off her audio from the external speakers. No need to have mella ears overhearing.

Would you like to take the tutorial now?

"Just give me the readout." When TOPA didn't respond immediately, Ember added, "Pretty please, with a cherry mashed into one of your delicate little circuit boards."

TOPA returned information without inflection, in the blandest monotone Ember had ever heard. **No current satellite data are available. Likelihood of being on Queen's equatorial region is 98 percent. To turn on local satellites and gain access to GPS location, please send an encrypted message to your current administrative head. Please include the reason for being in an equatorial zone and rate your current need of satellite interaction on a scale of one to ten.**

"Forget it," Ember muttered. "How many people are there here, in the wherever we are? Can you at least scan that without a satellite?"

There are one hundred and seven humans and fifty-two quinthropod beetles within a twenty-kilometer radius of your current location. Scans confirm thirty-six dwellings and agriculture of unknown status.

Well, that was all a hard nope, scientifically speaking. Tidally locked planets didn't work like this, and the mella sure as hell didn't work like this. Permanent settlements? Purposefully defective satellites? Fucking lakes and boats and topless women in some kind of 1970s Earth pulp fiction paradise? Forget the presidium. If the New Earth Council found out about this, they would be *pissed*.

A message from Dr. Nadia O'Grady has been received. Heading cannot be read without disabling the adult content filter. Would you like to disable this filter now?

Ember ignored TOPA. "None of us got clearance for easy colonies," she said, after debating several other questions while the ring of mella stared at her. They were very,

very patient, which meant she had to have something they really, really wanted. "We're on Queen because we've got vulvas, degrees, and robust immune systems. These types of ecosystems are supposed to be for people who can't hack lifelong camping inside a sandbox filled with beetle shit."

The mella who'd brought her in popped one of the cockiest grins Ember had ever seen and stood back up. "Do you want to debate ecosystems, or do you want the headband?"

Ember assessed the importance of impossible equatorial habitats and trees that thick and tall versus Taraniel's headband. Not a hard choice.

"Give it back."

"It's not yours."

Ember shot to her feet and promptly fell back onto the sand. Stun guns screwed with equilibrium for days, which, considering she'd only read about them, took her by surprise. "It *is* mine."

Another woman stepped up, shorter than Ember's mella, her light-brown hair pulled back into a ponytail. She wore sneakers—the kind that weren't practical even in a gym, jean shorts with little peonies embroidered (and unraveling) on them, and a plain black T-shirt. Her skin was a dark olive, but Ember couldn't tell if it was from being out in the sun side too long without a suit, or her base tone.

This mella didn't say anything, but then again, she didn't have to. Everyone spoke the language of eyes on Queen, a language that said they were all fucked, some more than others, and that as much happiness had to be wrung as possible from the sand and snow or risk becoming a living mummy. Choose one: dehydrated jerky or human popsicle.

Ponytail offered Ember a hand up. She took it and held on even when the mella dug sharp nails into her palm. Ember placed her right foot down too far onto the side and teetered, her equilibrium still whacked.

"How much?" she asked, pointing at the blue blip in the original mella's pocket.

Ponytail looked at Original, who pulled the strip of leather from a ridiculously shallow pocket common on Old Earth clothes and tossed it at Ember as if it were a half-eaten candy bar she didn't want to finish. Ember caught it, over-extended, and landed hard on her elbow in the grass, the blue clutched in her gloved hand. Her vision blurred for a moment and pain shot in the back of her head as red as the sun, but it didn't matter because the headband was still so smooth. The leather wasn't even cracked. It looked more brown than blue, of course, in the red sunlight, but god help her, it still smelled like Taraniel.

"How much?" Ember croaked. "How much for this and the spoon? For information on where you found them?"

Original dropped to her knees and stuck her freckled nose right up against Ember's face shield. Cracked face shield. Shit. No way to return to the main colony now without a flyer or a body bag.

The mella's breath bloomed across the glass. "The head-band is free. The spoon as well. We just want to talk." After a moment, she added, "We'd prefer if you didn't try to fuck us over with the colony. We'd *like* five days with you."

Someone behind Ember snickered.

"Grow up, Kate," Original said.

Days, money, whatever. Ember would give them her breath if they'd tell her where and how they'd got them.

"I agree. I agree to whatever terms you have. You want to break into the colony, you want to shoot the presidium, you want to steal the last shipment of vegetables. Fine. But give me my wife."

"Can we just kill her?" Ponytail asked. "She isn't worth it. How many of us has she killed?"

"To date, zero, although we could change that," Ember spat back at her. "You steal from the colonists. Your people voluntarily left the colony, which is your right, but then you steal from those who choose to stay and contribute.

Resources are limited. We kill you. You kill us. It isn't personal. Don't make it so."

"We don't kill colonists," Original said, exasperated.

"Awful lot of wanted posters for vegetable stealers," Ember countered evenly. "Our colonist numbers don't dwindle on their own."

Ember glared at Original, back into those damn eyes that looked like they wanted to pity her and then maybe hit her like a punch balloon.

"*Tell me about Taraniel.*" Ember stood up, shakily, like a sloppy drunk. "Or shoot me. Make a damn choice."

"A trade on good faith," Original said. "Information for you removing your helmet. Maybe then we can discuss the note."

"There's a *note*?"

Hadn't Original said that before? Out on the dune? Maybe?

"Take off your helmet and find out."

Ember lunged again, stupidly, but before her first foot could hit the ground (and inevitably give out), a cool sheet of plastic pressed into her hand from behind.

Ember didn't bother to say thank you. She fell to her knees. Her helmet was off a moment later, thrown to the ground with a crack that meant the shield was definitely gone. Her fingers scrabbled over the plastic, so desperate she was to touch Taraniel's words, to see them without TOPA's filters.

> *I love you.*
> *Trust them. Trust me.*

The soft skin under her eyes pulsed with the start of tears. Ember didn't need to be wasting water out here. Taraniel had never been one for long-winded correspondence, and she had to have been exhausted near the end, but still, just this?

"I'm sorry," Original said, almost as if she meant it. "She left another note for you. Well, a manifest, really, but I don't have it on me."

Ember couldn't process all the information. "How did she die? How long did she live?"

A woman with short black hair and olive skin, and dressed in cloth that might have once been part of a tangerine sari, approached. She offered Ember a plastic cup of water, her eyes defiant. Ember noted an elaborate crosshatching of white scars across the back of the woman's hand and onto her arm. The marks were short but wide and evenly spaced in rows of three, which was exactly the number of toes Queen's beetles had.

The random thought wasn't much use at the moment. As delicious as water sounded, Ember had no free hands as she wasn't ready yet to let go of the letter or the headband.

"The cancer took her only a few days ago," Original said.

For the first time in a long time, someone was speaking about Taraniel without sadness or pity, and it helped Ember steady her breathing. Taraniel didn't need a bunch of desert pirates to be proud of her, but for some asinine reason, Original's tone decreased Ember's desire to impale someone with a maple branch. Not a lot, but a little.

"She died in her sleep. She wasn't in any pain." Original paused, then added, "She missed you. You were always on her mind."

"Has she been buried? Burned?"

Original jutted her chin toward the lake. "Submerged. Her request."

Ember dropped the plastic sheet to the ground but kept staring at the space to the right of Original's head. If she imagined hard enough, maybe she would see Taraniel's ghost walk from the water. Right now, all her mind could come up

with were visions of her wife's bloated corpse being consumed, bite by bite, by whatever vertebrate lived in the impossible lake.

Ember should have felt several million things in that
moment. But all she could come up with was that Taraniel
had died, again, and she was fish food. Ember could have
had, what, another few weeks with her if Taraniel hadn't insisted upon dying alone? Well, alone and also with a bunch
of sun-drenched, tired-looking women in wrinkled clothing.
The mella had gotten Taraniel's last moments, and that was
bullshit.

"I hate you," Ember said, both to the mella and to Taraniel's ghost.

"We know, but it's done. You can only go forward. Taraniel wanted you to go forward. That's why we came for
you. To honor her."

"Go fuck yourself in a sand dune."

The dark, wriggling flame of masochistic hope inside
Ember's chest, which she'd birthed the day Taraniel walked
from the settlement, curled in on itself and extinguished.

Trust them. Trust me.

Ember picked up her helmet and pitched it into the
lake. She screamed—a sound from low in her throat that
ended with her jaw shaking and half-evaporated tears on her
cheeks. And then she was on her knees again. Spent. Somehow emptier than before.

"Gloves," Original said in a voice one would use with an
injured puppy. "And then the rest of it. You can't stay in that
suit here. It makes you a target, and you don't want to use
up the oxygen canisters for when you go back."

Ember nodded dully.

The crowd of women stepped back, and Original came
forward. Ember held out her hands and let Original pull her
gloves off, pinching the tip of each finger before tugging the
white leather. The fresh, temperate air raised the hair on the

backs of her hands. Soft, sandless, temperate wind ruffled the strands of hair that blew loose from her ponytail. On Earth, her hair had been cornsilk yellow. Under a red sun, especially in the dunes, it looked like old mud. After four weeks in a helmet, she probably looked as dead as Taraniel. A little less bloated, maybe. Definitely less fish-eaten.

"Dr. Schmitt?"

Ember shoved the headband into the pocket of her suit pants, unzipped, and let the jacket slide off into the sand. The heat of the day didn't hit her until she had it off—the rabbit leather's interior insulation protected against cold and hot—and she quickly overheated in the long-sleeved knit top she wore underneath. When Original still looked expectant, she stripped that off, too, leaving only the camisole tank she used in place of a bra. Anatomy was a funny thing, and she'd never had much need of support. She hesitated on the pants.

Original's eyes moved up and down, assessing Ember, her clothes, and possibly her chest. "Lose the pants too. It's too hot here for them. We can easily replace the leather. No shortage of Earth rabbits, especially on Queen."

It occurred to Ember that she'd not seen any rabbits since waking. Interesting, but not super relevant. "Only once you give me something else in their place."

She shrugged. "As you like. I'm Asher."

"It's a man's name." Ember stopped short of asking if she wanted different pronouns.

Most everyone used "she" at the colony, regardless, but it'd been different on Earth. It might be different here. They had three thousand colonists in a good year, depending on how often a colony supply ship brought immigrants and restock. But Queen was an all-women planet, by Old Earth definition, where woman meant you had a vulva. The end. Like a turn of the nineteenth-century white feminist utopia book. The rationale was probably bogus at the time, but

Ember wasn't privy to it, and it didn't really matter anymore. It was done. All of the original seed worlds had funny colonization requirement. Here on Queen, they could combine eggs of course—humans had been doing that on Earth well before the Collapse—but mainly relied on immigration and variation.

So, yes, they were *mostly* women, and a few men every now and again. It was an anatomical requirement, not a chromosome or gender identity requirement. And there were even fewer like Ember, who lurked in the intersex category that none of the Earth governmental officials had been quite sure what to do with. As long as base, external anatomy matched, you got in. Gender: irrelevant.

That was all pretty moot, however, when staring down mella on an impossible beach. Asher had stunned Ember. She held her wife's memory hostage. Ember had tried to suffocate her with sand. They were probably beyond polite pronoun exchanges.

"Asher is just a name. We know about you though. We're willing to accommodate if you want."

That surprised Ember, and Asher's words were way, *way* too soft. She appreciated being asked, but they could only dangle the Taraniel carrot for so long, and only Taraniel and her friend Varun Sinha knew about Ember's evolving feelings on gender. Which meant Asher knew too much about her. About her life. About her partial XY chromosomes and fluctuating hormones that bounced her between "male" and "female." About her and Taraniel.

"Nothing special here either. If you brought me here for breeding, I don't have fundamentally different equipment than you. And what I do have doesn't work well enough to make the effort worthwhile. I bleed like, twice a year."

"I love that you jump right to sex."

"Life is all about sex."

"Not on Queen. On Queen it's about survival."

Ember rubbed at her face, at the sweat there. "Well, that sure didn't work out for Taraniel, did it?"

Asher sighed and pointed west to a silver glint underneath a poorly made pole barn. Ember hadn't noticed the houses—plastic and old steel and embellished with torn T-shirts. Fifteen, maybe twenty of them. Another boat with a sail. A larger building with a double door made from stained bedsheets. Ten of the scraggliest-looking corn stalks she'd ever seen. Dirt, too, but rich with clay and sediment and small blooming things of red, orange, and sometimes, green. Just beyond those a building—a real one—made of cinderblock and aluminum, decorated in orange flowers, windows painted by tiny hands.

A school, Ember realized. A real, actual grade school.

How in the hell did the mella reproduce without a science facility?

And maples. Ember could still smell the sap, heady and fresh. If their maple trees were healthy enough to tap, then the mella had access to magic, not science. There was no way Queen's surface could support this type of ecosystem. She'd done a workup on it because, really, what else did she have to do? Taraniel had read it and tried so hard not to laugh. Hydrologists could turn anything into a joke on a dry planet, especially repeated references to "wood." Botanists had marginally more to do, what with the four whole tree species they'd managed to get growing on Queen. Ember had gotten two species to grow upright in the lab under controlled conditions. She'd sent them to New Earth with high hopes of licensing and return. Taraniel had even put in calls to several of her well-placed friends on the planet to try to help things along. Ember had only gotten a "rejected—poor seed stock" in response.

The point was, this ecosystem was impossible. Ferns sprouted in tufts along the lake. All red-leafed, some turning to purple. Ember's hand twitched involuntarily, and her fingers formed around an invisible spectrophotometer.

Someone had brought over and planted a damn Earth lilac bush.

The equator, Ember mouthed. Slowly. As soundlessly as she could and still be heard because everything around her smelled fragile.

"It's a strip, one and a half kilometers wide, that stretches all the way across the planet. We brought you here because Taraniel Schmitt, *your wife*, said you would help us leave Queen and return to Earth so we could have lives again." Asher smiled broadly, her perfect teeth gleaming in the unending sun. "Do you want to see her spaceship?"

Chapter Five

In September, there were six billion people left on Earth. In October, there were four. Private companies raced to fund stasis and generational ships, and world governments identified long-shot planets for colonization while the world starved.

Nadia

With TOPA turned off, Nadia had to watch the flyer's tiny clock through the mild distortion of her face shield. It only took two minutes to clear the dome, and another five to clear what was broadly considered Queen's habitable zone. Two and half hours later, heading west into waning light, the landscape turned rocky and cold, then snow-covered and frigid.

She'd watched the computer environmental readouts with growing anxiety as the temperature slipped exponentially downward and the last of the sunlight faded. Queen had no moons, but without light pollution from the colony, the stars reflected well off the unbroken snow. Twenty-three degrees Celsius, fifteen Celsius, negative twenty. The computer and Sinha's suit had flashed warnings at that temperature, and an automated recording inside the flyer had ordered them to turn back. Negative twenty didn't kill people, though, not people in envirosuits, and it wasn't nearly enough to take out their flyer. Nadia had begged, Sinha had sighed, but they kept going.

Forty-five minutes into their flight, the temperature bottomed at negative forty Celsius. The flyer could go to negative sixty before complete systems failure, though for a human body, negative forty was questionable. Nadia begged for one more degree. Just one. They were hundreds of kilometers from Ember still, but just one more degree, maybe, so she could feel like she'd tried everything.

Sinha had put his hands around his neck, looked up, and let his tongue hang to the side. As if she didn't know the potential for this turning into a suicide mission.

He couldn't hear her through his suit and her cowl, so she held up one finger and made a circle with the other hand.

"One more degree," she pleaded, though the words were useless. "You've got two before the coolant gets funny. One more degree and she's really lost, but right now, she could still be alive."

Sinha shook his head. The interior of the flyer had only dim lighting, but Nadia thought he looked apologetic as he reached for the console to reset the heading.

"Varun." Nadia yelled it, loud enough that he turned and looked back at her with wide eyes. Formality and honorifics wouldn't get her to Ember. Appealing to his friendship with her sister, the only one who called him by his first name, might. "Please!"

Varun's shoulders fell. His hands dropped to his sides, and they flew on into the dark, soundless, frozen wasteland.

Five minutes passed without the temperature moving more than a quarter degree in either direction. Ten minutes. At half an hour of (mostly) stable temperature, Nadia tapped Varun's shoulder, but he only shrugged and kept flying. Negative forty was doable, Nadia decided, if she had to get out of the flyer. Negative forty was *you'll regret it, but not immediately*, and a temperature that Ember could still be alive in if the tears to her envirosuit weren't too extensive.

At an hour of stable temperature, Varun put the flyer on auto and performed a diagnostic on the computer and external sensors. Nadia couldn't interpret the readouts, but when Varun looked back at her and shrugged again before resuming manual control, she assumed nothing had frozen yet. Even their exterior lighting, including the floodlamp, still worked.

They flew on, a progressive feeling of *not right* growing in Nadia's chest. Thank god she'd turned her TOPA off because she had about eighteen scans she wanted to perform. It'd be easy to get distracted out here in the bizarre climactic failure they were flying through, and the urge to call the director and flash data in her face would have been impossible to ignore. At least five of their weather satellites had to have failed to miss this change. It should have been all over the news feeds. Scientists should have been swarming the ice to get cores and whatever else the climatologists collected. Nadia remembered one good winter on Earth that involved Ember building a quarter of a snow fort before Nadia launched her body onto the wall and collapsed it. A vindictive fight ensued that ended with Nadia facedown, Ember sitting on her five-year-old back and gloating. Even that day, even in memory, the temperature had turned warmer as the hours progressed and the sun warmed the air. Not here. Likely because there was no sun.

Another hour passed with Nadia imagining all the different ways she could potentially unfreeze her sister, and all the ways she and Dr. Sinha—Varun—could die if the temperature dropped, say, five degrees in one go and the flyer dropped from the sky. Living tombs were interesting, maybe. They'd freeze out here, and the flyer would probably stay visible for a few months until snowdrifts ate it. She could end up an anthropological wonder. In five hundred years or so, Queen might have a museum to put her desiccated corpse into.

Twenty-five kilometers to target. Twelve. Five.

Target.

Still, the temperature held at minus forty.

A green light flashed inside Varun's suit, bleeding out through the face shield. An identical light strobed on the main dash. Varun glanced back over his shoulder at her and pointed down. Nadia nodded in assent. This was it. This was life, and consequences, and if Ember turned out to be already dead, Nadia had no Plan B.

The flyer landed.

Varun unbuckled his harness and pulled the cowl from his head. "She's about two meters down, according to her

GPS. The snow below us is already compacted with an ice layer on top. Doesn't look like there's been precipitation in a few weeks. I don't know how we will get her out. Wind is fast too. Fast enough to knock you over if you aren't paying attention."

"No beetle marks anywhere?" Nadia removed her own cowl and pressed her face right up against the flyer's viewscreen. Silver-and-white expanses of snow and ice gleamed in the triangular arc of the flood lamp. Nadia had a lot more experience on the sun side, but really, if she changed the colors around and ignored the temperature and that it was difficult to see well, the scenery didn't look all that different. This close to the equator, though, the ground was mostly a crunchy mix of icy snow with very little powder. Everywhere Nadia could see, the ground stretched flat to the horizon.

"None that I can see," Varun said, "but I can't see very far."

"Everything out here feels weird," Nadia said.

Varun didn't acknowledge her words, so Nadia crawled back over to her chair without another comment. If he didn't want to waste words on the temperature and how close they were to the equator, she wouldn't either. She didn't know him as well as Ember, and pissing him off with small talk could get her either jettisoned onto ice, or worse—she'd come into her lab one morning to find all the opaque white labels on her pristine glassware colored in with permanent marker. Academics could be vindictive as fuck.

"Even if there were beetles, with the wind the way it is, marks wouldn't last long," Varun said after a measured breath.

Nadia crossed her arms over her chest and frowned, the discomfort from a stagnant climate growing into the unsettling ripples she'd get when her sister read her ghost stories before bed, then banged on the shared wall between their bedrooms in the middle of the night. At least Nadia had been old enough not to wet herself. "Still, I mean, how the hell did she get out here, much less buried, without any marks? Not even scoring on the landscape? A suspicious lump maybe?"

"The beetles migrate, though we don't understand much about their patterns yet because we can only track them so far. They build permanent structures, too, but they get shared between migrating colonies and upkept through a symbiotic relationship with the rabbits. It could be that the beetles follow climactic occurrences like the one we are in now, although I have never heard of this before." He paused and squinted at the temperature readout. "Confirm temperature?" he asked his right shoulder.

"Varun, what's with the TOPA?" As long as he wasn't transmitting with his TOPA, Nadia didn't mind so much. If he did that, and anyone overheard and tracked their location, they were fucked.

His shoulder chirped a response Nadia couldn't quite make out.

"I find it distracting when I hear an AI in the helmet," Varun said. "I feel surrounded. I moved the processor and speaker into the suit proper. More importantly, the temperature reading from the flyer is correct. We're almost sitting on the equator. We should be dead. The ship should be dead." After a thoughtful moment he added, "I'm getting a paper out of this for sure."

Nadia shivered even in the heat of the flyer. "Maybe two, if we can defrost Ember. Does this crate do excavation?"

"If you don't mind it accidentally amputating her head or a leg, yes. Still might be a viable idea if we have to dig fast."

Nadia smacked his shoulder. "Of course we want to dig fast. She could be alive under there, but she'll definitely be dead if the weather reverses." That little factoid Nadia did not want to dwell on. "Shovels, then?"

"In the back, strapped to the wall in the starboard compartment. You'll want the pickaxes though. And I was talking about mella beetles, not the wild kind, although there's significant overlap between the two populations. Did you know the mella beetles have been trained to voice command? Can you imagine!"

Nadia stopped halfway through unbuckling. She decided to ignore the wide-eyed wonder on his face. "You don't think this is just a beetle thing? You read any out there?"

Varun shook his head, looking like a child who'd just had their new toy taken away. "Again, no, but that doesn't mean they're not there. We don't know how they survive. We don't know how the *rabbits* survive, for that matter, since they are descendants of European rabbits, *Oryctolagus cuniculus*, not snowshoe hares or another, hardier relation. The beetles can't be detected in groups less than two, so it's entirely possible the mella can't either. We wouldn't be able to see the snow-side beetles from a distance anyway. Their exoskeletons are too white."

Nadia mulled that thought for a long moment. "You have any problem with shooting them? The mella, I mean."

"No. They keep coming after the tech shipments from New Earth. Loss of that last centrifuge cost the colony a new antibacterial ointment one of the chemists was working on."

"Check." With the flyer hatch still closed, Nadia finished unbuckling and flopped over her chair into the holding compartment. Upon closer inspection, it was a lot dirtier than she'd realized, with ground in bits of beetle and viscera in the hard-to-clean corners. She edged on her knees over to the wall and felt along the perimeter until she found a loose panel. Here, she pushed and a long, narrow drawer popped out. Strapped to the bottom of the drawer were shovels, pickaxes, trowels, and a few handheld lasers. She unbuckled the large and medium pickaxes and tossed them over her chair.

"Ready," she said. "Pop the hatch or whatever."

Varun leaned over the back of his seat and pointed at her blue lab coat. "The only reason to go out dressed like that is because you have a death wish. I can dig. You can monitor the weather up here. Watch for bigfoot."

"Did you just make a joke?"

"I hollowed out a beetle carcass, shellacked the remains, stuffed the body cavity with malted milk balls, and left it on Dr. Schmitt's bed about two months ago. New Earth doesn't send that candy anymore. Those were the last ones on Queen. I have a wonderful sense of humor."

Nadia mimed vomiting, then tapped her face shield, ensuring TOPA was still powered down, climbed back onto her seat, and pulled the smaller shovel onto her lap. "I'll dig, too. She's my sister."

Varun almost managed a smile, or possibly suppressed a sneeze. "We'll do a blow first. See how much powder we can move. Hold up." He switched his suit TOPA on, and Nadia heard the AI click through into the flyer's computer. The ship rocked back for a split second, and then a blast of air shot from the thrusters.

The snow did move, perhaps half a meter uncovered. The airborne snow formed a cloud that waved across the icy ground. Nadia watched it disappear past the light from the ship. There weren't even any trees this far on the snow side to break up the monotony, since Ember's maples couldn't survive more than ten kilometers outside the habitable zone in any direction.

"Creepy, moonish landscape," Nadia muttered to herself. "You always have the worst vacation ideas, Ember."

"That's as good as it will get," Varun yelled through his face shield.

"Let's go," Nadia said and reached over Varun's chair to point at the hatch release.

Varun put his hand on the release panel but stopped just shy of depressing it. "You sure you don't want me to try connecting to her TOPA first? If she or the suit could turn on one of the exterior heaters, it would help our digging and reduce the probability of us hitting her with the pickaxes."

"If you connect to her TOPA while it's sending distress signals, everyone at the colony will know we're out here," Nadia said. "We don't need the figurehead rulers of Queen *or* their science director lackey breathing down our necks. Just *go.*"

Varun stopped arguing. The hatch opened and Nadia jumped out of the flyer, ignoring the air that was so cold it would soon make her exposed skin feel like it was on fire. Outside the flyer, the stillness could not be ignored. Tidally locked planets were known for their heavy winds, which was the whole reason the colony had a dome in the first place, but here near the equator, Nadia barely felt enough breeze to move her clothes. Outside the light halo from the flyer, stars dotted the sky in drops of brightness.

It'd be remarkable if it weren't so damn cold.

Varun crunched past her and pointed to an unremarkable spot on the snow. Without TOPA on, even in the mild wind, she'd never hear his words, but that was fine. She waited until he finished outlining a wide, vaguely human-shaped circle with orange spray paint before she sank her shovel in and started digging.

The first jab broke through the crust, but the snow underneath was wet and heavy. Nadia grunted as her muscles strained, her fingers and face warm and the rest of her well on its way to frostbite. Across from her, Varun gave up his pickaxe after a few passes in favor of a handheld laser that steamed the snow away in wide arcs. Smart. Nadia probably should have thought about the lasers that same way she should have thought about her suit.

After another minute of pickaxing, just as her toes began to burn, Nadia looked up to see Varun staring off into the horizon, the laser loose in his hands. Nadia followed his line of sight and saw...nothing. Only snow. Ice. The shivering that had started as a ripple in her shoulders turned to whole-body shaking.

"H-hey." Nadia stepped over and tapped him on the shoulder. She gestured wildly at the orange outline, her hand shaking. "Chop-chop, before I lose toes. The mella will attack, or they won't. Don't obsess." No way he could hear her words over the wind and through his face shield, but her body language drew a pretty clear picture.

He didn't respond, so she leaned in close enough to see that Varun's face shield was opaque, which meant he was busy with TOPA.

"Hey!" Nadia yelled, this time smacking the front of his shield hard enough to turn his head lightly. "What is it?"

Varun's shield glittered back into transparent. Through it, Nadia caught that surprised-yet-thoughtful expression of a scientist about to do something *really* stupid.

"No..." Nadia said as she took a step back and started to hop in place to keep warm. She wasn't entirely certain what she was saying no to just yet, but from the apology in Varun's eyes, it was going to be painful.

He tapped his face shield with a finger. Nadia shook her head and jumped higher. He tapped it again. Nadia hopped back, and in that exact moment, Varun clicked an override command. Her face shield sprang to life, and the generic TOPA filled it.

EMERGENCY OVERRIDE ACTIVATED. STATE INJURIES.

"Stupidity," Nadia said. "Clear the shield so I can see."

TOPA complied.

"Sorry, but I need to share data with you." Varun's voice sounded tinny through the comm. "Jack—that's my TOPA's name—just did a scan." He pointed to the lower left side of the outline, where, if Nadia squinted just right, she was pretty certain a frosty blue finger poked through the ice. "Our flyer doesn't emit enough light for us to get a lot of details. Jack picked up the hand. I didn't think you'd want to cut it."

"Ember!" Nadia knelt in the trough of ice and snow the laser had created, certain she would crack a tooth with the way her jaw shook, while Varun sent a "wait!" through the comm.

She used her hands to rake ice and snow from a clubbed fist and then an arm covered in thin white scars. "The fuck did they do to you?" Nadia hissed as she lost the feeling in her toes, and the burning moved up to her feet and ankles. Damn it, dying now was not an option. She felt a hand on her shoulder and heard Varun say something through the comm, but she was up to a shoulder now, then a neck, then the cowl and face shield of an envirosuit. Two of her fingernails tore off through the gloves, but she didn't care. The glass on Ember's shield was cracked beyond repair, but through it, Nadia could see a narrow nose, high cheekbones, glassy brown eyes.

"Ember!" Nadia punched a burning first into the snow. Her shivering stopped, which was a very bad sign. At least she was cognizant enough to realize it. "Damn it, Ember, what..."

Nadia put her face right up to the face shield. Her breath iced across the smooth surface.

There was a woman in there, but it wasn't Ember. Ember didn't have her ears pierced. Ember didn't have fringe. Ember would *never* wear a bangly necklace with a sea turtle carved onto a coconut shell.

"Well, what the fuck?" Nadia sat back on her heels and looked up at Varun. "It's not her, but someone went to moderate trouble to make it look like her. Am I supposed to be relieved or more terrified?"

He gestured to the flyer. "Get in. Get warm. Let's talk in there."

"Yeah, but shouldn't we..." Nadia pointed to the corpse, but Varun was already halfway to the ship. A few more moments wouldn't do significantly more damage to her body.

Nadia reached under the neckpiece of the face shield, muttering an apology to the dead woman, and depressed a finger onto one of the little round computer input junctions.

"Hey, TOPA?" Nadia had been able to feel the button thanks to her gloves, but the rest of her arm hadn't registered the pressure. Shit.

INTERNAL SCANS SHOW CRITICAL. PLEASE LIST INJURIES.

"Ignore injuries. Download the TOPA from this suit into mine and stop the caps lock."

Unable. Emergency override protocols in effect.

Nadia hissed. "Scan the other suit. The person inside it is dead. I am not. Download her TOPA, and I'll get back in the ship, and you can save my life. How about that?"

Download complete. Proceed to controlled environment if able.

Finally. Nadia stumbled back to the flyer. She couldn't feel her feet, which meant determining how hard to plant each of them in the compacted snow was not easy. Varun had to haul her into her seat but had warming packs ready. He'd removed his cowl and gloves and had the heater in the flyer turned up full blast.

"How far up?" he asked as he beat one of the heat packs against the wall to start the exothermic reaction.

Nadia tossed her cowl into the back of the flyer. "Just feet." She pulled off her boots and socks. "My arms will be fine on their own, but I've got no feeling below my ankles. You have ibuprofen?"

"Already on it." He held out two white tablets. Nadia took them and dry swallowed. No time to waste on asking for a cup of water. The pain pinpricks started the moment Varun placed the packs on her feet, but at least it was the good kind of pain that meant she probably didn't have too much necrotic tissue yet.

Still, the warming packs *burned*. Nadia sucked in her breath but managed not to curse. She'd never actually used a Bunsen burner but decided if she put her feet right over one, this would be the exact feeling.

"I got her TOPA in my suit," she said as Varun started in on her right foot. "As soon as you are—ow! I'm going to put your head into an autoclave when we get back."

"It'll get worse before it gets better," Varun said without a bit of apology in his tone. "If you send her TOPA to the ship, we can both talk to it."

Nadia clicked the commands as searing, blood-boiling heat trickled across her feet and into her toes. Flaying would have felt better. Amputation sounded more and more promising. Though it wasn't Ember's fault she wasn't a frozen snow mummy, Nadia briefly fantasized about coughing into her sterile laminar flow hood.

The ship's AI spoke, far too loudly.

GB-877 – Ember Schmitt. Mayday Mayday. See attached coordinates. Two minutes of power left, and I'm several meters under a snowdrift. Please send aid.

"Hey. Override," Nadia said. "Turn off the beacon. GB-993 out here with...whatever Varun's number is. The person is dead, and it's not Ember Schmitt. Check your memory files."

No files detected. No body detected. GB-877 Ember Schmitt is no longer in proximity of her envirosuit.

"Your person isn't Ember, and your person is also dead," Nadia barked at the ship. "That's why you're in our flyer. What's the last thing you have in your memory bank before us? You have to have something, and, Varun, I need more drugs now."

Varun wordlessly handed Nadia another two ibuprofen, which she shot into the back of her throat and swallowed like the pills had personally wronged her.

My activation date stamp is twenty hours old. I have GB-877 Ember Schmitt's personnel file and nothing else.

"Stop calling her that," Nadia snapped. "Her name is just Ember. And *someone* installed Ember's data in that suit. There had to be an authorization code. Can you find it? And turn off your damn beacon if you haven't already."

Distress beacon disabled. The data were transferred by another TOPA.

"Of course they were." Nadia slumped into her seat. She wiggled each of her toes in turn, debating in which she might have lost permanent sensation for no reason other than mella games. She still wanted to slice off both feet at the ankles. It felt like each of her toes was over a lit matchstick, which probably meant she'd be fine. "You have any ideas?" she asked Varun.

"Possibly. TOPA, can you still connect with the TOPA that transferred to you?"

That TOPA system is no longer functional. However, there is another TOPA on the network within one hundred kilometers of this location. It does not return an identifier code when pinged.

"Of course it doesn't." Nadia did not need more mystery or surprises. "We're already in a stupid amount of trouble. You want to haul the corpse back, go check out the mystery TOPA, or turn around, go home, and go get drunk? At least drunk, we might come up with a creative idea about where Ember is."

Varun turned to his side so he could meet Nadia's eyes. After a silence that hurt more than Nadia's toes, he said, "It'll be our jobs if we don't turn around. It might already be, if the director or any of the presidium are monitoring the TOPA networks."

"That's the kicker, isn't it? The mella are playing a game the presidium won't play back. Ember's not a giant popsicle yet. They want her for something; otherwise, why bother with this?" She massaged her ankles, which almost didn't hurt anymore. "That could be Ember out there in the unregistered TOPA. We're already out here. Maybe the temperature holds all the way to the equator."

"Even if it does, we can't do much in my flyer. We need to plan. We need supplies."

Nadia heard the unspoken *we need to think about this* as well. She readjusted the warming packs on her feet and loudly exhaled. "She's my sister, Varun."

"It's a big planetoid," he countered. "Are you a professional mella killer? I am not."

The rerouted TOPA spoke without warning. **Unusual heat signature detected one point seven kilometers from the active TOPA. Too far for chemical analysis, but BTU output is consistent with twenty-three different types of interstellar spaceships.**

Nadia's eyes bugged out, and even Varun coughed. "Spaceships on the snow side," Nadia said slowly, mind alight with possibilities that got increasingly darker the longer she thought about it. "Director didn't want us out here. No one is ever supposed to be out here. Ember is missing and probably maybe in that unregistered suit. You have a hypothesis? 'Cause I'm forming a few."

Varun sighed in defeat, clicked his safety harness into place, and gestured for Nadia to sit back. "That's two hours from here, Nadia. Forget the temperature. If we go out there, we won't have enough fuel to get back. You think the director will requisition a transcontinental flyer from the presidium to bring us back after all this? Who would volunteer to fly it?"

"That doesn't sound like a no." Nadia kicked her left leg, sending three warming packs over her seat and onto Varun's. She could feel all her toes again for sure, and the bottom of her foot positively bristled with pain. She rammed her feet back into her wool socks—a gift from Ember several years earlier that she wore even in the lab because she could—and did up her boots. Her feet could finish unthawing later, or the rest of her could finish freezing. It was bound to hurt like a bitch either way.

Two more hours of flying got them zero answers.

"Well, what in the hell are we going to do about this?" Nadia balanced next to Varun on his narrow flyer seat, staring gaped-mouthed out the main window. They'd switched the abandoned envirosuit TOPA off and buried it in the ship's storage files for future prodding. Now, they watched as the flyer, which was too old to have any form of AI installed, fed them environmental reports. Negative five degrees Celsius. Wind at six knots. Cold, with a light breeze, but not you'll-definitely-die weather. Not *equator* weather.

They were still roughly two kilometers from the snowside equator. They'd not gone any closer once Varun pointed out the midsized cruiser still visible as it left Queen's atmosphere, the hull lit with track lighting and stamped with a half-blue, half-green sphere—the symbol for New Earth. They'd promptly turned off all their exterior lighting, and Varun had landed manually. They couldn't see much with only starlight, but what they could see looked damn weird.

Nadia didn't think they'd ever take off again. Before her was her memory of Earth. But it wasn't fuzzy around the edges from age or too crisp as if she'd overlaid a picture from a book and gotten confused as to what was her real memory and what wasn't. There was grass under the flyer. It looked yellowish where they were, but it darkened into the rich chlorophyll-colored green as it moved toward the equator. Nadia remembered grass in the most abstract sense. She remembered it made her legs itch when she'd been forced to sit on it crisscross applesauce for the fourth of July. She remembered Ember taking a long, thick piece of grass from the wetland near the home, sticking it between her two thumbs, and blowing. She remembered that obnoxious, shrill sound of the grass whistle. Her legs itched. Her ears hurt. She couldn't seem to see straight.

Half a head turn and Nadia saw the outlines of trees taller than a human, with the red leaves of Queen. Those really stood out in the pale light. Trees had green leaves on Earth, she was pretty certain, and some were in the purple-red, but not the red-red, blood-red like these. As if the trees were hemorrhaging. But on the ground, there was no swell of red, just the progressively greener grass and... Nadia choked back a whimper. Creeks. Streams, maybe, depending upon how stable the climate was. Narrow, winding creeks disappeared across the horizon, visible because of the UV-spectrum lamps on tall posts scattered across the landscape, illuminating halos of perfect white light. She saw hundreds of lamps, increasing in number and forming clear pathways the closer they went to the equator. By the ship, the creeks had ice on the surface, but even a few meters out, the ice melted into softly flowing water, a hint of an algal bloom on the edges. Alive by artificial light and a miracle.

Nadia gazed along one of the creeks to the horizon. With the flyer's sensors under magnification, she could see buildings as well, made from what looked like high-end cinderblock, unpainted and gray. Flyers and real, actual spaceships patchworked across the grass, and towering trees surrounded the complex. There, the UV lamps sat every few meters, creating a cheerful if not somewhat classroom-like glow. She couldn't get a sense of size from the view, but the computer did have environmental readouts for her. Temperature at twenty-three degrees Celsius and the relative humidity at almost 80 percent. Wind at two knots. A quick, abrupt change she'd only ever seen outside the dome as the habitable zone transitioned into unlivable space.

"No wind. That never happens on tidally locked planets as far as I know," Nadia said, finally, as an oblong ship with four pods sticking off the main form like eyeballs landed within their visual range. That shape meant supply transport, and the bright-green color meant it had come from Europa. Also, there was green grass, and there was no snow, and if a bird hit their flyer right now, Nadia might throw up.

"Never gone out this far," Varun said in a monotone as he stared at the landing ship. "Never a need. Plenty of beetles near the dome."

Nadia pushed him with her hip. Vague figures jumped from the freshly landed ship, but even at this distance, their suits, *suits*, were obvious. No way they were mella, and no way in *hell* Ember was mixed up in a secret equatorial lab without telling her. Taraniel did weird shit late at night in the lab sometimes, but not Ember. Ember needed a solid ten hours of sleep a night and had no game face for secrets. Nadia and Ember had their differences, sure, but sisters shared that kind of shit.

"Stop with the beetles. We have to get closer."

"You still don't have a full suit," Varun pointed out.

"Hello?" Nadia flicked his left temple, and he jerked his head back, scowling. "It's a beautiful day on Queen, apparently. Never thought I'd get to say that. Now pop the hatch. We're going for a walk."

Chapter Six

In November, sixteen planets identified from the Kepler telescope and TESS satellite data were selected for terraforming. Extremists, voices amplified by worldwide panic, convinced governments to create utopian rules on the new worlds. Humans were given a chance to choose a society that mirrored their moral code. Those groups that didn't have enough voices to lobby were silenced or dumped on useless planets.

Not all the planets were as useless as first thought.

Ember

The mella had most of a ship. It had walls (gray), thrusters (four), and an interior (gray) that could seat maybe five. Six, if you didn't mind not having a harness and sitting on the floor. It had been a lifeboat pod before, with the telltale jellybean shape and hard plastic minimalist interior, but Ember didn't know enough about ships to guess whether or not it was capable of leaving Queen's atmosphere. Her stomach fluttered regardless, and not just because the last time she'd been on a ship, she'd almost died. There was a mess of a computer system near the only viewscreen. A nozzle in the wall just to the left of the screen could have been an early model 3D printer. There was a pocket door in the back that Ember didn't care to explore. If the ship had other features, they weren't apparent.

What it did have, in addition to a form of propulsion that gave Ember way too much hope, was Taraniel. It had the smell of her in small cabinets and her fingerprints across one of the control panels. It had strands of her honey-colored hair on the floor. Ember took deep breaths in the doorway to the small pod, barely able to stand upright. She had on Taraniel's old clothes, most of which had been hers before her wife conscripted them and hemmed the cuffs to fit her shorter frame. The essence of Taraniel wrapped around her, the clothes a shade too tight and too short now, Taraniel's echo reverberating in every welded joint of the ship.

Although she'd majored in hydrology, Taraniel had always loved mechanical engineering. Right there, right then, Ember could see Taraniel repairing the pod and dreaming about...well, leaving Queen. Leaving Queen with Ember.

Smiling in the sun that didn't burn. Breathing the air that didn't choke. Ember imagined her smiling with people who weren't bowed with the weight of her imminent death, who maybe had let her live her last days as carefree as when she'd come to Queen as a fresh, doe-eyed postdoc.

It was all *so much*. Ember felt nauseous, and hopeful, the thrills of excitement warring with memories of waking up with four hundred dead crewmates, while Ember swam in her own blood. There'd been a number of sticking points to her and Taraniel's plans to leave Queen, but a big one had always been Ember's deep desire to never step foot on a spaceship again.

"Take your time," Asher said, her voice low. "It's the only resource we have in excess."

"I hate time. It never comes out in my favor." Ember turned, shoving her shaking hands into her pants pockets, and tried to push past Asher. Their shoulders connected, and Asher held her ground, moving into Ember, forcing her back toward the chair.

Ember leaned in, Asher's shoulder digging into her collarbone. "Move," Ember said flatly.

"Dr. Schmitt, I would prefer you stay. Taraniel wanted you here. She said part of your lab work was exports. She mentioned codes. She mentioned coordinates. We need them if this thing is going to leave the atmosphere and go anywhere useful."

"No." If Taraniel had wanted Ember on a ghost ship spilling late-night fantasies about fleeing Queen, she could have left a damn note in their apartment, not with sand pirates.

The smell of Taraniel faded. Ember inhaled the scent of old plastic and propulsion fuel that proved a visceral reminder of her colony ship. She swallowed bile and ended up biting her tongue, the copper taste furthering the rising panic.

Ember beat her shoulder into Asher's, slamming into the other woman, forcing her to give ground. Asher stumbled. Her hand slapped the wall in search of support, and she stepped to the left, not clearing the doorway but no longer completely blocking it either.

Ember probably hadn't needed to hit Asher quite that hard. But then again, she really didn't want to be on Taraniel's ship. Any ship. Not yet anyway.

"You just going to ignore her, then?" Asher rubbed her shoulder. Her voice turned critical. Accusatory.

Ember took three deep breaths, letting her anger settle into a more manageable emotion. Whether that would end up being rage or despair, she didn't know. Her tongue continued to bleed. She felt like a lost, tattered beach towel.

"Just a few minutes. Look around. Touch things," Asher said.

"I don't want to."

"Dr. Schmitt—"

Despair won.

"What do you *want*?" Ember slammed a fist into the nearest chair. A waft of Taraniel's favorite soap released from the fabric and bored through Ember's heart. "You had her last month, *not me*. You got to watch her work. She gave you a damn ship! What else do you want? To rub it in that she was here?"

Asher's eyes closed for a moment, and Ember fantasized about punching her. Right between her eyes would make her head snap back. In the gut would send her to the floor. Taraniel wouldn't have liked either, but Taraniel wasn't here, and that was the point, wasn't it? Ember stood in shattered pieces and could glue memories together forever, but it would never be Taraniel.

Asher held her hands up like a surrender, but Ember heard too much hope in her voice to attempt politeness. "Dr.

Schmitt, maybe you could sit down, and we could talk about Taraniel's time here and her goals."

Right now, all Ember wanted was to get off the Taraniel funeral barge and feel solid ground under her feet again. "Our conversations are none of your business," she snarled at Asher. "And it's not fair to bring me here and use her memory to pull information."

Asher kept her hands up and shook her head. "No. It isn't fair. Nothing on Queen is fair."

"Don't patronize me. She should have been *home*. She should have been with her family. There, she could have had medical care and..."

Asher rubbed at her right arm, and Ember saw Taraniel with a PICC line, forcing a smile. Asher coughed, and Ember heard the racking sounds of her wife fighting an opportunistic infection. The sounds and smells of the Queen hospital crushed around her, depressed her breathing, made the air feel thick and useless.

Ember slumped into the chair. The plastic dug into her shoulder blades. Her pants slipped across the upholstered seat. The plastic smell dredged her memories.

"No one wants to die hooked up to machines," Asher whispered. "She said you respected her choice and her autonomy, what little of it she had left." She sat on the edge of the seat nearest Ember and clasped her hands in her lap. "Imagine her on our pristine beach. Imagine her slipping in between the small waves. Imagine her dying in joy."

Two other women entered the ship. They flanked Asher like a ridiculous honor guard. Asher greeted Kate by name, the woman's brown hair now braided and a look of deep disinterest on her face. The other was new, her black hair buzzed, her eyes kind.

They didn't speak, so Ember ignored them. She tried to focus on Taraniel in the ship. Taraniel in the water. Taraniel happy. And that helped, but only a little.

"She died here." Ember had meant it as a question, but it came out wobbly.

"Near here," responded Asher, and Kate made a jerking point with her thumb as her expression softened. "Just outside the door, around the twenty-seventh hour. No pain. We keep our drugs well supplied from the colony."

Ember refused to rise to the bait. Knowing Taraniel had had friends, and medication, and died while working on an impossible project they'd only ever seriously discussed while drunk eased the tightness in her chest. Taraniel'd had a ton of projects, however, and a few of them she never spoke to Ember about. It felt weird and a little slimy that she'd chosen *this* one to be her legacy.

Ember looked at the floor, trailing the smooth gray to the walls, then the ceiling. Paint. The next thing the mella needed to steal was definitely paint.

"I'm Nok," said the tall one with the pale white skin and the buzz cut. "Formerly of the colony myself. I've been with the mella two years as their entomologist. Their *good* entomologist. The three of us, along with Pui, who you've not met, worked with Taraniel on this ship. To leave Queen."

Ember dragged her voice and her temper down. "That's an old dream. An old memory. And a dangerous one."

Asher nodded and inclined her head at the door, and the other two women left, Nok giving Ember a light tap on the shoulder as she did so. "How did you meet her?" Asher asked. "Surely that's a safe memory."

Anger lit into irritation, then combusted into defiance. "She got assigned to me, drew the short straw. But she had a PhD in forest hydrology, and I was coming off a disaster colony ship with mass failures and my own geeky PhD in restoration ecology with a side of genetics. My sister's a hydrologist, too, so I knew the lingo. We had a lot of conversations."

Asher's eyebrow raised, and it perked Ember's vindictive side.

Ember sat upright, fished an old hair tie from Taraniel's pants where she'd also stashed her headband, and tied her hair back. "Yeah, it started as conversations about potential terraforming experiments, then turned into all-nighters about Earth. Easier to keep talking if you're exhausted, in the same bed—two sweating bodies in a huddle of blankets, giggling about the delight of lesbianism on an all-woman planet. Hydrologists know a lot about lubrication. Botanists know a lot about anatomy."

Asher looked like a maraschino cherry left too long outside the jar. Perfection.

Ember took the shot. "This thing can leave the ground?"

She really, really wanted the answer to be no.

Asher answered curtly. "Into space, I'd assume."

There went the idea of telling herself she wouldn't die on this ship because it couldn't go anywhere. "That's ridiculous."

It wasn't ridiculous. She and Taraniel had had a dozen conversations, maybe more, about spaceships and fleeing Queen, and Earth, both new and old.

"Did she tell you she was dying?" Ember asked.

"No." Asher finished gathering herself and swiveled her chair until her knees brushed Ember's. Ember grimaced and moved away. "Not for the first few days," Asher continued, "but most of us guessed. A child could have guessed."

"Well, she sure as hell never mentioned *this*." Ember gestured widely at the ship.

Still, they'd talked a lot in those lulls between stickiness and sleep. Days on Queen stacked end to end in one seemingly pointless experiment after another. Ember made a new tree; it got planted; it died. Her best trees got shipped off-world. Taraniel thought up a new irrigation system for crops; it got built; the mella, or the weather, or physics, killed it. Taraniel worked long hours late at night to try to make headway in terraforming research. Fewer successes meant fewer grants from New Earth governance. Less money meant fewer nonessentials. First, Ember couldn't find her brand of shampoo, and then, she couldn't find *any* brand of shampoo other than a governmental issue. Shelves lined with meats, cheese, and fruits turned first to canned goods, then to high-density meal supplement bars.

Ember had been so damn sure upon signing to Queen that she could bring, at the very least, some damn dandelions to the planet. Was there an ecosystem where the things didn't flourish? But even though early geological surveys of Queen had postulated richer soils under the sand, it was just...fucking *sand* and the occasional clay. It came from prehistoric granite and limestone structures that had once stood on Queen's surface. They made great concrete but were about as nutrient rich as the spaceship she was sitting in. So, there was no point, really, in any of them being here except as a holding pen for humans. Queen was never going to flourish. It was never going to enter into a galactic trade route. It was a bullshit planet colonized with bullshit promises, alternately roasting and freezing in its own juices.

Asher shifted in her chair. "She built this for you," Asher said.

"What will I do with a ship?" Ember countered sourly. "Can it leave the atmosphere? Where will you go, even if you have exit codes? Do you know the coordinates of any other colony world?" These were questions she and Taraniel had rehashed over and over.

There was a spark, too, hot and new, a spark from more secret, more careful conversations with Taraniel about fruit that sometimes came through shipments, about the natural lilac essential oil the last cargo pilot had given Ember when he tried to flirt. Conversations whispered just outside the dome with TOPA off and face shields down as the wind tried to eat their words and breath. Conversations about plants that had died on Earth popping up, revitalized, in the oddest of places, stamped with coordinates that could only be one world. A dead world.

"It flies," Asher said. "Dr. Schmitt made sure of that before... Before."

"I'd be surprised if it could fly from here to the lake and back." Ember walked to the main console and slid four fingers over the interface screen, sending little lights flickering in red and blue. A menu popped up, and she flipped through systems reports, not knowing enough about ships to make more than polite grunts of affirmation. She tried to suppress memories of her colony ship's cracked computer console. The dead TOPA. The bodies.

It was not the time for old trauma. The pod's manifest listed storage behind the cockpit for parts and foodstuffs. The nozzle in the wall was indeed a 3D print filament head, and it took various metal, plastic, and glass cartridges. The ship had a sublight drive, standard for pods of this type.

It had a T-drive.

It had a T-drive welded onto a piece of machinery the computer called a "wedge." When she clicked the T-drive icon, the whole ship rumbled and sputtered. Ember's ears popped. Her stomach twisted. She couldn't breathe.

"Where did she get the hyperdrive?" Ember gasped. "Where in the name of this godforsaken toenail fungus of a planet did *you* get the hyperdrive?"

The back part of Ember's brain reminded her to breathe, and she sucked in air like a five-year-old at their first swimming lesson.

Asher stood, widely planted her right hand on the interface, and curled her fingers in. The lights on the screen, the track lighting around the interior edges of the ship, and the T-drive all shut down in one giant exhalation. "We got the drive last year from the colonist ship that broke down. You remember? The refugee ship."

"The generational ship?" Ember asked, although she knew the answer. Another failed ship. Another mass death. Another memory she didn't want.

"Yes. With the composite crew. Ship broke near Jupiter. Thirty of the colonists got sent here—women and one boy child that the Resettlement Alliance called a girl."

Ember's face flushed with anger, and that helped with the terror. It hadn't just been the child the Resettlement Alliance had snubbed. To make up for the increase in population, the Alliance had also sent a paltry number of fresh vegetables, a few bolts of synthetic cloth, and—probably just because they could—fourteen pallets of toys. Not a menagerie of toys, of course, but cases of a three-pack sandcastle building set that included a bright-green bucket with yellow handle, a pale-orange shovel, and a tangerine starfish mold. The total number of bucket sets had come to 7,168. There were 200 children on Queen in a good year.

It had taken less than ten minutes for the mella to raid. The science complex sat on the opposite end of the settlement from the one landing pad, but Ember had felt the beetle humming, had watched her expensive three-liter beaker vibrate off the bench and destroy another in-progress experiment with birch saplings on the way down.

The mella had damaged the colonists' ship, taken the food, and left the damn buckets, which had later been melted down for printing filament. A missing T-drive never hit the newsfeed, but the presidium already looked like idiots by not preparing appropriately. Ember wouldn't have wanted her incompetence spread over the feeds either.

"God, this thing really can leave Queen, can't it?" Ember breathed.

Asher only smiled.

If Taraniel had built the ship, or fixed it, or whatever, and she'd left it here for Ember, there was only one thing Ember would do. She would for sure drag Nadia along because she'd never manage to keep her memories at bay without her sister's sniping. And she wouldn't be against inviting Dr. Varun Sinha along for the ride. He did well under pressure, autoclave or otherwise.

"You have a pilot?" Ember asked.

"TOPA can fly. But I have an engineer."

"I'm not going to be your pet botanist." Ember ran her right hand down the sleeve of Taraniel's shirt. The little fabric pills caught on her cracked skin, but the movement released a few molecules of familiar soap. This time, she inhaled the smell, held it in her nose, used it to brace her emotions.

Asher chuckled, stood, and leaned against the bulkhead. "I have no intention of terraforming anything, though I am amused you think five people could terraform a whole planet. Where did you get your PhD?"

"University of Fuck You."

Asher pulled out Taraniel's spoon, and Ember half expected it to find a way between her ribs. But Asher put it on one of the chairs as gingerly as one would a carton of eggs. "Could we stop? Please. We need to talk about ship mechanics and the mella crew. You've made our task a lot easier, but we didn't bring you here for this."

"You didn't bring me here. Taraniel did."

Taraniel's spell lifted. Ember wore her dead wife's clothes in a contraband mella ship with a stolen T-drive. It was hers, this ship, hers, and Taraniel's. And Nadia's because no matter how irritating, sisters did not get left behind. If this was what had driven her wife into the dunes, away from their last precious weeks together, then Ember would take it. Mella had never been part of their plan, and with limited seating, Ember had no intention of making them so now.

"Get off my ship," Ember said, keeping her voice low and cool.

Asher slapped her—fronthanded, across the cheek and nose—hard enough to send her out of her chair and onto her knees. "Your arrogance is obnoxious and trying," Asher warned, her voice deadly low. "We built this ship together. And *she* built it for you *and* us."

With her head still spinning, Ember shot up and rammed her shoulder into Asher's clavicle. Asher's fingernails found Ember's neck and tore. Ember grunted and continued to drive until Asher hit the wall, her head snapping back onto the plastic. She punched Asher's stomach. The mella gasped, but her nails still found Ember's arms and skin ripped as Asher doubled over.

"Don't you dare speak like you know her," Ember said, her voice cold as she took a step back and wiped blood from her neck. "You have no right to anything of hers, not her ship and definitely not her memory."

Asher shot upright and kneed Ember where an ovary should have been. Ember sucked in air, but from shock, not pain, and collapsed onto her knees as a ghostly Taraniel-yet-not voice played through the ship's audio and wiggled through Ember's head, throwing everything off balance.

Don't follow me, Ember. This is my choice.

"No," Ember whispered. They were Taraniel's whispered words from the morning she had left the colony, and Ember was clearly having some kind of auditory hallucination. She grasped the arms of the chair, digging her nails in. Ember had only tasted sand when Taraniel kissed her that final day. Her lips were warm, but the wind had stolen all the moisture. Taraniel was already a woman of paper—a delicate, ephemeral thing. She'd turned, and in two heartbeats, the sand had swallowed her. There hadn't been anything else to do.

You're bleeding on my floor.

Ember turned and caught the equally stunned expression on Asher's face. The ship's voice was also Taraniel's, a strange mix of higher-pitched computer audio and Taraniel's lighter, breathier lilt.

"I turned off the interface," Asher whispered as if the creepy Taraniel-AI couldn't hear every damn word they said. "Taraniel spent a lot of time alone in this ship, but I didn't think..."

I turned the interface back on. **Get up, Ember. You're embarrassing me.**

Ember got up, but deliberately, as she scanned the dark interface panel, Asher's tight body language, and the bolted chair that lay between her and the exit. She tried to regulate her breathing, tried to slow her mind. Taraniel was smart. Taraniel had an engineering background. Taraniel had worked on the pod. This, maybe, made sense. Maybe.

"Taraniel?" Ember asked and took an exploratory step toward the door.

A facsimile of, sure. A fax. A *fax*. The AI laughed with a riotous abandon that actual-Taraniel had never used.

Asher edged closer to Ember, insults forgotten in the atmosphere of weird. Ember found the hatch release panel, and the electronics whirred to life for almost a full second before the AI let out a high-pitched squeak that had Asher and Ember crouching and covering their ears.

Okay, okay. I'm sorry. I'll turn off the override alarm. It's my first time running solo. If I aim to be only half as creepy, will you two stop plotting ways to escape?

Ember would make no such promise and very much doubted Asher would either.

Neither answered, though they both stood back up, Ember's hand joining Asher's on the door panel.

Fine. But if it helps, I'm not Taraniel. There's no dead body hooked up to wires in my sub floor. I'm a personality imprint—a quickly done personality imprint—with a recorded voice and an immutable directive that involves both of you. I have memory files, too, because Taraniel thought it would help Ember. I also have the manifest she wanted you to look at.

"I've worked through my wife's death, mostly, but I am not prepared for her partial transformation into a ship,"

Ember said, much more blandly than the words had been in her mind. She certainly hadn't been prepared to hear Taraniel's voice again, however minutely distorted. Whatever the manifest was, she wasn't in the mood.

"We'd be more receptive if you'd open the door." Asher depressed the pad again. When nothing happened, she slammed her palm into it, growling under her breath.

Oh fine.

The hatch pushed out and hit the grassed ground with an anticlimactic thud. Bits of tree pollen wafted in, tickling Ember's nose. Asher took two steps down the hatch, tugging Ember's sleeve when she didn't immediately move to follow.

Ember pivoted, then turned back, trying to figure out where the camera or whatever optics sensor was located inside the pod. Maybe ships didn't care about being looked in the "eyes" when you spoke to them. With a Taraniel-ship, it seemed important.

"Taraniel?" Ember's voice sounded hopeful. If she could have smacked herself, she would have.

If that's the name you want to give me. The AI lowered its volume and smoothed its words in a near-perfect imitation of her late wife. It should have made Ember's arm hairs stand on end. It should have made her want to vomit.

It didn't, but she sure wasn't at ease either.

Would you like to read the manifest, Ember? It's a conversation Taraniel wanted to have with you.

"A conversation she couldn't have while she was alive?" Ember spat. The creepiness of Taraniel-as-a-ship settled in.

No, because there was nowhere to have it and no time. But the ship works. The mella can't leave without you though. None of this can happen without you and your coordinates and codes. The manifest will help settle your nerves and confusion.

Ember took note of her voice turning angry and decided not to bother fixing it. "What confusion? My codes are only for export shipments, not people, and the coordinates we have are...maybe to a world that isn't worth visiting. A shipping manifest isn't going to tell me anything new." She whispered the next words, not certain if Asher could hear. "Even if they indicate the location of Old Earth."

Which is exactly where Taraniel wanted you to go.

Ember frowned. "As I consistently told Taraniel, that is completely unmanageable and unreasonable. Earth was great and all, but Earth was also trashed. Trade one wasteland for another? Why?"

Because it isn't a wasteland. It's a paradise, and you know that, or at least, you guessed it. How many conversations did you have with Taraniel about the import licenses you had to sign? How many times did you stamp a box of tree seedlings from your lab with coordinates that didn't match any of the terraformed worlds? Why are there shipment codes for a world no one should care about?

Ember blinked once, letting her eyelids rest momentarily before the world filtered back in. Confusion was a state she didn't care for, in the lab or outside it. Sure, she and Taraniel had talked about licensing and imports and spreadsheets, but those were mundane aspects of Ember's job. They could dream about an Earth that never died, but that didn't refute cold, hard facts.

"I watched the ocean die. I saw forests decay to soupy puddles. You, Taraniel, think it was—what? Mass hallucination?"

No, not a hallucination. A lie by omission, perhaps, and infinitely perpetuated. But you could return to those flower fields you loved. Think about it.

"You have Old Earth coordinates?" Asher took a step inside the ship, her face incredulous. Apparently, she'd overheard. "Seriously?"

"No! We think...we thought... It's not verified. I mean, *maybe.*"

"Tell me." Asher stepped into her, far too close, her jaw set.

It's all right, Ember. The mella want off of here as much as we do. The mella elected Asher, Pui, Kate, and Nok to help me get the supplies for the ship. We built it together. We built it so we could go into space *together*, with the mella's blessings, so they could eventually return and get everyone off Queen. Including the colonists in the dome. The mella helped me live far longer and far better than I ever could have at the colony. You all belong on Old Earth. We all belong on Old Earth. No more stolen lives. You can take back all that Earth took away.

You can trust them.

Ember threw up her hands. No way she could pretend that slap hadn't hurt. "I don't trust any of you, but it doesn't matter because it was a pipe dream born out of pure conjecture. The presidium funds about 50 percent of my research, which means I have to take projects from them sometimes. Two projects ago, they wanted trees that thrived in salinized water. Last time, they wanted grass that grew on plastic. Every couple years, they make me box a few bins of experimental flora from my greenhouse, package it, and stamp it with numbers only. I take it to the depot. It ships. No big deal."

External packages get stamped with the destination planet though. Not just coordinates.

"True," Asher agreed as she bit her lower lip. "We've got a woman in the depot who lifts packages for us. Exported glass usually goes to the facility on Europa, with the packages stamped as such. The brown sand from most of the sun side gets sifted on Adair. Colonists may not get to know location codes of other colonized worlds, but the mella have a complete database. Well, almost complete."

"I don't think Earth has a lot of use for mutated sedge," Ember said sourly. "Earth is dead, and even if it wasn't, it's been half a century since the first ships left Earth. That isn't enough time to recover a planet. It's got to be less habitable than Queen."

"Taraniel said—"

"Even if it *is* habitable." Ember cut Asher off before she could add more fuel to a debate Ember and Taraniel had started long before the cancer diagnosis. "Once we get there and find, what, two acres of shitty trees, what do we do? Contact the presidium for transfer papers to a habitable planet? Come back to Queen and be in exactly the same place we are now? This is ridiculous. We have a ship. We could go *anywhere*. There's no need to go back to a sink-hole."

The AI sighed. The slip of electronics *sighed*, and Ember heard a whirr in the bulkhead to her left that sounded like a measured exhalation. **Earth is alive, Ember. Taraniel wanted to take you there with your sister and the mella and as much of her as possible.**

You can argue all you want, but this ship and I, by extension, are here to take you home.

Chapter Seven

From December and for six years thereafter, thousands fled Earth. Demand on the planet's resources eased. The procrastinators, the wealthy in their bunkers, the governmental scientists inherited, by default, a world shedding its skin to become a revitalized paradise.

They saw no reason to call the others home.

Nadia

"Taking off the envirosuit is a bad idea. I disagree with this idea." Varun stood outside the flyer and leaned back against a wing, shaking his head. He had his cowl off, but his envirosuit zipper still hugged his chin, and his boots were still laced as though he was going to run down a rabbit. Everything about his posture screamed uncomfortable, which kept people out of his lab at the science complex but would get him shot out here.

Nadia pointed to the building in the distance. They'd seen four more ships land and half a dozen take off while plotting in the flyer. When the ship told them the unregistered TOPA had entered the building, Nadia had made an executive decision that she knew Varun only followed because she outranked him academically.

Nadia had already shed the bits of the envirosuit she'd brought, along with her blue lab coat. She'd loosened her hair and teased her fingers through it from the roots out, hoping for a mad-scientist look but probably only managing unkempt. That would work fine. Her toes ached, and she shivered against the breeze in her black T-shirt and loose jeans, but she looked casual, she hoped. Like a mella back from a raid with new clothing and a smug attitude. Like she knew what she was doing out on the equator, entering into the Super-Secret Mella Hideout, which, if she made it back alive to report on, might get her promotion to full professor.

"You show up with TOPA blazing, and they're going to ask questions," Nadia argued. "You ever seen a mella wear an envirosuit, even a stolen, broken-down one? No. Chuck the suit. Untuck your collared shirt from your pants and maybe unzip your fly. Look like we're supposed to be here. Look cool."

"I am not cool."

Nadia reached over and unzipped Varun's envirosuit down to his collarbone. "We can't get back without refueling, so you're going to have to do something. Besides, we've found the mella base camp. Smile a little. Once we return with the GPS coordinates and the presidium come mop up, our discretionary accounts will never be empty again."

Nadia's smile turned grim. "We might accomplish some science. Imagine, culverts and pipes we only have to lay once. More...bug things for you. I don't know. Glassware. Forceps. Those tiny little pins you stick through the sand flies to mount them. What do you call those?"

Varun scowled, unclipped his gloves from his sleeves, and tossed them back into the flyer. "They are called insect pins. However, we do not look like mella, Dr. O'Grady."

"If you're going to be stuffy, they're going to know we're from the colony. Now, pants, boots, the whole collection. Move like it's tenure review, and I'm the head of your committee."

She paused, a thought niggling in the back of her mind. "Actually, I think I *am* the head of the departmental tenure committee this year. Huh." She waved sheepishly. There was no way him flying her out here, especially into a mella camp, wouldn't be seen as a gross imbalance of power. On the plus side, it pretty much removed all culpability from Varun. "I'll need your tenure packet next month. Just, uh, put it in my file on the server. When you can."

Varun stared at her.

"Time's wasting, Assistant Professor. Show me those standard-issue lab pants."

Varun inhaled loudly enough that Nadia heard snot click in his nose, but he unzipped and unstrapped the envirosuit and peeled it in layers from his body. He still had his white lab coat on underneath, which Nadia found hilarious, but he took it off without prompting. After that piece got flipped into the flyer, he looked much like Nadia—casual T-shirt, loose but not baggy pants. Varun didn't unzip his fly, but he did let Nadia rub a handful of slushy snow into his hair, which produced superb bedhead. "Now what?" he asked cautiously.

"Fuel. With this many people coming and going"—she pointed her finger and circled the ships on the ground and the two currently in the sky—"the mella won't be familiar with everyone. We just need to find the fuel."

She tapped his shoulder and walked toward the building, using her hips to generate as much scientist swagger as she could. The presidium had mandatory monthly mella update videos, and in them the women always looked confident. They lived in the desert and in the snow and slept with giant beetles. They wore colony textile scraps, but that pirate freedom clearly boosted the psyche. People in the colony always looked run-down and frizzy, even though they were the ones with reliable access to water and supplies. One could reasonably pick out a colonist from a mella lineup just by the slouching.

Nadia walked into the shipyard like she'd just gotten a big grant. She walked like she'd just come off a transport from New Earth, well fed and well clothed and ready to smack Queen into shape. Like she imagined a sand pirate would, full of freedom and a fuck-off attitude.

Varun, on the other hand, kept his head down, his eyes scanning the sand, and his shoulders hunched like a little boy being forced to wash up for dinner.

"Would you perk up?" she asked without slowing. "Imagine your lab publishes a dozen papers a year. Your autoclave has never broken. They need an architect familiar with Queen to design a new settlement. Pick whatever motivates you, run with it, and look engaged."

"Cranky old professor and irritating PhD student would also be convincing," he offered. "Plenty of the mella have

PhDs. Dr. Grant, our last organic chemist, defected two years ago." He looked up at her reproachfully. "Pretending to be defectors would be more plausible."

"I don't want to be recruited. I want to get fuel and leave. The ecosystem here isn't plausible, and that bothers me." She pointed down. The grass beneath Nadia's feet had transitioned to healthy green, but the soil looked like pale-white dust more than anything with rich organics in it. It felt smooth under her boots as if she were walking on powdered sugar.

"You underestimate the mella too much, and we'll be conscripted."

"Well, you can blame me after it happens." Nadia rolled the sleeves of her shirt up over her shoulders. She'd moved from chilly to sweating during their brief walk, and Varun's collar was now ringed with sweat.

They were half a kilometer at most from the main building but only a few meters from the closest ship. Shaped like a doughnut, this flyer had a substantial propulsion module on the interior of the ring. The entire thing was painted bubblegum-pink with little white polka dots. A lot of buildings and personal items were pink on Queen, but hotrod-pink, closer to magenta. Ember didn't care much for it, but Nadia found the color soothing in a strange way. Hot-pink felt feminine while still having an element of danger. This ship though. Nadia wrinkled her nose. Soft pinks, with or without polka dots, needed to stay on baby blankets. How could you take an adult serious in a ship painted like this?

"Do you want to just siphon the fuel from this one?" Varun asked, completely serious.

Nadia made a mental note to invite Varun out for beers once they found Ember. Nadia had a number of ongoing lab projects that needed the assistance of someone with a bit of flexibility.

"Maybe." They didn't have a hose or a container, but that didn't mean one couldn't be found.

Nadia peered up into what looked like the cockpit, judging from the clear window-like surface spanning two meters around the circumference. With the angle of light from a nearby lamp and the tint of the glass, she thought she could see the top of a chair but not much else. She moved to the backside of the flyer, then slid across the ring, belly first. She dropped into the center and put a hand on the round propulsion system. Cold. That seemed weird with all the air traffic about, so Nadia tapped the surface experimentally. A deep, hollow sound reverberated. Huh. Not the propulsion, then? Maybe a cargo hold, but that didn't make sense on a ship this small.

"This one isn't returning for another few hours," said a short woman who appeared from the north side of the flyer, startling Nadia. The woman had light-brown hair in the kind of pixie cut only grad students and toddlers could pull off, freckled pinkish skin, and a nose the shape of a small potato. Though she also wore a faded T-shirt, it had no logos, pit stains, or frayed hems. That didn't fit with what Nadia knew of mella, but she'd also never met one in person. The "Wanted" feeds and posters also made them out to be a lot taller and never so well dressed. This woman's pants were a deep indigo and pressed so that a line striped down the middle of her thighs to her ankles. A breeze wandered across the landscape, but the woman's hair didn't move at all, which spoke of gel and other haircare products Nadia hadn't seen in years.

"Oh," Nadia stammered, still not clear where the woman had popped up from. Mella on the propaganda videos always stabbed people a lot. This one didn't look stabby, and her pants were too tight to conceal a knife, so Nadia could probably relax. Her body did not agree.

"Yours break down or something?" the woman asked as she stood on tiptoe, looking for their ship.

"Yeah, we had to leave it back there." Nadia gestured vaguely back to Varun's flyer. "This one is..." Nadia pointed loosely at the doughnut ship. "It's real pink."

The woman shrugged halfheartedly. "You know how it is with the new ones. The other two they had on the lot for women had hearts."

Varun started to speak, then swallowed his words. Nadia nodded, although she had no idea what the woman was on about.

There were no ship lots on Queen, retail or otherwise. They had four hangars filled with ground flyers, which had the same crappy distance capabilities as Varun's, and one hangar with spare parts for spaceship repair. Queen didn't own a spaceship other than the presidium's personal transport ship. No one left Queen. People got assigned Queen, or they fled to Queen, but if anyone wanted to go somewhere else, it had to be with a visa, a passport, and a ticket on the one intergalactic transport ship that stopped by five times a year. Nadia's parents had never managed a visit in the decade they'd been defrosted on their world. Queen gave tourist visas about as often as Nadia got to shave her legs.

Compounding that issue, there were a lot of ships here. Mella rode beetles because colony ships weren't worth stealing. The ships sucked fuel, and their GPS turned spotty the farther out from the colony one got. Nadia didn't even know if Queen had satellites over the equators that the GPS could connect to. What would be the point? No one was supposed to be out here.

Mella aren't stupid enough to live on the equator. Ergo...

Oh, that was an invasive, concerning thought Nadia did not have time to unpack. Bad to make assumptions without data too. Which meant it was time to go collecting, and she'd always loved fieldwork.

Nadia leaned into the woman conspiratorially and whispered, "Our internal fuel gauge broke, and we need to refill. Is there an easy way to get to the pump without a ship?"

"Also, a toilet," Varun added, stepping up next to Nadia. He'd pitched his voice low enough that Nadia looked at him with what she hoped were her best bug-eyes. He met her gaze, but facial emotion had never been one of Varun's strong suits. Bathrooms weren't part of the plan, and he probably hadn't missed the implications of a shipyard. They needed a space to talk, alone, and a bathroom would do perfectly well.

Varun finally managed to look sheepish, which was really weird on a face that delivered bug facts like they were gospel and Nadia an eager convert. "I know where they are in the main building, but I don't think I'll make it there," he added. "I don't want to end up relieving myself near a water storage tank."

The woman opened her arms wide and grinned. "All the world's a stage. Though if he has to go—" She pointed at Varun and waggled her eyebrows. "—it'll have to be inside. Queen's satellites get a little too close on occasion, and there is no way of knowing when they might turn the cameras on. New Earth always seems to be changing the rules. The men's toilets are the third hallway on the right, and you can ask the receptionist at the front for a fuel car."

New Earth? What in hell did New Earth have to do with anything on Queen? The presidium were the ruling bodies, not an abstract government half a lifetime away. Another fun factoid to file away for later. Also...bathrooms? Everyone used the same bathroom on Queen. Otherwise, they wouldn't have been on the planet to begin with. They were mostly pit toilets anyway, with white ceramic foot guides and, in the science building, ceramic bowls set flush into the floor. Everything got fanned out no matter which way you squatted. It also meant there was no way to hide differences. Ember had spent many a drunken night ranting about privacy and urethra angles and general courtesy, but Nadia had never given it serious thought.

If there were men's toilets here, then there were men with more equipment than Varun. That was a big, big problem.

"Receptionist and inside. I have it. Thank you," said Nadia, and when she heard Varun take a step back, "No one wants to see dick anyway, especially on this planet. They're so sensitive."

"Hah!" The woman snorted and leaned with one hand against her ship. "He's lucky he got clearance at all. New Earth relaxed the visitor permits for the quartz scientists. Are you two manufacturers? I know a few were invited to address the conference. You dress almost as poorly as the colonists here do. We watched the feeds coming in."

Nope. Too much new information. Nadia's brain spun into overtime, and she reached back to Varun, grabbed his shirt, and squeezed. Varun's hand on her shoulder steadied her.

"We work with chitin, mostly," he said in a low, gruff voice. "Looking to expand into more lucrative areas." His bored scientist tone seemed to land perfectly.

"I'm Sal." The woman offered her hand, and Nadia shook it, giving Varun time to cover his half-formed, hands together, Thai-style wai with a smoothing of his T-shirt instead.

"Dr. Varun Sinha," he said as he shook her hand. "Entomologist."

"Well, don't be outbidding me now," Sal said with a smirk that turned the tips of Varun's ears red. "You scientists and your money. I'm from Europa though. Don't think I can't compete."

"I—"

Nadia didn't have time for awkward flirting. "We both need the facilities." She flashed a quick smile. "But we'll see you inside later. We can swap colonization tales then."

Sal nodded, casting a half-apologetic look to Varun. "Looking forward to it."

"Ma'am," Varun said with a nod.

"Double bed in the ship," Sal returned with a wink. "Much better services out here than in the colony proper. More varied equipment."

Nadia pressed another smile, tugged Varun's sleeve, and they walked briskly toward the main building. They were here for fuel, and for Ember, not whatever that was.

"I'd like to leave quickly," Nadia whispered as they walked. "Not that I'm not curious, but still." She turned to Varun. "Thoughts? Ember?"

"I have a number of hypotheses, currently, Dr. O'Grady; however, I can't reconcile Sal's comment about the presidium," Varun murmured. "If the presidium knows the mella have their secret base here, why are our sentries—why is Dr. Schmitt—risking their lives to find them? If these aren't mella, then we have much larger problems than a missing scientist. I don't like where any of the hypotheses take me."

"You're assuming Ember is tangled in all this." Nadia didn't like how saying that out loud made her stomach feel. Ember couldn't keep a secret worth a damn. Taraniel could, but Ember showed every emotion on her face like an overexcited puppy. Which meant either Ember hadn't come out here of her own volition, or she'd gotten better at lying. Nadia didn't like either.

"And the quartz," Nadia added as she continued to mull the Ember issues. "I'm not a soil scientist, and sure we have sand, but none of it is worthy of attention, especially not research attention. Mella sure don't care about it, so let's operate under a hypothesis that these are not mella. They aren't likely to be from on-planet, not with penis anyway, so who are they? Did they kidnap Ember? If so, why? And why fake her death far enough out that someone might go looking? It's like leaving a giant beacon saying 'Hey, people, work out here.'"

"If we stay, we could find out," Varun suggested.

"If we stay, we aren't looking for Ember," Nadia countered flatly. "Priorities."

"Yes, but cause and effect, Dr. O'Grady. One could lead to the other. But if neither leads to fuel, we will not have any options."

Nadia groaned. "Okay, fine. Fair. Inside for...ten minutes. Then we come back out here, siphon some idiot's tank, and..."

Varun put his hand on her shoulder, and Nadia fell silent. Once they got fuel, they had to head back, with or without Ember. Face the director's consequences. Figure everything out after.

Damn it. *Where* was Ember?

They both mulled as they wove around two other vehicles—clearly spaceships and both still warm and habited—until the building entrance came into view. It was shorter than Nadia had expected, with only two stories and half a dozen windows. The building's front façade glinted a pale green in the strong lamplight, the trim around the double entry doors and windows a sunset purple. They had to be straddling the equator now, and though only artificial light beat on Nadia's neck, the humid, temperate air stuck in her lungs. Here, the grass disappeared beneath paving stones, but the fill between each hexagonal shape was the same white powder. A steady stream of people brushed past them, barely nodding as they loaded and unloaded spaceships.

Nadia hadn't processed Sal's words until a group of four men exited the building. They laughed over a joke with a punchline Nadia heard as "and then she said, but how many?" Nadia lost the rest of the conversation as her eyes scrolled down. The men had no facial hair, and pronounced Adam's apples did crop up sometimes on females, but that pants bulge...distinctive. Nadia felt her face flush, then told her body to calm the fuck down.

"You get to do the talking," she whispered to Varun as the men passed them, oblivious to her sweating palms and billowing pheromones. "I'm almost forty, but if any of them talk to me I'll end up saying something suggestive. Wrong time of the month."

"I don't think it will be necessary."

He pushed open the right-side door, and the two of them stepped into a distorted memory of Earth. In the center of the rectangular entry room, a petite blonde woman with a pale, ruddy complexion sat behind a darkly stained wooden desk. Nadia counted seven pillars made from pink quartz, possibly an eighth behind a giant poster board that read "Purity You Cannot Believe. Feel the Silicon Dioxide of the Future." The full bottom third showed what looked like grainy snowballs placed in a circle. A free-standing banner read, in big black letters, "Bids Taken Throughout the Conference. Do Not Miss the Opportunity of Four Lifetimes."

Looking up at the ceiling, Nadia had to grab Varun for support. A gentle lattice of raw wood beams etched with gold filigree formed the dome. The floor appeared to be a continuous slab of rose quartz, just pink enough to make her think of undercooked hamburger. Nadia's stomach rumbled.

Varun pushed her forward as the desk lady smiled at them with bleached-brilliant teeth.

"Trade or conference?" the woman asked with an arch of eyebrows so heavily plucked Nadia couldn't tell if they were real or drawn on. "If conference, I need to see your badges before I can give you your packet. It will have your bidding cards in it if you're participating in the Queen sale."

The woman's words made no sense, and neither did her face. Nadia's stomach rumbled again, and exhaustion tingled in the corners of her eyes. It wasn't just the lack of food and hours in the flyer either. There'd been a point in her life when she'd had time for manicures and blowouts—little daily things for herself—but Queen hadn't had the supplies for nearly two years. Nadia had a quarter bottle of nail polish she hoarded, and even her razor had gone to metal recycling five months ago. When no one had access to hair dye or a working blow dryer, Nadia could pretend they didn't exist anymore. A visual reminder of all the things they didn't have on Queen—a planet with enough feminine preference to buy an entire city's worth of bikini wax in one go—pushed at Nadia's patience. If the people here had been mella, it might not have been so bad. If the mella had blush and fake eyelashes, it meant they'd stolen them from the colony, which meant there was a supply room somewhere Nadia could maybe find access to. Here, though, in this forbidden land of pink, Nadia had no idea. That made her grumpy. Mentally, she took a fat permanent marker and drew giant triangles over the woman's faint suggestion of eyebrows.

"We're here for business but hoping to catch a few of the conference-goers between panels," Varun said. "But we require facilities first. We also didn't budget fuel accordingly and need assistance with our flyer. We were told there is a fuel car?"

"Bathroom down the hall to the right," the woman said, pointing over her shoulder at a softly lit hallway that glowed the pink of North American girlhood. Nadia mentally added a mustache to the woman because Ember would have.

"Thank you very much." Varun stepped around the desk and made for the hallway, more confidence in his shoulders than Nadia had ever seen in the lab. He headed toward a door marked "Men" and pushed it open far enough so that Nadia could follow.

She took four steps into the white-tiled room—not a hint of pink here—and stepped directly into a man, slightly shorter than her, with white skin and curly brown hair that went just past his ears. Their shoulders bumped, and the man drew back, his eyebrows high with surprise.

"Women's is the next door down." He reached around, put a hand on the small of her back, and directed her out of the bathroom. Nadia suppressed a shiver and very quickly remembered the perks of an all-women planet.

"Off you go, then," the man said with a smile that made Nadia grind her teeth. He turned and disappeared toward the lobby.

Nadia took a breath, shook off the creepiness, and again made for the men's bathroom door. This time, a man with pants too loose for Nadia to make any assumptions pulled the door open a breath afterwards and nodded as he turned to go farther down the hall. He was white, like everyone they'd seen thus far on the equator. Further proof the people here were not mella since the mella came from the colony population in theory, and about 40 percent of the colonists were of Thai descent.

Nadia leaned against the wall and waited for the man to disappear, but he stayed in front of her, confusion on his face.

"You with the presidium?" the man asked and pointed to the name tag on his chest. His read "Dan – Newmark Electronics Product Development" with "Europa" in smaller font just below. "You look local. I've never met a resident outside the presidium and their entourage."

Nadia glanced down at her bare arms, weathered and freckled and distinctly olive in their undertones, especially when compared to Ember, who hated being out of her envirosuit, or this guy, who looked like he'd been birthed two days ago as a fully formed human.

"Presidium," she said as all the data points fell into place. "Lot of...sand...things."

There were no mella here. These people were too well fed and too nicely dressed. There were no beetles, no trails of stolen electronics, no *smells*. There was sand, however, and tech, which meant Nadia was standing in a conference hall with scientists and researchers and businesspeople, in the middle of trade and commerce the presidium said would never happen on Queen. *Could* never happen because Queen's sand was building sand, not electronics sand. Their concrete got used for only the most basic applications, though it was ridiculous, when she thought about it, to make concrete on one planet and haul it to another. Every colonized planet had to have sand, good quality or not. On the other hand, electronics sand—the fine, nearly pure white silicon dioxide—would be worth heavy export and commerce, and all of this.

Which meant Queen *was* a fucking paradise already, just an economic one, not a climactic one. They'd been lied to, the colonists, the scientists. Nadia wanted to punch the receptionist right in her pert nose and erase her eyebrows with a fistful of that expensive, bullshit sand.

"Hah," the man chortled. "Presidium. Funny. If you're taking orders, the primary conference room is out of cold water. Otherwise, you'd best get back to your ship. The rest of your group scuttled off with President Borchert like terrified crabs. A bathroom stop is a bold choice when a member of the presidium is that angry." He pressed his thin, pale lips together in a curt business smile and headed down the hall.

If a member of the presidium was here, things were even weirder. Nadia couldn't think of the last time one of the three-member presidium had left their building in the dome. They didn't travel.

Varun exited the bathroom as the businessman went through the fourth door on the left, right before a T-junction in the hall. "We could try the women's," he suggested. "Or find an alcove." His lips pursed when Nadia didn't immediately answer him. "Dr. O'Grady?"

"Come on." She grabbed Varun by the front of his shirt and pulled him down the corridor in the direction of the conference room. About thirty meters in front of them was a double door of green, tempered glass. Nadia could only make out blurry forms behind it, but as they got closer, tiptoeing even though the hall was empty, she could hear clapping.

"End of panel," Varun suggested when Nadia let go of his shirt. He smoothed the wrinkles away and very nearly glared at her. "They'll be coming out soon if there isn't another scheduled right after."

"Well, let's hope we get lucky." Nadia had never been to a conference in person but had digitally attended enough to know that a quarter of the room would be sleeping and another quarter hungover. These were academics. Not police officers. As long as she and Varun stayed in the back and kept quiet, chances were no one would care.

Nadia pushed the left side door open just enough so she could slip through. Varun followed with muted grumbling. Inside the hall, the lights were dim over the tiered seating, and no one bothered to turn as they edged along the back wall. Of the hundred or so seats, maybe three-quarters had a person in them. The stage was green glass as well, with a stained-glass podium that reflected brightly in the track lighting. A man with short, curly black hair and warm beige skin stood behind it, his head turned to the projection screen. The current slide on the screen was entirely text, black words on a white background, and he read them verbatim without inflection.

In the very front row, directly in the center and with no one sitting within a five-seat radius, was the very distinctive head of President Borchert. Nadia recognized the abomination that was her bowl-shaped haircut, though it had grown scraggly near the back. Borchert had her bright-blue suit jacket on—the one the presidium always wore for formal communications such as welcoming new colonists or telling everyone in the main cafeteria that Queen would no longer carry hot chocolate mix.

"Academic presentations are just as terrible in real life." Varun sighed. "I always thought they'd be livelier. Entomologists have so much to talk about. The insects on Queen, for instance, are more like true bugs than—"

Nadia stopped in a shadowed corner and pulled Varun up next to her, shushing him.

"...that we can expect four to five meters of silicon dioxide within a three-kilometer radius of the current mine site. Computer models show"— here he flipped to his next slide, which read only as a jumble of numbers in poor alignment— "based on a climate analysis, that similar veins of sand should be available on the sun side of the equator as well, although this is not confirmed and would be a gamble for prospective buyers. Therefore, we propose—"

"What do you think?"

Nadia shivered at the woman's voice, way too close to her ear. She turned to her left and could just make out someone standing next to her, maybe a handspan away, in a pencil skirt and blazer. The rest of her features were hidden in the darkness.

"About what?" Nadia asked in her best associate professor voice.

"There being enough sand on this planet to invest in. It's a big gamble, especially since we can refine lower-quality sand from other worlds, and the veins on Queen might be almost gone. The silicon dioxide here is just *so* pure. Did you hear the last guy talk about how the last time any of this purity was found, it was on Old Earth?"

Nadia stood there and blinked.

The woman giggled. *Giggled*? "Sorry. It's exciting to talk about this stuff with other people who care. I'm here for the business part of the conference. Snuck in to see what the academics are saying. We mostly get the digests from the panels."

"Uh," Nadia stammered. "Well, in terms of this paper—"

"We've been following the research from this lab for a long time," Varun smoothly cut in. "We're from Europa, and while our university isn't part of the bidding process, we are interested in the outcome. Newmark Electronics funds a significant portion of our research."

If Varun could lie this well, Nadia definitely needed to pay closer attention to his tenure dossier. He also sounded way too eager and a little like a first-year master's student.

"Newmark. Well, they do have a lot of hands in this, don't they? I'm part of the Kresky-Lieb Group. Our home offices are on Io and Proxima Centauri b." She paused, then added, "Proxima is tidally locked with a thick atmosphere, just like Queen, so the high winds are able to transfer heat around. Queen's ecosystem is only slightly varied, if I understood the presentation right, and the first colonists did terraforming that further altered the dynamic. Something affects your winds at the equator, but the rest functions like Proxima. Is this your first tidally locked planet?"

Varun must have looked as confused as Nadia felt. "No, ma'am," he responded in the same silken voice that raised bumps on Nadia's arms. "I was wondering, idly, how many tidally locked planets had thicker atmospheres? Most people would assume they only have the narrow habitable strip. I've heard the residents of Queen are generally of this same persuasion."

The woman shrugged, and Nadia thought she caught a quick hair flip as well. "The conference registration packets said the local population would be relocated to a new world once Queen sold. That's all I know about them. We so rarely hear about the exoplanets in Earth's solar system. I assume this one is just as desolate as the others. Even Proxima is nowhere to take a vacation. I hate having to split the year between the two corporate headquarters."

This time, she definitely flipped her hair, and Nadia's stomach flipped along with it. Could you even sell a planet? Planetoid? What did that *mean*?

"I don't suppose you've heard what Newmark plans to bid for the planetoid?" the woman asked. "Any thoughts on their max threshold? How much do they generally give you all, per grant?"

Nadia jumped in before Varun could bury them in more information she wouldn't know how to process. "In fact, we do have some numbers if you think Kresky-Lieb might be interested in research funding opportunities."

"I think that is a distinct possibility," the woman responded in a tone Nadia knew meant "no way in hell."

"Then we will go get our packets and be right back. We've been taking notes." Nadia took Varun by the hand this time and, with much more authority than she felt, left the conference room just as the audience began clapping for the end of the presentation. They slipped back through the glass doors, and Nadia squinted in the brightly lit auditorium.

"We need to go outside." A statistically significant portion of her wanted to storm back into the meeting and start yelling or at least sit in the back and silently seethe as academics debated how much her home was worth and the presidium sold Queen out from under the colonists. But there were only so many bluffs they could make and only so many times they'd pass before they got hauled to the presidium's main office. Ember wouldn't be in that meeting room, but she might be outside with the rest of the "locals." She might *be* a local, although if grief had driven her that far and Nadia hadn't noticed, she deserved to have her sister badge revoked.

"Dr. O'Grady—" Varun began.

"Ember," Nadia whispered fiercely. "Ember first."

Varun looked at her, eyes searching for the rest of the sentence, for the emotions that leaked from her like tears—emotions he always kept tightly locked away. Reaching an unspoken conclusion, Varun nodded and walked from the hall, through the foyer, and into the bright lamplight, not bothering to look back.

Nadia followed.

This time, the sand in the grass made her feet slip, made her mind slip, made her think of her fuzzy Earth memories. There was always unfairness in the galaxy because life was unfair. Queen had always been one flavor of unfairness for her and more an exasperated sigh for Ember. This went beyond unfair into wrong, and Nadia didn't have a great deal of experience with wrong. Scientists played by the rules. An experiment was statistically significant at $p < 0.05$ or less, or it was trash. If she broke her colleague's beaker, she gave them one of hers. They were in the shithole together, and that meant something.

This meant something, too, but Nadia didn't have a single hypothesis to throw at it that didn't end up with her and Varun being left out to die in the snow—or at least their suits thrown out while their bodies were whisked to who knew where. Selling Queen didn't register. She needed to disassemble, and for that, she needed her sister, and maybe also some pisco.

Varun tracked a path around the far side of the building because fuel still needed to happen. There, on the west side, where a creek meandered around a small riffle, a Queen standard-issue ground flyer sat on its struts with a fuel line stuck right into its port. The woman with her hand on the line turned to them first with a feral expression. She paused for exactly the same length of time they did, surveying their clothes, their hair, probably smelling them, too, before her mouth formed a lopsided grin.

"We come in peace," Nadia said without thinking.

"Well, I sure didn't. We need this for parts, and you have great timing." The mella hauled the fuel line out and tossed it at Nadia, turning it off only after Nadia's shirt got thoroughly doused in kerosene. "There's a gauge at the bottom of the fuel drum that alerts whoever runs this place when it gets low. You two have fun." She hopped up into her flyer and had the propulsion on before Nadia even processed what she'd said.

Varun pulled her back to a safe distance as the flyer lifted first laterally, hovering just above Nadia's eyeline, then shot off across the landscape, the force of it knocking Nadia and Varun onto their asses.

Either the kerosene fumes had Nadia lightheaded, or she'd thumped more than her butt on the way down. Either way, she didn't notice the police until she heard Varun grunt in surprise and felt her arms tugged backward, bound by a plastic cord.

"Wait," Nadia said, her head swimming as a woman with calloused hands dragged her to standing. "We just needed fuel. We made a wrong turn."

"Mella always seem to make wrong turns," the woman responded. "You violate the no-fly zone agreement between the presidium and the mella, you get brought in." She stepped in front of Nadia with a hand held over her nose.

"We are scientists," Varun stated, his voice dripping with academic disdain. "From the colony. We have every right to be here."

"You stink," the other police officer replied. "And you're mella in the wrong part of the equator. I don't care if you're the presidium's secret mistress. You violate the treaty, you're beetle food."

Chapter Eight

Scientists from across the terraformed worlds were tapped, unknowingly, for their expertise. Breeds of plants and animals, engineered or bred on alien worlds, were transported back to Earth to speed revitalization. Invasive, non-native—these words lost their stigma. Earth needed those that could survive, regardless of the effect on the fragile ecosystem.

Ember

Ember napped on the thick grass of the equator, her feet buried in white powder sand. The sun warmed her left side as it peeked just above healthy maple trees. Lights flickered behind her eyelids as she continued fighting with herself about returning to the ship and arguing with an AI, reading the shipping manifest and *then* arguing with an AI, or just stealing the damn ship and flying it without AI-Taraniel on the way to somewhere. Maybe Old Earth. Maybe just *not Queen.*

She yawned and stretched, flopping onto her back and reaching her arms over her head. A toe poked her side, just as the stretch was getting good. Ember squeaked and, more embarrassed than annoyed, took a handful of sand and threw it at the perpetrator.

Asher laughed as she spit sand from her mouth. "Good aim."

Ember growled and pulled the edges of her shirt back down. She smelled rice and friend peanuts, which meant dinnertime, and manifest time, and then talk to her dead-wife-in-a-ship time. She couldn't wait.

Sitting up sucked. Standing was worse because she had to see that bluish lake again, had to dig her feet from pristine sand and remind herself she had a shit ton of decisions to make in the next hour before the mella made them all for her. Flat-out stealing the ship looked better and better. Maybe Taraniel had programmed an AI pilot too. Maybe it wouldn't have a voice protocol and Ember could sit in silence to wherever she was going while she tried to think about anything other than her last trip into space.

Asher clasped her hands behind her back, looking expectant. She'd changed clothes into a tight T-shirt with most of the hem intact and a green, pocketed skirt that just hit her knees. Knowing she was a sucker for a circle skirt, Ember looked back at the lake. Asher was not a complication she needed.

"Dr. Schmitt?"

"I was considering a swim in the lake," Ember returned.

"Not advisable. Leeches. The ship would be upset, and then how would we get off this hellscape?"

"I don't want to go anywhere with you."

"Your wife, and your wife's ship, thought differently," Asher deadpanned. "Neither of whom you can throw sand at when angry. Not effectively. Could we focus on your wife's ship and resurrected planets?"

When Ember didn't immediately respond, Asher added, "I apologize for slapping you. I realize Taraniel's death is still fresh. I'm not very good at patience, but you do deserve a bit."

"I deserve that ship," Ember retorted, but it came out without malice. There was no reason to pretend Earth didn't fascinate her. She still wanted to punch Asher, but that was probably colony indoctrination talking. Taraniel had always been the more social one—dragging Ember to late-night lab parties where they mixed shots in tiny beakers and used the lab-grade ethanol for cheap drinks.

"Earth?" Asher prodded. "The old one? Talk to me. Taraniel said you had theories."

Ember let out a long breath. "No, we had daydreams. I don't know anything, really. Nothing more than you. Taraniel and I reminisced, dreamed, about Earth mostly when drunk, which usually happened after a grant rejection. New Earth Science Foundation is a bitch."

Asher smoothed a wrinkle from the front of her skirt. "You're both solid scientists though. You in particular, Dr.

Schmitt, are well published. I've seen your h-index. I know you had more contract work from New Earth than you could ever possibly do, so grants shouldn't have mattered. I know you make plants that are shipped all over the colony worlds. With that skill in such demand, why Queen, both then, and now?"

The hair on Ember's arm raised, and she had to consciously tell herself to stop bristling. "Why did *you* pick Queen?"

Asher didn't catch the warning. A genuine smile, no smugness at all, bloomed on her face. "Lesbian. It is our planet after all. I also don't really like authority, and I have a master's in theater tech so they may have thought I'd be decent at building short-term shelters. I lasted two years in the colony before I defected. The mella council nominated me to lead this excursion because I'm really good at last-minute patchwork planning. Theater will do that for you."

Ember focused across the lake to the little rowboat that bobbed on the edge. On Earth, the water would have shone the brightest blue. With red above, the color muted to an earthen turquoise, but it looked lovely nonetheless. It was a shame they'd melted down all those toy buckets. "You've read this shipping manifest Taraniel wanted me to read?" Ember had to work to keep the accusation from her voice.

Asher moved to Ember's side and squinted into the sunset. People at the colony didn't stand this close to her, not since Taraniel's death. Apparently, she wasn't a social pariah among outcasts. "Yes, but I could have guessed its contents before even seeing it. Nothing surprising. No mella is surprised by New Earth antics. Taraniel in the ship, however, no one expected. Your wife had a number of hidden talents."

"She was always good with her hands."

Asher chuckled. "I'd be lying if I said I wasn't envious of that kind of relationship."

Ah, right. The overture. Well, these kinds of things went one of two ways: immediate explosion or half a decade of slow burn. Ember wasn't really in the mood for either.

She blew out a long breath and spun around on the soft sand. A little girl, her chestnut hair in tight braids, skipped over and handed her a dish of roasted peanuts.

"Bear's specialty," Asher said, taking one and crunching loudly. "From the colony's last shipment."

"I assume it tastes better when it is stolen." Ember took the dish from the girl, who skipped off with a half twirl, her braids whipping around her head as she giggled.

"Was she born here?" Ember asked. "She looks the right age."

"Yes, and in the camp here too. She's one of ours."

Ember raised her eyebrows. "You have a reproduction lab out here?" She spun around again. "Where?"

"I don't think that's pertinent to the discussion. Do you?" Asher pointed at the tray. "Eat your dinner."

Ember snorted but pinched a few peanuts from the dish and ate, letting the salt and cinnamon roll around her tongue. What planet had managed to get cinnamon trees growing again? Who had decided that was a species worth saving, among the millions of others? Rubber trees had gone extinct, Ember was certain, and she'd thought the same about cinnamon, but clearly not since the spice maliciously bit her tongue like an aggrieved lover.

"Good?" Asher looked hopeful. Ember bristled for no decent reason.

"Yeah." She dumped the rest into her mouth, then washed it down with a cup of cold water Asher offered her. Ember hoped it didn't come from the lake with Taraniel's dead body. She felt tired. No more small talk. No more random flirting. It was time to get her wife—whatever remained of her—and leave.

"I'm going back to the ship," Ember said. "She and I...*it* and I, need to have a talk."

"And you need to see if the ship will let you fly without a crew?" Asher asked lightly.

"Invites only last as long as the person who issued them is alive." Ember handed both the dish and the cup back to Asher, making solid eye contact with the woman's chin and nowhere else, and walked back toward the ship.

"Hey!" Plastic thudded softly on sand, and Asher's slipping footsteps followed. "Dr. Schmitt, please reconsider."

Ember didn't slow. "No, thanks."

Asher continued to jog after her. "Don't you want more information? Don't you have a million questions you want answered?"

"Not by you," Ember said, turning to glare at Asher as she quickened her pace.

"But I have answers the ship doesn't have."

They reached the ship, and Ember rapped the side with a knuckle. "Hey. Let me in."

The hatch fell open, and Ember stepped inside, waving Asher back as she did so. "Get lost."

"I think this is a bad idea, Dr. Schmidt. At least let me come in with you."

"Private conversation. Go fuck yourself."

"Absolutely not at this time." Asher followed her inside, collapsed into the closest chair, and swung one of her legs over the right arm. "You don't get to be in here alone right now. We don't know enough about you. We need this ship, and we need you with it. No joyrides."

The hatch closed at Ember's command, and she glared at Asher, fists balled. Her stomach reminded her, loudly, that she hadn't had enough to eat, and what she'd managed to ingest was likely going to come up if she stayed on the ship too long.

Ember, you still haven't cleaned the floor from the last time.

Shit.

Ember deflated. Taraniel's voice—the ship's voice—sounded too close to her dead wife's you'll-sleep-on-the-couch tone. Ember sat in another chair, rear on the very edge, and stared up at the ceiling.

Ember?

"Hey," Ember said to the white composite above her. "You scare the crap out of me, and Asher's ready to declare us sorority sisters. I haven't had enough time to digest any of this." Ember frowned. "Speaking of—" She turned to Asher. "How long have I been here? Can we connect to my TOPA? I'm sure I've missed a check-in."

Asher's eyes went everywhere except Ember.

"Where is my suit?" Ember demanded.

Asher shrugged and crossed her arms. "Snow side, somewhere. You're dead as far as the colony thinks."

"What!?" Ember bolted from her chair, directly toward Asher. Her stomach sloshed. "You can't just—"

Ember, sit down.

Ember stopped moving forward, but she did not sit. "I have to call my sister. She has to know I'm not dead. We can negotiate the rest of this"—she gestured widely—"later. First, Nadia."

The AI cut in before Asher could speak. **Ember, Nadia's been arrested.**

The air around her chilled. She hadn't misheard, but she didn't want to hear either. Colonists did not get arrested on Queen. *Mella* got arrested. There wasn't even a jail on the planet, not that Ember knew of. What would she even be arrested for? Nadia held every aspect of a second, youngest child: attention-seeking, social, a big joker—especially in inappropriate places—but she didn't go around slicing wires or spiking drinks. Petty vandalism was practically a religion on Queen, so that couldn't be it.

Goddamn it, and she was still on a spaceship. Vomit came up, and she swallowed it, hoping there would not be an encore.

"Where? How? Why?"

Trespassing. Dr. Varun Sinha was arrested along with her for stealing fuel and a flyer. The transmission doesn't say where they are though. Ember, I'm so sorry.

Ember swore she heard worry in the AI's tone. Nadia and Taraniel had been close, as far as sisters-in-law went. A ship pining after a person felt ridiculous. She felt ridiculous even having a conversation with it.

"Varun is up here too? We have to get her. We have to get them." Ember stalked to the control panel and danced her fingers across the screen, having no clue how to use it. Her sister and her best friend playing rescue mission was not helpful in this exact moment. Her mouth kept watering, and she told her brain to shut up. "Ship...thing, whatever, we need to go there."

I don't know where "there" is, Ember.

"I do," said Asher. "She's probably in the detention facility over on the cold side of the equator. It's about one hundred kilometers from the conference center."

"The *what*?"

Asher stood and joined Ember at the main console. She brushed Ember's hand away from the screen and entered an alpha numeric string, offering Ember a half-smile as she did so.

Ember would have punched her right then and there if her wife's personality hadn't been watching.

"You need coordinates for either, AI. Or did Taraniel upload the mella GPS library?" Asher asked.

I have the library as well as her research files. The restricted channel shows a conference in progress at the center, so we should try to avoid that area. They're trying to court the new electronics startup that makes FTL processors and also appear to be auctioning...Queen. Except that can't be right. When I look up their net site, I see a lot of promises about mass-production FTL drives. Sounds like garbage, and also an investor dream. The Queen part could be a presidium PR stunt.

Ember felt like she'd opened a book in the middle and no one wanted to tell her what she'd missed in the beginning out of sheer spite and blurted out, "There is nothing on the equator!" A feeling of sheepishness followed because yelling at an AI would get her nowhere, and every time she lost her temper, Asher seemed to pay her more attention. "I mean, what more could this sinkhole possible have? Do the mella hold an entire strip of paradise?"

The AI let out a labored sigh with enough force that Ember very nearly hung her head. If Taraniel had been standing in front of her, she'd have felt bad enough to sleep on the couch or would have printed synthetic flowers.

Hey, the AI said, all soft gentleness. That sent Ember right back up to rage on her emotional roller coaster.

"You don't get to—"

Honey. Ember. I'm sorry. The pet names got programmed too. Taraniel loved you, but you're not a lot of use without background information. You need to sit down and talk with Asher or, at the very least, read that shipping manifest Taraniel saved for you.

"I want to find Nadia. I want to find Varun. I don't care about electronics conferences. Where would we even hold them? We don't have anything convention-sized in the colony." Ember recognized the AI's attempts at mani-pulation, at least, which made her even less inclined to read the manifest and made it more urgent to find Nadia. Sharp-tongued sisters were useful with mella kidnapping and dead-wife-in-AI issues.

Asher said, "They must have tracked your TOPA up there. She's an idiot for going past the freeze line. The colony doesn't do recovery that far, and she should have known that. It's the whole reason we stuck the dummy suit that far out to begin with. Chances are, it's our person who got them in trouble since Aya was supposed to bring back a flyer we could use for a few last-minute add-ons to the pod."

"You're—" Ember's tongue felt two sizes too big for her mouth as she stumbled over the right blend of indignation and incredulity.

"I'm sorry," Asher said. Her fallen shoulders and the way her eyes skirted the floor bled Ember's scathing retort away. "We didn't plan on colonists being up that far. But if she breached the snow equator perimeter, the presidium will never let her back out into the general population. The only people who get to go up that far are conference attendees, and they are all from off-world. It's where the conference center is, where Nadia is." Asher raised her head and said in a tone so gentle it could have soothed a hummingbird, "They're mella, now, just like you."

"No..." Ember paused, then mulled. Nadia wouldn't tolerate life away from the lab, and the science center was directly in the middle of the dome on Queen's temperate strip. Working outside the dome was not an option. Nadia had packed one of her four allotted suitcases with Earth glassware from undergraduate chem and all but smuggled it onto Queen. Ember could see herself lounging on a lake paradise, especially if Taraniel hadn't died, but Nadia? Her career path ended with her desiccated emeritus body found in a locked office by a persistent undergraduate.

Varun might be okay, maybe, if the mella had decent lab space and a desiccator big enough for beetle corpses.

Except the more Ember thought about a giant con-ference center stuck in the middle of a snow drift on arguably the most inhospitable place on Queen, the more concerning the idea became.

"Why is there a conference center on the cold side of the equator?"

Asher looked expectantly at the ceiling. Overhead, a small ship camera whirred.

Both sides of the equator are colonized, Ember. Mella on the sand side, and New Earth runs the cold side, via the figureheads of the presidium. The mella have a governmental agreement. The AI's voice turned back to business. **They started as a group of workers that helped set up the snow-side equatorial region when the initial survey workers found near pure silicon dioxide in the temperate strip. Which is when New Earth really took notice. It's as pure as the stuff Earth used to have. It requires so little re-fining and processing it is worth its weight in gold. Computer chips can be made from lower-grade sand, certainly, but it's much more time consuming and expensive, and there is a cost to the speed of the ships when they use lower-grade computer chips. Queen is remote enough to make the sand poten-tially not worth the effort, but it looks like New Earth wants to change that. Hence the conference.**

"But originally? Queen hadn't been platted as a high-commerce, high-value planet," Asher said, her voice almost a growl. "We were a gimmie for radicals, lesbians, and trou-blemakers. The colonists couldn't be caught prospering."

Queen turned into a high-level con job, courtesy of New Earth, which is another conversation we need to have. Later. For their silence, the workers got offered the sun-side equator, which had less sand, but since they don't officially exist, they can't get supplies. It was not an oversight. They could take the sun side, or they could be put on a ship to a new planet and start the terraforming process all over again. New Earth wanted them out of the way and out of communication.

Asher ran a hand through her hair. "Here, the presidium—and via them, New Earth—leave us alone and don't prosecute our little runs into the colony as long as we stay mum. Break the rules, you disappear, although escape has happened. We have four that managed to get out of the snow side and on one of our recon beetles and make it back. Every so often, we send someone up to check out the other side, or do some burying in the badlands in between."

Ember sank into her chair and bit the inside of her lip. "And Nadia is mixed up with it, the mella and the presidium?"

Asher shook her head. "Not us. We don't go to the snow side, remember. That's all the presidium and New Earth."

Ember decided she was officially screwed.

"We need to get them. Now."

"I'd be happy to take a trial run in this ship," Asher said. A smile blossomed on her face; Ember bristled. "And we owe Nadia a rescue. She shouldn't take the fall for our theft." Asher tapped the control panel, her fingertip hitting the side of Ember's hand.

She pushed Asher's hand away. Friendly was one thing; flirting was...just too soon when your wife's AI clone was literally hovering. "Too close. Personal space."

"I'll remember that next time you're spooning me to a tree. Are you volunteering to operate the ship?"

Ember's face flushed. "Listen—"

The ship cleared its "throat." **I can fly the ship. It's one of my features. Taraniel had basic starship training, and she downloaded manuals into me. Staying planetside is no biggie. Easy as pie. Smooth as buttercream.**

"And I have a crew." Asher leaned against a bulkhead and put her hands in her pockets, every centimeter of her dripping smugness and hotness, and it was a very bad combination. "You've already met a few of them." She raised her right eyebrow. "I can see it's getting harder for you to talk. How about we bring them aboard, and then, if you are in agreement, we can go for a little ride?"

Nok and two other women climbed into the ship, turning the primary space—the cockpit, Ember supposed—into something closer to a mosh pit. Each took a seat and swiveled to face Asher. They all wore pants (blue, red, and a version of lilac Ember thought might be stonewashed plum) and long-sleeved, black shirts with fluffy vests on over. The vests had rows of tiny, marginally uneven stitching, and the fur around the vest necks smelled very much like rabbit. Or something smelled like rabbit. Their boots were brown leather, new, and very expensive. Nok gave Ember a polite nod. Kate scowled, which seemed to be a perpetual thing for her. The third, Pui, Ember guessed, ignored her completely.

"You brought your packs?" Asher asked. She'd tied her hair back into a short ponytail and sat in her chair with her legs splayed. All business.

Ember swore she heard the AI snicker.

"And I packed several reference books," Nok added, sounding smug. "And I taught Kate"—she pointed to her left—"how to take proper notes, so if we get a chance to observe migration patterns, I want to take it."

"Unlikely to happen," Asher said, and Nok's hopeful expression turned crestfallen. "Nadia O'Grady is in detention at the snow-side facility. The AI estimates twelve hours to get there from here. Pui knows the facility and the layout. We'll be relying on her to guide us in."

Pui, wearing blue pants so tight they looked painted on, stood. She still didn't bother to look at Ember. "There will be some leeway in appearance due to the conference. The ship, here, will help, and Nok changed enough of the exterior that we'll pass a walk-by inspection. Kate." Pui pointed at Kate, who had on the not-quite-plum purple pants that clashed with basic human decency and looked two sizes too big in the waist. Her hair looked closer to red here in the ship. Or the mella had hair dye, and Nadia would be *pissed*. Ember squinted and leaned toward the woman covertly, or as covertly as one could in such a tiny space. Close enough to see the explosion of freckles across her cheeks. Not hair dye. Ember couldn't see a single discolored root.

Kate turned to Ember and glared. "Definite no, colony hack." She turned back to Asher. "I still know a few of the guards there and already pinged an inquiry. Kate and I loaded the bribe into the hold."

"I'm here for the unexpected and the science." Nok grinned. "I'm thrilled you've helped us with this opportunity. I've wanted an excuse to leave the camp and get back to fieldwork for ages."

"I didn't realize we were so inhospitable," Asher deadpanned.

"Unexpected what?" Ember cut in.

Nok's grin widened, and Ember felt decidedly uncomfortable. "Wildlife. It's not just beetles out there, though they're the biggest concern."

As far as Ember knew, the only vertebrates on Queen other than the native beetles, and humans, were the Earth rabbits. If they were a concern... Ember tried *really* hard not to laugh.

I've got Taraniel's access codes, the AI added in Taraniel's "I'm in charge of this lab meeting" voice, with a touch of "I see exactly what you're doing, Ember; please stop." **They won't help us in the breakout, but if we need to stop by the colony, we could get supplies. I can also get us clearance if Nadia wants to be returned to the colony.**

"But not me?" Ember sat up in her chair, bunnies forgotten, spaceship *almost* forgotten. Her throat still burned. "When did I become conscripted?"

The women looked at Asher. Asher stood, probably expecting Ember to start throwing punches again. Joke was on her. If they rescued Nadia and Ember had to stay at the mella camp, they'd all be listening to bad puns for eternity.

"Taraniel." Asher kept her face neutral while shifting her weight from one foot to the other.

There needed to be a moratorium on her wife's name. A two-year embargo, like on a PhD thesis almost ready to publish, but, really, some time was needed to forget the trauma of defense. Or everyone could just stop talking about Taraniel as if they knew her.

"Get out," Ember said to Asher, to the other women, to everyone. "Just get out for a goddamned minute."

Asher blanched. "I thought you wanted to—"

"*Out*," Ember demanded.

Could you give us a minute? Please?

"Will she be alive when I come back?" Asher asked the bulkhead.

The AI deadpanned, **If I were going to release toxic gas or electrocute any of you, it'd have been before you got blood on my floor.**

"Point." Asher shoved off the bulkhead, ushered the women to standing, and all but pushed them out the door. "No more than five minutes. We have a rapidly narrowing window."

I know. Five minutes.

The hatch shut, and the lock depressed. Ember didn't like locks. She'd never let Taraniel lock their door at night. The colony had no crime to speak of, and Ember needed to know she could get out. Locks kept people in. Trapped them. Suffocated them in blood and their own recycled excrement when AIs fucked up.

She swallowed hard. Not just because of bile. The idea of talking with her dead wife's ship was one thing; being locked inside it after it called you "honey" was entirely different. Still, she sat up straight. Face your fear and ghosts and dead lovers and all that jazz.

"I am going to rescue my sister, but everything about you upsets me," Ember said to the ceiling. "My wife is *dead*."

The AI's sigh came back deflated, and Ember swore she heard a note of hurt underneath. Once again, she felt like shit. "I disagree with your creation and all the bullshit tones you keep using to make me feel bad for you."

I didn't get much of a choice for existence. I'm...I'm not trying to take her place, Ember. That's not my purpose.

"Yet here we are."

The AI sighed, again. **Taraniel thought I could help, and I can. I'm a ship, but I'm her memories too. You have to grieve, but you don't have to forget. I can tell you the shape of the rock you two got married on. I can tell you how the recorded waterfall music sounded, how much Taraniel cried as you said your vows. I know—**

Nope. She wasn't doing this. She'd find another way to get to Nadia. Ember stormed to the door and banged so hard the vibrations radiated to her shoulders.

It didn't open. Ember breathed deeper, sucking in stale air that had been fine moments ago, but now there wasn't enough, and it was too hot, and she needed *out*.

Taraniel's voice came at her again, the hurt bleeding all over the words and slicing into calluses Ember had only begun to form. **I need you to trust me with our dream.**

The door refused to open no matter how many times Ember hit it. She felt lightheaded. A bruise started forming on her palm, and she mentally raked her fingers over the ceiling.

"It was *Taraniel's* dream and mine. Not yours. Taraniel is dead. *Dead.* Dead as most of my shipmates on the craft that brought me here, as dead as my sister is going to be. My sister is on Queen, so I am too. And I don't need to trust you. You are *not my damn wife.*"

The ship became maddeningly silent.

"Hey!" Ember smacked the hatch door.

No response.

"*Hey!*" Ember kicked the door, then turned and punched the nearest chair on the hard backing. Blood beaded on two scraped knuckles. Her vision spotted black. "I'm talking to you."

A confusing mix of fatigue and irritation dripped from the AI's voice. **I'm a free AI, Ember. I don't have to respond when users are callous assholes.**

If Ember could have stuck her head between a beetle's mandibles and let them chop her head off, she'd have done it. She didn't give a damn about TOPA, especially the weekly wiped, personality-free module. This AI didn't need to be any different, but she couldn't *not* respond to Taraniel's voice, and her wife had damn well known that. Knowing, deep down, this was Taraniel's manipulation and not the AI's made it really fucked up.

"I want to know why she made you."

I...I have ethics, and morality, and all the standard programming, but there's an override in all of it. I can use any motivation and means to get you into space and on the way to Earth. That was Taraniel's only goal—that you be free of Queen and back on the planet you both loved.

"So, if I told you to suck a bag of ship dicks you'd take off right now and jettison us into the atmosphere?"

That is one option, yes.

Ember whacked her head against the wall. They'd go around in circles for hours, just as she and real-Taraniel used to, if she didn't redirect. "I'd rather go get Nadia."

I'm fine with that for now.

"Well, fine." Ember stood, brushed off her pants, and sat back, gingerly, in one of the chairs. "But I'm not calling you Taraniel."

You could allow me to name myself.

Ember shrugged. "Sure. Whatever you want is fine. Let the others back in. We're done here." *Unlock the door*, she screamed into her head.

Thankfully, no retort came. The AI opened the hatch. Nok ran in, knapsacks over both shoulders, brows furrowed in a look familiar to any academic. She stowed her bags in a compartment in the wall, took her seat, and had her restraint fastened before Ember managed to find the other end of her lap buckle.

Kate came in next, rubbing her fingertips firmly across the sides of her pants and muttering to herself. Her fingers left deep gray stains in their wake that looked and smelled like oil. She sank into a chair, grumbled an unintelligible sentence, and snapped her harness into place, the buckle sliding through her fingers several times before she gained enough purchase to push it into its clasp.

Pui seemed in a much better mood, though she, too, carried a heavy assortment of mechanisms and paper charts that had on them a few constellations Ember recognized.

Asher came in last, eyed one of the remaining seats, then sidestepped over to Ember and, a little too casually, set four fingers on Ember's left shoulder. "Okay?" she asked in a near whisper. "We grabbed a few extra things while you were chatting."

Ember scowled at her over her shoulder. "What do you think?"

Asher winked at her and took her seat. Ember flushed in rage and embarrassment, a sizable portion of which stemmed from feeling like she was cheating on her wife, even though her wife had turned into an omnipotent spaceship.

"Take us up, AI," Asher said right after her final buckle snapped into place.

After a subtle jostle, Ember's ears popped, and she plugged her nose and blew to clear them. "It doesn't want to be called that," she said for a reason that definitely did not involve sympathy or empathy.

"Oh?" Asher kicked the back of Ember's chair.

I'm still deciding. "She" or "AI" will work for now. The interior ship lights flashed twice. **We've begun our trip. We are staying in the equatorial belt and will be out of mella territory in two hours. I will ping at the border.**

"Thanks." Asher pulled a cushion from a side pocket in her chair's headrest and curled it into her neck, using it as a prop against the side of her chair. "Get some sleep. We have a big day tomorrow."

The other women leaned back in their chairs or propped their heads on sweatshirts and small pillows.

Ember mouthed *bag of dicks* at the ceiling.

From the small audio port in the right side of her headrest came the tinny, distorted voice of Taraniel. **Your wife found your juvenile mouth sexy. She really liked your mouth for a variety of reasons. How about I list them?**

Ember pursed her lips and glared at the viewscreen, which showed only racing strips of green. "Champ? Buddy? Spot? Fido? Sox—"

The AI volume increased, loud enough that Kate, in the seat next, slit an eye open. **There's this thing you do with your tongue when you curled it right under her—**

Ember raked her hands over the small speaker, then cupped it with both palms finally. "Tara," she hissed. "Part of her, but not the whole thing. Okay?"

Maybe, the AI said, turning the volume back down. **I'll think about it.**

"I hate this planet," Ember said as she closed her eyes and tried to sleep.

Chapter Nine

New Earth never existed. Old Earth barely existed. For those who remained, New Earth rose from the ashes of the old, determined not only to rehabilitate but to control nature in every form.

Ember

"This is it."

Ember blinked back the remnant of a half-formed dream—a vestigial trapped feeling refusing to fade into her subconscious. If her heart ever slowed down, it'd be a miracle. She leaned forward against her harness and craned her neck to watch a flat, gray, one-story building glide across the viewer in a halo of artificial light, then disappear into snow and darkness.

Snow side. Right. No sun. The recycled air in the flyer had dried her eyes, and Ember tried to blink moisture back into existence. By their third fly-by, she gathered enough tears to make out the location coordinates and environmental data on the viewscreen. They'd passed out of the equatorial belt at around 9:00 p.m. and were five hours past the colony edge. Wind read at twenty-eight knots, and Ember could feel the push against the ship each time a gust struck.

The temperature reading on the viewscreen, however, was only negative ten. Ember squinted and double-checked. This far out, she expected well below negative fifty. They were still about an hour from the other side of the equator and...well, mild snow drifts barely covering grass tufts didn't look right. The physics of it all didn't check out, although she'd never been great at physics. Tidally locked planets didn't *do* this. They had sun on one side, no sun on the other, and a thin strip of decent land in between. Either they'd all been lied to about the planet, or they'd been lied to about physics. Ember hated both and seriously doubted the latter.

We've received clearance to land from Kate's contact. They've had us flying in circles until our

credentials cleared. We'll have to pass the inspection on our own though. Try to look important.

"Is everything on this planet a lie?" Ember asked, her thoughts slipping out. She felt vaguely lightheaded, which could have come from just waking up, pending motion sickness, or residual "you're probably going to die this time around; don't tempt fate twice-ness."

"Pretty much." Asher patted the bulkhead. "Go ahead and land us."

They set down on a landing pad lightly covered in drifting snow. The scenery outside dimmed as the ship powered down but did not turn completely dark. It took Ember a minute to realize their little pod had exterior track lighting on top of its floodlight. Pretty useless for space, but effective for attracting attention. The light had a slight blue tinge to it as well, making the snow look that much colder. She shivered, then turned her head to the side and puked.

Asher unbuckled the moment the landing struts hit and was in Ember's face a moment later. No one mentioned the vomit. "You don't talk," she said, her voice gentle but dripping authority that made Ember want to stick out her tongue like a ten-year-old. "The poor fit on the clothes helps, but you sound like a colonist. We all need to be mella. Colonists don't work with the research teams."

Her breath smelled like peanuts. There was no way Ember could take someone seriously who smelled like peanuts. "You're *all* colonists. Mella don't just spring fully formed from the sand."

Asher slapped her knee as she righted. "We were here way before you, Doctor. Remember that. Terraforming didn't spring fully formed from the sand. This is our world, and our treaty, and our interaction."

Ember unbuckled her harness, and when Asher put a hand on her shoulder, shrugged it off. Asher said, "You can debate with me later. If they want someone to come out of the flyer, you stay here where the AI can keep an eye on you." She looked up. "You got that?"

Aye-aye, Captain. Ember and I have a lot of catching up to do anyway.

Ember did not like how that sounded.

The inspector has arrived at the ship.

Asher looked at Ember with an I'm-not-kidding set to her mouth.

Ember smiled sweetly and loaded as much sarcasm into her words as she could. "Aye-aye, Captain."

"Great. Wonderful. Kate?" Asher said. "And AI, ship, whatever we're calling you, open the door, please."

Kate, a matching smear of oil now across her chin and still looking decidedly unhappy, stood as the hatch opened. A man with dull beige skin and slicked brown hair climbed inside. His nose wrinkled, no doubt from the lingering vomit smell the pod's charcoal scrubbers hadn't managed to remove. None of his clothes had the faintest hint of wrinkles. His coat had sharp edges and clean lines. His pants snapped as he took the final step and gave the impression of his whole body having just come out of an industrial press.

Ember was considerably unimpressed.

"I'm Edmond Ray, chief of staff for the external barracks. Mark's out sick, and the presidium sent me to fill in. Corrina says you have information? What are you after, and why aren't you talking directly to the presidium?"

Ember had been prepared for bored or maybe a little nervous. This guy spoke like he was the head of a criminal investigation and they were already convicted. That feeling of being in a game but only having read half the rulebook came back, and Ember sank into the cushionless chair, turning so she could be as close to the built-in speaker as possible.

You never did well with aggressive authority figures, the AI whispered through the chair. **You'll be all right. I promise.**

"I don't need soothing." Ember tried to keep her lips motionless and her voice as low as possible. "I need backstory."

Kate looked at Asher with clear panic. Asher stepped forward and hauled Kate back in one movement. "They're too busy to see us, and we have this." She handed Edmond a tablet. "We thought we shouldn't wait since it involves New Earth."

He scrolled, his eyes moving from disinterested to concerned. Slowly, painfully, his face turned the color of a cherry plum, which made Ember want to reach out and squash his head between her thumb and forefinger.

I wish you'd read the ship manifest first, the AI said.

"Please stop talking," Ember hissed. "I can't argue with you and follow their conversation too." Queen politics, Ember could take or leave, but information about New Earth? Anyone on Queen would have been interested in that. Hell, anyone in the terraformed galaxy would have been interested.

"What's this about then?" Edmond tapped the screen of the tablet and glared. "This isn't real. What do you think we'll give you for this? The tablet is worth more than the trash on it. Stop fucking wasting my time!"

"We took it from a colonist," Asher countered coolly. "It's not mella, and the presidium needs to know. Mark knew how to deal with this sort of thing, and we're not expecting anything monetary. We came here because Mark barters." She shoved her hands in her pockets, but her hands balled under the fabric. Another sound reason for Ember not to get involved with Asher—two people who emoted almost entirely in rage never worked out, friends or otherwise.

"Is Mark easier to work with?" Ember asked the chair.

Mark is easier to bribe, the AI responded. **Mark works directly for New Earth too. Edmond, we don't**

know a thing about, except that he's a colonist, apparently, if the presidium sent him. And if he is just a colonist, the info on the tablet won't mean a thing.

Edmond pinched the tablet screen hard enough to crack. "I'm not giving you anything for this."

"Come on now. We heard you had a conference going. We just wanted to listen in." Asher pointed at the tablet. "Mark is an information guy. The presidium thrives on information and gets off on colonists being kept like caged rabbits." Her voice lilted up. "These are the coordinates for New Earth, Edmond. *New Earth*. If one colonist has them, how long before they all do? You all need to nip this in the bud."

Ember wrinkled her nose and again leaned into the chair speaker. "Really? New Earth? You're going to bribe him with *that*?" She clenched her jaw and swallowed. Location of all terraformed worlds was tightly controlled. You only got coordinates once you cleared Queen's atmosphere, and you only cleared the atmosphere with a visa and a lot of money, which was why packages always got the planet name only. Visas didn't even get issued for New Earth. You either got in when the original lottery went up on Old Earth, or you didn't. But there was no option to immigrate. Hell, there was no option to tourist. You couldn't even *call* New Earth or send letters if you had relatives there. What had been the immigration requirements for New Earth anyway? Ember couldn't remember. Whatever they were, she hadn't even qualified to receive an application.

Those are your coordinates she's showing him, the ones that you stamp on your modified plant shipments. The ones that come in on the lilac products.

"You said those were Old Earth!" Ember turned the rest of her body too quickly toward the speaker and knocked her right knee against the armrest. "Ow. Fuck."

Nok shot her a warning look with one raised eyebrow and slowly shook her head. Academic disdain cut like a hot knife through butter. Kate flicked the back of her chair, which felt childish. Neither Asher nor Edmond seemed to notice.

According to Taraniel, *you* said they were Old Earth. Do you want me to replay her memory of the conversation?"

"Hearing my wife's memory in my wife's voice is not going to endear you to me."

Edmond tapped the tablet against his thigh and stuck his tongue into the corner of his cheek. "You're overplaying useless information." He shook his head. "And I want to know why. The little colony ducks wouldn't know what this was even if they did get it." He tossed the pad to the floor and clasped his hands behind his back like a little kid playing soldier. "We've already had one mella problem today, and I don't need another. I don't give a beetle's ass what's on that tablet. Come with me, all of you."

Asher stepped forward again, Pui just behind. Nok and Kate unfastened their harnesses but stayed sitting. Ember watched.

"We can come," Asher said. She picked up the tablet and brushed off the screen. "Inside, Corrina can vouch for the information, and Pui—" Asher pointed to her left, and Pui ran a hand through her short black hair and smiled. "—is a celestial cartographer. She can show you how to read the coordinates."

"I don't care about your damn tablet! All of you. Up." He tapped his left thigh.

A chair blocked Ember's view, so she had to lean back to see the handle of a holstered gun. She pursed her lips. Of course, he had a gun. Not a stun gun, or an avalanche mortar, or something marginally useful for life on the colony, but an actual Old Earth gun with the only use of snuffing out life. More concerning, when he tapped the holster, it pulled against the fabric of his starched pants, giving away a telltale bulge between his legs.

The slow buildup of pressure Ember had nursed since arriving in the mella camp exploded across her chest. She coughed, trying to mask her surprise and incredulity.

Try to breathe, Ember, the AI soothed. It clearly wasn't shocked by a penis on Queen.

"Our friend here has the flu." Asher put a condescending hand on Ember's head as Ember mentally sifted through every ridiculous possibility that could lead to an anatomical male on Queen. Not a qualified-on-a-technicality version like her. Nadia would be thrilled. "She should stay behind."

"The only way she stays behind is if she is dead," Edmond said. "Do you want to be the second group I sign a permanent detention order for today? You're coming to our head office now for questioning."

Detention? Nadia? Varun?

"Shit."

The word slipped out of Ember's mouth before she realized it was there. They didn't have time for chatting and posturing. Nadia could be bleeding out somewhere right now, while they argued over a tablet with Steve or whatever his name was. And, Jesus, how did this group expect to get off-planet with negotiation skills like *this*?

Asher held up her hands, and Ember caught the tightness in the mella's mouth. As she took a step back, her heel caught on the metal plate that bolted the chair to the floor. Asher's chest shuddered, and she tried to pass it off as a cough.

"Asher?" Ember asked, keeping her voice low.

"It's all right," Asher responded tightly. "Everything is fine. The head office is just outside."

"You'll go as far as I tell you to go. Now get up!" Edmond turned his eyes to Ember, and he looked predatory and ridiculous.

Asher's face turned pale and drawn. Pui, who Ember could see from the corner of her eye, dug her fingernails into her pants legs.

Men. Males. Posturing. Wasting precious time.

This, *this*, Ember knew, and she was damn sick of it. Nadia and Varun might be dying. The only penis-bearing men Ember wanted to see were those consensually courting her sister or Varun if he was ever allowed the surgery he wasn't sure he wanted. But both of them needed to be alive for either of those things to happen.

Ember unclipped her harness, then stood, brushing off Asher's cautioning hand. She rested a hand on the top of the chair and took a wide stance, hips jutting every so subtly forward. She pitched her voice down. Not too deep, it was already in the lower range for a woman, but enough that her throat rumbled when she spoke. It was a cool trick, the voice. Use it in a faculty meeting, and men took her more seriously. Use it on a voice call, and people didn't argue as much. Use it too much, and she ended up in her department head's office, being told the faculty found her "too intimidating" and "too aggressive." Of course, "for a woman" was always implied.

Ember knew all this, had fought it all her life. Here was a battle she came well prepared for.

Step one: challenge.

"You're too stupid to see what those coordinates are for. I haven't got time for this, or you. Move."

Edmond pulled the gun and leveled it at Ember's head. "You want to repeat that, bitch?"

Step two: authority.

"Try again." Ember held up a thumb, the skin scarred from hundreds of blood tests and screenings, hundreds of concerned medical practitioners trying to decide whether Queen would take her. If she was woman *enough*, or if they could overlook her hormones and bit of her anatomy, or if she'd be left to drown on Earth.

"Do you know how long I've been working here?" she continued. "Do you think I give a damn about some mid-management asshole? I've got a job, Steven, and you're fucking it up."

The tip of the gun dipped, but Edmond's face continued to redden.

"Do the damn test," Ember said.

Step three: freak them the hell out.

"I don't have the machine on me," he said, the bravado falling from his voice. He shut his mouth, but his lips continued to mime an internal monologue. What a dick.

"Hey, ship?" Ember yelled, her eyes never leaving Edmond's. "We have one?"

In the medical kit, just under the printer. The AI's voice came in flat monotone—a perfect imitation of a pristine TOPA.

Ember jerked her head left. "Pui, go get it."

"Ash?" Pui stuttered, her face complete bewilderment.

Ember kept her face still, her jaw clamped and slightly jutting, as she turned to Asher. Asher stared, weighing any number of retorts or challenges, then snapped her head to Pui and gave a low, deliberate nod.

The mella, Ember realized, had a hell of a lot more discipline than the colony scientists. It took Pui only a moment of rummaging, several metal objects hitting the floor, before a palm-sized rectangular tablet pushed into Ember's hand. In plastic wrap on the back were three cotton swabs on sticks. Ember pulled one from the packet, swabbed the inside of her cheek, and stuck the wet tip into the data port.

The machine beeped. Ember didn't bother with the readout, simply handed it to Edmond, whom she would never call by his real name because flustering him was far too easy. "Read it."

He moved the gun to one hand and took the tablet. There were only three lines of data on the screen. One had her gender marker as registered with the colony. One had her testosterone level; the third, her chromosomes.

The gun lowered.

Edmond looked at Ember, and she looked back. His eyebrows rose and he package-checked her, visually. Then his mouth dropped open in that confused incredulity that made people so incredibly stupid. She had the narrowest of windows to act, now, before Edmond's rational brain took over, and he started to question. Ember swiped the original tablet from Asher's hands and scanned the contents, hoping for an artifact that could either drive the deal home or get Edmond off the ship, keeping quiet as he did so.

The first thing displayed across the screen were the co-ordinates, with her signature, scrawled just above in a fingertip chicken scratch from a trackpad. Next, she read a list of import contents, each trailed by a permit number. At the top was the address for the presidium building, where the pallets were to be sent. The five-seat presidium (staffed by only three people because Queen sucked at more than just exports) routinely had packages and pallets shipped to their main building. Ember was responsible for plant pathogen inspection and occasionally general imports but didn't remember this particular shipment. As with all notes and manifests relating to the presidium, the actual contents had been locked. She scoured a list of fifteen separate pallets, each containing toiletries and foodstuffs Ember hadn't seen on Queen in a decade, if ever. She could almost hear Taraniel's voice whispering into her ear outside the dome:

"What about fungal detoxification? I read you can put some white rotting fungi in boxes in waterways, and they'll filter as well as help break down problematic elements. Fungi grow so quickly. How many boxes would it take, do you think, to clean Lake Superior? How many people could the largest freshwater lake in the world support? God, Ember. Did you ever swim in Lake Superior before the Collapse? The color. The cold. The endless blue."

She skimmed lower. There, at the very end of the note, after the list ended, were four handwritten sentences.

The coordinates check out, Ember. I ran them again, with the mella's tech. All of this came from Old Earth.

You were right.

Ember pretended to dust the cover of the tablet. In doing so she ran the pad of her thumb over the world "Old," pressing hard enough that the tiny processor highlighted it, then deleted it. It would have been nice to have time to process the whirlwind inside her chest right now, or how it felt like Taraniel was standing right behind her, peering over her shoulder, whispering in her ear, "*You were right.*"

"Did you read all of this?" she asked Edmond, shoving her emotions down far enough it'd take a geologist to find them. "Did you look at what is being shipped?"

"Yeah. Of course." He cleared his throat. "Of course, I did. I know my job."

"Then you have the reading comprehension skills of a toddler. Blueberries. Starfruit. Jackfruit. Roses. You know where they grow roses, Steven? Name me one terraformed planet that grows roses that *isn't* New Earth."

He didn't answer, but Ember saw his fingers twitch. She didn't know if roses grew anywhere on the colony planets, but then again, apparently neither did he.

"Forget the mella." Ember jerked her thumb over her shoulder, pointing at Asher. "They're not going anywhere. Colonists though, some have family on New Earth." In fact, Ember didn't know a single colonist with family on New Earth. That had been another conversation point between her and Taraniel. "You want them breaking out and knocking on New Earth's door to finally contact their long-lost relatives? Whose fault will that be, Steven, if they do? Not Mark's. He'd have traded the mella here for the manifest and not made me blow my damn cover, which the presidium spent *years* building so they could have a decent mella mole." And then, because she could, and because Edmond looked like he might wet himself, she grabbed her left breast and added, "And stop staring. They're not real."

The gun went back in the holster.

Men. Idiots. Of course her breasts were real. What had Nadia told her once? Little jiggle for a drink, double jiggle for a ring? Ugh. It was so much nicer when both parties in the relationship had breasts. At least then you had someone to complain to about not being able to comfortably sleep on your stomach.

Edmond sniffed, and his shoulders hunched. "Shit. Uh, what do you want to do?"

Ember folded her arms. "You could get lost and let me deal with these idiots. I'll take the manifest since I can't go back to the mella camp now anyway. Triage your damage. Go back to your desk and shut your mouth."

"You sure about them?" he asked, lip raised in question. "You got all of them?"

"Get lost, Steven. You're a pain in my ass and a double pain in my fake tits."

Edmond left with a curt nod, eyes skating one final time over her body. She knew his thoughts. She'd had them plenty of times, about herself, about other people. A head-ache built at the base of her skull, compounding the never-ending nausea. She was right. She'd been right about Old Earth, and now she had to go back, *had* to, and had to take all these clowns with her.

Ember counted to ten before slipping back down into her chair and swallowing a lump in her throat the size of a golf ball. So much for compressed emotions. "We all right, then?" she asked no one in particular. "It's time to rescue Nadia. We can talk about Earth later."

Pui shifted uncomfortably against the wall. Nok coughed. Kate was wide-eyed and incredulous. Asher came around to the front of Ember's chair, all trace of friendliness shot from her posture.

No one said anything.

Ember rolled her eyes and sat forward. She hated this conversation. She hated it the most with people who should have known her better. She'd happily debate gender until the cows came home, but biological sex was deeply personal, and there was nothing quite as demeaning as trying to explain how hormones worked (or didn't) to people who still thought the human race only came in XX—vulva and uterus—and XY—testes and penis.

"When we met, I thought you knew," she said. "You asked about pronouns."

Taraniel discussed it with Asher privately, the ship said in a disgruntled voice. Ember heard notes of protectiveness underneath, and for a moment, she didn't entirely hate the AI.

But this was all wasting time that Nadia didn't have, and mostly, Ember just wanted to scream at everyone to move on.

Get it together, Asher.

"I know." Asher held up one hand and closed her eyes for a long moment. "I've just never seen someone...disappear before. Like an actor, she was just, gone. How—"

This isn't the most sensitive setting to have this conversation. If Ember doesn't want to elaborate, I can answer general questions after we rescue Nadia.

Fine, another point to the AI. Relief washed over Ember—relief and gratitude. This wasn't a therapy session, and she had no interest in explaining the interaction of US socialization mechanics and archaic medical practices.

Thanks, Ember mouthed at the floor. To Asher she said irritably, "It's time to go."

Asher took another long, considering look at Ember. Her eyes flitted for one fraction of a moment to Ember's breasts.

Ember took a long, aggressive sigh and put a hand over the top of her left breast. "It's not a conversation for right now."

Asher nodded. One of her top teeth bit into her lower lip—a look Ember generally found endearing but, right now, set her on edge. After another moment, Asher squared her shoulders and raised her head. "I'm sorry," she said. "That was incredibly rude."

"Yes, it was."

Asher nodded again, grinding her lip. "I'll do better."

Ember shrugged. "Time to move on."

"From you, yes. From this? No." Asher walked to the hatch release panel and triggered the closing mechanism. "We passed inspection. You fooled one inspector, but you can't fool them all. Originally, I'd hoped to go in and meet our plant, Corrina, but I don't want Edmond-whatever asking more questions or double-guessing himself. Now we wait. Corrina has agreed to let Nadia and Varun out and show them the exit door. All we need to do is get them onto the ship before someone realizes what is going on."

"No."

Ember pushed past Asher, opened the door, and was down the ramp before the mella or the AI could react.

"Ember, you can't just walk into the—"

Ember didn't bother looking back. The wind hit her face, cold but not biting, and the snow slushed under her boots. She did not, at that moment, give two fucks about the mella or her wife-spaceship.

"You can stay here if you want. I'm going to get my sister."

Chapter Ten

Fresh water was no longer limited. Agriculture was established across dozens of planets and fed trillions. Rare Earth metals were found in abundance on colony worlds.

It was sand—pure enough for the chips used to power starship computers and a hundred other critical electronic components—that held humanity back. Most sand could be purified over time for such purposes, but Earth did not have time. Engineers and programmers stripped Earth first, scoured hundreds of new planets, and found a goldmine of usable, near-pure silicon dioxide on Queen—a throwaway planet with a throwaway population, suddenly burdened with an empire's precious resource.

Nadia

Nadia puked. It came up mostly protein bar and the stale water from Varun's flyer. She flipped onto her back, smacking Varun's stomach in the process. "Sorry." She wiped her mouth on the sleeve of her shirt and sat up, reminding herself that she could actually control her stomach, unlike Ember.

"I don't like gray walls." Varun stayed on his back, but at least his eyes were open. "They don't feel sterile. A laminar flow bench is sterile gray. Gray walls are concrete gray. You can't sterilize concrete."

"I don't think they're too worried about sterilization." Nadia surveyed the cell. If she and Varun stood side to side with their arms out, they could easily touch the walls, all uniform gray and bubble-textured. There was a drain in the back right corner and a spigot in the upper left that Nadia hoped was a showerhead. No bed, no light, except for what streamed from under the door, although the walls had a green glow, illuminating the cell enough to make out the outline of Varun's mustache.

"This wasn't how I thought this day would end. Any idea what time it is?"

Varun pulled himself to sitting and held up his forearm, an antique watch strapped across it. With a tap of an unseen switch, it glowed synthetic blue. "It's tomorrow. Early morning. I have samples that need to come out of the dryer today."

"You tried the door yet?"

The light on Varun's watch turned off. "No."

Of course not. Nadia stepped over his legs and tapped experimentally. No one screamed at her to quiet down, so she knocked again, louder. The third time, she banged with her fist. "Hey! Colonists have rights!" she yelled.

"I have samples!" Varun yelled in tandem.

The door pulled open on soundless hinges, and a short, lean woman with curly hair, wearing a jumpsuit with the blue-and-green New Earth logo, shot Nadia in the thigh with a Glock 22 police special.

Nadia held on to that detail, let it swirl in her head as she crumpled to the floor. Varun yelled, and the door slammed closed, but Nadia didn't feel any pain, not really. She felt cold, and wet, and the back part of her brain yelled about arteries and *how much it hurt*. But the rest of her wrestled over the Glock, and how her father had had the same gun in his job for the highway department, and she'd touched it once as a child, and he'd turned red, taken it, and it'd never shown up in the house again.

"Shouldn't have touched the Glock." Nadia giggled as Varun took off his pants and wrapped the legs around her thigh.

"Don't knock on the door again. And stop moving, or you'll bleed out."

"They just *shot* me."

Varun pushed her onto her back. She found his grim smile fascinating.

"Does anything in your pocket protector turn into secret agent lock-picking thingies?"

He finished the knot, gave the pant legs an extra tug that made Nadia gasp, then sat back on his haunches. "Please don't die."

"I already have tenure. Dying would be redundant."

Varun frowned, and Nadia tried to remember if tenure jokes were funny before you actually *got* tenure. "If you die your sibling will go the wrong way off that precipice she's on. Consider that as the beyond beckons."

Nadia squinted at Varun and the green haze of wall behind him. His words sounded silly and obtuse, which they always did, as if she was missing something important in them too. "Ember is kind of useless," Nadia agreed. "She didn't used to be. The Taraniel thing screwed us all up." She bit her lower lip. "My leg hurts."

"If it stops hurting, please tell me."

"Will you saw it off then?"

Varun fell back onto his butt, his bare skin making a slapping sound on the floor. Likely from her blood. Nadia blinked and thought about the sound. Definitely a lot of blood. Ember was going to be pissed.

"Sorry," Nadia said. "It'd be a lot different than ripping a leg off a beetle."

"And completely inappropriate."

The door pulled open again. This time, Nadia shut her mouth, and Varun pulled her back toward the drain with his sweaty hands under her armpits. The pants-tourniquet snagged on the textured flooring and pulled her leg with it.

"Oh, *god*," Nadia yelled as the back part of her brain joined the front, and her body decided it really did care about a bullet hole. "At least aim for my head this time!"

A different woman stood in the doorway, too backlit to make out many features other than the short haircut and narrow shoulders. She had the same jumpsuit, but it bore the presidium's logo. She had a gun as well, not a Glock this time, but one Nadia didn't recognize. She gestured with it to the right, down the hall.

Standing wasn't going to happen. Passing out was still on the table. Maybe one of the illegal men would pop in and carry her, and she could swoon like in the romance books her grandmother had left lying around when she was a kid. Romance novels and those little cheese cracker things. That had been a good time. Weird that she remembered that so sharply but had a hard time describing what the ocean smelled like.

"I don't have time for this," the woman in the hallway said. "I've got the hall cleared for five minutes. Your choice." She turned and walked away, leaving the door open and light blaring into the now-sticky room.

"I don't know what is going on, but I think we should take this opportunity before the guard with the Glock comes back." Varun wrapped Nadia's right arm around his shoulder and pulled her up. Terrible idea. The room spun like a bad circus ride. Nadia whimpered, which was a little too damsel-in-distress, even for her.

"Going to need a palanquin," she muttered. "With stain-resistant microfiber. Did the cavalry arrive?"

"Please just try to walk, Dr. O'Grady." Varun hauled her from the room, her right leg dragging uselessly and her left doing little deranged bunny hops.

This didn't feel like a good idea, but it didn't feel like a bad idea, either; therefore, Nadia didn't expend any energy arguing. If anyone could find the way from a bad situation to an equally bad one, it was an assistant professor.

"Move faster." The woman's voice carried from up the hall, although Nadia couldn't see her. Probably the blood loss.

Varun turned left down another brightly lit hallway of gray, doors etched every few meters into the endless expanse of cinderblock. It looked a lot like an undergraduate dorm, which made Nadia think of a university for mella, which made her wonder if the mascot would be a bad hemline.

Varun yanked her closer to him when she snickered. "If you could do at least a quarter of the work, I would appreciate it," he whispered.

With the mystery woman now just in front of them, Nadia could make out her straw-colored hair, pale skin, and high cheekbones. The group limped down another string of corridors before reaching a clear-walled little room with a computer console and an empty chair. Well, three of the walls were clear. The one opposite them had another gray cinderblock job.

"Through and out," the woman said. "Quickly. Willa will be back in under a minute." The little room had two doors on either side. She opened the first. Varun pulled Nadia through, her good leg catching on one of the chair wheels and dragging them both nearly to the floor, then pushed open the second door.

Their feet sank to the ankles in snow as they exited. Nadia looked up and blinked through fat white snowflakes that melted on her eyelashes like a fairytale. She shivered, and Varun brought his bare legs together, but it didn't feel *that* cold. It sure wasn't negative forty. Nadia had to really huff to see her breath. Bits of green popped up between the mounds of marshmallow-snow. Looking straight ahead, because turning her head was a lot of work, there were no other buildings except their one-story gray monstrosity, nor any flyers, spaceships, or other people. If she squinted, there might have been beetle antennae in the distance, or she'd lost more blood than she'd thought.

The door closed behind them with the loud *click* of an electronic lock. A heartbeat later, an alarm started to blare the most annoying *weee-do-WEEEEE-DO*, complete with flashing red lights coming from...she didn't know where. Everywhere. Nowhere. Whatever.

"Nadia?" Varun pointed. "Look."

Nadia sucked it up and turned her head. A gray escape pod sat to their left, a decent distance away. Light poured from its open hatch, staining the snow yellow with blue outlines. More mella shit. She wasn't interested.

Nadia shivered in Varun's grip and tried to weigh their options. Footsteps sounded from the other side of the door. Banging. Yelling. Abstract sounds that seemed silly when she was so lightheaded she might as well have had a hot-air balloon on her shoulders.

"Still close enough to the equator to feel its effects, but far enough that if we run, we probably die. It's a good balance point. They won't expect us to run far." Varun shifted Nadia's arm. "Want to try the mella? How do you feel?"

"Like the only one who got shot in the 'foot' doing this was me," she replied sourly. "Thoughts?"

"Escape?" He pointed again to the pod. "Mella better than the death back there?"

"Fucking *open the door*," a woman's voice called from the inside. "Why are all the exits locked? This isn't protocol!"

Nadia contemplated the ship-pod-thing and the mella running out of it. The woman waved and yelled something. Nadia couldn't parse either. Fat, wet flakes of snow kept falling in her eyes. She canted her head up. Varun's hair looked all but white and the snow surrounding them faintly pink with her blood. It was important to contribute to the decorative theme of the Super-Secret Commerce Section of Doom, Nadia mused, if only a bit.

"We could run," she agreed as the mella's shape became more visible. She couldn't see her face due to the snow and the hat the woman wore, but she was definitely mella—from the gait and the clothes and the fact that Nadia really just wanted to punch her. The woman waved wildly now, which would bring every guard in the complex if she kept shouting like that. If they could get out of the compound. What an idiot. "Or you could run, and I could be a distraction."

Varun looked at her like she was a giant beetle he was about to dissect but couldn't decide which end to start on.

"Err..." She edged her torso away. "So, Dr. Sinha—"

Varun wrinkled his nose and maybe, almost, laughed. "You don't take jokes well, Dr. O'Grady."

Nadia blew out a breath and sagged back into him. "Asshole."

Shouting came from behind them. Outside shouting. Guard shouting. Angry shouting. They'd probably found another exit. She and Varun should run. Part of her brain said to run. Part of it said to lie down in the snow and go to sleep. A very large part thought about cheese crackers.

The mella woman ran faster.

They should probably run, too, Nadia remembered, but Varun looked exhausted, and Nadia couldn't go anywhere without assistance. The mella it was then. Nadia pointed at the approaching woman.

"You could call me a 'son of a gun,'" Varun retorted dryly as he resumed hauling her forward.

"Fat chance. I'm the only one licensed to make puns on Queen."

"I'm probably just shooting blanks anyway."

Nadia groaned as she accidentally put weight on her bad leg. "I'm bleeding. Have a little sympathy before we get mella kidnapped. This clown is probably—"

The mella stopped an arm's length from Nadia and put her hands on her hips in the cockiest damn pose Nadia had ever seen. Well, outside of her sister, who had once explained lesbian courting dynamics and the importance of maintained eye contact, which Nadia thought would be low-level sexual harassment if a guy had been involved.

"What the hell happened to you!?"

Nadia snapped to attention so fast it felt like she'd pulled a tendon. The mella woman took off her hat, and there was Ember—her damn sister, Dr. Ember I'll-never-leave-the-sand-dunes-again Schmitt, trying to find her balance in the puffy snow. She teetered until she found footing, then finished kicking her way over, sending plumes of snow into Nadia's face as she did so.

"Dr. Schmitt!" Varun said, his voice all relief that made Nadia feel more incredulous. "Did you pay our bail?"

"Snow in the face really necessary?" Nadia asked over him. Pretty amazing how fast relief could turn to irritation. She brushed her front clean, sending powder into Ember's hair as she kneeled to poke at her leg.

"Is it anywhere else?" Ember asked, her words falling over one another. "Did it hit bone?"

"Gaaaah, *god*, Ember, it's a bullet wound; you don't have to verify it seventeen ways. Can we get on the ship now?"

"Do you know about how much blood you lost?" Ember asked as she stood and wrapped Nadia's other arm around her shoulder. With Ember and Varun helping, Nadia was able to partially canter toward the pod.

"Over there!" someone shouted from the prison building.

Nadia hobbled faster. "Do I look like a doctor?" she sniped back. "I'm sorry Varun didn't get a prison cup to measure it in."

The next sentry will pass in six minutes.

The voice came from a small communicator on Ember's hip. Nadia froze, which meant she was now being dragged. Varun's arms dropped to his sides, and she lost her grip on him. Pain shot farther up her side as her leg was forced to bear weight. Ember caught her on the way down, crushing Nadia awkwardly into her right hip and really not helping all that much.

"Shiiiiit, Ember?" Nadia whispered.

"We have to get up, Nadia. We have to *go*."

Please get them on board, Ember.

"Dr. Schmitt?" Varun asked. He took a tentative step toward the ship, then looked back at Ember with horrified hope.

"Really not the time." Ember hauled Nadia into a pseudo-carry hold that spoke of childhood swimming pool antics and pulled her across the snow and grass. Varun trailed silently behind. From behind her came the sound of running footsteps and locks clicking back into place.

Faster, Ember. We can take off the moment you are all on board.

"Fuck off," Ember whispered under her breath, right into Nadia's ear. Nadia's skin goosebumped with the colder air, her head lighter and her vision spottier. The shouting behind her became louder. Little zipping sounds raced past her, and Varun cursed in Hindi. Ember slogged her up the ramp, and Nadia crumpled into the cramped cockpit of a ship that had at least one zombie on board.

That was a little comforting now that she thought about it. If she died, maybe she'd get to come back too.

"Put her on this one. It reclines." A woman in tight pants gestured to a chair that looked exactly the same as all the others. Ember hauled her back up, and Nadia flopped down, exhausted as a different pain took over. She yelled at the pressure on the backside of her thigh until someone kicked the chair into recline mode, elevating her foot.

"Shitshitshit!" Nadia yelled, just as the pod whirred into action. She ground her teeth as her torso curled up in pain. "Shit, Ember, I don't want to die on your ghost ship."

Ember checked the tourniquet and patted Nadia's knee. It wasn't supposed to be condescending, but it sure felt like it. Also, Ember could have emoted a little more. Dead wives and soon-to-be-dead sisters, and *fuck*, her leg hurt.

"No fresh blood," Ember said. "I see an exit hole, so I think you'll be okay until we get clear. I'll get you painkillers. How do you feel, other than wanting to beat me with a poorly made beaker?"

Nadia had half a million puns at the ready but was too off-kilter to use any of them. She felt like a partially blended smoothie, and the next step was a shitty bone saw and a piece of hardtack.

"I hate everything right now." She tempered her tone because Varun had that sad-puppy look to him. "I'm also confused." Looking around, she didn't know anyone outside Ember and Varun. The ship wasn't a flyer, but the women (she assumed) in it were certainly mella. Mella rescue? Mella ransom? Where was Taraniel?

The ship bucked, and Nadia gripped the armrests. Her ears popped.

"Normal," Ember responded lightly. "I'll tell you more once we're safe. Could you try to rest for once in your life? No grants to write today, okay?"

"You suck at writing grants," Nadia retorted without malice.

"Everyone, get strapped in," one of the mella said. "Someone will have to sit on the floor. We can take a look at Dr. O'Grady's wound once we're past the perimeter. Go."

They'd have to work on names later. Ember secured Nadia's belt and knelt to her side. The rest of the harnesses clicked into place, and the ship surged forward. Nadia stuck her fingers in her ears, waiting for more popping, and rolled her jaw in circles as her stomach dropped with the ship's upward acceleration.

"Let me know if you need anything," Ember whispered as the pressure in the ship evened out.

Nadia jiggled her fingers in her ears and wiped them on her pants. She half turned on her side and looked at her sister incredulously. "Me? I need to know what happened to *you*, Miss TOPA-in-a-snowbank. Where is Taraniel? I know I heard her."

Ember licked her lips and looked up. Nadia followed but saw only ceiling.

Not fast enough! Brace!

The ship rocked to the left. Ember fell onto the floor, one hand managing to hold on to Nadia's handrest. The ship made a hard right turn, and Ember flew across the floor and into the opposite wall. Nadia's harness groaned. At least two of the other women cursed.

"Flyers?" the unnamed woman asked again.

It's a flyer from the compound we just left, and yes, the ship's nose shows the dopey, entwined, three-circle crest of the presidium. That's officially a government-sanctioned ship from a government-sanctioned facility.

And that was Taraniel again, her disembodied voice coming from an overhead speaker. Hypotheses clouded Nadia's mind, and the most disturbing one rose to the top, involving a brain in a jar with wires hooking it to the ship. Unlikely, but probably not too far from the truth. Nadia shivered. Ember...damn, she had to be an absolute mess. An actual zombie would have been easier to deal with. And what was the presidium doing putting up a building in the middle of nowhere? Did the conference attendees frequently need to be incarcerated?

"Can we get them on the comm, AI?"

They're not responding. They—

The ship accelerated, and Nadia's stomach rose in that horrible tickling way that meant they were falling. She lifted off the seat, harness digging into her neck and hips, hair falling straight up. Her toes and feet still burned from the frostbite, and her thigh throbbed with the change in pressure. If someone had offered to laser her leg off in that moment, Nadia would have accepted.

"Ember!" The ship abruptly changed direction, and Nadia whipped her head around to find her sister, who had a chair in a bear hug from behind. The chair fabric showed indents from Ember's fingernails, but there were lines, too, from where Ember had slipped. Was slipping. She'd turned toward Nadia, her eyes squeezed shut, her half-assed ponytail up like a chipmunk's.

"I'm fine!" Ember yelled in return. "Asher, what happened?"

The woman in charge—Asher—tried to get a hand on the main console, but was a bit too far away, and they were falling way too fast.

They're firing on us, Taraniel replied. **They *hit* us. Varun and Nadia definitely saw something they weren't supposed to**.

"Where are we going to land?" Asher pulled back and wrapped her hands under the handrests, her knuckles white.

Snow. Taraniel sounded worried. Nadia's mind still skittered over the whole ceiling voice thing—that Asher had called for an AI and how the situation had come to be. And how, in the name of the Great-Beetle-King-that-did-not-exist, Ember was dealing with it all.

A loud *pop* sounded from the back of the ship, and the fall leveled off. Nadia slammed back into her seat and was then pressed into the plastic as the ship continued its descent. She could only see half of the viewscreen-window (or whatever you called it on a spaceship that wasn't in space) because of the woman in front of her. What she did see was the start of a sunset, the endless white, and the concerning mountain peaks in the distance that they would hopefully be able to skim over and not crash into.

Trying to glide us into powder as much as possible, but we're too far from the equator. It'll mostly be ice.

"Only the one shot? Why not another if we have a chance at surviving the landing?" That was Varun. Nadia had near forgotten he was on board. She couldn't turn enough to see him, but he sounded worried, which meant he was not doing well at all. Not that any of them were, of course, but he wasn't buried into the backside of a chair, listening to his dead sister-in-law talk.

"What do you think it would be easier for a satellite to catch if it only does sporadic photography of the area?" Asher asked sharply. "Explosion or half-buried ship and some dead bodies?"

Please hold on!

The ship bounced when it hit the ground, like a child's rubber ball, each impact smashing Nadia's teeth together until she was certain one chipped. After seven or eight iterations, the pod rolled, generating a scraping sound like nails on an antique chalkboard until it lodged with a head-smacking jolt into the side of a snowdrift. At least they were right side up.

Ember? Ember, talk to me.

"Talk to me first!" Nadia unstrapped her harness and swiveled as far as she could without moving her right leg. She instantly regretted it. Black spots swam in front of her vision, and her equilibrium felt drunk. "You broken?"

"No, just bruised." Ember peel herself from the chair, unwound her legs, and shook out her wrists. She looked like slightly warmed-up porridge and blinked her eyes rapidly, no doubt lost in the same disorientation Nadia felt. Ember's cheek had a bruise blossoming, and there was a line of dried blood near her hairline, but otherwise, she looked pretty decent, all things considered. Head injuries they wouldn't know about for a while anyway.

"Can I get a systems report?" Asher tersely asked the ceiling.

Running diagnostics, the Taraniel-AI replied. **Right now, we've got our primary system down. Heat is gone. Propulsion probably too. I'll have a final report in an hour. I'm not allowed to assign any more processing power to diagnostics until I know Ember is fine**.

Asher cursed, and at least one of the words was "Taraniel."

"My head hurts. Fuck." Ember flopped onto her back, then turned to Nadia and gave the most shit-eating grin she'd ever seen. "Surprise! Sorry we didn't call ahead. There's a clot on my mind."

"Zero points for creativity since I used that one two weeks ago. Two points for style and because you didn't have a seatbelt. Also, I think you should know that Queen is for sale, and we all have to move." Nadia smiled despite trying to look serious.

"Uh. You look pretty banged up," Ember responded, her tone turning serious. "You're not making sense, and that sale thing can't be real. It has to be a stunt. Pui has field medic training, I think she said, and can help you with the med kit. I need a minute."

"Yeah, well, you look like hell, but an entirely different kind than when we last spoke." Nadia lowered her voice, even though she felt silly doing so. "Where is Taraniel?"

Ember again pointed to the ceiling and grimaced. "Taraniel put a personality clone into the ship's AI." Her finger tracked to Asher. "This mella stunned me after I buried her in sand and then dragged me to a secret hidden mella base. We're going to use this ship to get off Queen, apparently— if we don't die first—then fly to Earth, do something I'm not super clear on, and come back for everyone else. Very exciting. Never going to happen. It'll work well with your pain-fueled conspiracy theory. Want to come?"

Would someone check Ember's head? I think she might have a concussion.

"No, I'll do it. Sister thing." Nadia lowered her voice. "I'm serious though, sis. Our planet is being *sold*."

Ember stared. "Okay, you win. Now look at my head."

Tight Pants started to crouch as well but stopped when Asher put a hand on her shoulder. They both sat back down, and Asher watched Nadia, enough tension in her jaw to break a glacier.

Nadia slid her right leg gingerly off the footrest. She gasped when she bent her knee, and her vision temporarily dotted, but it didn't take much to half kneel next to Ember. Her sister shot her a clear I'm-fine-and-*will*-punch-you look, which Nadia ignored, blowing a breath right between her eyes.

"Ahh! Fungus-face! What the fuck?" Ember rubbed at the bridge of her nose. "What's that supposed to check? I'm not the one who got shot."

"Your reflexes. How old are you?"

"Old enough to have locked you in that closet when you were seven."

"What's my married name?"

Ember rolled her eyes. "You're going to bring O'Grady into this? He liked *golf*. Never marry someone who likes golf."

"And what's your wife's name?"

Ember's eyes turned cold. She pulled herself up on the chair in front of her, then wove to the front of the cockpit, where she stared at the snow-covered screen. "We have a distress beacon we can activate? And would one of you please check on my sister's leg? Pui?"

Tight Pants—Pui—got up again and pulled a first aid packet from a pocket under her seat. "I'm an astronomer with four hours of field medicine and blood makes me faint. I'll try."

"Super," Nadia said. "So, can we talk about this leaving Queen thing? Because we can't leave Queen. We need to defend Queen, or something like that. There's a conference on the cold side, and they are auctioning off our planet because of some sand."

That brought stillness to the cockpit while Pui poked awkwardly at Ember's temple.

"Ow!" Ember said as Pui's middle finger found a tender spot on the back of her head.

Pui, the AI cautioned, and the skin on Ember's neck goosefleshed.

Nadia scowled at the ceiling. "Can Tara change her voice or something?"

No, I can't, the AI said sharply. **And I can't take back my embargoed processing power on "probably fine."**

Ember shot an I-told-you-so look at Nadia. Nadia almost told her she resembled a spooked chipmunk, then decided that wasn't fair since she could feel the fatigue on her own face.

"Your confirmation is troubling," Asher said, "and we can send it back to the mella council to discuss. But for us—" She stuck her hands on her hips. "We're leaving. Queen can sort itself out."

Nadia was too tired to fight. She moved both her legs and sat on her backside. Hopefully, they had more ibuprofen because that and adrenaline had to be the only thing keeping her upright. She looked over Pui's shoulder as she riffled through a moldy canvas bag with a red cross stamped on either end and caught Asher staring pointedly at Ember. Her sister had that kicked-puppy sadness that was both adorable and infuriating. If the ship AI had had eyes, no doubt it would have goggled too.

Pui poked another random place on Ember's head, and Ember cursed.

"Did I get an answer on the beacon?" she asked.

Ember—

"*Beacon?*"

The AI continued to sound worried even as it complied. **The flyer is hovering above, and they're blocking all the comm channels. We also can't get any satellites due to where they've positioned themselves and since we're still closer to *their* side of the equator than ours.**

Ember leaned against the screen and closed her eyes. "Fine. Okay. Plan B?"

"The plan was not to get shot." Asher walked over and leaned next to Ember—a little too close, Nadia thought. She'd need to watch that. "Our contingency is that if we don't show up, we got caught, and not to waste any resources coming to get us. The mella council has all our data from Taraniel. We're expendable, except for Ember's exit codes."

"So we die *and* we lose our planet," Nadia muttered.

Everyone else remained silent and in their seats except for Pui, who appeared fifty seconds from passing out and had somehow gotten blood smeared across her right thigh. Ember seemed as if she might either explode or deflate.

"Ember is fine," Pui declared. She wiped her hand against a wall, leaving red streaks. "I think. Nadia, you're next."

"Has the flyer sent any transmissions, AI?" Asher asked the ceiling. "Are you capable of monitoring that?"

Yes, I am, and no, they have not. They're hovering and waiting, with no heat signatures for additional weaponry visible. My guess is they are waiting for us to exit. If they wanted to arrest us and haul us back, they'd have done so already.

"They want something," Asher agreed grimly. "And they've never hesitated to arrest mella before, for any infraction."

"So they don't want us captured." A woman reached into a side compartment and removed a thick, handmade sweater in green. She tossed it to Pui, then pulled an identical brown one for herself. Varun had already been given a pair of jeans, which he straightened out with gentlemanly distaste. Nadia just really wanted a shower.

"I'm Kate. The AI is Tara. Catch up and put this on. They want us dead. Or, not us so much as our colonists here." Kate jabbed a finger in the direction of Ember and Nadia. "Because if these three go back to the colony, they blow the whole farce up. Which I *get*," she added when Asher scowled at her, "because I don't want to adopt several thousand colonists into our camp either. Especially not when they decide you've corrupted their dome, chase you all out, and bring in a fresh batch. *Again.*"

"Move the cynicism down at least two notches, Kate," Asher said. "Now isn't the time."

"I'll just save it till we're dead from exposure."

Ember—

"I think we should sleep," Ember said before the AI could respond with more honey-laced concern. "It's almost three in the morning, and since the flyer doesn't seem interested in more than hovering, maybe a few hours will help us come up with a plan." She wove back to Nadia and sat next to her.

Nadia grabbed her hand, and Ember put up with the squeezing without complaint as Pui cut Nadia's pant leg off and rinsed the wound with alcohol.

"Gahhhhhhh," Nadia said through gritted teeth. "Tell me you have drugs."

Pui finally smiled and handed four bottles to Ember. "We have many, many drugs. You decide. I don't know what most of them do."

"Well?"

"Painkillers *and* sleep aids." Ember poured four ibuprofen into Nadia's hand. "Asher can bring the water."

Asher didn't look particularly pleased to be given orders but moved anyway. "If the flyer does decide to call for backup, or gets bored with waiting and incinerates us, we are sitting ducks."

We are no longer capable of moving without substantial repair.

"Not it," Kate called. Her eyes were closed, her head snugged onto her right shoulder. "I can't...I can't think straight right now. I think my head rebounded too hard during one of those bounces. I need at least an hour to sort out, maybe more, before I can crawl through the pod's innards and see what is what."

I can provide a full diagnostic report now, Tara offered cheerfully.

Kate pinched the bridge of her nose and grimaced. "Great. Do that. In like...an hour or two. If they wanted us dead, they'd already have taken the next shot."

Ember's head fell back, and she let out a long breath of hot air. "I agree. We could go outside and freeze to death, but the pod can't move without repair, so I don't think we have many options, and I'm too tired to think." She lifted her head and quirked a smile at Nadia. The smile was zero percent convincing.

"Fine." Asher slid farther into her chair and covered her eyes with her arm. "But if we die it's not my fault."

Nadia dry swallowed and ignored Asher. "You doing okay?" she asked Ember. "A quarter of your face is purple. Do lesbians like purple?"

Pui's smile turned to a grimace as she removed the shreds of Nadia's pants, dressed her leg, and helped her into a pair of soft cotton pants with a drawstring, staining all of it with Nadia's blood.

Ember's mouth quirked. "Yes. It'll take a lot of pharmaceuticals for me to sleep, especially after your news about the conference. I *do* care, but—" Ember pointed up at the ceiling, and Nadia swore she heard Taraniel sigh.

I could turn my camera and audio sensors off while you sleep, Ember, if that would help. I agree with staying inside the pod until you have formed a plan. There is a significant chance the flyer would pick you off one by one if you exit the ship.

Nadia snorted. "Yes, turn off the inside stuff. I think that would help all of us. Just, uh, scan the perimeter and whatnot."

In the ensuing silence, Nadia imagined Taraniel's disembodied head staring at her through the ceiling, her mouth quirking as she tried to decide whether to beg someone to run a cranial scan on Ember. Taraniel had always been way overprotective of Ember, which Nadia deeply approved of. As a little sister, Nadia had worshipped the ground Ember walked on. As a big sister, she thought Ember had a stubborn streak that would get her killed.

Aye-aye, little sis, the AI said, the words clipped and generic.

A loud click came from overhead, then from the front of the cockpit. Nadia decided to pretend those were the sounds of the AI shifting from internal to external, and not switching to some secret alternate camera.

"Taraniel always did love having a 'little' sister," Ember said under her breath. "How are you doing with all of this? How is your leg?"

Nadia stared at Ember. "I think you should share those sleep aids, big sister." Nadia held out her hand.

Ember gave Nadia the whole bottle. "Happily. Sweet dreams, Nadia Ann—"

Nadia scooted her shoulder closer to Ember and glared. "If you finish that thought, I will slap you, creepy AI or not."

Ember grinned.

"Missed you, too, asshole," Nadia said. She popped back a pill, closed her eyes, and slept.

Chapter Eleven

The discovery of the electronics-grade silicon dioxide on Queen during the equatorial terraforming project came too late. The domed settlement had already been established, the land within terraformed, a culture blossoming. Earth governance—a group of loosely elected leaders from the remaining functional countries—asked the colonists to relocate first. Then bribed. Then begged.

Finally, they forced.

The colonists fought back.

Ember

Ember hadn't had a good night's sleep since Earth, though there'd been a handful of years spooned around Taraniel that it'd been okay. She awoke well before anyone else, Nadia so soundly asleep that drool leaked from the corner of her mouth and into her hair.

Ember took the corner of her sleeve and wiped off as much as she could. She'd spent a lot of time braiding that hair, or pulling it, depending on the situation. Nadia had such a sensitive scalp. No need to exacerbate their problems with tangles.

Her sister didn't stir, even when Ember cautiously lifted her head to put her folded blanket under it. Even when Ember warmed her own hands with her breath and put them over Nadia's, trying to gauge how cold her sister was in the thin colony shirt and only moderately thicker mella pants. Nadia's fingers felt cool but not icy. Ember could only just see her breath if she deeply exhaled. She'd fallen asleep before the AI's report was ready but didn't need it to see they were screwed.

Ember didn't know anything about spaceship mechanics. If it didn't use photosynthate she'd, tra-ditionally, tuned out. But the residual heat trapped inside the flyer wouldn't last forever. They needed heat, which meant they needed the greater ship systems working, not just the AI, which sounded like it ran on its own independent power source. Kate was their engineer, right? Wasn't that what she'd said during their foray to the snow side where conferences and intergalactic politics were playing out? Meh. They needed another option, a quicker option than tinkering, and they needed it soon.

Ember threaded around chairs and flailed limbs to the back of the cockpit. She slid her hand into the crescent indent in the door and tried to slide it right. It didn't budge.

"Hey," Ember whispered to the wall. "Unlock the door."

The AI didn't answer.

"AI," Ember tried again.

More silence.

"Tara. You there?"

When the ship still didn't respond, Ember put her palm on the scan pad to the left of the door and watched the gel beneath turn red. Of course, she wasn't keyed to access any of the ship, but it had to have sent a message to—

Ember?

Ember didn't like how the AI's voice made her feel as though she was drowning in sunlight. Other parts of her body responded, too, which was a whole separate problem. At least the AI had whispered. Ember needed a few minutes alone before the crew woke.

"Could you open the door?"

Of course.

The pad turned green. This time when Ember tugged on the door, it slid easily into its pocket. Cold air hit her face, and she shivered. Breath and bodies had kept the tiny cockpit warm. Here... Plastic bins lined the walls, although the remains of metal rails showed they likely held a series of bunk beds at one point. The space wasn't large—maybe forty square meters and around twice her height. The bins were stacked in columns and then entire columns strapped to the floor, giving a strange cityscape look to the room.

She slipped between the stacks, tapping sides but not bothering to unstrap anything and check contents. They either contained supplies that would keep them alive, or they didn't, and there was no point wasting what time she did have. She found a place near the back, three sides closed in by bins, and sat with her feet tucked under, like she was preparing for prayer.

Mostly she was just cold.

"You still there?" Ember asked the ceiling.

The voice came louder now that the door was shut. Still, it sounded way too gentle. **I can go again if you'd like.**

"No. How long do we have before the temperature in here drops past...I don't know...tolerable for someone with blood loss?"

It depends on how much everyone moves around. Half a day, maybe a bit longer. Several days for those with thicker clothing.

"The flyer above us? What is it doing?"

Hovering.

"Do any of the ship systems work other than you?"

Tara sighed, and this time, it didn't feel weird. **You don't know enough about how spaceships work to explain this well. Asher has the full report. I could heat the ship for two more days at this current low level, or I could keep filtering the air for silica and other particulates one more day. I could push us off the ground for maybe...five minutes before we crashed back to the snow. I could run fourteen days of solid system diagnostics. I could send one thousand and seventy-three text messages or one-sixteenth that number of video calls through to the colony. Etcetera. I'm prioritizing the air.**

"Sound call. Guess that takes Earth off the table for now, huh?" She tried to make it sound like a joke, but the end of her sentence lilted instead, the words turning shrill.

Why are you fighting so hard to stay on Queen? Especially after what Nadia said? Your reasonable fear of being in stasis again can be dealt with. We won't use stasis capsules again, and we have anti-

anxiety drugs that can help. Taraniel made sure the mella packed them. The AI's voice gentled. **Taraniel knew you would be nervous. She compiled a few music playlists and even suggested three virtual reality sim games you could still play while on medication.**

Medication? *That* was the AI's answer to Ember's flashbacks? She'd had plenty of drugs in stasis, too, and they hadn't helped shit.

"I don't want to stay on Queen. *No one* wants to stay on Queen. If the colonists get relocated, that sounds like a reward, not something to fight. But I'm not equipped to join pirates and scientists into space, either, and I'm not prepared to take *myself* into space. I'd be terrible company."

No one is asking you to lead. Just provide the coordinates. Help get the clearance. I have instructions for how to help manage you.

"Manage me?" Heat rose in her face, and she decided arguing along this course would get her nowhere fast. Better to debate the tangibles. Coordinates, she had. Well, maybe. There was a lot of conjecture there. Clearance—that came from the presidium. While Ember had, on a number of occasions, walked into their suite to yell over manhandling of her seedlings or conscripted plantings, going to them and wheedling clearance off-world had absolutely no way of succeeding.

"I'm not ready to agree to that," Ember said after a pause that seemed to stretch as far as the snow outside. "I want out of here first. Out of the snow."

The AI's tone came back neutral. **Understandable.**

She definitely wasn't going into space with the... whatever it was between her and the ship. Ember had enough awkward tension in her. Add to that the mella crew and her sister in the same cramped living space—time sucks and arguments with an AI would get them killed.

Ember folded her hands on her lap and took a deep breath—in through the nose, out through the mouth. A similar sound came from the AI. Ember's mood soured.

"I wish you would quit doing that."

Doing what? Ember, I'm not trying to upset you.

"Then stop sounding so damn human."

I am exactly what Taraniel programmed me to be.

The voice that responded was Taraniel after a fight—a fight where Ember lost her temper about another set of dirty clothes left on the floor, or after Ember woke up to find dishes still soaking in a basin of cold, gray water. Hurt. It—she, Ember really had to start thinking of it as an intelligence and not just part of the ship—sounded hurt and at least 15 percent indignant because Taraniel had always been quick to apologize but was just as absentminded a scientist as the rest of them.

"You are a poor copy."

The indignation dropped away, and the voice became barely more than a whisper. **I suppose.**

Ember felt terrible again. She put her hands on the floor and leaned back, staring up at the ceiling.

"Shit. I...I'm sorry. That was low."

The AI didn't respond.

"Did you pick a name yet?" Ember asked, trying to prod the conversation along. "You should have one before we all die wedged into an ice slick."

I like Tara. Half a name for half a person, right?

Ouch. Still, "person" seemed like a reach. Not the time to debate, however. Angry AIs in snow drifts got her and her sister killed in short order. "It's a good name. I like it."

Thanks.

Round and round and never finding the point. Ember took another long breath. "I'm trying to find space in my brain for you and my wife. It isn't going well. I'm sorry."

She shivered then, the cold seep noticeable as her breath condensed around her face in a dusky cloud. "Why am I taking mella to Earth, old or new? Taraniel and I never discussed this."

Things change, Ember. Taraniel made a choice to use her last days to save you. She contacted the mella. She worked with them on the ship. On me. She was determined to get you off Queen with friends who could help you reestablish your old lives.

"On Old Earth?" Ember whispered incredulously. "We don't have any *proof*. Not substantial proof. You can explain roses a hundred ways. Earth is the easiest explanation, but it isn't the only one."

There is a solid way to find out.

"We're never going to get off Queen," Ember countered.

I think you'd be surprised what the mella are capable of.

Ember sat back against a stack of bins and deflated. "Why you? Why this?" She pointed at the ceiling.

Taraniel wanted you to have a part of her there because she didn't think you'd take her death well. And because you, alone, wouldn't be able to make the journey to Earth. Taraniel...she had plans for Earth too. The cancer delayed some, but she didn't want your life delayed anymore.

"I'm fine," Ember snapped. "I'd have been fine." The last part sounded childish, especially since Ember would *not* have been fine, alone, for months in space. Ember kept her groan to herself.

No response came from Taraniel.

"It isn't fair to judge me from beyond the grave."

I doubt Taraniel is judging you. I am because I'm supposed to be helping you as much as I can.

"While also manipulating me so I do what you want."

What *Taraniel* wanted.

"Argh!" Ember ran her hands through her hair and slapped the floor. "Is there even a difference?"

No, not really. Tara's voice melted into softness. **I think that's the point.**

Expertly played and expertly defeated—the way most of Ember's and Taraniel's discussions went.

"Our marriage license does not contain a clause for becoming a ship."

Tara's voice turned ribbing. **For better or for worse though. You're living the worse. I can help you get to the better. Also**—Tara's voice turned conspiratorial—**Taraniel didn't expect you to mourn her forever.**

"Stop. This is not what I want to talk about."

What would you prefer?

Ember slumped. "Nothing. I'm tired of moving backward. So, I guess this is okay. I guess. For now." And it was, kind of, which felt bizarre but also comforting in that if she died out here, at least Taraniel—Tara—would be around to walk her through it.

Ember stood and put her hand on a bare patch of wall. The wall sucked the last of the warmth from her body. Her teeth started chattering. "Okay?"

Always. Tara's voice turned light. **Be nicer to Nadia. She got shot for you.**

"Yeah, yeah." Ember waved dismissively at the ceiling but smiled. "She can take it."

I know she can. You, on the other hand, wilt when she's sharp, and I don't currently have breasts for you to bury your face in.

Ember flushed, the warmth flowing from her ears to her fingertips. She didn't spend enough time in *those* memories, or any memories, really, other than Taraniel's last days. Another point to the AI.

"Dr. Schmitt?" The bins muffled Varun's voice.

Saved by the scientist. Guessing he felt too timid to step inside, Ember stepped from her makeshift room and walked to the door.

"Everyone up?" she asked as he came into view. For a man who'd just been sprung from prison, Varun looked downright perky. His thick black hair was still combed just so, and he had maybe a centimeter more of facial hair than the last time she'd seen him. Ember swore she could see the start of a smile around the corners of his mouth. "You look good. Testosterone?"

Varun nodded, his mouth twitching. "Yes. They resupplied finally. There's extra, if you want."

Ember shook her head. That was another private conversation she didn't really want to be having on a stranded ship. "No thank you. The rest of the crew?"

"Just Pui and Kate and I are up. Asher, Nok, and Nadia are sleeping soundly. It's warmer in there still, with all the bodies." A light shiver ran across his shoulders. "I thought I might bring everyone in here and discuss our current situation once they wake. Hypothesize options."

Ember's brain still lagged on the farther future. "Would you go back?" The question came out before she'd finished forming it mentally. "To Earth. The old one. If you could."

Varun blinked, then canted his head. "Yes."

"Really?" Ember took a step toward him and folded her arms across her chest.

A smile engulfed his face, lit his eyes in a way Ember had never seen. "How many planets have humans terraformed, Dr. Schmitt? How many ecosystems, never meant to support us, have we twisted to our will? Imagine, with the tech we currently have, how easy it would be to terraform Old Earth."

"But Queen is our home. It has been for years."

"Queen is bullshit. If the presidium offered me a relocation voucher, I'd take it without thinking. And so would all the colonists, I am certain."

Ember had to mull that for a long moment, while Tara chuckled in the background. "If I told you I was taking this ship and going. That I wanted you along..."

"Yes."

Huh.

"So..." Ember squinted. Varun seldom looked this confident, and while it was good to see him smiling, enthusiasm for a dead planet seemed overkill. "Am I missing something?"

Varun's eyes lit up brighter, and he grinned. *Grinned.* It looked about as natural as a jack-o'-lantern. "Those aren't mountains out there." His mouth twitched again as he tried, unsuccessfully, to suppress his smile. "They're beetle mounds."

Ember tried to remember what the mountains had looked like as they crashed into them but could gather a blurry image at best. They'd looked white. They'd looked pointy. They were tall. It was cold as fuck outside, and it was soon to be cold as fuck in the ship. That was about it. "How can you tell? Was your PhD dissertation on weird Queen arthropod structures?"

Varun rallied, squaring his shoulders even more and puffing like a balloon. "Yes, more or less, as well as their phosphorescent capabilities." He held up a finger. "First, there are no mountains on Queen. Hills, yes, but no mountains. Second—"

"Don't argue semantics."

Varun let out a *pfft* and continued, holding up a second finger. "Second, what really matters are the small pock marks you can see near the base of the mounds. Those are the entry points, which the beetles back fill for warmth and open when they want to leave. The inside of the mounds is like a proper bark beetle gallery on Earth. Of course, the Queen beetles aren't even marginally related to anything on Earth, not even technically in Kingdom. The beetles haul the sand from the sun side, we think, since the ground here should be too frozen to dig. The new data I've collected this trip should prove my hypothesis that the sand-side beetles and snow-side beetles are, in fact, the same species, with minor mutational differences."

Varun paused for a breath and clasped his hands in front of himself. "Well?"

"It's fascinating," Ember drawled, trying to find the point. "What good does that information do us now?"

"The mella ride beetles, Dr. Schmitt. The beetles are believed to traverse incredible distances. They can pull twenty to thirty times their body weight. We harness a few, and we can pull the flyer back to the colony, gliding on the snow and ice the whole way. There, we can repair it, and you can"—he made a fluttering movement with his hand—"take us into the stars."

"I haven't—"

The door behind Varun slid open, and Pui and Kate entered, bringing a breeze of warmer, stale air with them.

"Everyone is up," Kate said in a monotone, point back over her shoulder. The door remained open, and just beyond, Ember could see Nadia stretching her back and Asher's head bobbing behind Pui's. "What's going on with beetles now?"

"Beetle rides," Ember said. "Or beetle carriage. Take your pick."

Asher pursed her lips and pushed into the hold. "How does that help us with the flyer overhead? We leave this ship, and we'll get blasted."

Everyone looked at Varun.

He blinked. "None of you have any idea how beetles work, do you?"

"I study plants, Varun," Ember said dryly. "The only bugs I care about are the ones I have to spray."

Varun scowled in the way only an uptight academic could. "Hypothesis—the flyer isn't shooting us because an explosion would get caught on a satellite and fed into the colony. Follow up—if colonists see an explosion outside the habitable zone, they will ask uncomfortable questions. Tertiary—the flyer will avoid explosions at all cost. Finally—mella lives have insignificant value."

"Hey," Kate said. "Watch it."

"*Science*," Varun countered, "doesn't care about your feelings. Neither do I at the moment. I've got eggs hatching in the lab in two days that I need data on, and I don't want to die. Therefore, I propose you, mella, Asher, whomever is managing this crew, to send the beetles at the flyer and-or have the beetles carry us back. Our only other option is to sit here and slowly freeze to death."

"I don't think they have that kind of control over them," Ember said. She turned to Asher. "Right?"

Asher looked incredulous. "Well, a pet one, sure. We have a few at the camp that are voice command trained and will do just about anything for food, but you're talking about wild beetles here, Mr.... Actually, I don't know your name at all."

Ember jumped in before Varun started awkwardly stammering. "My colleague and friend, Dr. Varun Sinha. He's our architect turned entomologist."

Asher leaned into the bulkhead. "Talk to Nok. She's our entomologist turned wildlife wrangler. I don't work with the beetles at the camp, but from what I've seen, they take a few months to even warm up to people." Her eyes flicked to the ceiling. "We don't do magic on Queen, despite what it may look like on occasion."

"Still waking up," Nok called from the cockpit with an audible yawn. "Give me a minute before we make beetle decisions."

Varun bristled. "I have no interest in how you work with beetles on the equator." He paused, scratched at the stubble on his beard, and snorted. "That's a lie. I do, in fact, have questions, but they're not pertinent to this discussion. I propose we bait the beetles to the flyer."

"With what?" Ember asked.

Nok walked, bleary eyed and wrinkled, into the hold. "Please don't say pheromones."

Varun's eyebrow rose. "Pheromones," he said smugly. "All of life, across any planet, is driven by pheromones. Surely, we're not the only ones who have taken a chemistry class?" The barb was distinctly for Nok. The mella yawned in response.

Asher pushed from the wall and scowled at Varun. "Stop it, both of you. Dr. Sinha, do you have any pheromone spray on you? You can be smug as hell about entomological BS, but it won't fix our problem."

"Why would anyone leave the colony with a giant coleoptera-esque target in their pocket?" Varun asked. "How long has it been since you worked in a lab?"

Please, everyone. Taraniel's meetings-are-a-waste-of-time voice came on. **Varun, these people are my friends. I do trust them.**

"You are an artificial intelligence set to sound and act like Dr. Schmitt's wife for reasons as of yet unexplained. I do not trust *you*."

"I agree on that point," Nok added.

"Well, I do." Ember's voice forced itself up without consultation with her brain. For a half moment, it felt like a betrayal of Taraniel's memory, but then it felt like one more thing Nadia could rib her about later, once they were no longer living popsicles.

Varun studied her.

She quirked the side of her mouth and shrugged. "I have data you don't."

"You might also have a concussion!" Nadia yelled from somewhere in the cockpit.

"Fine. I have data *and* potentially a concussion. That doesn't invalidate the data."

"Fair." Varun turned back to Asher. "No, I don't have any of their sex pheromones on me. I do, however, know where they are stored in their galleries. Collecting will be a problem, but the bigger problem is getting into the gallery from here. We're not far—maybe a two-minute sprint from the nearest one. But that's two minutes dodging air attacks as I'm guessing the flyer won't have an issue firing on *us* since we wouldn't make a visible explosion. This part of the plan I cannot help with." Begrudgingly and very slowly, Varun turned and took a step toward Nok. "Dr....?"

"Dr. Nok."

Ember could hear Varun's eye roll.

"Thoughts?" he asked Nok.

"I think colony academics couldn't find their way through a beetle gallery with a GPS and a good flashlight."

"No chance Ember's sex bluff will work again?" Kate asked. "With the flyer. Not with the beetles. Obviously." Her brow wrinkled. "Unless it would?"

Pui giggled.

"I don't have a penis to go waving around outside if that's what you're asking," Ember retorted. "The only man in here is Varun."

Kate held up her hands. "Just checking."

"What are we checking?" Nadia entered the already cramped storage space, shadow-eyed, limping, her hair a partially matted mess against one side of her head.

"Varun would like us to break into a beetle gallery and steal pheromones so we can take out the flyer. I've professed loyalty to my dead wife's personality imprint, and we have all come to terms with the fact that I do not have a penis. Good morning. How's your leg?"

"Oh, is that all?" Nadia limped to Ember, purposefully bumped their shoulders together, then stood at her side. "Leg hurts. Don't want to talk about it. And the ship can't fly us, like, another twenty feet? Or whatever that is in meters?"

Five, maybe. But otherwise, I'm grounded.

"Her name's Tara," Ember said to Nadia in as flat a voice as she could manage. Nadia's mouth opened, and Ember held up a finger. "No retorts until we're elbow-deep in pheromone. Then you can cut loose."

"And me without my Sunday shoes. Ah, well." Nadia looked around the room. "Who's in charge?"

Asher thumped the wall. "Me. And I don't want anyone making a suicide run across snow. Do the galleries only go up?" She looked first to Nok, then Varun, then back again. "Or do they spread? Do they go under?"

Varun considered.

"I...have only been in ours before," Nok admitted, a faint pink coloring her cheeks. "And tamed beetles aren't likely to make the same kind of structures, specifically because we keep ours penned. There hasn't been a chance to explore wild-type ones."

Ember sighed. "They can't be that different, right? Just underground cave systems?"

Varun said, "That would be consistent with what I have seen, although I've only received permits to survey abandoned ones." After a thoughtful pause, he added, "The only thing living in those are rabbits." His eyes flicked up to Nok. "I'm willing to share coauthorship on a paper if you'd like to collaborate on this."

Nadia muttered, "Jesus Christ save us from assistant professors," under her breath.

Nok raised an eyebrow. "I'd share regardless because I don't want to die. But I appreciate the offer." She moved closer to Varun, into his personal space. They eyed each other for a long moment; it was the most academic assessment Ember had seen since leaving Earth. If they'd had smartphones, they'd be checking each other's h-indexes. Out here, there was only street cred and looming death.

"Coauthors." Varun held out his hand.

"Coauthors," Nok said, shaking it.

"Can we move on? How do we check your hypotheses?" Kate asked. "Can the ship dig?"

"Ugggh. No more digging." Nadia leaned against the wall, her face way too pale.

"With that leg, you're not digging anything," Ember muttered.

"Your concussion still talking?" Nadia shot back.

I do have scanners, you know, Tara cut in, frustrated. **They can't go far with how much power we have, but I can tell you we've got about a meter of snow and ground under us, and a thin but stable layer of ice before I read void space. I've made a crappy map that may or may not help. I could do better if you don't mind losing the last bit of life support. If you go into the cockpit, I'll bring the map up on the screen.**

"That's useful." Asher turned and left the room, and the rest of the mella followed silently.

Ember wrapped her sister's arm around her shoulders and helped her limp to a chair in the cockpit. There, the screen showed a simplistic black-and-white, two-dimension image of a tunnel system.

Here—Tara lit a tunnel line on the left side of the screen in green—**is the closest connection to the main**

mound that I can find. I can't scan the mounds without digging into reserves you all need to keep warm. If we can get in, it is also unlikely that I can guide you back except for maybe the last thirty meters. I also cannot tell you where to go once you exhaust the map provided here.

"We'll want the biggest chamber, likely central to the mound." Varun pushed in front of everyone else and traced a finger through one of the tunnels on the screen. "The smell will be apparent as it concentrates, even to human noses."

Nok joined him at the screen. "We might be able to navigate via smell as well," she added. "Move in as it concentrates, move out as it wanes."

"Is *that* why your lab smells, Varun?" Nadia asked. "Oh, god. Next time we get a charcoal filter in, it's going to you."

"I'm touched, Dr. O'Grady."

He was clearly not touched.

"But how do we get down there?" Ember leaned onto Nadia's chair. The start of a headache tickled the base of her skull. Great. Maybe she did have a concussion after all.

Kate tapped the wall. "Hey, ship, Tara, can you get off the ground at all?"

Maybe a meter before I crash back down.

"How many times do you think you could do that?" Kate asked. "Up and down. Crashing."

A whistling sound came through the ship speakers. **Ten, maybe, until the bottom plating brakes off or the thrusters give out or until I can no longer keep heating the cockpit. Taraniel's programming won't let me actively kill Ember, however, so plan on eight crashes before I go into keep-Ember-alive-at-all-cost mode.**

Nadia's eyes narrowed as she looked from Ember to the ceiling and back again. "Are you telling me that you would just—"

I don't think you want that confirmation.

"Nope. Definitely don't."

"Flopping around like a big fish until we break through is going to bring a lot of beetle attention," Ember interjected.

"But it might also scare the immediate beetles off." Varun sat in one of the chairs and continued to study the map. "Having a hoard of angry beetles will be useful when the pheromones arrive, however."

Ember nodded, the plan coalescing while her fingertips began to tingle from the cold. "So, Asher just needs to keep the beetles from destroying the ship long enough for you to bring the pheromones back. Maybe five minutes? Twenty?"

Nok shook her head. "Definitely longer than that."

"An hour," Varun countered, nodding in agreement. "Probably not more. I need people I know with me. No offense, Dr. Nok. I'd take Dr. O'Grady, too, if not for the leg."

Nok did not appear to take offense. "I can gather complementary data from the ship. I like the idea of splitting eyes."

Nadia muttered something unintelligible, and Ember lightly slapped her shoulder.

"No, you're not going," she said. "I'm going. When you get shot, you lose your right to run around in the snow like a rabid toddler."

"This should fall under the ship's protection clause," Nadia shot back. "Don't you think, Tara?"

The odds of survival if no one goes out are zero percent. I can't calculate whether Ember should stay or go because I don't know enough about Varun. I've got too much missing data. Therefore, I abstain.

That added another layer to Ember's shivering. Taraniel had never been this weird. A bit secretive sometimes, but not...this.

"I'll go." Asher bent down and fished her vest from the floor. "Dr. Sinha, Dr. Schmitt, you'll want to swap clothes with Pui and Nok."

Varun made a tsking gesture as Asher zipped her vest. "It will be much warmer in the galleries. Save the winter gear in case the beetles get in here. Keep Dr. O'Grady warm; she already has frostbite."

"I can go, Asher," Kate said, her voice confused. "Don't you want to stay here and coordinate or protect the ship or some other captain thing?"

Asher's face contorted from agreement to frustration to, upon making eye contact with her, a look that was sure to be big trouble later.

"You have to stay and fuss with the ship," Asher said eventually. "Whatever repairs you can manage. Taraniel and I chose to bring an engineer for a reason. Pui, however—"

Asher needs to go with Ember, Tara confirmed in as close to a standard TOPA voice as Ember had yet heard her use. **Pui has to stay. You're expendable, Asher. The ship medic is not**.

"It's like just when you think she can't get creepier, she manages this." Nadia looked wryly at Ember. Ember shrugged. Taraniel had always had a distinct sense of humor.

Asher took off her vest and handed it to Nadia, along with a pair of gloves and an extra wool sweater she'd put on before sleeping. "Guess we don't get a choice. Sit down. Everyone strap in. Ember, you here." Asher pointed at her chair. "I'll hump the furniture this time. Tara?"

Yes?

"Once everyone is secured, let's start before any of us can think up the inevitable shitty consequences."

Copy.

Harnesses clicked into place. Asher wrapped arms and legs around Kate's chair, eyes wide open, ready to bark the next command. Ember briefly wondered why she hadn't chosen Ember's chair to spoon, realized that was not a path her mind needed to go down, and closed her eyes as well.

The thrusters fired.

The pod wobbled into the air and fell back to the snow.

Ember's head cracked forward, and she heard, quite distinctively, the ground break apart.

Chapter Twelve

Queen's original colonists lost.

Earth blossomed again. Industry boomed. Queen's raw materials could no longer be ignored.

New colonists came—the originals pushed from the dome, from their work, from their lives. The new colonists had heavily monitored inputs and restricted communication. They were bright minds who would further Earth's needs but not take Earth's resources.

Earth, finally, had won.

Ember

Four attempts. It took four attempts of the worst roller coaster ride of Ember's life to punch down into the gallery. No fire from above, of course, because to any rational person, it likely looked as if they were trying to end their own lives, not save them.

Finally, the ground gave way enough that the pod sank into frozen sand, into a tunnel barely bigger than the ship. Debris covered the viewscreen, and Tara made no attempt to clear it. The pod stabilized with a slight tilt to the right; then Ember heard a long mechanical exhalation.

That's it, except for minimal life support, Tara said.

Ember heard the worry, so carefully concealed only someone who had slept with Taraniel the night before a conference presentation would have been able to decode it.

Ember patted her chair armrest—Tara had to have noticed—and asked as she unbuckled, "If the ground is this thin and breakable, how likely is it that the ceiling caves in when we're walking?"

Asher peeled herself from the back of Kate's chair, knuckles white, looking a bit green. Nobleness was cute, Ember decided. Stupid, but cute.

Asher pushed a small access panel aside, right above the hatch, and removed a handful of headlamps. She handed one to Ember, eyes darting to Ember's, then away. Ember wrapped it around her forehead and put her emotions in a chokehold. If they were already at the "avoiding eye contact because there was something to avoid" stage, she needed to cool off. Beetle galleries were terrible first dates.

It's almost nineteen degrees Celsius in the tunnel system. You'll be fine without your envirosuit, Dr. Sinha, if you're interested.

Asher handed out the rest of the headlamps, including to those who were staying in the ship. She pulled one over her own head and clicked it onto the lowest brightness.

Varun shook his head, headlamp bobbing. He was already at the hatch door, practically salivating. Ember stood, fought a quick wave of black spots in front of her eyes, and staggered her way over to him.

"Hey, Ember." Nadia didn't stand, but she did, irritatingly, clap her hands twice.

Ember turned her headlamp to the blindingly white, flashing setting before turning around. "What?"

Nadia put her hands in front of her face. "Gahh. Don't die. They don't have tenure in heaven."

Ember stuck out her tongue but turned the light off. "Try not to get shot again. Play nice with the other children."

Her first sentence had Nadia almost smiling. The second sent her right back into a scowl.

"You don't even deserve a pun right now, Lamphead."

"Great, then we can go." Asher edged in front of Varun, who'd hit the access panel at least twelve times already, and put her palm on it. "We're ready, Tara. How much time do we have?"

I have one hour of heat left, three of air filtration. It will be a very uncomfortable ride back. I'm also glad you're ready because so are the beetles. Nine approaching.

"Out then, while we still can."

"They don't eat people," Nok called out from the back room. "No recorded instances in the colony or the mella camps."

Ember did not find that comforting.

The hatch descended, and Asher grabbed them both and ran down the plank.

"Be safe!" Nadia called out after.

"I only have one more bottle of antiseptic!" Pui added.

Ember didn't have time to respond. The hatch shut and all around her was red clay, softly dripping water onto a ground marred with claw marks the length of her forearm. She clicked her headlamp back on, just a soft glow this time. The three headlamps swung around as people got their bearings, and it took Ember a minute to realize why the tunnel walls looked like they were pocked with stars.

Bunnies.

Oh, god, she'd forgotten about the rabbits.

The headlamps reflected in their eyes, creating sharp pinpricks of light. Hundreds of the things stared at them, ears erect, eyes wide, little white cotton tails fluffing from their butts. They covered the clay in fuzzy clumps, stalled in their panic as they waited for one of the humans to spring. A big white one leaned in close to Ember's boot, its left ear bent and its red eyes shining in the pod's lighting.

You need to move, Ember, Tara chirped from the comm on her belt. **They're just bunnies.**

"They're staring at us," Ember countered, taking tentative steps toward Varun, whose head slowly rotated as he mouthed a count. "You could have reminded me."

I didn't think common knowledge needed reminders. *Please* move.

"Agreed." Asher brushed past her and kicked a foot toward the nearest clump of fur. The rabbits hopped to the tunnel wall in a synchronized arc, stood on their hind legs, and continued to watch.

Varun turned sharply, having finished whatever he was doing, and disappeared around the curve of the tunnel.

Asher halfheartedly swatted at Ember's shoulder, but there was a clear *can we get moving* in her eyes.

"Dr. Schmitt," Asher said. "Please."

"I'm coming." Ember followed Asher out of the tunnel in long strides, keeping her eyes on the creepy rabbits for as long as she could. The scratching sound of the approaching beetles grew deeper, settling into a trill Ember could feel in her bones.

They progressed in a wandering line, no one speaking, the air thick with humidity. The sounds of the beetles didn't increase, but evidence of their approach showed everywhere. Water puddles on the floor rippled. Loose sections of the clay wall shook and crumbled. Varun stumbled, caught himself on the wall, and fell farther when he couldn't find a handhold.

Ember helped him up, but in doing so, made the mistake of looking at the ground. Rabbits buffered the corridors, staring, standing. They were every color she remembered from her childhood: brown, white, that funny gray-blue color. Most had smaller, erect ears, but here and there, she saw lops—big ones with ears that dragged on the ground and small ones that looked like they could fit into the palm of her hand.

Ember didn't feel terrified at all. Slightly nauseous, maybe. Concerned, sure. Mildly allergic, possibly. She kept walking. The walls kept shuddering. A clicking sound whispered in the stagnant air, first a tickle, then a symphony.

Varun yelled and pulled her and Asher to the ground.

The beetles came.

Beetles were white, on the snow side. She'd forgotten that. In the headlamp light, they looked like ghosts. They ran across the ceiling, their toes embedded in the soft clay, their mother-of-pearl wing casings blinding. They stampeded over the trio like a herd of spooked deer, much less graceful and a hell of a lot bigger. Even squatting, antennae still batted at Ember's face. One of the beetles lost its right-side footing and half fell from the ceiling, smacking into Varun's shoulder and pressing him belly-first to the ground. The beetle's abdomen hit Asher in the back of the head, and she disappeared from the periphery of Ember's vision.

"Varun! Asher! Are you—"

Ember didn't see the beetle right in front of her. One of its antennae caught her in the mouth. She grabbed at it, thinking to clasp and push it out of the way before she lost an eye. But her sleeve snagged, for some reason, on the coarse scales of the antenna, and she got pulled up off her feet and dragged several meters back toward the ship before the fabric tore.

Forty-five minutes left. That's to get there *and* back. Please hurry.

"Please hold!" Ember fell to the ground, landing on her backside, vision momentarily spotty. She managed to avoid squishing any rabbits, but two hopped onto her legs the second she settled. They stood on their hind legs and turned their heads, each staring at her with one beady, unblinking eye.

The last beetle passed overhead. The clicking faded to a low purr, then cut off altogether.

Now Ember did feel distinctly like puking. Too much head trauma. She stood as soon as the beetles had passed, bobbing as she got to her feet. One of the rabbits squeaked as it fell off her leg like a castoff Easter toy. She could hear Varun in front of her but not see him, not in the distorted cone of sight she got from her headlamp. He was yelling with excitement and terror.

Ember turned to the right, and Asher came into focus, backed into the clay with a beetle staring at her while it hung upside down from the ceiling. Its thin, reedy tongue stuck out and lapped the air as Asher kept impressive eye contact with its mandibles.

Ember was not jealous of a beetle, she told herself. That would be ridiculous. Also, she was wasting time. Rabbits wove around Asher's legs, occasionally hopping to head height, one smacking her with a forepaw in the cheek. The beetle's tongue with its embedded needle-like spines contacted Asher's forehead, drawing a line of blood across her brown skin.

Asher kept her eyes on the beetle.

Forty-three minutes.

Ember ran.

The rabbits refused to move from her path, and she tripped, catching herself once on the wall, fingers embedding into soft wetness, and then on a cluster of rabbits that acted like a fluffy springboard when she face-planted.

I need you all to hurry up, Tara said into Ember's comm, her voice distracted and irritable.

Ember didn't have the headspace to respond. She pushed up from the floor, jumped the pile of bunny rabbits, and grabbed at the nearest dangling antenna with an "AHHHHH!" She'd grown up reading her father's old collection of Tarzan books from his childhood—ones with the barely clad men and women on the cover and yellowing pages. Since it was never too late to live a childhood dream, Ember brought her legs to her stomach and swung to Asher, ignoring how dangerously close her hip skimmed to the beetle's left mandible.

She planted firmly on a rabbit's foot. The damn thing nipped at her, enough to rip a hole in her pants, so she picked the bunny up and swept it back into its friends. There was precious little space between Asher and the mandibles, yet Ember wedged herself in, definitely not terrified at all of a punctured lung.

"Ta-da!" Ember said as she took Asher's wrist. Dizziness batted at her vision, but it couldn't combat how smug she felt in that moment. "Time to go. Tara's getting bossy."

She ducked under the mandibles, pulling Asher with her. Wet beetle tongue hit one of her arms, which felt like a wet feather dipped in hardening gelatin. A spine sputtered across her sleeve, separating fabric. She swallowed bile.

The beetle chittered, and several fluffy things pawed at her legs, but Ember pulled Asher forward, toward the sound of Varun's voice and away from the beetle. She made a conscious decision to release Asher's wrist and take her hand instead once they cleared the mandibles and broke into a run.

Their boots dug into the soft clay as they ran, Asher's breath visibly hot in the still chilled air of the gallery. The beetle didn't follow. Instead, it continued to skitter toward the ship, down the corridor Ember had just come from. Ember pulled Asher around a corner, and Varun came back into sight.

"Okay?" Ember asked as they slowed.

Asher stared at her, eyes locked, for too long.

Ember stared back. Her stomach dropped or spasmed or whatever it was called when one realized the inevitability of a situation.

Well, fuck.

The rabbits, unfortunately, did not appreciate the moment. They hadn't followed the beetle. Or they had, and there was just an endless supply of them. They batted at Ember's shins as Asher cursed and kicked a leg up, breaking eye contact.

"Damn thing bit me!" she said.

"We should go." Ember inclined her head in the direction she'd last seen Varun. "They're the universe's dinner. Ignore them."

The side of Asher's mouth quirked.

Ember started walking again, tripping immediately over another cluster of rabbits. Asher tried to catch her, but two more rabbits jumped onto her pant leg, and she fell, along with Ember, into the soft clay. Their legs didn't tangle.

They didn't end up anywhere near each other, but that didn't stop both of them from bursting into laughter.

"This is obnoxious," Ember said.

Asher nodded. "Little bit."

The beetles have reached the pod and are attacking. Our track lighting got them upset. I turned it off, but they won't stop. I've moved your time estimate to twenty minutes or less because one of these things is going to impale our hull.

"Damn it, Tara," Ember said in a voice she'd never have used on Taraniel because *that* voice would have earned her several nights on the couch, along with the "donation" of two of her best beakers to Taraniel's lab.

Move, Tara demanded.

Ember turned off the comm.

"Ember?" Varun's voice called from down the tunnel. "You coming?"

"Yeah!" she called back. This time, Ember kicked at the rabbits as she stood. She offered Asher a hand up, and the mella took it.

"That's not Taraniel," Asher whispered as they crept around the bend, kicking out their feet as they did so, scattering the rabbits.

Ember bit into her lower lip. "I know. Sounds like a duck, but doesn't walk like one. But Taraniel gave her a job, and we're not making it easier."

Asher stopped abruptly enough that Ember got pulled back. They continued to hold hands far longer than necessary. Ember turned, careful to keep her headlamp to the right of Asher's face.

"We're going to Old Earth, right?" Asher's voice had the smallest shake to it and way, way too much hope. The other colonists on Ember's ship had had hope, too, and look where that had gotten them. Ember licked her lower lip, trying to avoid the question, and belatedly realized her lip had split. She sucked in a breath at the sudden sting and the inevitability of her answer.

"Yeah. Yeah, I'll get us there. I don't really know how, but after this—" Ember pointed to the ceiling. "Well, it's not like I have a choice."

"You do about some things."

Ember looked up at the ceiling. "Not a good time, Asher." She tugged Asher's hand and looked away, which felt like a blend of emotional avoidance and self-preservation.

Asher started walking again. It took maybe another thirty seconds for Varun to come into view again, leaning against a wall as he waited for them, his face eager.

"There are at least fifteen papers begging to be written about this tunnel alone," he whispered at them in delight. "Pack formation has never been observed like that before."

We don't have time for science, Tara reminded them all through Varun's comm. **I need you back here ASAP. Ember, turn me back on.**

"No," Ember said, leaning into Asher's comm to do so.

Varun rolled his eyes, then nudged the nearest rabbit from his path and continued forward. Ember dropped Asher's hand, risking longer eye contact to bring up just a hint of a smirk, turned, and followed Varun.

We've got one set of mandibles punctured through the hull and stuck. Pui is trying to saw them off, and Kate thinks she can repair the holes so the ship can still go into space, but, Jesus, would you three hurry?

They ran as hard as they could, the rabbits keeping to the edges, only moving if Asher or Varun moved to touch them. The ground began to slope upward, and Ember shivered in the humidity. Her mouth tasted like copper. She must have bitten a cheek too.

I need you back here in about five minutes, Tara said as they entered a gallery with five offshoots. **Or I don't think the pod will be recoverable.**

"That's not very specific," Varun said distractedly as he sniffed the air. He pointed to the far-right tunnel. "To the right and up. We're not far." He leaned into his collar comm. "Would you confirm, please, Dr. Nok?"

"You're off the map," Nok returned, her voice warped into a higher pitch. "And you're near the end of Tara's range as well. She can't spare the power to boost the signal."

"She's still recording though, right?"

"Yeah." Ember heard a clicking in the background before Nok resumed speaking. "We're generating a map as you move, but whatever is ahead, we can't see."

"Well then, is anyone else concerned we haven't seen more beetles?" Ember asked. They entered the wider tunnel, and she moved next to Asher, planning on very firm, resolute eye contact that would stop her stomach somersaults from the whole subtle lesbian-eye-contact flirting thing. When Asher turned to her with a quirked smile and a wink, Ember let out a measured breath.

"Do you like looking for trouble, Dr. Schmitt?" Asher asked.

Ember's legs felt like overcooked spaghetti. Also, she hated spaghetti.

She certainly does like looking *at* it, doesn't she? Can you *please* keep moving?

"If we could avoid a hundred-beetle pileup in the main chamber or wherever we're going, I'd like that," Ember responded. "But I don't...I mean, I'm prepared for a bit of trouble too. Yeah. Earth beetles were always a bit of trouble, too, weren't they? Like, mountain pine beetle."

Asher looked at her like she'd grown another head.

Varun kicked a clump of clay to the left of his foot, completely ignoring the secondary conversation going on around him. "These aren't really coleoptera, Dr. Schmitt," he said. "They're solitary in their tunnels for the most part, except for predation issues or stress, potentially both of which the ship is providing. We're not searching for a queen. They aren't ants. We're looking for...that."

Varun stepped into a large...chamber, for lack of a better word. Clay mounds brushed the ceiling, looking far too close to stalagmites. Ember brought her head close to one, letting the headlamp light the claw mark patterns across the circumference. They were too evenly spaced and too repeating in size and angle to be random, and Ember didn't like where those thoughts led.

"Shit," Asher breathed. "Ember, look."

Ember peeled herself from the stalagmite and focused on the center of the room. A ring of rabbits stood on their hind legs, ears plastered to their backs, hopping in a circle. Their little front paws swished in front of their bodies, casting weird bunny magic and managing to be adorable and creepy all at the same time. Within the bunny circle lay an egg roughly half the size of Ember, white and oval-shaped, and partially submerged in a pile of rabbit droppings. The ends of decayed maple branches poked out from the rabbit shit. *Ember's* maples.

"Dr. Nok!" Varun cried into his collar. "I read your papers on beetle-rabbit interactions and the role of fungi. Theory *confirmed.*" Varun cheered. He dropped to one knee and lightly pumped a fist. A similar whoop came over the comm from Nok. Ember turned her comm back on.

"Dr. Schmitt, did you ever read *my* paper on fungal symbiosis and how the Earth rabbit population pushed radial evolution in the Queen click beetle population?" Varun asked.

"No," Ember said flatly. "Do the bunnies have sharp teeth? And is that a beetle egg? That's all I want to know about right now."

Varun looked back at her with a disappointed scowl. "Of course not. Where would you get that idea from? Rabbits are Earth imports—brought along as food sources and too often smuggled onto planets as pets."

"They're dancing," Asher added. She poked Ember's sleeve, her eyes wide. "You see that too, right?"

"Definitely." Ember turned back to Varun. "I thought we needed pheromones, not baby beetles?"

"Not an egg!" Nok said triumphantly. "That's an immature form of *Mutinus elegans*!"

One of Asher's eyebrows raised.

Ember shrugged. "Different kind of beetle I guess?"

Varun's frown deepened. "No, Dr. Schmitt. It's a variety of stinkhorn fungus. It was grown on a number of colony ships because it is pathogenic to a range of human food pathogens, such as E. coli and salmonella. I have some in my lab. You've made lewd comments on them at least four times."

Ember had zero memory of stinkhorn fungi in Varun's lab, but then again, she'd only the vaguest idea what they looked like.

Nok chuckled. "And we have hypothesized for years that fungi wouldn't stay confined to the lab, no matter how good the protocols and no matter how inhospitable Queen's environment. I've sequenced out fungal remains in beetle carcasses before—"

"As have I," Varun cut in, his words speeding up as Nok's infectious joy spread. "And I sequenced it out to Phallaceae but could never get further—"

"*And now here we are!*" Nok finished up with an audible squeak, and something crashed in the background.

"There's an intellectual orgasm happening right now," Nadia cut in on Asher's comm. "Over a penis-shaped mushroom that smells like ass, by two scientists who I don't think care for penis. Please tell me you're enjoying this as much as

I am, Ember. Also, if you don't get back here soon, we're going to be skewered."

Ember snorted. Phallaceae. Of course. How very appropriate for Queen. To everyone, she said, "Okay, so what do I do? Queen's rabbits worship a stinkhorn fungus. That's lovely. Where are the pheromones? I assumed *on* a beetle but, maybe, no?"

You are supposed to be hurrying,

Varun's eyes lit up, and everyone ignored the TOPA. "So, if we were to wait another few days, the fruiting body would emerge and slowly grow into a phallus shape. There'd be this sticky green slime on it that, on Earth, would attract flies and such, though here, I guess just rabbits. I hypothesize the rabbits have adapted to this since there is little else they can scavenge out here. But this, *this* is what we need." He pointed at the egg, around which the rabbits continued their circular hopping. "The beetle pheromones are minimal—their glands for production are tiny in comparison to their size—and we always hypothesized there was a queen or something akin in the main chamber with more...well, smell. Bigger glands. Something to keep the populations growing and mating. Something we could harvest. But *this*." He reached out toward the egg as if he wanted to caress it but pulled his hand back before his fingertips got anywhere close. "This makes sense too. It makes sense in a very Queen way, in that the glands on the beetles are so small they could very easily be vestigial, and they've used *our* fungi as a work around." And then, in the most generous academic showing Ember had ever seen, he said, eyes alight, "Do you want to tell them, Dr. Nok?"

"Yes! They're using the chemicals from the fungi in a mating ritual, and the bunnies are the farmers."

Varun turned to Ember. Her headlamp reflected off his irises, making him look like a possessed junior professor instead of just an excited one. "Like how leaf cutter ants on Earth farmed fungi to eat, but here, the rabbits grow the fungi on their scat, and there are three organisms involved, not just two!"

Ember really did not care for rabbits, and Varun knew how she felt about fungi. "Can I just go take it, then?" she asked. "So we can get back to the ship?"

"I'd really prefer you didn't." Asher put a warning hand on Ember's arm. Ember didn't shrug it off.

"They're bunnies," she said.

"They're farmers for the beetles," Varun countered. "Primary hypothesis—they farm the fungus and get to eat the raw fruiting form, I bet, in exchange for use of the tunnels. And the beetles use the scented slime for sex attraction rituals. It's *beautiful*."

"Perfection," Nok added from the comm.

Ember heard Nadia fake-gagging in the background. Asher real-time gagged off to her left.

Would someone please get the egg thing? Kate went out to bait the beetles farther down, but I haven't heard from her since, and we've got three still thumping the pod. Maybe Asher? I need you back in two minutes. *Please*.

Ember didn't need a name for that Taraniel tone. Regardless, it had taken them at least fifteen minutes to get out this far. Which was less than they'd originally thought, but there was no way they'd make it back in two. She pushed sideways through the rabbit circle, trying not to touch them. Rabbits bumped into her shins but kept their balance, grunting but not biting. A few short, quick steps and a hop, and she broke through the line and stepped onto a thin maple branch. The wood, deeply decayed, pushed to stringy white under her boot.

Ember shuddered at the texture, like stale mashed potatoes. Her next step put her in firm-but-not-hard rabbit droppings, which mercifully, didn't have an odor. Here, at least, she was close enough to reach for the egg. She squatted, careful to keep her ass from touching shit, extended her arm, and prodded the egg with her middle finger.

It felt more like a soft-boiled egg after the shell had been removed. She grimaced at the texture. She slid her hand to the base, searching for a way to lift it when she heard a chorus of *thump thump thump.*

"Ember," Asher called out.

"Huh?" Ember pulled her hand away. The rabbits had stopped their dance and were sitting on their haunches, drumming a back leg. Again, their heads turned, each of them glaring at her with just one eye.

She definitely hated rabbits as much as she hated fungi.

"Do we need the whole thing?" she asked over the low vibration wobbling up from the ground. "It's about the size of my torso, and I'm not sure I can carry it alone." Ember decided to ignore the bunnies and put a hand on either side of the egg, right at the base, and tried to pull up.

The egg remained firmly attached to the ground.

A rabbit lunged at her ankle and growled. Ember mimed kicking it, and it scuttled back, ears slicked to its sides. Another rabbit on the opposite side did the same thing. Ember ignored it.

"The whole thing," Varun said.

Ember looked at him over her shoulder. He held a small recording device, the grin on his face only worn by scientists sure they were about to get a building named after them.

"We need to hurry, Ember," Asher added. "Please."

"Ugh. Fine."

Ember took another step into the rabbit droppings, leaned into the white mass, and pulled up. She inserted her fingernails into the soft, slippery flesh and jiggled the egg a few times, but it held fast to the ground. Frowning, she got down onto her knees and dug into the shit and maples, breaking the mycelium apart that connected it together. Detritus (that was a nice name for it, sure) built up under her fingernails, and the smell of rotten apples filled the air. The mycelium slid through her fingers as she separated it, flopping onto the rabbit droppings and spraying green, sticky water onto her face and shirt.

Gross. Mycology was so, so gross.

She pushed the egg over, finally, with a low buzz that sounded too much like a broken zipper. It fell to its side, and Ember wrapped her arms around it, pulled it into her chest, and prepared to stand.

The bunnies attacked.

They launched at Ember, nails digging in through the fabric of her shirt and pants, back feet raking across her skin. They grunted and bit at her in quick, successive jabs, plucking the fabric and opening tiny holes. A set of very flat teeth found the skin at her side and clamped down, pulling as the rabbit backed away.

"Ahh!" Ember yelled. She kept her arms around the egg, stood with the thing balanced on her hip, and tried to jiggle the rabbits off. They weren't breaking skin—thank the sand dunes for small favors and lack of canine teeth—but it still hurt and betrayed pretty much every childhood memory she had of her friend's pet rabbit, Buttons.

"Damn it." Asher pulled balls of fluff from Ember's pants and the persistent hanger-on from her shirt. They rebound back, smacking into her legs, grunting, tearing at her socks and ankles.

I need you here now! Tara yelled through all comms simultaneously.

"Run!" Asher told Ember, giving her back a push. "To the ship."

"I can't outrun rabbits!" But Ember broke into a run, anyway, because anything was better than being slowly nipped to death. Asher flanked her, pushing the egg back into Ember's arms every time it threatened to slip.

"Taraniel?" Varun put the recorder back into his pocket, his voice maddeningly calm as he ran behind her. Ember was ready to rethink their friendship on the spot, but hearing someone else say her wife's name, in conjunction with the rabbit hopping up to head height to growl at her, kept her quiet. "Do you have an audio database?"

It's Tara, and, yes, I do.

"Would you please play a wolf howl?"

The long, throaty sound of a wolf played at Ember's hip. It raised the hair on her arm. though she'd heard plenty of the same when camping with her family on Presque Isle, Michigan, as a kid. Tara chased that sound with the screech of a hawk, upping the volume until the call rebounded through the tunnel.

The rabbits fled, bolting in every direction, away from Ember. A few burrowed down into the clay but most scattered. A cluster of seven, however—Ember thought they might be the group that had been dancing—backed away but watched her, noses twitching, eyes wide, tails erect.

Varun called out a directional change. Tara suggested a different route. Varun consented.

Ember kept running. The rabbits disappeared except for the group just ahead, watching and wary.

And then, of course, the beetles came back.

Ember heard them before she saw them. A discordant clicking vibrated the walls of the tunnel, and claws clicked on partially-dry clay. She wormed her fingers deeper into the mycelium, and wetness leaked down her arms.

"I think I broke something," she said as Asher pushed her into the wall just as the first beetle barreled toward them.

In the poor, directional light of their headlamps, it looked yellow, its antennae casting shadow puppets on the clay walls. Mandibles opened, and Ember vaguely heard Tara saying something through Asher's comm. Asher's fingers scratched at her arms as she pressed into the egg, reaching for Ember. Ember's back pushed into the clay. Humidity and sweat drenched Ember's shirt, as did the tacky liquid bleeding onto her from the fungus egg.

Ember took a moment to register that Asher's breath no longer smelled like peanuts, that the freckles across her nose looked like the constellation Gemini before silence snapped her back to the present.

The beetle had stopped. A thin tongue flicked from its mouth and lapped the air. It'd been almost comical when it was happening to Asher. Now, with a fungus bleeding all over Ember, it was wet, and gross, and the mandibles looked ten times sharper.

"Please tell me I don't smell like food," Ember hissed at Varun.

"No. You smell like courtship. The beetles don't eat fungi; they eat... We aren't sure. But not fungi. There weren't any fungi before humans colonized Queen."

The beetle let out a long, high-pitched click, and its tongue flicked Ember's left arm. The fabric tore, and wetness ran down her arm.

"Varun!"

"Ride it." Asher pushed to the side, her back now against the wall as well, her brow furrowed. "We don't have time to run. Give it the egg; then get on its back and ride the thing."

Ember turned to Asher, incredulous.

Asher pushed her shoulder, forcing Ember to take an unbalanced step forward. The egg pitched forward from Ember's arms. The beetle caught it on top of its mandibles, wrapping and cradling with its tongue. It skittered back, giving Ember enough room to breathe and panic.

The beetle stared at Ember. She glared back, green slime dripping from her arms and onto her boots. She ran a hand down her right arm, trying to flick the slime away, but when she pulled her hand off, the line of fungus goop smacked the beetle right between the antennae. The line of slime hung in the air for a moment before snapping in half, punching Ember in the face with the smell of rot as it did so.

"Stop playing," Asher said. "Put your feet and hands in the joints where the leg parts meet to step up. There's a depression between the head and the thorax where you can sit, or the thorax and abdomen. It's easiest, without a harness, to lock your heels behind the hard outer wing plate and pray." Asher cupped her hands and knelt. "Now. Don't overthink it."

Ember managed a small step forward. The beetle cocked its head at her like a curious bunny. A curious bunny with a face full of fungus slime.

"Go on," Asher said under her breath as she smirked. "Impress me. It's not going to buck you or anything. The egg is too precious. Besides, I'll bet you got enough fungus juice on you that it thinks you're just another egg."

"That is possible," Varun added.

Please do *not* ride the beetle, Ember, Taraniel said in her do-not-argue-with-me voice.

Ember had never responded super well to that voice. She stepped into Asher's hands and let herself be buoyed onto the beetle's back. Sliding her fingers over the striated chitin, she found a joint and gripped. The remaining fungus slime on her arms and hands absorbed into the beetle's exoskeleton, which helped with her grip. Asher pushed on one of Ember's heels, and she used the leverage to settle into the thorax depression, hooking the heels of her boots and skirting her fingers just under the head plate.

"Should it have been that easy?" Ember called down to Asher and Varun. "I'm not even slimy anymore except for a patch near my right elbow. My clothes are still soaked though."

Hurry, Tara pleaded.

"Don't ask stupid questions," Asher called back up with a wink.

The beetle's antennae turned to her. Ember tried to flatten herself into the shell, but the antennae followed, patting her as though she were a kid it was trying to put to sleep.

"What are you two going to do?" she asked as the beetle clicks turned into more of a hum. The walls seemed to be humming in response, which Ember did not care for. She turned and looked down the tunnel, casting her headlamp in a wide arc.

She saw only clay. No reflecting rabbit eyes.

The hum became a rumble. Ember's stomach flipped.

"We'll follow," Varun said, his voice clipped. "Get back to the ship. We can figure out how to get the egg away then. You'd better go."

"Kate!"

Ember couldn't see the mella, but Asher ran down another corridor as a chorus of click beetles emerged from the darkness in front of them. They came on the ground this time, two abreast, clicking wildly, their tongues flicking out like snakes.

"Run!" Ember yelled down at Varun. "Follow Asher." She tried to kick her heels into the beetle as she would a horse, but it still didn't move. Beetles swarmed around them, not touching her beetle but streaming into the tunnel Varun and Asher had just disappeared into. "They're coming!" Ember yelled, and into her collar, said, "If that's the tunnel that goes back, be ready, Tara."

***Please* get off that beetle!**

"Check your logic. Better than being on the ground." Ember clicked off her collar comm again. The slime on her elbow felt thicker now, probably because it was drying. She flung her arm right, sending a mess of the wet stuff off and down into the rabbit-less corridor.

Amazingly, improbably, and disgustingly, the beetle turned. It climbed halfway up the wall, toes digging into the clay, nearly dislodging her before it came back down to face the opposite direction. It let out a short bleep of a click before breaking into the lopsided run that made the things look so damn ridiculous in the sand. Any hope of directing the beetle left in that moment. Ember gripped and cursed as it wove through the maze of tunnels, spewing red clay and bunnies in its wake.

She probably shouldn't have turned the comm off, but there was no way she could free a hand to turn it back on now. The only thing Ember could do was hold on and not look down as they moved...up. Her ears popped, and every time she lifted her head from its smushed position against the beetle head, she saw a significant incline. The beetle's toes sank deeper into the clay as they progressed, the sounds turning from scratching to thudding until they were climbing instead of running. Ember's legs slipped from the thorax cliff and slid, her fingers the only thing anchoring her to the beetle. Her head snapped right, and her chin hit the comm button, thank god.

"Tara," she wheezed through the adrenaline rush. The beetle stopped clicking as the wall turned convex. Ember hung like a little kid on a chin-up bar. She would not look down. Memories of penny drops and broken wrists flitted across her mind.

You...colony...back at the pod. Heat...air...here. Tara's voice, distorted and stretched from distance, was further distorted by the raucous noise of beetle toes in clay and Ember's own labored breathing.

"I'm getting there as fast as I can!" The wall flattened, and Ember managed to swing one leg back under the wing case. She didn't have enough upper body strength to pull herself further, and when she tried to flatten back onto the beetle's back, she hit her headlamp. The elastic contracted from her head, and the whole thing fell off and down, taking way too long before it hit the tunnel floor below.

Sight was overrated, Ember decided. Heights and giant beetles were a lot less terrifying if you couldn't see.

Sounds, however, sounds were critical. Ember kept her forehead pressed to the beetle as the incline eased. In the distance, more clicking and thumping of rabbit feet echoed through the tunnel. Her beetle resumed its own weird noises as the temperature and humidity started to drop. A slow breeze blew across her skin, picking through the small tears in her clothes. Beetles—three? twenty?—joined them, climbing up the walls in a tightly packed formation—not visible, but clearly there in the tickling brushes of other antennae on her arms and legs.

The beetles continued climbing up toward the surface.

The clicking became deafening.

The incline eased. Her beetle stopped, and Ember scrambled her right leg back under the thorax. She'd just found a place to hook her ankle around when her beetle reared. As she slid halfway under the wing casing, the beetle's head smashed into the ceiling above them. Snow and clay rained down; then there was light—pale, diffuse, marginal light as they burst from the gallery and into the freezing morning.

I can see you! Thirty-six meters up, on a small ledge. Nice work.

"I haven't done shit," Ember muttered.

Beetles streamed past her, climbing down the gallery walls and swarming the snow. The thick lines made it impossible to count how many there were, their exoskeletons the color of cooked white eggshells blending into the snow. The rabbits, though, those Ember could see clearly as they streamed from below ground.

There was the pod, nestled into its depression and half-covered in snow. It wasn't far, but the minimal sunlight cast a sickening orange glow on the snow that turned her stomach more than the beetle ride had. Above, the governmental flyer hovered, its tip rotating from the pod to the beetles, probably just as terrified as they were. The flyer could only see the top of their pod, the rest of it well meshed into the broken ground.

"Dr. Schmitt?" Nok's voice came tentatively over the comm. "I'd suggest you move."

"Why? What—"

The snow was decayed orange peel one minute and the color of old blood the next. Hundreds of beetles, thousands of beetles, snow side *and* sand side, pushed from the gallery walls and covered the landscape. More rabbits followed, hopping between toes and skittering legs, some of them riding the beetles in the most bizarre rodeo. Ember's feet got pushed from their catchment as her beetle's wings unfolded, and the damn thing took flight, launching itself from the ledge and into the air with far more grace than she would have expected.

"I didn't know they flew!" she yelled. "Tara, what the hell?"

"This is Varun," the comm said. "Can you get the beetle to the flyer?"

The wind stung Ember's eyes, and she blinked back half-frozen tears. "Damn it, Varun. Does any part of what is happening look like I am in control?"

"Yes, okay, hold on." The comm clicked off. The beetle dove, and Ember yelled as she slid too far forward, her fingers unable to hold. A blinking yellow light caught her eyes from below. They were angling toward the downed pod which had all its lights on—track lighting, flood lights, emergency chasers—all blinking in tandem in a repeating pattern.

All across the ground, beetle butts lit up yellow in response. They were supposed to be...what color? Blue? Ember tried to protect her face from the wind. White?

The pattern morphed, but Ember didn't have time to parse it. The ground beetles took flight, joining her in the sky in a flock.

Flock? Swarm? Warren? Did it matter?

"What the hell did you tell them, Varun?" Ember screamed into the frozen air, her fingers increasingly numb.

"That you're the best mate option," Varun responded. "That is Dr. Nok's and my hypothesis." His voice hit the wrong octave, and Ember's stomach sank. "If you can get to the flyer, that would be ideal. Although, if you fly another five minutes, we could record a few more formations and get another paper."

"Fly and do *what*?"

"Get out of the sky, Ember," Nadia yelled. "Tara's going to have a ship-heart attack, and so am I."

"I'm open to suggestions!" Ember yelled back.

No one responded.

Well, fine. This time, when her beetle took another dive, Ember loosened cold fingers and let herself slide forward. Her feet flipped in front, and she flipped too. She then grabbed the underside of the head as her feet dangled in the beetle's eyes. It pitched left, and she slid with it, hands skimming the chitin, the sharp edge separating her skin. She kicked her legs, trying to find purchase. The exoskeleton was too slick, however, despite its mild striations. She kicked again, tried to dig her heel in, and screamed a few times for good measure. The beetle turned upside down and then flew in circles, confused, angry, or simply trying to dislodge her; she couldn't tell.

She found purchase, finally, as a booted toe struck the soft mycelium of the fungal egg and buried inside.

The beetle screamed. Beetles were not supposed to scream. Ember lost her grip and slid down, crashing, sinking into the mycelial egg, surrounded by a rotten apple smell laced with the distinct odor of bread mold. She hit a solid, cylindrical thing—probably the forming mushroom—and wrapped herself around it, spitting tacky fluid from her mouth. It was a truly fantastic coincidence that she'd already lost her headlamp.

"Ember?" Asher's voice chirped, muted, through the comm. "You're coming up on the colony flyer now. Any chance you could get the beetles to go down a bit? Maybe attack?"

Ember kicked at the white and green around her. "Tell me when we're just above. I'll see what I can do."

I don't like the tone in your voice. That's your "don't ask me too many questions because you won't like the answer" voice.

"So, don't ask any questions." Ember raked her broken, gunked fingernails at the bottom of the egg. Mycelium peeled and separated. Lights flickered among the mesh. In terms of stupid things she'd done in her life, this ranked equal to the time she and Taraniel had snuck out of the colony dome and had very loud sex in the entry to an abandoned beetle gallery. She hadn't seen any rabbits then, but that didn't mean they weren't there.

That was a good memory. It was good to die with a good memory.

"Now!" Asher said.

Ember kicked her heel into the brightest, thinnest spot at the base of the egg, and fell.

Chapter Thirteen

Ember

Ember hit the windshield of the colony flyer in a belly flop, her chin rebounding off the sapphire and smacking into her shoulder. Her neck popped. Her comm cracked and splintered apart, and a piece of plastic definitely went up her nose. Warmth spread under her skin as she coughed—the feeling of a burst vein—but the warmth felt delicious against the frigid air and the ice on the flyer's windshield.

It took the flyer pilot or whomever was on the other side of the windshield a moment longer than Ember to realize what had happened. Ember managed to turn enough to see through the sapphire to the wide-eyed, gape-mouthed woman in a New Earth uniform before the flyer canted in the air and its thrusters surged, sending the ship forward and toward the birthing sunset.

Ember groaned as she slid down the windshield, the fungus slime hardening and freezing in the air. It gave mild traction to her fingers that wasn't nearly enough to counter the air that hit her as the flyer accelerated.

The initial thrust molded her farther into the windshield. The pilot wised up far faster than Ember would have liked, turning the flyer, then flipping it over. Ember's fingers popped off, and she slicked off the windshield into a complete, terrifying free fall just as her beetle rammed the flyer in the exact place Ember's body had just been plastered.

Icy wind tore at her clothes and ripped through the rabbit tears in the fabric, stripping heat from her body. For a minute, everything looked gray and red; then Ember squeezed her eyes shut and told herself to not panic, to imagine falling into a bath of hot chocolate, or a candy floss cloud, or anything other than snow and rabbits because she was *definitely* going to die, but at least there'd be Taraniel on the other end.

A deafening *crack* sounded from above. Ember let the wind peel her eyelids back just as her beetle contacted the flyer two more times, leaving two sizable dents, before the flyer righted and changed course.

Another beetle flew past, catching the side of her shirt and turning her partially over. She made the mistake of turning her focus to the oncoming ground, neck muscles spasming and a fresh wave of warmth exploding under her skin. Snow and bunnies came increasingly into focus, and Varun's mustache. Fuck.

Ember screamed, finally. It seemed an appropriate time. Then the most disgusting strip of fleshy blue went around her waist and thighs and yanked her *up*.

Beetle tongue. Of course.

The tongue's spiny barbs slid into clothes and skin and, yes, held her in place but also felt like getting a tattoo while drunk. Her hips ached from the force stopping her descent, and red bloomed, slowly, in a belt around her midsection and a halo around her upper thighs.

She'd stopped descending but spun wildly, the horizon looping around her head as beetle saliva and fungus blood and *her* blood mixed and froze in the cold air. She puked, maybe more than once. The beetle whipped her back and forth on her blue tether like a doggy chew toy as short, clear little hair-barbs pushed deeper into her skin.

She puked again.

They didn't have enough antiseptic for this, and Nadia would kill her if she died.

Ember told herself to stop puking, which her body agreed with. She closed her eyes and waited for the next direction change. Then, using her inertia, she flipped up, grabbed the tongue with her hands, impaling them on spikes, and managed a semi-sitting position.

"Cut it out!" she yelled at the beetle. Hand skin was way too sensitive to have twenty or so needles embedded in it, but if she let her eyes water, she'd cry snowflakes. "I said stop!"

Ember flicked one of her goopy boots at a mandible. A half-congealed slick of fungus slop hit the beetle's...eye? Maybe? Whatever it was, the thing stopped clicking, which Ember hadn't realized it'd been doing. Hearing loss. What was hearing loss on top of mass impalement, really?

Ember's spinning slowed to mild rotation. She stared at her beetle, took in the little black dot on its right mandible, the near-iridescent shine to its exoskeleton. In the sunset, it reflected the pink of a seashell. Its wings, now that she could see them properly, shone in a rainbow of refracted light as they beat the air. Its eyes looked way more human than insect as it glared at her with barely tempered irritation. That was fair. She'd broken its sex toy. Hopefully, she wasn't the replacement.

The beetle seemed content to hover, wings thrumming like an Old Earth hummingbird, Ember dangling and dripping blood onto the snow at least ten meters below. Every part of her hurt, including her heart as she thought about Taraniel and how much fun she'd have had hearing about Ember Tarzan-ing in to save the damsel and riding a giant beetle to almost-certain death. Death was stupid, she decided as she slowly rotated in the breeze. Stupid and cold.

Clicking sounded off to Ember's right. She craned her neck and reclined halfway back—god, the tongue spines pulled from her skin, sliding seamlessly out and sliding back in again with the subtlest pressure—until she could track the other beetles. There were four of them, flying in a tight swarm shaped like a distorted diamond. They'd trapped the presidium flyer in the center. It shot at them, first with a projectile weapon Ember didn't recognize. When the beetles proved too agile for that, the flyer tried to slam into their bodies.

Ember had a moment to contemplate formation mechanics in giant insects before the four beetles closed the space between them and, in tandem, attacked the flyer. One grasped the back end, the thrusters, with its mandibles. Metal crunched. Beetle butts glowed a weird, diffuse blue, and the three others hooked their toes into the ship. The first beetle let go, and the conglomerate spiraled toward the ground, thrusters whining and the people inside no doubt screaming.

Ember was also screaming, she realized. She shut her mouth.

The entire thing was over way too fast. Her beetle began descending right as the ship hit snow. Ember managed to turn her head before the crash, but she still heard the cry of metal folding on ice and the triumphant clicking of beetles. The rabbits, too, joined in, thousands of furry feet beating the ice in long trills that distorted in the wind. It sounded like a bone saw, which Ember had used once in an undergrad anatomy lab. It sounded like the plunge of a drill bit into a hollow door. She'd flirted with carpentry one summer to help pay rent.

It sounded like the end of her and Nadia's and Varun's academic careers, their labs dissected and given to research scientists and adjuncts out of spite and bitterness.

Ember pressed fingertips into the blue tongue, the sharp pain of the spines pushing into bone and clearing her head. The ground got progressively closer. First, she could only make out the top of the mella pod, then the furrows in Asher's forehead. Taraniel had had those same furrows. Ember couldn't feel her own face, she realized as her ass hit snow when the beetle landed. She couldn't feel her fingers, either, despite their being impaled.

The beetle's ass turned off. The tongue unwound, and Ember screamed again because the spines were not coming out straight, and having that many tiny spines pulled from your body, especially while you were lying on half of them, *fucking hurt.*

By the time the tongue had finished respooling, Ember had whole-body shivers and had moved beyond sticky into drenched. She curled into a fetal position in the reddening snow, shaking, trying to breathe down into her torso instead of the winter air.

"Flyer down," she managed between chattering teeth as the crunching of footsteps approached. The blood from her fingers was going to clot them to her arms as she hugged herself, and she'd have to break the scabs to move, but moving seemed like a lot of effort anyhow. Besides, she didn't know if anyone could hear her, especially with Tara's comm cracked to hell. Didn't matter. "Beetles secured. Not bad for an assistant professor. I deserve one of Varun's fleakers because then I can lord it over Nadia from now until eternity."

The footsteps came faster, seeming to run with as much caution as they could muster. Ember could only shiver in response.

"Jesus, how are you alive?"

A metallic blanket fell over her torso. Asher tucked it around her sides and legs, cocooning Ember, before shoving her arms under and lifting her. Nok grabbed her legs. Ember lurched into the air and ground her teeth together, unreasonably concerned about Asher seeing her half-frozen—a half-frozen brain went to really weird places—and let the two carry her to the pod.

The blanket worked quickly. Or her blood was flowing faster. As she warmed and the feeling came back in her fingers, Ember stopped worrying about the awkward carry and what Asher's sweat smelled like (unexpectedly fruity, or maybe that was just her). The remaining beetle in the sky landed, and the rabbits—*god*, there were so many rabbits—hopped alongside them. One of them jumped up on her chest, and Ember *oofed* as it walked over her collarbone and peered at her, its nose wiggling like a cartoon bomb about to detonate.

They reached the edge of the gallery hole, and Ember got set, almost gently, on the ground. The rabbit did not get up.

Nok tucked the blanket back around her legs and mouthed *you're a badass*. Coming from a scientist's mouth, combined with the blood loss, it was hilarious. But Ember suspected being a badass would not keep the colonists from giving her a giant caterpillar brow and drooping mustache when her face eventually joined the rest of the mella on the wanted posters.

"I want a shower," Ember groaned. She wrestled her way out of the blanket, tossing the rabbit off as she did so. It hopped right back on. With the stiffness around her midsection, she hoped at least some of the punctures had clotted. It wasn't as if any of them were that large. "And a massage. And a beer."

"One of those things exists on Queen, and we can discuss it later." Asher knelt next to her. "You're a mess. Can you walk at all?"

"Yes. Probably." Ember sat up. The rabbit hopped right back onto her lap and stood on its hind legs, bringing its nose up to hers and tickling her face with its long whiskers. From the corner of her eye, she saw a handful of other rabbits forming another circle around her.

Ember rolled her head back onto her shoulders, emitting more popping noises, and looked up at Asher and Nok. Both grimaced. The flyer had gone down, and there'd been a New Earth pilot in it. Someone was dead, damn it. They were eventually going to have to talk about that.

"What now? Rub myself all over our pod so the beetles want to fuck it and not me?" Ember asked. "I smell like never-ending autumn in a fruit orchard."

"Unless you want to ride on the windshield the whole way home," Asher returned evenly. "Though, without heat, I don't think it'd be that much colder. The only system left up is Tara, who has a separate power supply, which she can reroute to other systems. I don't think that's wise though. Even she won't last the night. We have plenty of emergency blankets in the back, so if we all take a few, we should survive the trip back, assuming the beetles assist."

"That wouldn't work." Varun popped up from the side of the crater and offered Ember a hand. She took it, scattering indignant rabbits around her, and ground her teeth as his grip popped soft scabs off her palm. "Not the blanket part, the ship part. The most ideal scenario was bringing the egg inside and using the exterior lighting to functionally hold it hostage until we got back to the colony or the mella encampment. Now—" He eyed Ember's soaked clothing, green from fungus slime, red from her blood. "—I'm not certain what to do."

Ember started to shiver again. At a loud *thump*, she turned just in time to look a rabbit in the eye before it fell back to the ground. She no longer regretted every meal of rabbit stew she'd had in the dome. "Why do they keep doing that?"

"You smell like fungus," Varun answered. Nok nodded in agreement. "Earth rabbits have one job here on Queen, and you killed theirs. Chances are they don't want to be kicked from their warren."

Ember wrapped the blanket tighter and peered over the ledge at the battered pod below. Even if the heat wasn't working, it *had* to be warmer than this. "Can we please go inside the ship and talk about this? It's fucking freezing out here. At least in there, we don't have the wind."

"We can certainly try." Varun sat and slipped down into the hole the pod had made. He landed on the roof, boots making a hollow thudding noise, then slid the rest of the way. The hatch to the ship opened, and a blast of warm air drifted up, turning Ember's clothes stickier. Nok followed him and disappeared into the ship.

"Need some help?" Asher inclined her head at the pod. "Your muscles okay to jump? The crash wasn't too long ago. Your equilibrium is probably still wonky."

What was it called when one part of the brain basically stopped working and the part that took over was clearly drunk?

The shaking, Ember realized, wasn't entirely from the cold. Her muscles screamed with tears, her head pounded, and her skin itched. Her hands looked red and puffy, and she vaguely remembered being told as a kid that she had a few fungi allergies.

"Yes, that would be useful," she said.

Asher's smile looked too much like triumph.

Ember rolled her eyes and harrumphed onto the snow. Asher wrapped her arms under Ember's armpits again, and Ember straightened her body and slid to the side of opening. Instead of landing like Varun, her feet hit the side of the ship, slipped out from under her, and she streaked on her belly down the height of the pod, landing in a clump on the hatch door.

"Shit. Sorry!" Asher called from above. "You okay?"

"Still smooth I see," Nadia called from the inside.

Pui and Nok came out and got Ember to her feet, then led her inside and onto one of the cockpit chairs. She made a squelching sound when she sat and hunched her shoulders, trying not to think about fungus, and rotting apples, and how she was at the center of a disgusting Venn diagram of the two.

"Do we have spare clothes in here?" Ember asked. She shifted onto her left hip, the plastic underneath her dragging her shirt and making a sound far too close to a bodily function. "Also, Pui, I'd like that last bottle of antiseptic."

Pui appeared at her side, brown plastic bottle stamped DETTOL in one hand, a wad of cloth in the other. "Please take off your clothes. The sooner we get you cleaned, the sooner you get warm. I can work fast."

Ember pulled herself from the chair and grabbed her right sleeve halfheartedly. It felt like the weight of the sunset was in her eyelids. She just wanted to sleep.

"At least you're making 'scents' after that fall." Nadia grinned at her from her chair, an emergency blanket tucked tightly up to her chin. Her face looked ashen gray. Ember's stomach dropped. She pulled her shirt off her head, stood, and dropped her pants, cursing as the scabs stuck to the fabric.

"What happened?" Ember asked once she'd managed to stop shaking.

Nadia shrugged, her grin drooping. "Beetles. Mella. Your wife."

Pui started dabbing with antiseptic, and that pain was worse than being stabbed in the first place.

"I'm ready to go back to the sun side any time," Ember muttered as Pui circled a particularly angry puncture wound on her left hipbone.

Kate came around from behind Ember's chair, a stack of cloth in her arms. "Here. We've plenty more in the back. And Nadia is as stable as we can make her. I agree we need to get back to the equator. The *good* equator. Then we need to talk. This ship is toast. I've repaired what I can, but no way it can go into space. I'm good, but I'm not *that* good."

Which would explain why the inside of the ship smelled like burnt metal in addition to sweaty bodies.

"You need to take off your underwear," Pui prodded, sounding like every ounce of joy had been leached from her insides.

Ember's eyes went to Asher. The mella's jaw was set, her eyes narrow as if she'd just been told her birthday party had been cancelled. Relief and sadness tumbled through Ember.

"Tara's okay though?" she asked.

Everyone very politely turned around as the hatch door closed. Just before it clicked shut, a handful of rabbits—eight, maybe—wedged through the fist-sized crack as if every bone in their tiny bodies were made from mayonnaise.

I'm stable, and I'm a TOPA derivative. I can be moved easily to another ship. For now, I'll move my attention to the exterior scanners. Tara added softly, **I'm glad you're okay, Ember.**

"How is she okay?" Nadia whispered, loud enough for Ember to hear.

The rabbits, once again, circled Ember.

She agreed. Tara's assessment didn't seem accurate at all. Still, as long as the bunnies didn't grow fangs or start licking her, she was probably fine.

Ember pushed her underwear down, and Pui finished swabbing in short order, which was good because her shivers had turned quickly to whole-body shakes. Once she got the go-ahead, Ember redressed as quickly as she could. She didn't care at all for the stonewashed jeans, but the "Earth First. We'll Log the Other Planets Later" T-shirt fit and felt like a decent enough statement for her mood.

She kicked the wet clothing to the hatch. The rabbits collectively tracked the movement, ears turning in the direction of the clothes. Two of them hopped to the pile, sniffed it, and turned back to the others, noses wiggling.

Ember collapsed back into her chair, one eye still on Nadia and her ashen face. "Okay, now I smell maybe 70 percent less like fungus. Varun, can we do something useful with the clothes? Do you know the light code for 'we'll wring the scent out so you can have a mating orgy if you drag us back to the colony first'?"

"I can get tangentially close to that, but I don't know if the clothes alone would do it."

"We could get close," Nok offered, stepping up to Varun with renewed confidence. "I have ideas. Also, Dr. Sinha, you're the new colony entomologist, correct?"

Varun gave a long nod.

Nok huffed a laugh. "I was the last one. Defected two years into the job because the pay sucked and the mella stole my glassware shipment. At that point, I cared more about the round-bottom flasks and my new rotovap than I did the colony."

Varun stuck his tongue into his cheek, an expression Ember knew from late-night Monopoly tournaments. "I dislike the idea of defection, and yet, here I am. I'm interested in hearing your ideas; however, I think we should be sure to plan thoroughly before we rise to action."

Ooh, a thinly veiled slight.

Nadia chortled, and Ember wrinkled her nose. Nok assessed Varun, and Varun assessed Nok, and the rest of the mella looked exceedingly bored.

"Well, can we at least try *something*?" Ember prompted when the conversation stalled. "And you two can compare pinned collections later?"

"I agree," Kate said from the storage room behind the cockpit. She turned around, also looking pale, her lips a little too red. All the snark and fight had bled from her body as she collapsed limply into a chair, a slight tremble to her hands. She didn't seem to have any cuts or bruising, but if Kate had been beetle bait, well, Ember knew how that felt.

"Given how much is still on you, I suggest you go out there and offer the clothing to them," Pui said with a yawn that Ember definitely felt. "Your beetle didn't want to kill you." She paused. "You know, I was in the astronomy complex before the presidium decided it needed to be an independent hydrology building and sold all the telescopes worth anything to Europa. My minor was in agriculture though. For my last two years at the colony, before I defected, I built drought-resistant wheat from the genes up." She shoved the Dettol and rags into a hidden compartment behind her head, then turned back to stare pointedly at Ember. "Guess how many of my plants are still here on Queen?"

Ember didn't have to guess, so she stayed silent.

"If it matters, I'm a computer scientist," Kate called from the back room, her voice shaking. "Double major in electrical engineering, PhD in biomaterials. I altered your TOPA and envirosuit. Also—" Kate took a deep breath, and a hint of color returned to her pale cheeks. "I'm glad your beetle didn't kill you. Cool flying, even if you did end up covered in fungus."

Ember forced a laugh. "I'd prefer it didn't mate with me either."

"Prude," Nadia retorted, her eyes full of mischief. She almost didn't resemble a revitalized corpse.

Could we send the rabbits out with it? Tara's voice sounded tired. Ais didn't get tired, which meant Tara was exasperated or worried, both of which meant an argument loomed.

"We don't entirely understand the rabbit role in the pheromone process." Varun spoke to the ceiling. "With that said, it's no worse than any other idea, especially if we pair it with my theory on the role of light in Queen beetle communications. The rabbits should follow the clothes, and that should get the beetles interested. Following that success, if we can find the right sequence of colors—" His voice faltered. "—we might get out of here."

It actually sounded like a great idea. Like one of the best ideas in the world, really, because it got the damn rabbits off the ship. Ember wasn't sure how much more aggressive nose wiggling she could take. She could still feel their flat little teeth on her ankles and sharp claws digging into her back. Her cuts stung, but the blanket had warmed her up enough to be irrational.

"Wonderful," she said. "Tara, open the hatch, would you?"

There was a long pause in which Ember felt certain Tara and Asher had managed telepathy. Asher glared at an overhead camera, and it glared back, as much as an inanimate piece of plastic could. Ember pushed the blanket off, stood, and broke through the ring of rabbits. She grabbed her clothes—shirt, pants, socks, and underwear. Asher muttered, the hatch opened, and Ember tossed the clothes high and over her shoulder. They landed on an awkward clump on top of the pod and promptly froze to the exterior, the fungus goop morphed to a disgusting glue in the frigid wind.

Three rabbits hopped first to the edge of the hole the ship sat in, then launched themselves at the pod. Two made it, scrambling with sharp little claws until they slid into the frozen clothing pile and burrowed inside.

Rabbits were in her underwear. Ember needed to not contemplate that.

"Tara, I'm going to input a flashing sequence for your main lighting," Varun said. "Nok, you have any input?"

"Yes. Here, let me show you." Nok joined Varun at the console, and the two retreated into conspiring whispers.

I'm ready when Ember is.

Ember stood at the apex of the hatch ramp and watched the beetle she'd ridden crawl down the side of the earth until it came up parallel with the flyer. The wind outside further chilled the air in her nose, and she grabbed her emergency blanket and wrapped it around her shoulders like a cape. Beetles lined the upper ridge, some crawling on top of others, their little toes scrabbling to find purchase on the striated exoskeletons of their neighbors. The remaining rabbits hopped, all at exactly the same time, to her beetle. Her beetle scuttled to the pod, touched an antenna to the pile of clothes/bunnies, and lit its abdomen light yellow, like a damn lightning bug.

The rest of the beetles lit up the same color.

"Now, please," Varun said.

The white flood light on the front of the pod turned off. The track lighting around the ship circumference flashed green, then sputtered into a repeating sequence, bright enough that Ember had to shut her eyes

"Can we harness one now or something?" she asked as lights flashed through her closed eyelids.

No one responded, but she heard the sound of toes scraping clay. Fur brushed past her ankle. She opened her eyes just as Tara called **Ember!** And her beetle scuttled down the hole, scattered a handful of rabbits, and clicked its way to the base of the ramp.

Shit. Shit shit shit. Ember tried to back into the pod but came up against another body. Nok's hand fell on her shoulder, and she turned, giving the woman an incredulous look.

"Move!" Ember hissed.

"Badass," Nok whispered.

Antennae fell on Ember's shoulders, one on each side, and Nok's hand fell away.

"Varun needs you to stay put," she said.

"Tell Varun," Ember said in a low voice, when she really just wanted to yell that Varun needed to go fuck himself, "that I'd like to get back on the ship now."

"Just give it a minute," Varun called out. Apparently, they hadn't been quiet. "For science."

The beetle's light began to blink in tandem with the pod track lighting.

"If I give you my PhD, will you let me back on the ship?"

"I'll give you one of my fleakers if you stay put for another minute."

Ember growled but stayed. The track lighting changed patterns; the beetle's changed as well. The floodlight turned back on, green, and the beetle's light turned red. Ember looked up at scattered clicks from the beetles above, thinking there might be a warren of rabbits peeking between beetle legs, but there was only mottled white exoskeletons. The rabbits that had hopped around her legs just moments ago had also disappeared, leaving behind a few tumbleweeds of loose fur and her trampled clothing.

"Yellow is for mating," Nok said, her hand still hovering near Ember's shoulder, just to the left of the beetle antenna. "I used to work on the beetle project, too, years ago. I've got a double PhD in entomology and bacteriology. Relax for a minute. We've got them off the mating part. Red is for migration. They've got spectral shifts we can't perceive in there that Tara is copying with the ship. Your beetle is a flock leader, which is why it had a green light. Right now, Dr. Sinha is negotiating who gets to decide where we are going."

Varun also came up behind her, his voice too loud as he said, "And I know the four cardinal directions, and I'm suggesting directions to the mella's encampment since I don't think the colony would appreciate our current cohort landing in the dome."

"The light is shifting back to yellow though," Ember said, pointing at the beetle. "Why?"

"Probably a negotiation," Nok suggested.

"You have to have New Earth approval for human trials," Nadia yelled to them. "Remember that before you consider feeding Ember to the bugs."

Varun bristled. Nok laughed.

Ember got tired of waiting. The emergency blanket concentrated the rotten apple smell, and her body heat had turned the fungus goop from a viscous material to a liquid. She smelled, she was dripping, and a beetle was playing antenna-footsie with her shoulders. She'd hit her gross threshold for the day.

She reached out, steadfastly ignoring the mandibles that spread apart as her hand neared, and patted the beetle on its head. The angled red sunlight reflected pastel orange on the off-white exoskeleton, making the beetle look more like a mutated My Little Pony than an actual insect. That was a cute idea. She'd loved those plastic pastel toys as a child, even after Nadia gave most of her collection thorough haircuts.

Slightly less freaked out, Ember ran both hands through her matted, sticky hair. She pulled clumps of fungus ick out, flicked away the solids, and mashed the rest between her palms, trying to warm it back to runny. God, but it smelled foul, and even after warming, it still had the consistency of half-cooked eggs. When it looked like her hands had been encased in a tub of warm margarine, Ember stepped closer to the beetle and rubbed her palms on the exoskeleton, between the eyes, where she thought a forehead might be. A translucent green circle of slime remained. As she pulled away, strands clung to her palm like the world's most disgusting cobweb.

The beetle's light turned off.

Ember shoved her hands into her pockets, and the beetle backed away.

"Off means 'I'll follow directions,' right?" Ember asked. Fungus goop threatened to congeal her hands to the cotton lining of her pants. She balled her fists and tried to forget how bad she smelled.

"Lights off, Tara." Varun stepped away from Ember, and Nok's hand came down. The ship went dark, leaving the triangular wedge of white that spilled from the open hatch as the only light source. "No light means they're listening."

Her beetle continued to back away, and Ember finally retreated into the ship, exhaustion hitting as her adrenaline ran out.

Varun spun a chair out for her, and she fell into it, sliding halfway down until Nadia's familiar hand squeezed her elbow. Ember let herself sink deeper into the cushioning. Her eyes closed, and someone put another emergency blanket on her. Sleep. She really, *really* needed to sleep, even more than she needed a shower.

"There's a possibility we may have to gift you to the beetle colony or find something of equal value in exchange," Varun said, and Ember didn't care to find out if he was serious or not. "No need to worry about that right now though. We're a long, long beetle ride away from home. With Tara's power rerouted to the lights, Kate says we can keep them on the whole way back."

"You look like how I feel," Nadia said. "Complete shit. Also—damn with the beetle riding and the fungus ripping. Mom'll have a heart attack when I tell her the story. Remember how badly she panicked that time she visited you in Toronto during your postdoc, and you two got caught up in that riot but, like, it was just a few protestors, and the whole thing was *super* peaceful and she lost her shit? Yeah, this will be a hundred times better."

Ember groaned at the memory. She opened her eyes, shook her head at Nadia, and tried to wring more fungus juice from her hair. It was still dripping despite the chill in the ship, and she had a sudden, visceral image of her head gluing itself to the chair as she slept. This time, all she managed to pull out were strands of her own hair.

"I'm going to shave your head when we get back," Nadia whispered to her.

"I'm going to let you," Ember returned. "And we can light the residuals on fire in Varun's lab so the planetoid's beetles all come visit and he never has to go scavenging carcasses ever again."

Varun cleared his throat. Nok appeared at his side, loops of cable and leather gripped in her hand.

"So," Nok said, looking hopefully at Ember, "we have to decide who is going to try to harness your beetle."

Ember definitely eye-rolled Nok in response. "Not it," she murmured as her eyelids closed, and she slid, mercifully, into sleep.

Chapter Fourteen

Nadia

A morning dawned with solid daylight instead of a perpetual bleeding sunrise. It looked alien from inside the mella base, and Nadia wasn't sure how to feel about the beach thing, or Taraniel turning into an AI, the Queen for sale thing, or that her damn sister was still asleep when she could have really used someone to disassemble with. Also, Varun would be absolutely insufferable now in faculty meetings with all the beetle data, assuming the colony let them back in.

The colony *had* to let them back in. Nadia fought down a wave of panic. There were no mella universities, and it wasn't as though she could get a transfer to another planet. Tenure was secure, but it wasn't *mella* secure. If Nadia was going to royally screw herself out of her dream, she wanted to do it properly, with several sharpie markers and choice words for the science director.

Nadia yawned, stretching her arms into the tangerine sky. She'd slept well enough on the pod, under three emergency blankets, listening to Ember's snoring. Their harnessed, fungus-smeared beetle had gotten them within spitting distance of the mella camp, a few of its buddies helping, and then riders on trained beetles had done the rest. Mercifully, Ember hadn't needed to be a human sacrifice. The whole pod now stank of rotten apples. Ember would never be able to remove the unique bouquet she now carried.

Nadia had spent two hours in the mella hospital, which was just as well stocked as the colony hospital, if not better. Now, with drugs in her system and a patched leg, she felt as spunky as a full professor ignoring a faculty meeting.

Asher came out of the nearest building—two stories, cinderblock, no windows—trailed by Kate and Pui. They walked along the lake's edge, directly to Nadia, who managed a polite-yet-academic wave.

"Afternoon," Asher greeted her.

One of the problems with Queen was that you had no idea what time it was without a watch. Nadia did not, as a rule, like to wear anything on her wrists that would have to be taken off when working in a lab. "Yeah. How soon until we can go home?"

"Flyer's shot," Kate said and sighed as she sat in the sand. Pushing her legs out straight, she stared into the sunlight. "I've got it going as a short-range ground flyer again, but no way it's going into space. And you're not going anywhere unless you take a beetle."

"Or you come with us to Earth." Asher dredged the sentence up, loaded with a heaviness and optimism that made the muscles in Nadia's shoulders bunch.

"You don't have a ship anymore, remember. Besides, you really want to go back to Earth? *Earth,* Earth? Can't you let that asinine dream die with your broken pod over there?"

Nadia plopped onto the sand. An old boat bobbed on the gentle waves of the lake. She'd already analyzed the water: drinkable, not brackish, no concerning algal stuff. But Queen didn't have algae, so that made sense. The topographic maps she'd had recharged-Tara pull up didn't have any information on the groundwater structure at the equator, and Nadia didn't like hypothesizing on the lake's origin. Hypotheses without any data were pointless at best and highly unpublishable.

Asher and Pui sat next to her, in a line with Kate. Pui patted her hand and offered a small smile, which Nadia returned halfheartedly.

A little kid came by and gave Pui a gap-toothed smile. She was maybe eight or nine, with short, black hair and beige skin. She dumped an armload of twigs in front of them, just at the edge of the water. Maples—Nadia realized—but none she recognized from Ember's lab. The kid doused the limbs with a clear, odorless liquid, then struck a match and squealed with joy when the haphazard pile burst into flame.

Nadia scooted back. Everyone else stayed put, including the kid, and watched the flames of a small campfire rise skyward.

"We'll find a new ship. We found one, after all." Asher's voice did not sound as confident as Nadia thought it should if she was really going to keep chasing and selling the Earth dream. "Besides, you're not curious?" Asher asked. An ember jumped from the twigs and danced near Nadia's hand. "Earth has been lying to us, all of us, since the beginning. They had to have been. Forget the lies you were told at the colony. If Earth is alive, then we all have a right to know."

"Do we though?" Nadia blew a strand of hair from her face. "We collectively fucked up that planet. Some people stayed behind to bring it back. Maybe it's their planet now. It's not like we don't have our own." *And I have a job here. A good job I worked my ass off for, as did Ember. As did Taraniel. No one would willingly leave all that behind, even grumpy colonists.* "This is our home."

Asher turned to her, and Pui emitted a weird, guttural laugh. "You don't care at all?" Asher asked. "About the lies? The subterfuge?" She pointed back toward the colony. "You're living a lie, squared. The presidium has you bust your butt on this sandstorm from hell so they could steal your science to repair Earth. Your research, Ember's research—it was supposed to be going to help other worlds. And now the presidium is shipping *us* to other worlds." Asher's voice got louder. "And yet, Jesus, we don't even know if there *are* other successful worlds! If all your research was going to Old Earth, who was helping the other colonized planets?"

Nadia's gaze turned cold. "I chose this sandstorm from hell. So did all of you."

"But you shouldn't have had to. That's my point." Asher stood and kicked a plume of sand at the fire. The flames stuttered and dipped low. The girl frowned, stuck her tongue out at Asher, and ran off. "Once we have a new ship, we won't have to choose it either."

"I appreciate Nadia choosing Queen." Ember came toward them, Varun at her side. She looked like hell, her hair tangled, the dopey mella clothes they'd given her hanging at all the wrong angles. Downwind, Nadia only caught the faintest hint of apples and had to admit it was a damn good thing the mella stole toiletries as well as tech. Varun looked great, but Varun always looked great, which Nadia kind of got and was also kind of jealous of. It rankled how he could find mustache gel anywhere, but she couldn't even manage eyeliner.

Asher stepped back and made room for Ember in the fire ring. Pui nodded appreciatively at Varun. Varun blushed. Then she watched Ember as Ember watched Asher, her body strung with a tension Nadia definitely understood. About damn time for a rebound, and her sister deserved it. Sex was about the only decent thing on Queen, assuming you weren't hunting a very particular phenotype.

Nadia patted the sand next to her. Ember turned to her, eyes wide and relieved, and sat. Varun did the same.

"Thirsty?" Nadia asked her sister sweetly.

"Shut up."

"I have water," Pui offered, oblivious, and tossed a plastic bottle over the dying fire. Nadia caught it. The bottle was warm, but she handed it to Ember anyway, a toothy grin on her face.

"You sure? Nothing cures a dry spell quite like—"

Ember snatched the bottle from her and threw it into the sand. It lodged at a forty-five-degree angle, the red sunlight hitting the plastic and refracting a kaleidoscope of oranges. Nadia saw what she needed to—that her sister's fingers were their normal color, and she could still move all of them despite the scabs. No frostbite necrosis, no infections, and it seemed she had no significant concussion. Nadia was down a pinkie toe on her left foot, but she hadn't ridden a giant beetle, so Ember was damn lucky.

"I'm not ready for this much water," Ember said.

"Yes, we're all aware of that." Asher sighed, picked up the bottle, and took a drink. "But a sip won't kill you. Transparent innuendo aside, Earth is what we need to talk about. Earth, and finding a ship."

"Excuse me, then, because I'm tired of this conversation. I already said I'd take you all there. The ship isn't my problem."

"Taraniel wanted—" Asher began.

"I know what my wife wanted. But since she chose *you* to make it happen, and I just rode a flying beetle, I'm tagging out for a while. I need a nap. I need…" Ember sighed, stood, and shoved her hands into her pockets. She flashed Nadia a halfhearted smile as she walked past.

Nadia gave a brief thought to following her, but she recognized the fatigue in her sister's eyes, saw the way they tracked ever so briefly to Asher, then darted away. They could be lovingly snippy with each later, once Ember took the vulnerability down a notch. Or after she got laid.

"I'm ready to sign up." Varun squinted at Asher and wiped the sand from his hands onto his envirosuit pants. He'd put the outfit back on minus the face shield, which made no rational sense since the climate in the mella strip was downright comfortable. "I have a flyer, too, smaller than the pod, although most of its space is storage. It would need modifications. However, it is at the equator, or was when we left it. It's likely been impounded."

"Which means it won't be any easier to steal than the others, so we might as well go for a big one." Asher looked thoughtful. "We'd planned on Ember, Nadia, Pui, Kate, Nok, and myself for this initial run. If successful, we'd send for the rest of the mella, or come back and get them ourselves. No point in killing us all in one go if we fall into a black hole. We'd need an extra seat for you, Dr. Sinha. Though, of course, you are welcome to come." She gazed directly at Nok, who, after a long moment, nodded in agreement.

"I can take the seats and the supplies from the pod and find another chair easily enough," Kate offered, crossing her arms. She'd changed into a worn pair of denim coveralls, and Nadia counted three grease streaks across her chin. "We still need a shell and a working propulsion system. And it has to have been made to go into space in the first place. We don't have the facilities to go from ground flyer to space-ship."

"However we do it, I'd like to leave as soon as possible before Ember has a chance to second- or third-guess her-self." Asher chewed the inside of her cheek.

Pui got to her feet and brushed the sand from her back-side. "Could we steal the presidium's private ship? Outside of the conference, that's the only ship I know of on Queen that is spaceworthy."

Kate's eyes lit up like a Christmas tree and she slapped Pui across the shoulder.

"Ow," Pui said and took a step away from Kate.

"I think this is a *fantastic* plan if we could work out the specifics. What do you think, Ash?" Kate ran her hands down the front of her coveralls, and her eyes got the same faraway look Varun's did when someone asked him a question about Queen beetle genetics.

"Workable," Nadia cut in, "if we don't mind being shot."

Everyone's attention turned sharply to her.

"It sucks," Nadia said flatly, "if you're after my opinion on that. I think we should stay here and fight the presidium. What are we going to do on Earth anyway? Farm? Muck toxic waste? We don't have a plan."

"I was thinking of leveraging you and your sister's status as scientists." Asher looked devious. Nadia hoped Ember found that endearing because it just bugged the hell out of her.

"Sibling," Varun said, his voice quiet but forceful—serious, all of a sudden, in the beating sunlight.

Nadia wrinkled her nose. "Huh?"

Asher cocked her head to the side. Varun's mouth turned into a frown.

"You've had it explained," he said, "at much embarrassment to Ember. You should honor that information."

Nadia had no idea what he was talking about. She looked at Asher, whose brow knit in concentration, her lips pursed.

"So..." Asher started, searching for words. "She didn't say anything about pronouns. I asked."

Varun continued to stare at the whole group as if they were really dim rabbits.

"Ember's a girl." Nadia said it defiantly because who the hell was Varun to come in and question Ember's own damn sister?

"Maybe when you were growing up. But organisms evolve." He turned his chilly eyes on Nadia. Her skin prickled. "Have you talked about it? Recently?"

They'd never talked about, not directly. Not that Nadia could remember. During the exodus testing, they'd been too young to get into the weeds about Ember's chromosome discovery, and then there was the ship debacle and Nadia ending up "older." And, well, when you were fighting for your science, fighting to survive, genetic mosaicism wasn't a high priority.

"I'll talk to her," Asher said. "You have my word."

Damn it; now Asher was all serious too. Nadia snorted. Now wasn't the time, and their last conversation was way more important than her sister's biological sex.

"Back to the scientist thing. And the answer is absolutely not. I know what you're thinking, and *no.*"

Asher tapped Pui's wrist and pointed to the longhouse, where Nadia had gone for medical care. The white building had a red cross painted every eight centimeters or so across its midsection. "Pui, would you restock the medicine cabinet while we have the panels off the pod?"

Pui stood still for a moment longer than Nadia thought necessary, even to make a point, then stalked off.

"Kate, would you oversee more repairs?"

Kate wrinkled her nose and tilted her head. "Why? It'll never go into space."

"It needs another chair at least."

A tickle ran up Nadia's spine as Kate brightened, saluted, and left in the direction of the pod. Varun looked back over his shoulder with a long, reproachful look to Nadia before following Kate to the pod.

Damn it, now wasn't the time.

Asher turned to Nadia and didn't say a damn thing.

"Ember is my sister and I am not leaving Queen," Nadia said, sounding exactly as juvenile as she'd intended. She crossed her arms and blinked into the reflected light from the water. A ten-minute conversation about Earth interspersed with a tour of the equatorial mella camp did not endear her to the cause. They'd barely had time to shower and eat, much less contemplate intergalactic subterfuge. There was plenty of subterfuge on Queen already. Also, Nadia could still see little flakes of dried fungus-whatever clinging to Ember's hair, even at this distance. Neither of them was prepared for a however-month-long trip in very close quarters with no recreation or solid sanitation options. Scientists, as a whole, did not play well together, especially in tight spaces.

"Queen isn't *that* bad," Nadia argued. "We have food. We have shelter. We, or at least the colonists, have jobs and decent health insurance, and my lab is good enough. Did Ember or Taraniel tell you what happened on Ember's way out here?"

Asher shrugged. "A number of the other colonists died. I didn't press for more information."

"A number? Yes, that number was five hundred seventy-three. There were five hundred seventy-seven people on that colony ship, tucked into stasis chambers. *Four* defrosted correctly. *Four* had properly functioning pods. The other three were already dead from various, in theory, unrelated illnesses. And you want Ember to get back on one of those things and make the journey that should have killed her the first time. And that ship was *meant* for interstellar travel." Nadia pointed back at the pod. A handful of mella buzzed around it, sparks flying and packages being brought inside. Ember stood just outside it, staring hard at the viewscreen window, the dried fungus flakes difficult to see. "Interstellar ships are flying coffins, in more ways than one."

"Taraniel said—"

Nadia was in no mood to hear about Ember's dead wife. She turned from the mella and the lake and stalked toward

Ember. "Hey!" she called out, waving her arms up over her head like she was flagging down a runaway plane.

Asher didn't call after her and Ember, too, ignored her.

Nadia wove around the side of a brick building (did they have any brick buildings at the colony?) and finally got close enough to Ember to be heard. "Hey! No more of this"—she pointed at the pod—"lesbian emotional moping. No more Taraniel, or Tara, or mella for the moment. Are you seriously going to take these clowns back to Earth? You buy their story? And what are we going to do when we get there?"

Ember turned to her. Melancholy flashed under the fatigue. "Tara is convincing. Probably because Taraniel programmed her. This was our idea, you know. The mella aren't proposing anything new. And for Taraniel and me, the plan was always...you know... House. Some land. Just quiet living, cleaning up a patch of earth, maybe planting a forest or two."

Ember's eyes got soft and wistful.

"It's fucking suicide!" Nadia ran fingers through her ponytail in exasperation. "How are you getting this land? How are you getting through Earth's almost certain defenses? And don't tell me all your emotional baggage from your last spaceship trip has evaporated with your newfound focus on Asher's breasts."

Nadia expected Ember to blush but got a chuckle instead.

"I have not, for the record, made any type of study of Asher's breasts," Ember said. "And, Nadia..." Ember looked up at the bloody sky. "We can't go back to the colony. If you want to science again, it'll have to be on another world, or here at the mella camp." She leaned against the nose of the pod. "Don't you want to go home?"

Nadia stomped her foot. "This is my home!"

"You don't have to come."

"And if I don't, who looks after you?" Nadia regretted the words the moment they left her mouth. All the amusement dropped from Ember's face, her eyes hardening. "Shit, Ember. I didn't mean that."

"I'm not an invalid, and I didn't ask you to come to Queen," Ember said flatly.

"We're *sisters*."

Ember's gaze skittered across the grass to the lake. Nadia had been told who was in that lake, and a muscle twitched in her face. "I'm going back to Earth. They've got my trees and my memories. Not all of them, but most. Taraniel always said...she always said worry about the *when* later. That we had to get there first." Ember shrugged. "And Tara"—she thumped the pod with her palm—"isn't going to accept anything other than a yes."

"Can we discuss how weird that is? Is it Tara manipulating you, or is it— Jesus, Ember, have you considered—" Nadia took a moment to reassemble her thoughts. She didn't like the warning look on Ember's face. "It's a ship. Taraniel imprint or not, we could light it on fire right now and solve the problem."

The edges of Ember's mouth crinkle upward. "You know that New Earth–Old Earth gives 50 percent of its grants to on-world scientists. Think of what you could do with that kind of money. Think of the waterways that need revitalizing on Earth. I bet Lake Superior needs a hydrologist with big grant money, stat, to clean up those once-pristine beaches. Taraniel seemed certain we could get jobs there. That they'd welcome remote scientists, especially those who'd worked on the plants saving our homeworld."

"Maybe. But who's going to hire us, Ember? H-indexes aside, we're from Queen. Have you been to an academic conference recently? Because I sure haven't, aside from the one on the equator. And our grant rates are abysmal." Nadia stared down at her feet. She'd dug her toes into the sand. Bits of the fine white particulate had sifted through the lacing rivets and now tickled between her toes. She didn't like the manipulation, and she didn't like the prospect of Ember on another spaceship, and she really didn't want to have to work her way up the tenure ladder again. If they were doing this, they had to be all in. No half-assed beetle riding, no patchy mella clothes, no complaining when you lost a few toes to frostbite.

"Hey, Ember?"

"Yeah?"

"This whole idea is dumb."

Ember snorted. "I am aware of that. But I'm not going to light the last piece of my late wife on fire, and Tara isn't going to let up until we agree to go to Earth. And I have. Agreed. Just so you know."

Nadia gazed at her sister. Blinking. Digesting. "I guess I have to go too, then," she finally managed to choke out.

"Nadia, you don't have to come."

Nadia waved her hands in front of her face and scowled. "I do. Because you are going to just...crash Old Earth without a plan. You are so impulsive it hurts."

"I'm not—"

A shockwave thundered through the ground. Nadia grabbed Ember's shoulders to steady them both. Behind her, several children screamed. Smoke plumed, and the whine of flyers ripped the air. Nadia heard the unmistakable sound of cinderblock cracking. Four—no, five—flyers flew directly overhead, their noses pointed to the few mella buildings.

"Flyers!" Nok called, running up to them and grabbing Nadia's hand. "Half a dozen at least. Presidium logos. They're aiming live rounds everywhere! Buildings, people, *everywhere.*"

"The presidium followed us?" Nadia took Ember's hand and let Nok tug them through the smoke and screaming mella. A whistle of weapons discharge blew past her ear, and she stumbled. Keeping up with Nok's pace seemed impossible with her very tender bullet hole.

"You okay, Nadia?"

"We're being shot at! Of course, I'm not okay. Don't ask stupid questions during a firefight."

The flyers moved into a tight diamond formation and opened fire, together, on the mella school. Cinderblock shattered. The vague silhouette Nadia could make out in the smoke, crumbled.

"Faster!" Nok yelled. "Varun! Over here!"

Varun speedwalked in a very upright, very Varun manner, over to them, his face waxen.

Ember wrapped an arm around Nadia's waist, supporting her bad leg. "Nok, how did they find us?" Ember asked as Nok wound them around pocks of blackened grass. To where, Nadia had no idea, but anywhere was better than where they were now. "We took out their flyer, and we came back through the badlands where they don't have the satellites recording, according to Pui. How did they track us without satellites? No one here has TOPA or anything that could act as a beacon, so how—"

"Varun!" Nadia's eyes went as wide as a beetle's as she screamed his name. Shit. Shit shit *shit*. How had they both forgotten? Varun whipped around, his mouth morphing from frown to an *O* of surprise. "Your TOPA is still on, isn't it?"

"TOPA is just in the helmet though," Ember said way too calmly. "So what—"

"No, because he moved it to his damn collar piece. Damn it, Varun!"

Varun's hands scrambled at his suit. Nadia shrugged out of Ember's arm, spun on Varun, and tore at the collar. "Turn off, TURN OFF," Varun yelled into the embedded speaker by his right shoulder. Nadia's fingers found the hidden pressure seam under his armpit and had the suit half off before Varun said, "TOPA, shut down!"

The tips of Varun's ears start to pink as unintelligible words whispered back at him through the suit. "My commands have been overridden. TOPA won't respond."

"Take the suit off, Dr. Sinha!" Nok doubled back, and together, she and Varun dug at the remaining seam clasps. They pulled the bulky material from his body, stripped his envirosuit pants down and off his legs (he still had on a crisp pair of Dockers underneath), and tossed the whole mess into the dirt and smoke.

"This is what relocation looks like," Nok spat. She grabbed Varun's shaking hand and once again broke into a run. "We need to get to the flyer. Asher and the others will already be there. Come on!"

A loud *crack* thundered across the landscape. New smells rose from the smoke, burning Nadia's nose and throat. Sand persisted in clogging the air, making it impossible to see more than a few meters away. As they continued to run, Nadia started seeing more pocked earth, more burned grass. She saw bodies—mangled, crisped, many too small to be adults. Her stomach turned, and what had been just eye irritation morphed to tears.

Why?

A row of LED lights blinked yellow and blue as the flyers cruised lower.

"They're landing!" Nok yelled as she pulled them through the cloud of sand and people and corpses. Two of the flyers settled just in front of them, cutting off their path. Nok and Varun turned left, but Ember grabbed Nadia's hand and bolted right.

Nadia's leg gave out.

She and Nadia crashed into each other, then onto the ground as a cluster of live rounds sputtered far too close. Sand filled her nose and mouth, and she coughed and spit, her eyes watering as she tried to clear them with her fingers. Stupid move. She only rubbed in more grit. Ember dragged her up, and her eyes cleared enough to see the ramp to the pod hovering a few meters above the ground. Ember gave her a push forward, and Nadia hesitated for only a moment. She looked back long enough to confirm that there were bodies moving toward them, and said bodies were vaguely Varun and Nok–shaped. She then jumped, grabbed the edge of the ramp, and pulled herself up, flopping like a dead fish onto the floor of the cockpit.

The inside of the flyer was warm. Bright. Half-dazed, she turned to Ember, who sat beside her on the floor. Blood covered her sister's right side, from her hair to her boots. Not her own—it was too sandy, and Ember didn't have a single tear in her clothing—but that didn't matter.

Ember stared at her right hand, the sticky, half-congealed sand-blood mixture quickly cementing to her skin. This was not a good time for memories.

"Ember," Nadia began.

"The last time I was covered in blood was when the stasis chamber defrosted," Ember said in a low, dead voice. "Some of my PICC lines were pulled out improperly by the malfunctioning AI. I fucking hate AIs. I had open veins. My capsule lid wouldn't open, Nadia. I kept pounding and pounding. I was swimming. Drowning. In my own blood. Begging for an AI to hear me."

I can hear you, Ember, Tara said, and Nadia's arms goosefleshed.

Nok dove into the hatchway, landing on Ember and knocking the wind from her chest in a huff. Ember's eyes snapped back into focus, which was excellent because Nadia had no idea on how to counsel on PTSD. Taraniel was supposed to have made Ember see a therapist for it. That clearly hadn't happened.

"Sorry," Nok said as she awkwardly got to her feet. Ember sat up and scooted from the hatch entrance. Tara had the interior fans pushing air out, minimizing the sand that swirled in, but the mella crew and Varun still brought plenty with them when they pulled themselves, one by one, into the pod. Asher was the last to enter.

Strap in. Now. The hatch closed, and the ship's interior air filters whirred into overdrive.

"Just blood, sis," Nadia whispered as she stood and offered Ember a hand up. She helped her into the nearest chair, making sure every section of the five-point harness clicked into place.

"The rest of the mella are heading to our underground bunkers," Asher said as she coughed, and inertia pinned them all to their seats. "We took over part of an old beetle gallery several years back."

Those are drones from the colony. They're being run only by AI and this is, according to their chatter, their second stop. Their first is encrypted.

Their *second* stop? Nadia's mouth went dry. Her sister was covered in blood. The ground was covered in blood. Queen was covered in blood. Blood blood *blood*. And for what? Some stupid sand?

"The colonists?" Nadia asked shrilly. The pod was flying now, and sand stretched endlessly across the viewscreen. "Are they alive?"

I don't know.

"Jesus, well find out!" she yelled.

"It doesn't matter right now," said Asher. "Ideas?" Her eyes rested pointedly on Ember, who was lost in a memory Nadia couldn't begin to imagine.

Ember blinked and shook her head. "If these ships are here, they aren't with the presidium or the colony. We should go to the colony. The presidium has ships, and we could see if the flyers went there first."

"Agreed!" Nadia squeezed her shoulder and handed her a half-soiled cloth she'd found under her chair. They had to get back to the colony. Had to check. Had to *know*.

Ember raked the cotton over her skin, scrubbing the blood, and dug under her fingernails for any remains. "I have Queen's atmosphere exit codes." The cloth had become so clogged with blood that it stopped wiping and started smearing. "But I'm supposed to be dead, according to the colony registry. At least that's what Nadia told me. My codes might be dead too. They were only for shipment of promising saplings, and only cargo exit codes, not passenger ships. We need backups. We also need a ship. At the very least, Nadia and I can distract the presidium and their people while you all 'acquire' one. Our h-indexes are high enough to get us an audience, and I've done enough shipments for them that they're used to me calling in at all hours. I doubt we'll get codes from them, but we could be a good distraction."

"We could just steal it outright," Asher countered, her eyes narrowing to slits. "We don't have to dump you and Dr. O'Grady on the presidium's lap to do it."

Ember tossed the now fully soiled cloth at Nadia, who swatted it to the floor. The color had come back to her face, and Nadia saw life in her eyes again. Thank god.

"What do you think they're going to do to us?" she asked. "You think they'd just shoot their top hydrologist and the botanist who has apparently been handmaking the forests of Earth? We're not..." Nadia stopped, but Asher had already gone cold. Pui, Nok, and Kate all stared at her, and Ember snorted. The sound of gunfire faded, finally.

"Sorry," Nadia murmured.

You have no value if Queen's science program is being disassembled to ship you all off-world. Taraniel thought—

"Taraniel is dead," Ember snapped, the sharp words startling Nadia. Ember's emotions had bounced back faster than a yo-yo. "Taking us to the colony, whether to steal a ship or check on our friends, is one step closer to Earth. It'll fulfill your directive, and I'll keep my word to Taraniel. So how about you stop arguing, and just do it?"

Nadia felt the pod change headings. Sand cleared from the viewscreen within minutes, leaving only a view of patchy grass transitioning to small sand dunes.

Yes, Dr. Schmitt, said Tara in a standard issue TOPA accent. The interior lights dimmed.

Nadia, exhausted, fell asleep.

Ember? Dr. Schmitt? Can you hear me? God, where did all the blood come from?

Oh my god the line from her neck is out. Her thigh as well. The suspension fluid has her blood in it. Get a team here. NOW!

She can't breathe.

I don't know how to fix her vitals.

Dr. Schmitt? Dr. Schmitt, say something!

She isn't responding!

Ember's beetle appears to have followed us here, along with two others.

Tara's voice cut through Ember's dream. Memory. Nightmare. Whatever. It felt like her head had been removed and replaced with two rocks bashing together. Ember forced her eyelids open, the lashes goopy from sand and tears. The obnoxiously large clock on the viewscreen read: *7h 21m 46 s post departure.*

"Nothing we can do, really," Varun said. "They're beetles, not people. Technically, they're not even beetles. They're giant lightning bugs that *look* like beetles and use phosphorescence and oxygen in a manner completely unique to Queen."

"If the beetles aren't hurting anything, ignore them." Asher came up behind Ember's chair and tapped her once on the shoulder. Ember managed a throaty grunt and re-pressed the urge to wipe her eyes. If Asher had found her attractive covered in fungus, a little eye goop wouldn't be a dealbreaker.

"The port authority accepted my code, so we've got an entrance quadrant. Also means we still have a ground port authority." Varun unfastened his harness and stood next to the viewscreen.

The pod decelerated as it dropped into the hexagonal opening in the colony's dome. Ember saw flashes of beetle wings as buildings slipped past her peripheral vision. Housing barracks. Primary school. Commissary. Everything closed, lights out, not a sign of life, but it was also the middle of the night.

They passed the science complex that she and Nadia would never get to step foot in again. Varun would be sad but would probably recover. Nadia would be pissed. Ember...wasn't sure. Her lab, and her section of the building, had echoes of Taraniel in every corner. The pod *was* Taraniel in a weird, ghostly way.

"Tara?" Ember asked as she caught the concern in Nadia's eyes. The knots returned to her stomach.

I don't see any sign of damage here, Ember. No distress codes. No unusual communication traffic. There are heat signatures in the barracks. People are sleeping. They are alive.

Ember couldn't decide whether to be relieved or not.

The pod looped over an artificial hill of brown grass and a handful of sad, flattened maple trees and landed in a hexagonal courtyard. The presidium building loomed directly in front of them. It looked as dumpy as anything else on Queen, set apart only by its towering five stories. Colony rules dictated no other building could be taller—a political decision that had probably started off fine but quickly screwed the colony since the protective dome was a fixed circumference. If one couldn't build out, the only other option was up.

The presidium building exterior had a browning white-wash, and dead maple trees lined either side of the footpath to the main double doors. A very talented gardener had managed to weave the branches together while the trees still had water in them. It was probably supposed to be delight-fully ornamental. Instead, the trees clung to one another in their death throes—frozen in time during their last scream for life.

Originally, the whole thing had been set up as a parlia-mentary unit. The five-member presidium were supposed to have been elected from the populace after the first batch sent from New Earth. But the colony hadn't been around long enough; not enough people had wanted the job, and the original three jokers were still in power. As far as Ember knew, they'd never cared to train any subgovernment offi-cials who might take over after their (hopefully) eventual death either. They reported to some office on New Earth, which reported to some other head in New Earth govern-ance. New Earth, vaguely, controlled the colonies. And that was about as much as Ember understood of the whole thing.

The beetles landed the pod with a jostle, and the buzz-ing of their wings stopped. When the pod hatch opened, the smells of the colony wafted in—the sterility and mild despair giving the unwelcome feeling that Ember had come home and had better like it.

Ember unstrapped her harness in tandem with Nadia, and they walked, wordlessly, to the hatch. She passed Asher's chair, and at a brush to her sleeve, Ember turned to wink at her before following Nadia down the ramp and into the presidium courtyard. If Ember was brave enough to storm the presidium building, she was brave enough to make a pass.

Probably.

Outside, the air was still. One of the beetles—the one she'd ridden, she thought, though the sunset light on their pearlized exoskeletons made it hard to tell—took four steps toward her and drooped its antennae until they touched both her shoulders.

"Mom'll never let you keep it," Nadia said. "Remember what happened to our hamster?"

Ember did remember their ill-fated plan to teach Chippy to run through an obstacle course on their lawn without first enclosing the course or remembering that the neighborhood had a large number of semiferal cats. Ember took the antennae in her hands, this time mindful of the scales and her freshly scarred hands, and led the beetle back to the pod. It clicked at her, and its butt flashed yellow, but it stayed.

At least there were no rabbits around. Thank goodness for small favors.

"You good?" Ember called into the pod.

Kate's head popped out, a smirk on her face almost as good as Nadia's. "We know how to steal things, Dr. Schmitt." She made a shooing motion with her hands. "Go talk to the presidium. Maybe bring up why half of you is caked in dried blood."

"Varun?" Nadia asked.

"Beetles!" Varun yelled from inside. "Prime research opportunity!"

Nadia wiggled her eyebrows. "Entomologists are kind of cute."

"You always did have a soft spot for men. We should go."

Nadia started up the path, and Ember followed, her eyes scanning the aborted tree limbs for any sign of life. These had been early versions of the variety that eventually got shipped out. They'd done well as saplings, but they never formed proper heartwood, and something in one of her edits had stripped the number of living cells in the sapwood down below half a percent. They had a five-year life expectancy inside the dome and six months, max, outside. Still, they'd been her first success on Queen—enough so that the presidium had planted them and not removed their gnarled husks. Hopefully, a bit of that goodwill remained.

"Plan?" Nadia asked as they neared the double doors. "Also, thank god for Queen's lack of security."

"I'm sure the satellites have us already." Ember rapped on the door with her palm. The resulting thud sounded hollow and too loud in the still air.

"They have butlers or something?" Nadia asked, pressing her ear against the door. "It's the middle of the night."

"There should be an attendant on duty. Last time—"

The doors opened in tandem. A tall, willowy woman stood behind them, a deep frown etched onto her face. She wore the same stonewashed jeans Ember had on, except her T-shirt read LIVE AID on the front in peeling black letters, with the top half of a guitar folded over and stuck back onto itself. She had a short mop of curls that fell just to her eyebrows, the coloring that in-between red-brown Ember could never seem to correctly parse, and her skin appeared paler than Ember's in the low sunlight. Her name badge—a plastic square—read "Maxine" and looked recycled from an old diner. From the curve to the woman's shoulders and her sleepy eyes, Ember would have sworn she was facing a mella if she didn't know better.

"What?" Maxine asked in a low, tired voice. Her eyes tracked to Nadia, skimmed away disinterested, then opened wider when they fell on Ember. "I know you." She said the word "you" with a drawl. "Weren't you here last month with a new seedling variety?"

"I also do quarantine and inspection for all the presidium imports. Can we come in? There was a problem with their last shipment, and I thought they'd want to know."

"A problem involving blood?" Maxine's eyes bulged as she shook her head. "And her?" She pointed a thumb at Nadia, who rolled her eyes.

"I'm your hydrologist," Nadia said. "And my pipes are torn up near the dark side badlands. I investigated, and turns out, the badlands aren't so bad, if you get my snow-drift. I think we should probably talk about that."

Ember caught a flicker of...she didn't know what, in Maxine's eyes before the woman nodded, turned, and gestured for them to follow.

The inside of the presidium complex hadn't changed in the seven years Ember had been allowed to visit it. Raw cinderblock remained on the inside, unpainted and unfinished. One staircase climbed the right side, no curves on the handrail, no rounded spindles in the banister, just straight, unforgiving lines. The staircase climbed the entire five stories with a landing at every floor that led to a long loft. Although the electric lights were turned dim, Ember could see tables and chairs in each loft, and all were empty.

"It'd be good to wake the presidium," Ember said as they moved to the foot of the staircase. "I don't think this can wait until morning."

"It'll wait as long as they need it to," Maxine responded. "Stay here." She left them at the foot of the stairs and disappeared into a door just under them.

Nadia turned to Ember the moment Maxine's footsteps faded away. "Your explanation was half-assed. Mine is better. No way they're going to ignore a colonist, with their secrets."

"Point. Doesn't matter though. We just need them in the same room, and we need them distracted."

Nadia kicked her halfheartedly in the shin. "Acknowledge my victory."

Ember pushed her away. "You're excellent. You're wonderful. How old are you again?"

"Asshole," Nadia muttered under her breath, but Ember caught the lopsided smile too. Nadia opened her mouth again in what was certain to be a retort, but cocked her head. Her brows furrowed. "Do you hear a scratching?"

Ember turned her head in the same direction and closed her eyes. Too many days outside the dome, even with the face shield, had deadened her finer hearing, but there was only stillness. "No. What?"

"Scratching," Nadia said after a long pause. "Like nails on an emery board." She shuddered. "Worst sound in the world."

All Ember could hear was the sound of footsteps coming from underneath the stairs. The door opened, flung out harder than was necessary, and Maxine appeared, her curls tousled and an extra level of irritation on her face.

"Come back tomorrow," she said, eyes heavy on Ember. "Both of you. Or wait in the third floor flat until one of the presidium is awake. They don't care."

"Not a single one of them is up?" Nadia asked before Ember could get anything out. "Seriously? I have the secrets of Queen *in my brain* and they want to wait until morning?"

Maxine pointed at the double door, the right side of which was still ajar, spilling a wedge of red sunlight onto the polished concrete floor. "President Johnson thanks you for pointing out the need for a new gate sentry since ours is clearly napping somewhere."

"President Johnson can go and—"

Ember put a hand over Nadia's mouth. Her sister licked her hand, a long, wet draw of her tongue, but Ember held it there anyway. Now, she *did* hear scratching—a sound like thick, chitinous toes on cinderblock.

"The presidium aren't going to get to sleep much longer," Ember said. She dragged her hand off of Nadia's mouth and wiped the spit onto her sister's chin and down the front of her wrinkled shirt. Nadia called her something profane. Ember ignored it.

She turned just in time to see a long, segmented beetle leg, lightly white and candied in the sun's red glow, move past the gap in the door.

Maxine gasped. Nadia failed to swallow a snicker. Two little toes clapped the concrete, then hooked around the door and pulled it open. Another leg followed, and then the square head of Ember's beetle—the mark under its eye distinct—pushed past the doorframe.

"I have to make a call!" Maxine ran back under the stairs just as Ember's beetle tried to wedge its thorax through the opening. It lodged between the frame and the side of the closed door, let out a series of what sounded like irritated clicks, and rammed its head to the left.

The hollow core door crumpled in on itself, staying on its hinges but folding in the middle where the beetle's head had made contact. There still wasn't enough room, so the beetle pulled itself out, opened its wing case, and flew at the door, crashing it off its hinges and blowing wood and bits of metal at Nadia and Ember. The frame separated from the cinderblock, and the cinderblock crumbled, leaving an opening closer to the size of a garage door than an entry door.

Ember pushed Nadia into the staircase, covering her sister's front with her own. She expected shrapnel but got only the light slap of beetle antennae on her cheek, the scales raising a thin scrape that had to have drawn a line of blood. Ember didn't want to think about blood again.

Rabbits followed.

Streaming into the building, they alternately hopped and glided on the smooth floor. They weren't the ones from outside the dome, however. These were the colony's pet and meat rabbits, distinct in their lop ears for the pets and giant, bloated bodies for the meat rabbits. The two disparate sizes would have been comical if Ember'd had time to process. But the other two snow beetles followed, an entire goddamn warren of lop-eared rabbits riding the smallest of the three.

Rabbits lopped up the steep staircase. They bounded across the floor and wedged under the door gaps, their little cotton tails wiggling and then disappearing. They skittered into the few chairs and sofas scattered across the main entryway, shredding cloth and chewing wood. A loose electric cable that ran from a corner outlet and up a wall to an antique lamp—a relic of Earth Ember didn't miss at all—was stripped and chewed through in under a minute by a black mini lop with a pink bow glued to the top of its head.

Maxine burst from the staircase door with two other women behind her, both in the same nondescript jeans and T-shirts, both equally disheveled. Ember recognized the shorter one with her black hair in a crew cut as President Johnson, and the taller one with the neat black braids as President Frimpong.

"Get them out!" Maxine yelled. She tried to grab a ginger rabbit by its midsection, but the little fluff ball slid through her hands like water. The smallest beetle—the one with all the damn rabbits still on it—took offense and hooked Maxine with its front left leg, sweeping her from her feet and slamming her into the staircase, from which she did not get up.

"Enough!" Johnson yelled as she made ineffectual shooing motions at the rabbits streaming across her feet. Frimpong plastered her back against the wall, eyes squeezed shut. Both had stopped, stupidly, far too close to the open staircase door.

"You have to evacuate the building!" Ember yelled. "Where is President Borchert?"

"She's not here!" Frimpong yelled as rabbits swarmed her legs, hopping and grunting at her.

"Maxine is down, and I don't think she's breathing!" Johnson called from Maxine's side. "Dr. Schmitt, this is uncalled for. All of it. What do you want?"

Ember's mind raced as fast as her heart. The presidium, as a rule, did not leave their building. Everything was brought to them. All their communication information was here. They were the communications hub for Queen, the ruling body, and the transit authority, all rolled into one centrally located package. They'd never even bopped over to the science complex to check on Ember's greenhouse or Nadia's newest computer modeling workups. The science director was their person on the ground. The presidium stayed put. So, where in hell was President Borchert?

How long did it take to steal a ship?

"Well, we wouldn't be here if you hadn't opened fire on the mella," Ember managed as she pushed her beetle's head back from where it was trying to nuzzle her side aggressively. "Are you going to kill colonists, next? Right here in the dome?"

"What are you talking about?" Johnson demanded, glaring at Ember while Frimpong lightly slapped either side of Maxine's cheeks. The prone woman groaned, but her eyes stayed closed.

"If you don't tell us, we can sick Snuzzle here on you." Nadia peeled herself from the wall and the mass of butterball rabbits flopping at her feet and pointed at Ember's beetle. "These things eat people."

"They do not!" Ember countered, just as "Snuzzle's" blue tongue snaked out and around her waist. The hair-fine spines slipped too easily past her scabs and the sensitive skin and nearly made her yell. "Damn it, back off!"

Snuzzle did not back off, nor did it retract its tongue. Its butt did turn red, though, which Ember did not like at all. Now was not the time to migrate. Now was the time to get answers since they had to kill time.

"They might try to mate with you though," Ember added as she tried to slide her fingers between the tongue and her shirt, avoiding as many spines as she could. The spines dug into her sensitive skin, and the mucous coating its tongue seeped far too quickly through her shirt, cold and sticky. At least it darkened her clothing, hiding the inevitable bloodstains. "I don't know about the rabbits. Why are you killing mella?"

"We don't care about the mella!" wailed Frimpong. In the time between Maxine hitting the staircase and Ember being belted by beetle tongue, rabbits had toppled her to the floor. Now the woman lay curled on her side in a fetal position, crying as a dozen white rabbits—all white, no other colors—thumped one back foot into her body.

Ember considered the possibility that she might be dreaming, or drunk, or both.

"Well, if you didn't send flyers to shoot up their camp like a bad Wild West movie, who *did*?" Nadia asked. She managed to grip a meat rabbit with one arm under its front legs, the other cradling its butt, and sidestepped over to Johnson, who knelt beside Maxine. Nadia held the rabbit out in as threatening a gesture as possible, noting the way the rabbit kept licking her fingers. "Talk!"

"Dr. O'Grady—" President Johnson said, far too calmly as she eased Maxine into a sitting position. Maxine coughed, and her eyelids flitted open. She took in the rabbits, the beetles, and Ember, caught in a giant tongue, and promptly passed out again.

"Dr. O'Grady," Johnson said again, "the presidium complex has three flyers. Three! We have our personal one and two smaller versions made mostly for hauling cargo. That is it. We don't have any weapons. And we would *never* kill mella, no matter how irritating they got. They're *people*."

"No, you'd just incarcerate them in the badlands and shoot them if they get out of line. You're so lying," Nadia spat.

"Conference? Prison?" Ember yelled. "Is President Borchert at one of those? Or do you not know about that either?"

"Borchert *was* at the conference!" Nadia said as she jostled the rabbit in her hands menacingly at Johnson. "I saw her myself. Front row."

"The prison on the snow side isn't staffed by us. New Earth sends specially trained guards for it. And President

Borchert was...requested." Johnson stuttered the last word. "She went to the conference but got on a ship two days ago for New Earth." She mopped her face with a sweaty hand. "We don't...we can't leave this house, professors. We fill our days with paperwork and exports, some of which you apparently now know about, but we do *not* send flyers to kill colonists, old or new! Now *please* remove the beetles and rabbits."

Ember stopped struggling and stared at Johnson. Frimpong sat up, moaned, and scooted until her back was against the wall. No one went to New Earth. New Earth governance didn't request people; they requested things. But Johnson and Frimpong were shaking too much, and they were far too pale to be lying. Which meant...what exactly?

Ember balled her hands and rubbed them on her thighs. Damn it, she wanted someone to blame for those little bodies in the sand at the mella camp!

"Ember?" Nadia pointed at the slowly pooling blood at Ember's feet.

Ember snapped back to her task. She had the tongue pushed down to her hips now, most of the spines out, but the remaining ones still in at an angle. If she pushed it much farther, she'd lose her pants. She'd lost track of the other two beetles but could hear their toes scraping, around a corner and somewhere above her head. A quick glance confirmed one of them had taken flight and was scratching (digging?) at the ceiling.

Bits of concrete rained into her eyes. She wiped at them, forgetting the slime on her hands, and managed to end up with a burning, popping sensation across most of her face. The cut across her cheek stung.

Nadia dropped her rabbit and came back over to Ember, the rabbits clearing a path for her in a way that was definitely not creepy at all. The presidium and Maxine stayed exactly where they were. Maxine whimpered.

"You okay? Because this"—Nadia spun her finger in a circle around her head—"is not okay. Because if it's not our presidium screwing with us, but *New Earth*..."

"We don't have any confirmation of that," Frimpong said, but her voice sounded tired and utterly unconvincing.

Ember pushed one more time. The tongue slid from her, pants with it, down to her ankles. Little rivulets of blood ran over her legs, each of the tiny puncture wounds like fire.

Nadia punched her in the arm before her mind could wander. "Focus."

The nudity might have bothered Ember more if circumstances had been different, but really, this whole scenario reset the bar on nudity nightmares.

"I think we should go to the conference," Ember drawled as she tried to sort facts from conjecture. "I think..." She paused and glanced at the presidium and Maxine, huddling on the floor. Disoriented. Upset. Ineffectual.

Ember pulled her (now wet) pants back up, stepped out of the tongue circle, and pointed to the mangled doors. "Let's head back to the pod."

"Please remove the rabbits." Frimpong kicked at a small gray lop that just grunted in response and nipped her ankle. "Please!"

"They'll probably follow us. Probably. *You*—" Ember pointed at Johnson, then at Frimpong. "—need to get aid to the mella camp. Now. We'll send you coordinates if you really, truly don't know where it is. Help those people you supposedly care about, and hope the flyers that were stamped with *your* symbols don't come for the dome."

Ember walked to the door, Nadia just behind, and Snuzzle clicking to her right. More clicking followed, along with the sounds of wings folding into their casings. They exited the building, and neither looked back.

The light breeze blowing through the colony chilled the whatever-it-was from the beetle tongue on Ember's face and pants and wafted the smell of wet feet. Beetle mouth. So gross. She patted the left side of Snuzzle's thorax. Her hip hurt again, and her hands were wet. She should have worn gloves, with the scabs so fresh. Right now, the best she could do was not look at her hands.

"Holy. Crap." Nadia pointed east.

Fifty meters from them, just off the path and on top of three of Ember's (now extra) dead and crumpled maple trees, sat a flyer in the loosest sense of the word. It looked more like a deformed lilac bush than a continuous piece of plastic, with thick, spindly *things* branching off a vaguely cylindrical central axis. The old pod, one quarter the size, sat on the ground next to it, like a trashy car on a used car lot the dealer used to upsell you the most expensive piece of shit they could.

It had a hatch, though, the same as the pod. Kate leaned against the frame of the hatch, arms crossed, expression smug, a socket wrench in the hammer loop of her decaying carpenter jeans.

"Comes with *fifteen* chairs," Kate said as Nadia and Ember climbed the ramp, neither managing to speak. "Didn't need to unbolt anything, and we've already moved the supplies. The presidium's personal flyer is a beauty. Ready?"

Ember stepped into the flyer and thought she might get a sunburn on the spot. The inside had lights everywhere. Little white LEDs glinted from the ceiling, the walls, the floor, the access panels. The walls were deep midnight blue, the chairs a shade lighter, the crown molding green. The TOPA interface stretched in a panel across the widest point of the cockpit.

The chairs were bolted in two tiered semicircles, the back row on a riser. Each had thick padding and a cupholder. Kate pushed past Nadia and strapped herself into the second from the right, second tier chair. Pui, Nok, and Varun were already seated in the first tier, with one empty chair between each of them.

"This is...bright," Nadia said.

"How did it go?" Asher asked. She pushed up from the wall across from them and uncrossed her arms. Ember took note of the little tooth-shaped indents in her lower lip. "You're bleeding."

Pui got up. Ember waved her back down.

"I'm fine. Just more beetle tongue."

The word *Tara* formed on Asher's lips.

"Don't you dare," Ember hissed. "I am fine. You can look yourself later, if you want."

That had way more innuendo than Ember had planned. Warmth rose in her cheeks. "Anyway, the presidium didn't do it. New Earth stinks more and more."

Varun's eyes opened wide in alarm. "Do you think they'll come for the dome?"

Nadia shook her head. "They'd already be here if they were coming. Someone is trying to pin this on the presidium, and the presidium would never attack the main colonists. The dome is safe, at least for now." She took a breath so deep Ember thought she might pop a seam on her snug-fitting T-shirt. "Queen is my home, but this, this is all bullshit. If we want to leave, as much as I don't want to say it, now is kind of the time."

"Skipping the conference?" Ember asked, surprised. "There are answers there."

Nadia held up a finger as Asher moved to the main control panel. "I want to do damage. Yes. But I have deep reservations about leaving the mella—"

"We voted on this plan of action," Asher cut in, her tone hardening. "And we always knew an air strike was a possibility."

"And I don't feel good about leaving the colonists." Nadia glared at Asher. "I don't think we should hang around the conference, no matter what information we might turn up, but I *do* think, instead of having everyone just wait around for our *one* dinky, obnoxious spaceship to get to Earth and back, what if we tore this whole façade down, using the galaxy's best scientists to do it?"

Ember's brain finally caught up with Nadia's. "Oh, god. Can you image what an upset it would be if the galaxy's tech elite found out Old Earth had turned into an exclusive paradise they can't access?"

"Or," Nadia added, matching Ember's grin, "just to consider, but what if we brought them with us? To Earth." Nadia's eyes took on a perfect mad-scientist gleam. "Tell them the secret; take them to Old Earth. *Show* them the lie. We crash Earth with the galaxy's best scientists and most of the tech money and *damn*, Ember. There's no way they aren't letting us back in. We'll have the biggest secret in the galaxy on our lips and two or three dozen scientists frothing to get back home."

"Home," Ember said and crinkled her nose, her voice turned wistful. "It could work."

Nadia put an arm around Ember's shoulder and kicked at her sister's left toe with a dusty boot. "With Queen's best and most rakish-looking scientists on the case? Please. It's a 'shoe-in.'"

Ember rolled her eyes. "Weak, O'Grady."

"I'll do better toe-morrow. What do you think, Asher?"

"I'd like to leave as soon as possible, but Nadia's plan has merit. We have a lot higher chance of getting let onto Earth if we have half the galaxy's pissed-off scientists with us. But if we're going to delay, I think we should make the most of it. I like the idea of backup codes. If we can get to one of the mining sites, we can pull export exit codes from the computers there. It'd be good insurance while you try to convince a bunch of scientists that Earth exists." She lifted her chin and spoke to the ceiling. "Kate, you finished?"

"Tara's snug as a bug in a flashy rug," Kate said. "Took five minutes to transfer her. We just finished. Taraniel made a very compressed TOPA imprint."

"Do I want to know how you got the presidium's only interstellar ship?" Ember cut in.

Asher smirked. "They have a hangar. We have codes. We steal from you people *all the time*. Someday, the presidium is going to have to get better security software, although since there were only two ships, really, not a lot of choices."

Nadia gave a sigh that sounded like a punctured helium balloon. "Well, we definitely won't be getting our glassware back now. Any chance you stole Varun's fleakers while you were out?"

Asher ignored her. "Tara, take us outside the dome and toward the conference center. Stop about twenty kilometers out. Land, and we can transfer Ember and maybe Varun to beetleback." She turned back to Ember. "You'll make a bigger impression coming in on a beetle than on a ship."

No. We don't need the scientists to leave Queen. We should leave right now. Ember, are you bleeding again?

Ember was *not* in the mood for overprotective AI-wives. And while she wasn't keen on riding a beetle again, the more she thought about crashing a conference while riding Snuzzle, the more she liked it. If Asher took Pui and the ship and got backup codes, that would help settle everyone's nerves.

"It's just beetle spit," she said. "Focus. We need those scientists to have a shot at not being kicked off of Earth. Taraniel wanted us to live there, not get shot to pieces the moment we entered its atmosphere. Check your programming."

Ember counted to fifteen before Tara returned.

Fine. But you've set up a conflict in my mandate that I don't like and can't rectify.

Whatever the result, it couldn't possibly be more unexpected than riding a beetle while being chased by bunnies.

"Great. Then let's go crash a conference, disillusion a bunch of scientists, and then...then we go back to Earth."

Chapter Fifteen

Ember

"Here. Land here." Nadia pushed Asher out of the way and tapped a finger on the viewscreen, which showed snow just beginning to transition to patches of brown grass. Ember unfastened her harness and stretched her arms.

"We're close to where Varun and I touched down originally, just outside the perimeter of the conference area," Nadia continued. "We shouldn't get any closer with this number of beetles. Their wings sound like an army of machine guns. We can all land, stretch, then mount our beetles and break into groups."

Asher muttered under her breath.

"Oh, relax," Nadia said with a slap to her back. "You're still in charge."

Asher flushed, and her eyes flicked to Ember. Ember smothered a smile.

"Land, Tara," Asher said with a cough. She stood and handed Nok a rabbit leather harness as the pod decelerated.

Ember turned to watch the snowy grass come into focus, dotted with bare ground. She checked the thermometer readings on the left side of the screen: 8C. Cold, but not frigid.

Asher had her hand on the hatch release panel the moment the landing struts hit.

"Get the harness on like we discussed, Nok. Nadia is with me and Pui. Kate and Nok are going with Ember and Varun. Questions?"

"We'll need about ten minutes for Ember to figure out beetle steering," Nok said.

"We have ideas," Varun added brightly. "Ready, Ember?"

"No."

The hatch opened. Asher took a step onto it, paused, then turned sideways. "Taraniel said you were hotheaded. 'Stupidly brave,' I think were words she used." Asher again bit into her lower lip, and her eyes burned into Ember's. "I'd love to see that."

"Aheh." Ember sounded like a teenager at a middle school dance. She hurried down the ramp and into the slushy field, where she wouldn't be tempted to make increasingly less awkward eye contact.

I don't like this. We are wasting time. We should just leave, Ember.

"No."

Snuzzle and the other two beetles stood in a loose triangle to the north of the ship, antennae to abdomen, clicking at one another. Kate and Varun joined her at the base of the ramp. Nok came down and jogged to the beetles, harnesses in hand.

"Asher?" Ember called back into the ship when her stomach started doing flips. Nothing about riding Snuzzle again meshed with her desire to stay alive. "You're sure you can get to the dig site and back in under an hour?"

Asher appeared at the ship opening as she shoved a handheld comm into her pocket. "Sorry. The mella council just sent a message. We had about fifty fatalities, mostly children." Her voice turned cold. "I think the mella are beyond hit and run at this point. The presidium may not be responsible, but they're complacent if nothing else. There's going to be a reckoning once the mella are on their feet again. But we have the council's blessing to move forward with our plan for Earth."

Ember nodded and took two very hesitant steps toward Snuzzle. "All right. So. Beetles? I don't want to do this again, by the way."

"Oh, come on," Asher said. Her eyebrows wiggled as she came down the ramp. "We've got non-TOPA envirosuits you can use, and wild beetles migrate and are used to following a leader. It could work. You look good in an envirosuit."

"Looking good in an envirosuit does not mean I can direct Snuzzle."

"Have you tried?" Asher asked.

"Fuck you." The words came without malice, though, as Ember tried to picture what that might look like—the riding, not the fucking. Were the antennae long enough or flexible enough to be pulled back and used like reins? There was no way she was flying to the opposite side of the equator wrapped in a barbed blue tongue. But beetleback, with a firm, gloved grip on each antenna...

A cool cylinder of metal pressed into her hip. "This will help," Varun suggested. "A flashlight. We put a color filter on it. Triple blink in yellow should get its attention. It says, 'I'd like a mating performance,' loosely translated."

"You're certain it's not 'I'm ready to make beetle babies'?"

Nok returned to the group, chuckling. "No. That's what being covered in pheromone says. You already did that. Beetles are all harnessed and ready to go."

Snuzzle took flight without prompting.

"Lovely." Ember flicked the flashlight three times, counting to five between each click.

Snuzzle's butt flashed green, once, but didn't change altitude.

"Do it again. Faster this time," Nok prodded. "He's probably just being playful."

"He?" Ember asked as she repeated the flashlight display. "How do you know?"

"I've recorded thirteen different genital configurations on the Queen beetles. Don't overthink it. Use whatever you want. He's a giant firefly that rolls around in stinkhorn fungus to have a good time."

"Fair point."

Ember finished the sequence, and this time, Snuzzle dropped with more grace than Ember had ever seen the thing use before, even when it had her in its tongue. Its—his—wings fluttered closed, and he reared his front legs up, dangled in the air for a minute, then landed again.

"Now do two long, two short flashes. Same color."

Ember did so, interpreting "long" and "short" to the best of her ability. Science was supposed to be specific.

"What did I tell it?" Ember took a step back as Snuzzle came toward her, its antennae spinning in wide arcs.

"That you've made a selection."

"What?" She spun on Nok, but Snuzzle got to her first, antennae once again on her shoulders and one of his eyes less than an eyelash length from her nose.

"Ahh!" Ember yelled just as Varun yelled, "Got it!" A shudder of red light came from the spaceship. The beetle lit orange, clicked once, and backed off far enough that Ember no longer felt like she might contract beetle herpes.

"That's the unsure signal, we think," said Varun. "You're demanding courtship." Then Varun *smiled*, the asshole, and said, "It's like lesbian slow-burn romance. Make the beetle really work for it."

There were at least seventeen retorts she wanted to use but instead asked, "Can you flash the same to all three? Do beetles orgy?"

"Yes. In unlimited numbers."

"Great. Hey, Asher?"

Asher's voice came from somewhere behind Snuzzle. "Yeah? Right here. You wanted an orgy?"

Wow did Ember not want to respond to that. "Bring me one of those envirosuits?"

"The ones you look good in?" Asher asked.

"Whatever. Yes. Just bring me one."

Ember kept her eyes on Snuzzle despite the orange and yellow blinking in her periphery. Like living inside a clementine, she mused, that was also hosting a rave.

"Suit." Leather pressed into one of Ember's open hands. She didn't take her eyes from Snuzzle, who had once again drawn way too close. Ember's mind kept slipping into conjecture about what would happen with that tongue if she looked away, or with the mandibles that hadn't eaten her yet, but hey, the night was young.

Ember pulled the tight white leather up her legs, being as mindful as she could of the embedded electronics within. She only lost her balance once trying to find a foot hole but managed to keep her head up and her eyes locked on target. She tightened the ankle openings, petting one of the rabbits as she did so for absolutely no logical reason, then put her arms through the rest of the suit and fastened it up to her chin. She pulled the attached gloves over her hands and broke eye contact with Snuzzle just long enough to have the stupidly bulky helmet placed over her head.

The world became tinged with yellow as the suit's visor filtered color. Someone snapped the helmet into the neck clasps, and sterile, dry air poured through two vents near her nose. Ember took a deep breath and flexed her arms experimentally. The suit was a reasonable fit, although she had a limited range of movement in her shoulders.

She clicked her upper and lower right molars together. No sign of TOPA, but a display did pop up on the inside of her face shield, presenting a menu of options. Ember mulled them for a minute before letting out a long breath and tapping on her face shield with a gloved finger.

Asher came around to her front, taking care not to cut off Ember's view of Snuzzle, and popped the sapphire of the face shield out in a move so practiced and fluid Ember had to blink a few times before she could talk.

"What's up?" Asher asked. "You do, in fact, look fine." A smile ghosted across her face. "Beautiful, even." Her voice dropped. Softened. "Please be careful out there."

Ember's stomach fluttered in a way that hadn't happened since Taraniel. She couldn't decide if she should be excited about that or not. "Later, Asher. Right now, I can't work a suit while manually flying a beetle." She paused, testing the words she was about to use. "Can Tara route through here and run the ship at the same time? Or can you clone her and put her in the suit?"

Asher's right eyebrow raised. "You want *two* digital dead wives?"

"I need help!" Ember's eyes flicked to Asher's for a moment. One of Snuzzle's antennae drooped. "Quickly, before they lose interest. Although I still don't see why *I* have to do the leading."

"Because you're already mated to the lead beetle. Hold on. I'll see what Kate can manage." Ember heard a muffled

"Hey, Kate" just before Asher reseated the sapphire and Ember's world turned yellow again.

What to do in the interim? Curious, Ember reached out and placed a hand on Snuzzle's right antenna, stopping its spinning. It hit her palm like a whip, the leather only partially deadening the sting. Ember cursed but held on.

Snuzzle stepped into her, too close for her to see the wide-set eyes but so close that she was directly between its mandibles. The other antenna stopped twirling and bopped her, tentatively, on the shoulder.

Ember grasped it and flexed them both experimentally, first left and right, then up and down. The scaling grabbed at her gloves, but otherwise, the tissue felt flexible, like a thick outdoor-rated extension cord from Earth. She turned the first few centimeters of the right one to point at Snuzzle's face.

The beetle sat down.

Ember was unaware beetles could sit. They weren't dogs. Yet Snuzzle had clearly folded its back two legs underneath and had the light-up part of its abdomen in the grass.

A hand tapped on her face shield, but she waved whomever it was away. Keeping the right antenna folded, she curved the left as well.

Snuzzle lay down on the ground.

This made no sense. *No sense.* Directionality had to be a uniquely human thing, and Snuzzle had no reason to follow any type of command, implied, interpreted, or otherwise, since his only stake in this was reproduction.

Ember released both antennae slowly, uncurling one finger at a time until she finally pulled her hands back. The antennae stayed curved, and Snuzzle stayed down.

Ember grinned. "Ride 'em, cowgirl," she whispered into the face shield.

Good thing I didn't turn the exterior speakers on. Ember, I don't want you doing this.

Tara's voice—*Taraniel's voice*—startled Ember enough that she flubbed her first step forward, stepping on rabbit tail. The little lop grunted and lunged at her ankle as she pulled up but stopped short of actually biting.

"Stop. You don't get a vote. You're just here to ferret verbal commands." Ember finally broke eye contact with Snuzzle, waited several breaths to see if the beetle would move or maybe eat her, then, when nothing happened, walked to the nearest bent leg and pushed her hand against it. Firm. Stable. It had little elbow joints, or whatever they were called on beetles, and the way the legs collapsed into five segments, bending at ninety-degree angles at the joint, made each leg a convenient staircase.

Taraniel doesn't want you doing this. Think about her.

"Remove the yellow filter," Ember said. "It's too hard to see the edges of the legs from the grass on the white beetles. And don't you dare tell me what my wife would have wanted."

The face shield view changed to real color. Tara fumed with fake, pointed breathing. Ember hunched her shoulders at the sound. It grated, and now wasn't the time to fight over beetles.

Tara stayed mercifully silent.

Ember shook the whole conversation from her head and focused on climbing Snuzzle's leg without slipping off. Her boots were the mella-issued ones, and their grip was too worn to prevent sliding on lightly striated exoskeleton. Still, Ember managed to stay mostly upright until she hit the junction of leg to thorax.

"Think I can hop it?" she asked as she eyed the distance between herself and the ridge where the beetle's head met the thorax, and the junction where thorax met abdomen. She pointed to the head joint. "That's where I rode before."

No. Can you jump half your height? It isn't safe.

"Taraniel didn't do testy," Ember shot back. "Taraniel did quiet passive aggressive. You're becoming more irritating than my original suit TOPA." She ran her gloved hands against the exoskeleton and tried to dig her nails in as she had before. It failed miserably.

You only saw one side of her.

What the hell did that mean? Ember jumped. She reached for the curvature of the thorax right as it met the head, remembering the textured ridge she'd used before for grip. Her fingers found it, and she dangled for several heartbeats, trying to find purchase for her toes before Snuzzle straightened his left legs.

Ember's body slid to the right. She loosened her grip enough to control the slide until she was roughly on top of the central thorax. Once there, she pulled her legs up under herself as much as she could and clicked her tongue in what she hoped was a reasonable imitation of Snuzzle's irritated click from the presidium complex.

Snuzzle didn't move.

"I'm bad at this!" Ember yelled, even though there was no way anyone could hear her through the helmet. "Can I get some lighting? Tara?"

"Just calm down, Ember. You look pretty all right," Nadia called up to Ember from near Snuzzle's toes. She'd let her hair out of its ponytail, and it whipped around her face and into her mouth, where she spat it out in very Nadia-like disdain. While they were fussing with harnesses and beetle steering, rabbits had arrived, and Nadia used the side of her foot to sweep a cluster of them away from Snuzzle.

"You okay?" Ember asked. "Shouldn't you be on the ship?"

"We can't go anywhere until you do. Also, sister time." Nadia stood on her tiptoes and leaned in. "This is kind of it, Ember. We go to Earth...we go to Old Earth and that is *it*. It'll be years before we can get back here, or find them when they inevitably scatter across the colonized worlds. Are you ready? Like, *ready* ready? You're willingly getting on a spaceship. I've seen you panic on a flyer. What are you going to do in space? Have you thought about that? Asher says it's almost eight months to Earth."

"Panic. But at least we won't be frozen."

"Argh. Stop deflecting. Not being frozen doesn't mean things won't go wrong." Nadia turned and leaned against Snuzzle's abdomen. "Circumstances can change in a heartbeat. You shouldn't have to go through that again, even if it's what Taraniel wanted."

Ember flipped up her face shield with a sigh that was one part sore muscles and fatigue and a hundred parts *don't tell me what to do.* "What *we* wanted. And it... I wouldn't have done it without her. Her, or you." She batted at her left calf, cursed, then looked right back at Nadia. The furrow between Nadia's eyebrows meant she was not okay, but she was sucking it up for Ember's sake. Damn Schmitt stubbornness.

"Are you ready, sis?" Ember asked

Nadia clicked off her headlamp, bathing them in patchy darkness broken only by the wandering lights of the mella. She saluted Ember. "Always ready to follow you, Ember. You know that. Always have been. Crapsack world to crapsack world."

"Tenure won't forgive this."

Nadia scoffed. "Please. We are way beyond tenure. I have to keep you from puking all over our new stolen spaceship ruining your chances with Asher, who doesn't entirely suck. That's way more work than grant writing. Besides, what are little-big sisters for, if not moral support?"

"Headaches, mostly." Ember thought she caught a smile. "I'm really glad you're always here, Nadia Ann. Thank you."

Nadia flushed and turned her headlamp back on, blinding Ember. "Yeah yeah yeah."

Ember snorted. "Get back to the ship. We are short on time."

"Yes, in a few minutes. Bathroom breaks, I think." In a lower voice, Nadia added, "Asher *really* likes to be in control. I don't know where you fall in that kind of dynamic, but just so you know."

Ember rubbed her calves, which were already starting to twinge. "Jesus, Nadia. You know where you're going?"

"Asher does. They've done a few failed raids on the mining sites before, apparently. Here's hoping we have more success. Varun offered to go, but they want him with Nok in case the beetles get weird."

"You should leave now, then." Ember scratched at her scalp and took a long, deep breath of cool air. Strands of her braided hair had come loose and likely looked like one of the thirty thousand rabbits running across the snow had made a nest in it. She smelled like blood and had a slight tremor to her right hand. Ridiculousness, all of it, the posturing and pretending. Her sister was just as fucking petrified as she was. They were about to overthrow a conference. They were about to storm a planet.

"Nadia?"

"When we hit space, that first night, I'm going to sneeze in your hair while you're sleeping. And I'm going to watch you sleep and make sure you don't have weird nightmares and shit, and we're going to crash the party on Earth just like I did with the brand-new hybrid car Mom got you for your sixteenth birthday. Wrap that planet right around a telephone pole and grin like only a joyriding tween can."

Ember stared at her. Nadia stared back. Rabbits clawed and grunted and hopped over Nadia's boots, and the wind remained mildly unpleasant.

Finally, achingly, Ember dissolved into laughter.

"*Jesus*, Nadia."

Nadia laughed, too, and it felt like neither of them had done that, really laughed since Earth. Or at least since Taraniel's death. "So, let's go. Really go and do this."

Ember sobered and pushed her face shield back into place. "Once we get to the conference, it'll be fifteen minutes, maybe half an hour before we've done our part. You can't take much longer. Get those codes and get back to me. *Fast.*"

"You're so damn bossy," Nadia said with a grin. She saluted. "We'll do our best to meet your timetable. Fungus-face?"

Ember glared at her, but it had only joy underneath. "What?"

"Be careful."

God, she loved her sister, every pun-filled, brash, irritating part of her. "Yeah, yeah. You too. It'll be more fun to journey to Earth with living-you than corpse-you."

"Hah!" Nadia waved curtly, spun, and limped back to the ship.

Ember watched her until she disappeared into it and the hatch closed. Both her calves cramped at the same time. When she tried to shift her weight to her left leg, her feet slid out from under her. Her hands slipped, the leather tearing and sending warning lights across the inside of her face shield. She kicked her toes against Snuzzle's exoskeleton in the vain hope that Queen's beetles might be genetically related to horses—trained Earth horses—and only stopped when she saw a blaze of red from above.

The pod hovered directly over her, the track lighting chasing a band of white and orange. Snuzzle knelt into the grass, then lay, flattening out as he did so. Ember let out a long sigh of relief and pulled herself up to sitting. She wedged her feet and ankles back under the thorax curve, checked her ripped gloves for blood (none, thank god), and leaned forward until her belly lay on the top of Snuzzle's head.

From there, she could just grab the tip of the right antennae if she reached out with her left arm, then pushed off with one of her feet. Snuzzle let out one loud click but didn't move, and Ember managed to grasp the antenna and then work herself back into her "seat." She held both like she was in a bizarre arcade game—one that no one had ever played before because it looked like it would eat your quarters and stop halfway through for no reason whatsoever.

Ember. Now, Tara did sound exactly like Taraniel. Ember bristled. Every ounce of sisterly joy Nadia had managed to fill her with seeped from her pores.

"I can see your manipulation a kilometer away."

Not safe. It's still an hour to the conference center. What if you fall asleep? What if you fall off? You're not stable.

"Guess you'd better keep me awake." Ember lightly pulled both antennae straight up. Snuzzle, miraculously, stood. Ember did it again, and his wing casing opened, pushing her forward into a forty-five-degree sitting position. It wasn't uncomfortable at the moment, but she didn't know if she could sustain it for seven hours.

Ember—

"Do your job and keep me alive."

Snuzzle pushed from the ground, directly up. His wings buzzed to life in the same second, and once again, Ember was flying on beetleback, the ground dizzy beneath her, her last meal threatening to escape out the wrong orifice.

"Compass, please," Ember said as her face shield tried to make sense of what she was doing and flipped between the layout for flyer, running, or stationary. "I can see Nadia's stream, but which way does Asher want to go? We're equidistant, right? From this point, between the conference and the mining site?"

The voice that came back was entirely TOPA. **She says to stay on the equator and go west. Ready for your lighting?**

"My...oh." The ring of tiny LEDs around Ember's wrists and, she assumed, the band that ran across the top of her helmet lit beetle-green and blinked in a repeating three-blip pattern. Ember looked back over her shoulder to see Snuzzle's butt matching the color and pattern.

A plume of air shot upward, giving Ember the momentary feeling of pressure as the other two beetles took flight as well. They stayed on either side of Snuzzle, both with rabbits perched on their exoskeletons, the little furry ears popping out from underneath the same thorax curve where Ember had wedged her feet.

The whole circus hovered then, waiting.

Tara, finally, manifested a rose compass up on Ember's face shield. It pointed northeast. Unhelpful. Ember bent the antennae left, making sure to track them in a wide arc as she did so.

Snuzzle clicked and turned in the corresponding direction. Dead west. The other beetles mimicked. In her peripheral vision, Ember could make out Varun and Nok together on the bigger one, Kate alone on the small, brown-speckled one.

She pushed the tips of the antennae around and left them pointing forward. Then she leaned down, pressing her body into the exoskeleton. Snuzzle's clicks dropped away, and a low thrumming sound started from behind.

They sped west.

Extended flying while plastered to the back of a giant beetle, covered in fungus or not, was hell.

Ember didn't have to steer. Snuzzle stayed on course beautifully, and it was a small relief that the beetle didn't respond to body movement. Well, not *minor* body movement. Twenty minutes in, Ember's back had twinged so badly she had to straighten, and Snuzzle had veered, and they'd both ended up half lodged in mushy snow.

At the thirty-minute mark, when Ember's right calf and left foot charley-horsed at the same time, she admitted defeat. She clicked her back molars, and her audio feed turned on. "Someone distract me, please."

Tara's voice was the last she wanted to hear, so, of course, it was the one that responded. **We are almost to our site. For you. I have audio recordings from Taraniel. She left you seventeen, none of which you've listened to.**

Tara's voice sounded distinct, if not snippy. Maybe. Maybe Ember was forgetting how Taraniel had sounded in life. Now, Tara sounded more like how Varun might speak while trying to half carry her home after a sad game of beer pong (they had no bars on Queen, so the games were always sad). Or how Nadia might speak during the rare times they weren't playfully sniping at each other.

Still, the idea of the recordings. The image of Taraniel, in the ship, making them day after day as her body gave out. A muscle in Ember's neck spasmed.

"Is it a mandate for you to play them?" she asked.

No.

"Do it."

A low thrum of static blasted from the internal speaker before Taraniel's voice filled Ember's head. Tara turned the viewscreen dark, the letters **I'll watch** scrolling across in white.

Taraniel spoke, and Ember's heart skipped.

Hey, love. This is my...fifth? I think? recording to you. I've already covered all the big stuff, so I thought I'd remind you that Varun still has our last bottle of pisco, and you were adamant he not drink it all. And that now you can fold your shirts fresh out of the dryer the way you want, no more refolding. Taraniel laughed. *All the stupid things people fight over in a marriage.*

One thing I don't want to fight over is Earth. The mella know what they need to know, but I still don't think it's right, what's happened on Queen. You don't deserve to be here. You deserved a choice. A lot of people deserved a choice. I know the AI is pushy—and I've got override codes for her if you need—but she's been instructed to not release my last message until you're at least off-world. I need you to do that for me, Ember, if nothing else. You've got to get out of here. You can't keep having your research stolen, your hope stolen, and both taken to a world I'll never get to see again.

Go home, Ember.

The recording abruptly cut off. Ember's faceplate fizzed back to transparency, but she had no interest in the landscape.

Do you want another one? Tara asked, hesitantly, in a voice that Ember realized sounded nothing like Taraniel. It sounded like an echo on a poor voice recording, hollow and sad, where Taraniel had been animated, passionate, driven.

I can give you all but the last.

"No. Not right now."

Do you need someone? I can put Asher on. Or Nadia or Varun. Nok, Pui, or Kate, even, if you want to talk about computers or beetles.

"No." Ember then whispered, "I'd forgotten what her voice sounded like. I'd forgotten the depth to it. I just need a minute."

Of course.

The little yellow light that stayed lit when the suit AI was active went out. Alone, truly alone, Ember rested her forehead on Snuzzle. She let tears fall then, splashing onto the face shield where the suit could absorb them readily.

There weren't as many as Ember had thought there would be. Five minutes, maybe, before she lifted her head again. She set her eyes on the horizon, rotated her ankles as much as she could, and clicked her teeth to get the AI's attention.

"Play them all, Tara. In order, as many as we have time for. I'm ready."

Chapter Sixteen

Nadia

Snow reflected light. Grass did not. Hence, it was clear when they hit the habitable strip of the snow-side equator. Three minutes past the boundary, and a halo of artificial light flared in the distance. It was deep night, or early morning, which meant when they flew over the well-lit buildings and ship parking lots, there were no signs of life. T-shaped clusters of two-story buildings were visible from the viewscreen, as well as paved circles of concrete filled with hexagonal, standard-issue New Earth spaceships (which she recognized from the waning supply shipments), and three small ponds that may have also qualified as lakes.

"Do ships regularly fly over?" she asked herself. "How weird do we look?"

A hollow *thunk* answered her. A little gray rabbit sat at Nadia's feet with small, mouse-like ears and a pink nose.

"Are you kidding me? How are there rabbits on this ship? Did you sneak on in the settlement?"

The rabbit thumped again.

Nadia sighed. "Right. Don't talk about it. I don't want to know. Hey, Asher? Did you know we have rabbits on board?"

"Six of them," Asher answered distractedly as she fussed with a console to her right. "Pui thinks there may be more. Ignore them. We're landing."

The rabbit slipped under her chair with one final thump.

"Uh-huh." She turned back to the viewscreen. The ship's track lighting illuminated for about ten meters in every direction, and just to the north of them, Nadia caught a glint of silvery-blue.

Another lake.

The ship drifted lower, which seemed stupid since anyone monitoring the skies would pick them up no matter what speed they came in at. The ship lighting sparkled off stagnant water, surrounding machinery she only remembered from books. Old, lightly rusting, yellow machines with buckets filled with sand so white it reflected the ship's light the same as snow. Excavators. Loaders. A landing pad five times the size of the one at the conference center had three spaceships parked on it—each with cargo holds that made up three quarters of the ships. There had to be a hundred of the machines stationed in her line of sight alone, clustered around lakes that couldn't have been natural.

Ship sensors don't detect anyone or anything moving around. The miners and everyone else associated with this site should be at the conference.

The hatch opened. Asher and Pui walked out, Pui tugging on Nadia's unfastened coat zipper as she followed them. At least two of the rabbits darted out with them and disappeared into the snow. Nadia stepped outside, but even unzipped, she was almost too warm in the insulated boots, pants, and coat the mella had insisted she wear. Yet it was cold, clearly. Ice cracked on the lake surfaces, and she had snow up to her ankles, but the breeze carried enough warmth—however impossibly—that it didn't feel like the snot was freezing inside her nose, and she seemed in no danger of losing her remaining toes.

One large building loomed in front of them—dark gray, unlit, and way too creepy. The outside was cinderblock. Not surprising. It had two stories but no windows, just a bay door on the second floor and a ramp leading up to it. Nadia took the ramp and tried the door handle, pulling up tentatively and then, when that didn't budge it or make a horrible squeaking sound, more firmly.

A squeal loud enough to be the death throes of a beetle came from what sounded like rusted metal. The door still didn't move.

"You couldn't wait for Pui to clear the alarms?" Asher asked irritably as she came up the ramp, Pui trailing her. Asher pointed up, and Nadia noted the panel to the left of the door and another just above head height. Great. Digital locks *and* they were on *Candid Camera*.

"Sorry. We're committed to this one now." Nadia gestured to the camera.

"Your parents should have worked on patience more with both you and Dr. Schmitt." Pui edged past both of them and stuck a round piece of plastic about the size of Nadia's thumbnail on the front of the main panel. "Tara. You're on. Once we're in, I'll go directly to their server and hook you in. Hopefully, we can breeze through their security to get the export codes. Kate's better with machines, but if you can work with genes, you can work with any encryption. At least that's what my PI used to tell me."

It's open. I've got the cameras down, too, but they're continuous feed. If anyone is watching, they know we're here.

"And Ember?" Asher asked as the door pulled sideways into a pocket in the wall. It slid sideways and to the right, not up like Nadia expected.

Haven't heard yet and was told to not speak until spoken to.

Nadia snorted.

The door clicked into place and rows of LED ceiling lights lit simultaneously. They pushed forward onto a plastic catwalk that ran the circumference of the circular building. Filling the inside of the building all the way up to the catwalk was white sand. It lay mounded in small hills, spilling across the doorway, the catwalk, and some of it sticking to the walls in fine granules.

Pui wormed around Asher and ran ahead to a computer console embedded in a wall about twenty meters from the entry door. She pressed the little plastic piece against the wall, and a green light illuminated from within. "Give me ten!" she called back, not bothering to look at them. "We've got encryptions."

Asher leaned against the wall, arms across her chest, and closed her eyes. Nadia squinted into the darkness. There was so much sand. How the beetles didn't have a massive gallery out here was beyond her comprehension. Every beetle on the planetoid should have been actively colonizing the area, which meant whoever ran the place had likely either chased them out or was doing something to keep them out. Nadia shivered.

"Better make that fifteen minutes," Pui said, her voice strained. "I didn't expect the shipping information to be as well guarded as the finance reports, but they're all in the same place."

"I think you have twelve at the most, Pui," Asher responded, not opening her eyes.

Nadia continued staring at the white sea beneath her feet, a decidedly eerie prickling moving up her arms. Even under the thick boots, the sand felt slick, like satin. Nothing like the main sand of Queen. She could *feel* the price of the stuff. Also, there were no beetle mounds. No flocks or herds or whatever they were called. Maybe the sand was too slick for building? Maybe this was outside their migration area? *Maybe the presidium was as cutthroat with wildlife as they were with grant funding.*

"Okay, okay, we're finally making headway. Give me five."

Nadia barely heard her. The beetle question kept bugging her. The more she thought about it, the creepier it became. She moved farther into the silo, into shadow where she hoped Asher and Pui couldn't hear, and whispered into her collar, "Hey, Tara. Do you know, or does Nok or Varun, why I don't see any beetle mounds up here?"

I'll transfer your question.

Nadia did half a lap around the silo before Nok answered. "That's a very complicated question, Dr. O'Grady. Perhaps another time."

"Make time," Nadia insisted. "This is *weird*. Why are there no beetles here?"

"It's possible they just make more underground structures—"

Irrelevant, Tara cut in, her voice cold and nothing at all like the Taraniel Nadia had known. **Please wait for communication. Until further notice, this comm will not function.**

With a click, Nadia's comm went dead.

A weight dropped in her stomach.

"Asher?" She jogged back to the other women, the hairs on her arm standing up and a very unpleasant tingle in her spine. "We have a problem."

"Done!" Pui plucked the plastic disc from the wall and grinned triumphantly. "The presidium has five unique export codes they use for shipping the sand, depending on destination, and I have all of them. At least one should work. Let's go."

Asher pushed from the wall and jogged with Pui back out the door.

"Hey. Asher!"

She caught up with them just as they exited. "Asher!" Nadia slapped the mella in the shoulder. "Tara just cut me off. The comm is dead. Do you hear me?"

They stepped outside into the cool air, which sent shivers across Nadia's skin and made her nose itch. She hadn't realized how warm it had gotten in the silo with all the sand insulation.

"I hear you." Asher pointed to an indent in the snow, right where the presidium ship had landed. The ship, *their* ship, was gone. And just beyond its imprint sat a row of gleaming, hexagonal colony flyers. Ten of them, all parked in a perfectly straight line.

"Asher?"

"We're fucked," Asher deadpanned. "They pinged on the one satellite the mella have access to, about ten seconds ago. I just got the notification. Nothing we can do. Go!"

Dozens of streetlamps buzzed to life, obliterating the dark and shadows. Flyer hatches opened, and people in jumpsuits with New Earth logos spilled out.

Nadia turned off her headlamp and ran.

Her leg was nowhere near healed, but she managed to get down off the ramp, back behind the silo, and into a triangular wedge of shadow at the T-junction of another building without seeing another human.

"Tara?" she asked, breathless and in more pain than she'd anticipated.

No response came from the comm.

She heard shouts. Names she didn't recognize. Heard the sound of live ammunition, and it was suddenly very hard to breathe. When footsteps got too close for comfort, she limp-sprinted across what passed for a road and buried herself underneath one of the diggers. From the corner of her eye, Nadia thought she saw a Pui-shaped form wiggle under another vehicle to the west.

"*Tara!*" she hissed into her shoulder.

Again, no response.

Nadia's brain bathed her in the Ember-is-in-trouble-and-you-can't-help hormone. Most people got fight or flight. Nadia only got *where is Ember?* It felt a lot like panic, but the kind of raw, heady panic of a PhD defense. Nothing to be done, just get through it. Remember that Ember had survived her childhood, adolescence, and the disaster colony ship through sheer dumb luck. No sense in it running out now.

"And I'll screw you, and your mom, and *her* mom!" Nadia watched as Asher's boots marched down the ramp, surrounded by multiple pairs of polished black rubber. *Rubber.* They didn't have rubber on Queen or anywhere else in the colonized worlds because rubber came from rubber trees, which grew only on Earth. You could get a few specialty products—small souvenir things—made from a few of the lower production plants, like dandelions, but that many boots that looked that new did not come from Earth's most useful weed.

If Nadia had had any lingering doubts about being screwed over by her homeworld, they were definitely gone now.

Two pairs of boots went with Asher, back around the other side of the building. The rest scattered. The video feed had likely shown all three of them. Damn it. And it definitely had Nadia's face. There was no way they'd give up with only Asher.

A pair of black boots approached her loader. It stopped near the cab, and Nadia heard the door open, heard a woman mutter, "Nope," under her breath before she jumped back to the sand. A hand came into Nadia's view as the woman began to kneel down, and so she did what any good scientist with indefinite tenure and a solid publication and grant record would do.

She panicked.

Nadia leapt out from the opposite side of the loader just as the woman's face appeared. She sprinted (badly) deeper into the cluster of silos, having no idea which way to go but figuring as long as she was *running*, she wasn't in a cell and about to be shot again.

The woman called out to her, and a bunch of other voices—some distinctly male—called out too. A rabbit darted in front of her and pivoted right. What the hell? Why not. Nadia changed course and followed. She cleared another silo, detoured around a small pond-lake thing, and managed to put on a burst of speed despite her leg feeling like it had a red-hot poker embedded in it as another black-booted woman surprised her from the backside of a storage shed as she passed by.

Then she was in open field, the sand mixed with light snow, a hill roughly five times her height looming dead ahead. The rabbit crested the hill and disappeared. There was no way Nadia was running up that hill, not before the Boots caught her. Not with a shot leg.

She was absolutely fucked.

Nadia stopped, gasping and heaving. Ready to meet the inevitable head-on and reassess from there when...when an absolute *mess* of beetles belched from the ground, running right at her.

A hand grabbed her coat, and she pulled against it, her gloved fingers frantically tearing at the buttons and zipper to get free.

"Hey!" Nadia waved her arms and did her best impression of a beetle click. "Over here!"

Rabbits wove in and out of scuttling beetle toes. Nadia counted at least twelve snow-side beetles and hundreds of rabbits, some riding the beetles but most just hopping, and wiggling, and turning the snowy ground into an undulating mass of fur.

Two more women reached her and each took an arm. Unable to break free, Nadia went limp instead. The women didn't let go but fell with her, knees embedding in slush.

"Help!" Nadia called, frantic, and smacked her tongue as loudly as she could against her upper palate.

A squarish beetle with mother-of-pearl wings and jet-black antennae broke to the head of the colony and charged.

His mandibles would have been right at head/neck height had they been standing. Instead, Nadia and her three captors got a view of beetle legs tearing up snow and sand and a horde of rabbits slithering between the debris. The lead beetle's ass went blue, and Nadia tore an arm free enough to turn her headlamp back on.

Rabbits hit them first—a stream of frantic fur and sharp nails. They launched themselves onto the humans, nipping at hair and clothes and skin as they ran past. One raked claws across Nadia's cheek. Another sank teeth firmly enough that she felt a rush of warmth on her calf. The women holding her yelled in surprise, and their grip loosened as they were consumed by the wave of rabbits racing over them. Nadia pulled one arm completely free, then the other.

The hold on her back didn't release until the lead beetle—Nadia had already mentally named him "Digger"—barreled into all four of them. Exoskeleton hit her jaw, and Nadia saw stars before she pressed back into the woman behind her, flattening them enough that the bottom of Digger's abdomen just missed their heads. The women who had been on either side, holding Nadia's arms, had fanned out too widely. Digger's legs clipped both of them, knocking them back and into the slush.

Digger stopped directly above Nadia. She looked up into mottled white exoskeleton tinged with blue light and squirmed away from the woman beneath her and out from under the beetle. Her jaw hurt. Her leg hurt. This beetle was a damn superhero.

"You're under arrest," the woman said with zero conviction.

"You're under a beetle," Nadia returned. "I win."

The woman groaned, but no hands grabbed at her, and since she didn't hear anyone yelling, Nadia tried to drag herself up one of Digger's legs. She missed the first joint three times before Digger got the picture and knelt, hopefully not squishing Nadia's erstwhile captor in the process.

She didn't waste time gawking or thinking about how she had *no earthly idea* how to ride a beetle, especially without a harness. She especially didn't want to think about how much of Ember's fungus had managed to end up on her; she had no other idea why the beetle was being so jovial. She clawed her way up legs and wing casing, secured herself behind Digger's thorax, grabbed his antennae, and tried her best to imitate Ember's movements. They shot into the air for several seconds before Digger turned to the left and sped from the mining site.

Nadia knew, in that moment, she was definitely going to freeze to death on the back of a giant beetle, stinky mella clothes or not.

She kept her eyes closed for at least seven heartbeats. Maybe more. She opened them when her fingertips started tingling, which meant frostbite *again*. Just to her right, Nadia thought she saw a flutter in the air. She urged Digger toward it. The flutter persisted, a pinprick of light blinking in an out of existence. It took another seven heartbeats before Nadia realized it was another rider on beetleback, flying at the roughly the same breakneck speed they were, although Nadia was gaining. There were other flutters, too, these without lights. The rest of the flock? There had to be...she didn't know... A dozen? Two dozen more beetles out there, tailing the rider as well.

"Hey!" Nadia called, though the wind ate her words. She didn't know the commands for "fly faster" in beetle-antennae speak, but Digger seemed just as eager to catch his friends as she was. Nadia had to press her forehead down onto his exoskeleton when he put on a burst of speed. The coldness in the air couldn't be ignored. They were leaving the equatorial region, and Nadia was not suited for it, literally.

Hah. Well, maybe she was in no danger of freezing if she could still make puns.

She'd lost feeling in her fingertips by the time they caught up with the other beetle. Digger brought them right up beside it. The swarm tailed them close behind. They were mostly snow-side beetles, their mother-of-pearl exoskeletons much easier to see in the poor lighting, with a few brown ones mixed in. Her headlamp reflected off hundreds of pairs of eyes as well, all sparkling from head to thorax and thorax to abdomen joints. So, so many rabbits.

The rider turned, but in the dark, only her headlamp was visible.

"It's Nadia!" she yelled. Even at this distance it would be difficult to hear over the buzzing of beetle wings.

She couldn't hear the rider's response, but their headlamp blinked three times.

If the other rider was attempting Morse code, they were both screwed.

Nadia blinked lamp three times as well, because why not, and continued following the other beetle. It had to be Pui because Asher was in custody, though Nadia was pretty certain they were going toward the conference center. Hopefully.

She just had to hold on and hope they reached Ember before she fell off or froze to death. And hope the flyers hadn't come for her sister as well.

Chapter Seventeen

Ember

There was a fundamental difference, Ember decided, between what you thought a crowd of disgruntled conference attendees would look like, and what they actually looked like. She'd expected panic and frantic pleas for assistance and explanation. What Ember had before her, however, were maybe fifty bleary-eyed business-academics, all staring at her as if she'd presented mediocre results at a low-level conference and the moderator had let her run overtime.

They were functionally penned into the square by Nok, Varun, and Kate, still astride their beetles. Somewhere in the past ten minutes, they'd picked up a few new beetles as well, all snow-side white, all with rabbits peeking from under their wing casings. They'd fanned out in a semicircle, using the conference building as a perimeter.

"Nok? Varun? Kate?" Ember spoke into her collar. "Everyone out?"

"No one left in the main complex," Nok returned distractedly.

Ember leaned back against one of Snuzzle's legs and let out a long breath. They'd set down on the roof of the main conference building, and with the ample street lighting, the damage from Snuzzle's toes to the roof were clearly visible. In the main plaza area below—a rounded circle of pavement from which six sidewalks fanned to six other, less impressive, structures—the academics sat or meandered in small clusters. At least two had their hands up and were looking at Ember expectantly. They'd had their hands up for at least five minutes now, which made them more patient than Ember had ever been.

"Nadia?" Ember asked.

Still hacking the computer at the mining site.

"Okay, but were there complications?"

Flyers. Stay on task.

"What?" Ember hissed. "What's going on?"

You should leave as soon as possible.

A woman from the crowd yelled up at her, "The panels don't start for another three hours, and the auction is after that. Go back to bed!"

At least, that was what Ember thought the woman said. She got back on Snuzzle and made the appropriate antennae movements, she thought, for the beetle to fly down and join the others in the plaza. Leave as soon as possible...they'd only just arrived. Ember hadn't even started talking yet. She needed a plan, and she needed it fast.

Snuzzle hopped instead, landing in the center of the crowd and scattering them like...well, bugs. The conference attendees didn't scream, just jogged from the contact area as if giant beetles threatened to sit on them every day.

Ember had been to all of two academic conferences, both during her PhD, and both of which she'd fallen asleep during at least four sessions. Fashion hadn't changed much, she noted as she approached the largest group. They still wore the same beige-colored slacks, some in rigid button-up cotton and some in polos. Anything with a collar, she remembered, was viable. Some of the people had skirts, and all had sensible shoes, which was good because even the temperate zones of Queen weren't made for dress footwear.

"Are you *all* here for the electronics conference?" she asked. "No one works here or runs the center?"

A man in the front of the group hooked his thumb under his name badge and pushed it up from his shirt. It read: "Dr. Prof. Samuel Smith. Newmark Electronics, Castille, Europa."

"Europa." Ember nodded. "Big tech circuit there."

She knew literally nothing about Europa or its commerce.

"I'm the moderator for the morning sessions. If there isn't an emergency, can we go back in?"

Leave it to academics and business people to make the loudest person in charge.

"Uh, no." Ember searched for proper academic motivation. She needed to get things moving. "There's a beetle swarming issue, as you can see."

"Well, did anyone get called?" a pajama-clad woman asked.

"Yes. That's us. We're Queen's beetle cowgirls. Cowboys too," she added sheepishly as she made an exaggerated wave to Varun, who returned it with only half the enthusiasm.

"That wasn't on the excursion list." Another small cluster of people approached Ember, curiosity overcoming common sense. One got too close to Snuzzle's mandibles, and he snapped them together, barely missing the man's chest. The man fell onto his backside, gasping, but with the wide eyes of someone who was going to find a way to turn the experience into a paper, one way or the other.

Excursion? God help her, that was perfect. It would give Asher, Pui, and Nadia more time if she could go to them. Plus, everyone at the conference was here for the sand. Getting them to visit a mining site shouldn't be a hard sell at all. She just needed to get fifty-some scientists onto beetleback. Then keep them on beetleback and away from any pending flyers. How hard could that be?

It was definitely not the best plan, but it was *a* plan, and it didn't involve waiting for Nadia, or for New Earth/presidium/whatever ships to come shoot them like fish in a barrel.

"Since we have a few hours, and you're all up, any of you want an additional excursion? Free of charge."

Kate shot her a *please-do-not* look, which Ember ignored. Into her collar, she whispered, "Tara, how many can we sit per beetle?"

I don't have that kind of information in my databanks, and I think you are playing with fire. Just talk to them here.

"Noted and ignored." Ember returned her attention to the crowd, which was already forming two loose lines in front of Snuzzle. Ember still felt the deep need to *move,* to *action.* "Right! So, if you're interested in seeing how the silicon dioxide is mined and how the beetles fit in, please queue in front of your preferred mount."

The lines broke apart and reformed in orderly rows, the scientists arguing over even distribution versus weight distribution based on size of each beetle. Not a single person went back to their rooms.

"Kate, Varun, Nok, could you please help harness?" Ember asked into her collar. "Nok still has the extra leather?"

"This was not its intended use," Nok replied. "But yes, we can."

"Ember, I think this idea has not been fully formed," Varun added. "These are wild beetles. It's unethical to have us riding them, much less scientists who trust us."

"You want to just tell them the truth now?" Ember hissed into the comm. "All of it? And what if the flyers come? If Nadia doesn't join us soon, we'll have to put them on beetleback anyway, but then they'll be half in shock and more likely to fall off."

"You should tell them something, Dr. Schmitt," Varun countered. "Leading them on and lying will lose you authority."

"Yeah fine," Ember muttered. Louder, she said, "Any of you bloggers? Have working devices?"

A few people shook their heads. "Not allowed," a woman told her as she passed. She had her pale-yellow polo unbuttoned as far as it would go, showing the mildest hint of cleavage. Her pants were that pale-khaki color that always made Ember think of middle school dances. "Strict media rules for this conference, but the ones on Queen always are secretive. They've blocked our comms, and we won't be able to send anything until we are back on our ships and outside the atmosphere. We heard the colonists are fragile and part of a long-term experiment in isolationism."

"Sort of like the Earth experiment?" Ember asked.

The woman stopped walking and turned to face Ember. Several other heads did as well.

"What Earth experiment?" a man called out, only the top of his head visible in the crowd, his brown hair half smoothed on one side, tufted like a dandelion on the other.

"You know. Where they've been rehabilitating Earth. 'Cause some people never left. I don't know if they ran out of colony worlds or what, but Queen could easily support four or five times its current population." Which Ember didn't actually think was true, but facts were only marginally relevant right now.

"We did get a tutorial on how the mella survive." That came from a person being pushed onto beetleback by Nok as Varun secured the harness on a wide peanut-colored beetle. "I never followed astronomy much, but I was particularly fascinated by the milder regions on the equators, the initial settlements, and the eventual placement of the colony on the north pole."

"I loved the part about the winds," said the woman who sat behind them. She looked the most awake out of anyone Ember had yet seen, but she also had on a royal-blue cocktail dress and brown sandals, so Ember doubted she'd gone to bed at all. "They've got a simulator inside the complex you can step into. Incredible pressure. And we got to try on one of the colonist's envirosuits, too, and turn the TOPA on!" She squealed like a first-term freshman at their first college bender. "I watched a special on television about it before the Collapse, though it was just a hypothesis back then, about how the winds would bring hot air from the sun side, cold air from the dark side, and they'd meet and blend into pockets of habitability. Really, Queen is a fantastic educational tourist destination."

"Yeah, it's great, but I'm saving for Earth." Ember drove the conversation back on track.

"I thought New Earth wasn't taking tourist visas currently?" a man with one of those dopey beige brimmed hats asked from atop a smaller, more chocolate-colored beetle. Two other people were wedged on either side of him, and all of them had death grips on the harness and juvenile glee in their eyes.

Ember?

"Not a good time," she whispered to the comm.

Ember, I'm picking up comm chatter from twenty flyers. Half are going north, following Nadia's group; the other half are definitely headed toward you. They aren't colony flyers. They've been told to control the situation using whatever means

necessary. It sounded very much like the AI took a deep breath. **You're in danger. I'm coming for you.**

Ember's heart stuttered in her chest, and her palms started sweating. "Did you tell Asher?"

When Tara didn't reply, Ember slapped her face shield, sending a *thud* reverberating around her head. "Tara!"

I'm coming for you. Stay where you are.

"Tara, *tell Asher. Do not leave them*!"

I am coming for you.

Damn it! Ember ripped her helmet off and tossed it into the crowd, where it was ignored. At least she knew which way to fly now, assuming she could figure out directions without Tara. Her cuff lights had a backup comm because Asher was thorough, but Ember had to turn it manually on and off, which meant Tara couldn't blast her whenever she wanted.

"We have to leave immediately," Ember yelled into the crowd. "Please find your seats, er, mounts."

Shit. Nadia was in trouble. *Shit.* Rushing the boarding and strapping on and whatever they had to do to get the scientist's moving would result in injuries and probably death and...just...she didn't have any other options! She could have them hide, maybe, back in their beds and hope the unknown flyers didn't come for them the way they'd come for the mella. But they'd come here. The owner of those flyers— New Earth—had no idea how much they'd told the scientists.

She, and the mella, had consigned these people to death the moment they'd arrived.

Shit.

"So *is* New Earth taking tourist visas?" dopey-hat man asked again.

"No, they're not taking visas; you're right." Ember paused partially for effect and partially because her heart beat so loudly she had a hard time hearing her own words. Her heartbeat slowed. Marginally. The scientists continued to mount, making delighted sounds to one another, taking notes, at least one of them orally teasing out a paper introduction. None chose her beetle. With her smell of rotten apples and potential beetle mating future, that was a wise choice.

Ember got a confirmation first from Varun, then Nok, then finally Kate, and did a quick head count. Forty-two humans strapped across ten beetles, and a host of rabbits had wedged themselves back in as well. Leather straps wound around wrists, around hips. Feet struggled to find purchase.

Ember knew for sure, in that moment, that there was no way they'd make it to Nadia without at least a few people falling off. Not at the speed they had to fly. Hell, she had a decent chance of falling off now, too, sans helmet. She squirmed against the exoskeleton as the last person strapped themselves down. Fuck Tara and her protocols, and fuck Taraniel for not giving her the overrides until she was off the planet. This was Nadia's *life* they were playing with, as well as the lives of the galaxy's best scientists!

For them to have half a chance of surviving, she needed people awake, with more adrenaline running than just "pleasure cruise," and she needed them on board with the greater plan before they hit Queen's orbit.

"I assume you all know that New Earth is just a front for Old Earth. We ship out to Earth regularly. It's the primary job of the colony scientists to develop plants and tech to rehabilitate Earth. Not that any of us get to live on it, but still. A handful of us from Queen are going back to Earth. We're going to live with the tech we created and reclaim the land that used to be ours. We want you to come with us."

Aim taken.

Shot fired.

Explosion immediate.

A clamor of voices broke out, each presenting a host of facts as to why she was wrong. Ember climbed onto Snuzzle, grabbed the antennae, and sent the command for "up." Snuzzle hopped twice, and then his wing casing spread. Clear, silvery wings reflected the artificial lighting for only a moment before they were airborne. The other beetles followed to the delight and terror of the academics as their own beetles took off.

"North!" Ember yelled at Snuzzle, though he obviously couldn't understand her words.

"These people are not stable," Varun yelled through the comm as they gained altitude and the air turned from pleasant to chilly. Which Ember knew. She heard the screaming and wanted to join in herself since the wind, without the helmet, was frigid. She opened her mouth, but shut it again at the low thrumming sound of a flyer. She let go of Snuzzle with her right hand and slammed her wrist onto the scalloped point at the backside of his head, turning the comm on.

"Tara!"

Another seven minutes out! Tara yelled back at her. **Fly faster, sweetheart. *Please* fly faster.**

The AI's voice was Taraniel's exactly, and Ember coughed on panic that burrowed into her stomach, making her feel faint. Flying faster meant more people dying but maybe saving them all from being shot out of the sky. Scientists weren't trained to make decisions like this. She leaned into Snuzzle and flattened herself, not that her body would be a significant drag on a beetle this size, but then again, maybe it was. She turned her head to the right, and from the corner of her eye, floodlights pierced the dark, so much brighter than her little headlamp and the ships flying so much faster.

Since they were on the snow side, it seemed appropriate that her heart froze in her chest.

The ships resembled little purple fireflies at first, a memory that almost made Ember smile as the wind turned colder and the conference lights winked out of existence. But the light grew to a beachball size too quickly, and very soon after, Ember had to close her eyes against the glare.

"I've got a guy who...shit! Ember! We lost one!" Kate cried out into the comm, but Ember didn't open her eyes to look back. Death was coming. She'd seen it at the mella camp. But they'd been mella, and she'd had years of indoctrination helping her rationalize all that. Scientist deaths would not go down easy. Her sister's death, if it happened, would hollow her out enough for Varun's remaining malted milk ball supply.

Asher's death...

The flyers opened fire.

They had live rounds again. Bullets screamed into the wind. She opened her eyes as the flyers interspersed with the beetle swarm, and one flyer took direct aim at a wing and shredded the delicate tissue with bullets.

The beetle clicked, its legs flailing as it turned casing-side down and plummeted to the ground. The rabbits and the people on it screamed in unison as they fell, the sounds eerily similar, and then they were gone, lost to the darkness below. A scream grew in Ember's throat as well, but she swallowed it, terrified of spooking Snuzzle. Damn it, those were *humans* that now ink-splattered across the snow. They weren't mella; they weren't colonists; they were just stupid, naïve scientists who had absolutely no idea what was going on.

More gunfire. More screams. The flyers were in front of them now, flying backward, their lights blinding. Ember couldn't see a damn thing, and the lights hurt even with her eyes closed. Snuzzle's clicking had turned to a low hum, but she wasn't being bucked off, so maybe photosensitivity only went so far.

Maybe, Ember realized, the flyer lights were purple.

"What does purple mean, Varun? Do beetles do purple?"

Varun's voice came back as smug as Nadia's the day she'd gotten her tenure letter. "They do! It means *prey*."

"How do I tell them to...attack? Eat?"

"Don't do anything," Nok said. "You just have to stop interacting."

"Wonderful. Tell everyone to hold on." Ember opened her eyes, very briefly, into the blinding light, and smiled. Then she slid her hands from Snuzzle's antennae, hooked them both under the leather harness, and rested her forehead on Snuzzle's head.

Snuzzle dove.

His wings slicked straight back, like a hawk going for a mouse. Ember hadn't realized they were above the flyers but wasn't going to chance looking, or changing her position, or anything that might change Snuzzle's course. They impacted something hard enough that her head came up and slammed down on Snuzzle's head. Ember managed to bite her tongue and tasted copper. Another gunshot ripped the air, and then the blinding light was gone.

"Anyone see anything?" she asked her wrist. Every single one of her bones hurt as though they'd been used as a child's percussion set.

"Ten flyers, six beetles remaining, minus yours," Kate returned, her voice triumphant. "The odds aren't terrible, and the beetles don't seem to care as much about surviving. We've lost scientists, but...wait; hold on."

Ember heard another loud clang, as beetle impacted reinforced plastic. There was a definitive crunching noise that, when Ember opened her eyes, turned out to be a beetle with a flyer between its mandibles.

She almost cheered.

Despite its imminent death, the flyer opened fire.

This time the crunch came from disintegrating chitin. The beetle's toes clutch at the air as the conference goers gripped uselessly at joints and the harness.

Gunfire again. The beetle to Ember's left lost its head in a concentrated effort from two flyers. Rabbits hopped off its back the moment it began to fall, landing on the main screen of one of the flyers before the beetle went into a roll and dislodged them.

Again, the scream formed in her throat. This time, she let it free.

Another batch of identical flyers came up over the horizon. Ember's stomach sank, and the copper taste continued to flood her mouth.

"Kate!" Ember called.

"Nok's down with her beetle," Kate returned. "And the ten scientists on it. Haven't heard who has survived, but I doubt all of them did. Varun's is injured and, I think, landed? He's not responding, so I don't know about his riders either."

"The other ten have found us," Ember said. "Did they find Nadia first? Asher? They could be in one of those ships! Tara, where are you, and *where is Nadia*?"

I'm here! Tara flew into the middle of the swarm, her track lighting illuminated green and in a repeating sequence that hurt Ember's eyes. Snuzzle responded immediately and stopped chasing a flyer, turned, and chased Tara instead. The remaining the beetles fell in line behind.

Tara led them in a series of tight loops and jogs that the presidium ship was much more capable of than the bulkier flyers and that the beetles didn't seem to mind at all. Every time they got close to one, Tara's track lighting changed, and one of the beetles extended a few legs and punched their toes through the hull or the sapphire of the viewscreen. One of the snow-side beetles managed to drag its toes down like a can opener before the change in momentum peeled the leg from its body. The beetle screamed. The flyer split in two, and people in distinct blue-and-green New Earth uniforms fell to their deaths. None of them looked like Nadia, thank god. Ember couldn't imagine Nadia's body being among those left in the snow today.

"Tara!" Ember screamed. "Where is my sister?" And where was Asher, for that matter? Pui?

I have a directive imbalance.

"Well turn it off and *think*."

Fifteen to five plus a stolen ship were still terrible odds, even with three of the flyers spiraling to the ground, a beetle attached to each one, their wings open and driving the flyers into the ground.

"Tara, make them stop!" Ember pushed Snuzzle closer to the ground, scanning the bodies and the wreckage. What color had Nadia been wearing? Would she recognize her sister if she was smeared across the snow?

A flyer turned toward her before Tara looped back around. Snuzzle didn't veer, but another beetle rammed the side of the ship with its mandibles, skewering the flyer clean through. The flyer and beetle hit the ground in a large plume of sand and snow. The beetle shot back skyward immediately after impact. The flyer did not.

"Turn off your lighting!" Ember screamed uselessly. There was no way anyone could hear her with the wind and the ships and the buzzing of beetle wings. "We've got people on the ground, and you are *going to kill my sister*."

Two more flyers veered to Ember, one coming from her left, one on her right. Tara's track lighting sequence did not change color, but the pattern alternated to four long dashes. An eggshell-white beetle maybe half the size of the rest shot like a bullet from the line and rammed the backside of the west flyer. The beetle fell away, spinning drunkenly for a moment before finding its equilibrium. The flyer puttered, hanging in the air while its thrusters sputtered, then dropped like a stone to the ground.

Snuzzle turned to face the remaining flyer and flew straight at it. It veered, as if the pilot had a last-minute change of heart, and turned ten degrees and accelerated. Except, with that heading change, it would still sheer off a few of Snuzzle's legs. Ember screamed though her throat was raw. She tried to direct her beetle away, but he was intent on ramming. She had a passing thought about sliding off Snuzzle and chancing the (certain death) free fall, when Varun's voice came over her comm.

"Dr. Schmitt, *look*."

Ember couldn't tell where Varun was pointing, so she sat up and wildly twisted her head. Flyers, changing course, were coming at her, coming at Varun on his beetle, the passengers flailing and probably screaming. And below them, wreckage lay on the snow, bodies, broken ships, red.

From behind her, another swarm of beetles approached, at least two of which had riders.

Mella? *Asher*?

The flyer barreling toward Ember turned another ten degrees and skated above her, so close Ember could see the call sign painted on its hull. Close enough she could have spit on the viewscreen and mooned the pilot if she'd wanted. Tara's track lighting continued its repeating sequence, and the new beetles peeled off and clamped onto the remaining flyers, dragging them to the earth. One down. Two. Five. Crushed metal and smoke littered the ground.

More blood.

Ten breaths and the only flyer still in the air was one that had just tried to ram Ember. It flew erratically, thrusters alternating between full blast and full shut off, and listed decidedly to port. A beetle cautiously tailed it but didn't engage, which was the first instance of self-preservation Ember had seen in the species. Also, Ember wanted a taste of whatever that pilot was drinking.

"*Tara!*" she called into her wrist. "Those riders—"

"Jesus, you are *so bad* at flying!" Nadia's voice crackled over the comm, and Ember swallowed her words in relief. "Flying under the radar mean anything to you?" Nadia continued. "And I'm on one of these beetles. Pui too. Try to be careful."

"Kate and Nok!" Ember managed to say as irritation stacked on top of her adrenaline. "They're grounded or down there or something. Where the hell were you?"

"They've got Asher, but we were doing what you asked, Icarus. We've got a bunch of export codes, and some beetles think we're the second coming. You're welcome. Now let's take out this last flyer and find Asher."

I've got a comm request from the remaining flyer.

"I'm here. My pilot isn't cooperating. Hold on." Asher's voice sounded fuzzy and distorted as it came from Ember's wrist comm, like a radio dial poorly tuned. The last flyer shot upward in a tight corkscrew, let out a massive blast of exhaust, then began a slow descent.

"That'll do it. I think."

Ember sucked in air. Her heart rate spiked and settled. She directed Snuzzle as close to the flyer's screen as she could. She didn't need visual confirmation Asher was in there, but she didn't mind the idea of confirmation that she was in one piece.

"Asher?" Ember asked her comm when she was within spitting distance of the slowly looping flyer.

"You look *very* nice in that flight suit, Dr. Schmitt. Especially on a beetle."

"You—"

A flyer on the ground exploded in a firework of orange and red.

Ember, you need to land and board me. No more time wasting.

Ember was done with bossy AIs, especially ones intruding on private conversations. "I'm not landing Snuzzle until you agree that all of us are leaving this planet together. Together. With the scientists." Her mind flicked to the scientists, to their bodies, to what they owed the people they'd dragged into their mess. She felt sick. She felt dizzy. She felt like she'd deeply violated every conflict-of-interest statement she'd ever signed and every ethics course she'd ever taken.

I have another conflict.

"Fucking deal with it. You left people behind. That isn't going to happen again."

Tara clicked off, audibly. She stayed silent for a long moment, then clicked back on.

I'm going to help her, and we'll start searching for Kate and Varun. Their comms are still pinging me, so it won't take long. Please land, Ember.

"Are you all right, Asher?"

I cut her comm. Land and board, and you can talk to her.

Ember fumed but directed Snuzzle down. Landing, she could do. Explaining seemed unlikely, especially to a group of scientists who had to be scared shitless.

Change your heading twenty-seven degrees. Nok and Kate are with the remaining scientists and beetles about three kilometers west. We can pick them up there.

The lights on Ember's left wrist went out, then on, then out, until Snuzzle had sufficiently course corrected. Tara moved to their port side, Asher's flyer just behind.

As she was no longer actively falling off her beetle, Ember's mind skipped back to the snow. To the blood on the snow. To the broken bodies of scientists and the little mella children. *All this*, she thought as her stomach sank low. *All this because of sand and a planet that is our collective human heritage.* It was shit. Absolute shit.

Another grounded flyer burst into flames. Her suit picked up the sounds of human screams. Every ounce of potential optimism drained from Ember's body.

"We can't pick all of them up," Nadia said over the comm. "I've just landed, and damn, I didn't realize the conference was so big. We lost way, way too many, but even with those, there have to be a good two dozen people."

They'd started out with forty-two. Mella deaths weren't worth this. Earth lies weren't worth this. These scientists had gotten better planets, but they didn't deserve to die for it.

Ember leaned toward her comm and tried to steady her voice. It came out just as guilt-ridden as it sounded in her head. "We can't leave them to freeze. We'll have to make multiple trips to...somewhere."

"The mining site?" Nadia suggested. "There are plenty of buildings they can shelter in until we sort out the ship issue. It's about a ten-minute flight from here I think."

"Yeah, but who's going to get them from the mining site? What do we do if they don't want to go back to Earth with us, after this?" Ember had always just assumed. After being shot, however, and watching their colleagues die...

"My people can," Asher cut in. "And, Tara, stop cutting me off, or I will tell Kate to wipe the personality imprint clean off."

You don't have that capability.

"Try me. Also, New Earth Governance aren't as smart as they think they are," Asher continued. "Half our buildings and stores were underground, and plenty made it there during the attack. We have five mella on their way in a ground flyer with supplies, but it'll be a day or so, depending on weather and the presidium security and that's *if* we can figure out how to transport them."

Ember pushed down on Snuzzle's antennae, and the beetle landed gracefully on the snow next to a small herd of people. They had wide eyes. Windswept hair. Terror on their faces. Smoke from exploded flyers rose on the horizon. Bright red covered skin and clothes.

"Shit," she muttered to herself. "What are we going to do?"

Nadia ran across the snow, her hair and eyes wild from the wind and excitement. She scaled Ember's beetle and slapped her on the shoulder. "I'm really glad you're alive," she whispered into Ember's ear, "but smash whatever it is you're feeling down right now. Emotions are for later." She then slid down the thorax.

"Form a line!" Nadia yelled into the confused, heavily panicked crowd. "Back on beetles but this time, no spaceships!"

Four people immediately came up to Snuzzle, all with the same wide-eyed, bedraggled look. Shock, Ember realized. They were in shock. She probably was too. There'd be time for screaming later, probably. In space. That seemed like a good place to scream—into an endless void—about losing friends and knowledge and their humanity. Ember gave them a hand up and tried to remind herself that they weren't *all* dead. The scientists sat in a line behind her, each spooned against the backside of the next.

"Mind if I ride too?" Asher, with a split lip and a partially blackened eye, gazed up at her. She'd lost her cowl and envirosuit jacket and stood, shivering, at Snuzzle's toes.

Ember had to think hard about her next words. She almost immediately said *no, we're full up*, but A) they weren't full up; there was space for at least three more behind the last scientist, B) having Asher spooned behind her made her belly twist in a way that no longer felt like it violated Taraniel's memory, and C) Asher would be a very good guilt distraction.

"Scoot back a bit," Ember said over her shoulder to the scientist behind her. The line dutifully moved back without a grumble, likely because of terror and trauma and being half-frozen. Ember offered Asher a hand once she was half-way up a leg, which Asher took though Ember doubted she needed it. Even through the gloves Asher's hand felt warm, which was clearly all in Ember's head, but she didn't care.

"Where do you want me to hold?" Asher asked. Her voice came out low, matter-of-fact, but right by Ember's left ear.

The scientist had been holding on to her shoulders. Ember didn't even contemplate her response. "Around my waist."

Asher's hands found her hips, glided over the leather, then locked together just under her navel. She felt the mella's breath on her neck, hot, humid, and a little too fast. *Very* hot, in fact. It stung the skin of her neck and made the rest gooseflesh. Ember leaned back, just enough to feel Asher's chin on her shoulder.

"Warmer?" Asher asked without inflection.

"Shut up." Ember told herself not to grin. It didn't help.

"No," Asher whispered.

"We're responsible for a lot of death," Ember said, which was definitively a mood killer.

"Did you shoot down the beetles?" Asher asked.

Ember scowled. "No. But I put the scientists on the beetles."

Asher pushed forward until her lips touched Ember's ear. "You didn't kill anyone. You didn't fire the shots; you didn't aim the weapons."

"Tara—" Ember started to argue.

"Is a problem we have to deal with. Later."

Ember was tired of later, and losing arguments sucked. She turned her head to the side just as Asher pulled back.

"Dr. Schmitt?"

Ember kissed her. It was one part reckless abandon and twenty-seven parts a need for human contact that wasn't Nadia. Asher didn't pull away and leaned in enthusiastically while scientists grumbled behind them.

She tasted like salt, and wind, and sand. One of her hands slid from Ember's waist to her left breast and cupped it. Ember covered Asher's hand with her own, and Ember let the dead scientists, and the upcoming spaceship, and all the blood slide into the corner of her mind. Just for a moment. Just for one fucking moment. She felt warm. The way Asher kept nipping at her lower lip made her warm in a lot of places.

Also, she felt *happy*.

When the last scientist had mounted, Tara turned the flyer north, changed the track lighting to solid green, and went back to the sky. Ember reluctantly pulled from Asher, though the mella snuck a lingering kiss onto Ember's jaw as she retreated.

"I love a person in uniform," Asher whispered. She tugged at the collar of Ember's envirosuit.

Ember bit down on her lower lip and smiled.

"Come on. Off. Get inside the main complex." Nadia's voice boomed across the snow fields (sand fields? It looked too grainy for snow) as the beetles touched down. Tara flew in just overhead, her track lighting off, her voice smug with accomplishment.

I've got Kate and Nok, as well as ten of the scientists. I didn't have enough space for the bodies, and there are a few. We can go back later for them if we need to. I did what you asked, Ember.

Asher's arms slid away from Ember as she righted herself. Lips had maybe just brushed her neck, or it maybe was a loose strand of Asher's hair. Her skin was too chilled to tell. "I don't think we'll have time," Ember said. "We need to care for the living."

Asher looked at Ember, mildly perplexed, as she slid off Snuzzle and helped the scientists down.

"A pissed-off AI is a good way to die in space," Ember muttered under her breath as she slid down the opposite side of the exoskeleton. Plus, they really didn't have time. It was either get out now, while everything was blood and confusion, or try to clean up and get executed mella-style by New Earth later. Nadia was right. Emotions had to wait.

Ember joined Varun and helped him untangle a short woman with long blonde hair and a torn pair of Dockers (the tag was still attached) from a beetle leg joint. Ember helped the woman straighten her clothes, hoping her voice sounded soothing and confident as she tried to calm the woman's panicked questions.

Tara landed the presidium ship far too close to Ember— close enough that Ember's face flushed with the heat from the flyer's exhaust. The hatch opened, and Kate came out first, her hair a mass of looped tangles and her clothes scorched from who-knew what. Nok followed, her (nonexistent) hair obviously fine and her clothes 75 percent less burned. Kate walked over to Ember and Varun, took the beetle's detached lead from Varun, and coiled it around her arm.

"Well, that sucked," Kate said, her voice flat. Blood dripped from her chin onto the front of her envirosuit. She, too, had lost her helmet and cowl. Nok still had hers, but the cowl's screen had shattered, and a few fragments still clung, the edges jagged and angry. "They're willing to kill investors. We are absolutely dead."

"I demand to know what is going on!" Explorer Hat Man pushed through the crowd of beetles and humans, flicked his name badge, and crossed his arms. "Newmark Electronics will want answers when the comms are restored. What happened out there and what is going on with Earth?"

A chorus of agreement came from the scattered, shivering scientists. Ember groaned. In the game of Top Ten Things They Didn't Have Time For, this had to be at least number two. But she owed them answers, and she owed them a lot of lost lives.

"Go inside," Ember said, pointing to the silo door where Nadia and Pui stood. She started shivering again as the flyer's engines cooled. "Once we get your injuries sorted, I'll make a formal announcement about Earth. The invitation stands, of course."

"And the ships?" he demanded.

"Pirates."

He left with his small cohort and fell into the line on the ramp to the silo door, looking way more defeated than Ember wanted.

A new rush of warm air across Ember's neck made her look skyward. Her hands momentarily stopped shaking. Snuzzle was just above her, gaining altitude and joining the flock of beetles already sprinkling the dark sky.

"Where are they going?" Ember walked, eyes up, toward the silo and climbed the ramp. The beetles flew in formation, and Ember wondered if there would be rabbits, too, perched at various places on their bodies. She caught sight of Snuzzle at the back of the formation, his little light blinking a slow yellow. Which she kind of got. They *were* fungusmated, she supposed. It was still a pretty shitty goodbye.

"There is a colony near here," Nadia answered as she joined Ember at the door. "Maybe they're checking out a new home. That's what we should be doing too."

I'd like you to get on the ship, Ember.

"I thought we talked about you giving me orders."

Nadia's voice soured. "Can we turn her off yet? You know she *shut down* on me, right?"

Ember was very aware of that, and a handful of other incidents she couldn't assemble into a logical thought pattern. Getting on a spaceship, kissing Asher—she didn't have enough space in her brain for an AI with problematic programming.

"Tara," Ember said firmly into her comm. "Can you reach the scientists' ships?"

I need you to get onto the ship, Tara whispered firmly into Ember and Nadia's comm, low enough that no one near them turned their heads at the slightly metallic voice.

"Fuck you." The words were slow, deadly. Words she'd never have said to her wife. "You want me on that ship, you will do what I ask. Can you or can you not get the scientists in contact with their ships?"

Ember counted to ten before Tara responded. **Yes. Scientists aren't known for their attention to detail outside the lab. None of the ships are locked down. Most still have open data feeds to their respective homeworlds to monitor meetings and experiments. Their comms might be blocked, but mine isn't. Not on this presidium ship.**

"Great. Nadia?"

"Yeah, gotcha. I'll wrangle Pui and Varun and let the scientists make calls."

"Thank you," Ember said with a half-smile to her sister.

You're welcome. Now get on the ship.

Ember would definitely paint a face somewhere on a bulkhead during their space journey, just so she could throw things at it.

"Do they have clearance codes to land?" Nadia asked, brow furrowed. "The science ships, I mean."

You don't need codes to land on Queen. Just to leave. I've picked up another flyer on an approach, however. Unmarked, with no ID. It's about ten minutes out. I need you on my ship. Now. *Now.*

Tara's voice held a very clear tone of *or else*. Ember bristled, but a tickle ran up her spine, too, that she really didn't like.

"Pui?" Ember called back into the silo. "Can they all walk?"

"In various definitions," Pui called back. "Yes."

"No winter clothing though, sis," Nadia reminded her. "And we're too far from the new beetle site to recapture any. If more ships come, this is where we have to meet them."

Ember.

Nadia pushed her back, hard enough to force her to step forward down the ramp. "Go. I'll help patch up the scientists. Get on the ship and wait so Tara leaves us alone."

Weren't you just complaining about me not paying enough attention to you?

"Ember," Nadia pleaded.

"Oh fine." Ember stomped down the ramp and over to the flyer. Inside, the air felt dry and warm, so warm Ember considered removing her envirosuit jacket. Exhaustion beat around the corners of her mind, twirling with the intense heat, so Ember just stripped off her gloves and sank into a reclining chair with a groan.

The small of her back twinged. Her right calf threatened to charley horse. Ember hissed and sat up, rubbing at the muscle and cursing. "Too much beetle riding," she spat. "Never again."

"So, is this a bad time to talk?"

Ember's head jerked left. Asher stood against the viewscreen, her clothes covered by a new envirosuit. She had the helmet off and had managed to partially tame her hair, but her lip was still swollen, and she had a deep weariness around her non-blackened eye.

"Hey," Ember said, which was again a shitty way to start a conversation.

If the science ships left now, they could be here in just over five minutes, Tara announced. **The other flyer has not approached and is hovering a kilometer out. It is sending encrypted broadcasts of exactly the same length in one-minute increments. Likely a repeating message. I can't decode it—I don't have that type of programming. The ship bears the presidium's symbol but is smaller than our ship. You need to leave.**

"I..." Ember launched herself to sitting. A very unsettling thought speared itself through her brain. "Hey, hey Asher? Have you considered that the presidium may not know the truth about New Earth either? That they might *want* New Earth off their backs? That they might want to leave that gilded coffin they're sequestered in?"

"I mean..."

To expedite our process, Ember, would you please put your exit code into my system? Then I can send it to the orbital station when we hit the atmosphere and we won't lose more time.

Ember rolled her eyes at Tara's frustration but tapped the alpha-numeric string into the main console as she spoke to Asher. "Listen. They said their flyers don't have weapons, but they could still be a great distraction. What if...they're protecting us now? They're hovering far enough that they could dissuade other flyers before we're in sensor range, right? Maybe? What if it's a repeating message that says something like, 'already checked here, go look somewhere else'?"

The more she thought about it, the more everything made a sick sort of sense. There were the presidium's faces when they stormed their building. There was the confusion, the way Edmond had acted versus what she knew of Mark. The conference. The sudden disappearance of President Borchert, the only one of the presidium allowed to leave... It made a lot of sense.

Ember stood up, the pain in her calf forgotten. The chair snapped back into position, and she made a point of meeting Asher's eyes. "They've seen the stamps on the packaging. They've seen the coordinates. They've guessed. I'll bet they guessed a long time ago. And then the command to relocate probably came down, and I'll bet they were confused. I wonder if they even knew Queen was being sold? But then with the attack on the mella camp..."

Asher nodded. Her eyes moved from wide shock to heavy-lidded frustration. Finally, she sat down. "It makes sense. If you were a super-secret Earth government hell-bent on keeping people away, would you tell some mid-level bureaucrats on a lucrative world that Earth was alive?"

"Everyone on this planet is just a pawn," Ember said under her breath.

"Yes. And if that ship isn't going to attack, we don't worry about it." Asher's voice lowered. "Our only problem, right now, is convincing those scientists to come with us. We're a sad boat of refugees without them."

"Ember?" Nadia's voice came through the comm, triumphant and exhausted. "They're coming. The science ships are coming. I don't know who is going home and who is going with us, but they've come as a group and are in the upper atmosphere. We've got a few landed near us already. We're loading them as quickly as we can."

Ember caught the whine of ship engines and realized they had a whole new problem and possibly an excellent opportunity. That would be a lot of ships leaving at once. It'd be hard for the port authority to deal with the traffic. They wouldn't have time to check all the codes before the scientists started sending comms to their companies and Big Money started complaining about delays. And no matter how many codes Pui had managed to download, Ember doubted it would be enough for every single ship they were trying to get off-world.

"Asher," Ember said, her eyes opening wide.

Asher stared at her like she was a very shiny bug. Her lips were red, Ember realized. Cherry red. Lipstick red. Was Asher wearing *lipstick*?

Irrelevant, though Ember's eyes couldn't seem to find anything else to look at.

"Asher, do you know much about the space port authority?"

"Just that you need an approved exit code to get out, and a ton of paperwork. If it were as easy as flying away, we'd have done it years ago. The whole point in getting you, aside from Taraniel's attachment, was because she thought the codes you had for exporting materials might pass on a small spaceship. We could have stolen these codes before, but having *you* explain to the port authority was always going to carry more weight. No one gives a fuck about a mella, even with a correct exit code."

Ember pried at a tangle in her hair, caught of whiff of fungus/blood/beetle spit bouquet, and shoved her hand into her hip pocket. "Tara, I want to talk to the scientists. Open the comms on all the suits."

You should be heading into orbit.

"*Just do it.*"

No.

The unease that had been batting the edges of Ember's mind blossomed into panic. The hatch to the ship closed, a metallic clicking reverberating through the cockpit. The rear of the ship jostled, and Ember heard yelling. The thrusters fired before Asher and Ember were out of their seats.

Asher ran to the controls. "Tara! Stop this nonsense! Don't you dare take off without the crew!"

Ember ran to the hatch door, pounding and cursing. "Tara! We can't leave without them. We can't man this ship for eight months with just two people, not realistically. We *cannot* leave Nadia behind!"

"Open the damn door!" Asher smashed her hand into the interface. She kicked the lower console. Ember tore at the hatch door with her fingernails. When that (obviously) didn't work, she dove for the panel with the red cross and riffled through med kits, hoping to find something sharp, something hot, or a combination of the two.

It is time to leave.

"No!" Ember and Asher yelled in unison.

The ship jostled, and Ember's ears popped as it lifted from the ground. Having found only bandages, gauze, and alcohol, Ember ran to the console, to Asher, and helped her try to pry an aluminum panel from under the touch screen. An electric current shot them both back, off their feet, and onto their backs. Ember saw stars and the bodies of dead scientists. She heard Asher groan. She smelled cooked hair. She tasted blood and bile.

"Tara," she managed to raggedly choke up from her sore throat.

"This wasn't part of Taraniel's plan," Asher said.

Ember's vision cleared enough to see Asher struggle to her knees, a twitch in her right hand as she offered it to Ember.

My plans are flexible.

Ember took Asher's hand, and together, they stood on shaking legs.

"*You* are not Taraniel," Asher snapped. "You're supposed to follow *her* plans.

I have one immutable directive, and we are meeting it. Now.

Ember's vision stopped swimming. She turned to the viewer and saw wisps of white. Her ears popped again. Her stomach dropped as she started to shake.

"You can't leave Nadia behind!" Ember punched the ceiling. She'd have gone for the aluminum panel again, but white sparks still jumped across its surface. "You can't leave any of them."

The port authority has accepted your code. Tara's voice came out a horrifying blend of TOPA and Taraniel. Too smug. Too tight. Like microwaved butter about to explode.

The scene on the viewer bled to darkness and stars.

Ember sank into a chair. The back part of her brain sent her images of red blood, of limited air, of drowning in nothing as her chest crushed. Asher's lips weren't cherry-colored anymore, but blood-colored, death-colored.

The screen went dark—not the dark of space, but black and without stars.

Strap in, Tara commanded.

Ember's eyes darted to Asher's. They both raced for the panel, electrocution be damned. Tara turned up the gravity in the same moment. Ember and Asher fell to their knees. Ember struggled to breathe, as if a weighted blanket wrapped her lungs. A high-pitched whine came from above, and the interior lights dimmed so briefly Ember might have imagined it...

Then everything stilled.

"Tara," Asher growled. "Let us up."

The gravity eased enough that the two could get to their feet. Cautiously, Asher edged to the main interface and tapped a series of commands. Ember stood behind her, watching readouts she couldn't interpret.

"You have to be kidding me." Asher spun around, her eyes wild, her mouth agape. "We're in hyperspace! You left *everyone* behind!"

Ember felt her own mouth fall open. She had no idea what to do with that information. It was impossible to use a comm in hyperspace, impossible to *see* anything in hyperspace, just black, black, unending black. Asher's lips were still so red, and they were on a spaceship, in *space*, in *hyperspace*. And they didn't have a medic. And they didn't have an engineer. And they didn't have Nadia. And without Ember to talk to the port authority... Jesus, Tara had abandoned the scientists, the mella, Nadia, to the whims of New Earth and their trigger-happy flyers.

Ember backed into a wall. She pushed her palms into her thighs and cinched her eyes shut, and tried to think. "Tara, you at least sent them the coordinates, right? To Earth?"

No.

"She didn't," Asher grumbled, "but Pui mapped the coordinates from the manifest. She knows the location. They can meet us there. That's something. Except..." She squinted at the screen. "This readout says four ships exited hyperspace just before Tara fired the hyperdrive. Their identifiers read New Earth." She punched the back of a padded chair and cursed.

"Tara, you have to take us back!" Ember pushed from the wall but didn't open her eyes. She was too afraid she'd see blood, real or imagined. "We have to go back."

We will not exit hyperdrive until we require refueling.

"How soon is that?" Asher snapped.

Two and a half months.

In two and a half months...how far would they be? *Where* would they be? If the scientists and the mella and Nadia and Varun needed rescuing, there'd be no way.

"The codes." Asher leaned into Ember, whispering in her ear. Ember opened her eyes. Asher's lips still looked like blood. Her skin felt rough and chapped from Queen's weather, but warm. "You had override codes for Tara, right? In Taraniel's last message?"

Ember slapped the bulkhead above her. "Give me Taraniel's last message, Tara," Ember demanded. "She said it would be released once we left Queen. We've met that directive."

I've decided to alter that directive. It counters my protocol to keep you safe and take you to Earth. You cannot be trusted to make your own decisions. I will make them for you until Earth. If you persist in trying to damage the ship, or turn me off, I will drop the oxygen levels so low until you pass out, and I will only raise them long enough for you to eat and drink. Tara's voice turned sour. **Do not make me functionally induce cryosleep in you, Ember. I don't want to cause you that kind of pain.**

"You *can't*," Ember started, then trailed off, unsure what else to say. Clearly Tara *could* do just about anything she wanted.

The audio clicked off so loudly it sounded like Tara had walked off and slammed a door shut.

Ember looked at the ship, with its deep-blue interior walls, plush chairs, and green molding. She sat, again, in the nearest seat and kicked it back into full recline. God, the shitty padding felt like a cartoon cloud. Fatigue blossomed from the corners of her mind and washed across her body. She wanted to vomit. She wanted to cry. Memories threatened to drown her, and her damn sister had been left behind. Again.

"They'll be killed. Incarcerated and then killed. Asher—" Ember breathed into the too-warm air and left her last sentence unfinished.

Asher sat in the chair next to her, the rigid same tightness back in her shoulders and face as when they'd fought in the dunes. "Nadia can take care of herself," Asher said softly. "Varun, Nok, Pui, and Kate, they're a hell of a crew. And those spaceships aren't going to destroy the tech elite of the colonized worlds." She brushed a finger across Ember's cheek. "The scientists were already in contact outside Queen, remember? The colonies know. Everyone knows.

They will be okay, somehow. I promise. And when our people get away—and they *will*—they will meet us on Earth. We're just going to get there first."

Ember pursed her lips. "Even if that's true, I don't know if *we* will be all right."

"Maybe not. But"—Asher's voice lilted—"we, we have two and a half months to sort things out."

Ember met her eyes, and there was a promise there that said, *We will deconstruct the AI and spread its personality across three galaxies.*

"We'll take it one day at a time," Asher continued. "You'll be okay. No cryosleep. I promise."

Cryosleep. *Cryosleep*. She couldn't do that again. She could *not*. "But even if we get there alive, and Nadia makes it past those unknown spaceships, we'll still have to go back for the others, or wait for them to get to Earth. We could be there months, if not years, before anyone else."

"There's a good chance."

Asher's chair creaked, and Ember felt the brush of synthetic fabric over the top of her hand. "What do you want to do, Dr. Schmitt?" Asher asked. "Head directly there? Wait for our first fueling stop and contact someone if we can, assuming Tara lets us do anything? Fight? Try to break the ship right now and probably end up being partially suffocated?"

"Nadia'll head to Earth directly. Even if her ship doesn't have to stop for fuel, she won't let them linger. Once she gets clearance, she'll turn her academic myopia on Earth."

"I didn't ask what Nadia wanted. I asked what *you* wanted. You and I both know your sister will catch up. Hell, she could get there before us, if Tara fucks with us enough."

Ah, curse words. Nadia would have been proud. She popped one eye open and caught Asher's smirk. If there hadn't been an unstable AI with her dead wife's personality imprint watching them, Ember would have kissed her right there, memories and all.

"They'll be all right, Ember," Asher said in a soft, breathy voice. "Tell me what you want to do."

"I want..." Ember rubbed the bridge of her nose and gave a long sigh. The memories ebbed as Asher's words settled. Nadia could take care of herself. She could herd the scientists just fine, too, especially with Varun and Nok there. Asher was right; they weren't in life-threatening danger, at least not immediately. There were too many important scientists and too much media attention already. Things would be complicated when they emerged from hyperspace, but they wouldn't be impossible.

And she and Asher? They were already on a ship. They were headed to Earth. They had a plan that would probably work. It would just take more herding than she'd originally thought and far more deprogramming than she had the skill for, but in two and a half months, she ought to be able to learn. This wasn't a problem, just an...unexpected complication. Reprogram Tara, and they'd be fine. How hard could it be?

Right now, however, Ember needed to relax. To process. To do breathing exercises and get a solid ten hours of sleep. As long as they didn't directly threaten Tara, they'd probably be allowed a fair amount of freedom.

Maybe it was time to give Asher more than ten seconds of glancing eye contact too. Nothing said romance like being sequestered on a possessed ship for months, right?

"I want...I want to sleep. Then I want to shower for a day because I still smell like rotting apples. Then?" She bit into her lower lip and raised her head from the cushioning so she could stare, properly, at the black screen. Her stomach started to roll, and she told it to shut up. Her mind wandered to Nadia's chances of survival, and she jerked it back to the present. "I want Old Earth, New Earth, Just Earth. Whatever. I want...oh fuck it, Asher. Ignore the fuel stops. Ignore the comms." She slammed her head back onto the chair and screwed her eyes shut as tight as she could manage.

She wanted to say, *Let's take out this creepy AI and take control of the ship. Then let's fuck like Queen bunnies until we get to Earth.* Instead, she said something that was equally true, if not devoid of specifics.

"Let's do whatever we can to get home."

Acknowledgements

As always, infinite thanks to RE Advanced, the best critique and friend group on this planet. To my editor, Elizabetta, for taking on another one of my weird books (bunnies!), and to my sister, from whom I liberally borrowed much verbal snark. The puns in this book are almost entirely via Rosiee Thor, who took in my semi-coherent texts and turned them into eyerolling puns in seconds.

A big thank you as well to my Patreon supporters. You keep me writing, and you keep the power on. THANK YOU!

No thanks are given to my robot vacuum, Sally Shark, who ate approximately 1000 phone charging cables during the writing of this book.

About J.S. Fields

J.S. Fields is a scientist who has spent too much time around organic solvents. They enjoy roller derby, woodturning, making chain mail by hand, and cultivating fungi in the backs of minivans.

Email
chlorociboria@gmail.com

Twitter
@Galactoglucoman

Website
www.jsfieldsbooks.com

Patreon
www.patreon.com/jsfields

Other NineStar books by this author

The Alchemical Duology
Foxfire in the Snow

Ardulum Series
Ardulum: First Don
Ardulum: Second Don
Ardulum: Third Don
Tales from Ardulum

Connect with NineStar Press

www.ninestarpress.com

www.facebook.com/ninestarpress

www.facebook.com/groups/NineStarNiche

www.twitter.com/ninestarpress

www.instagram.com/ninestarpress